# The One My H

## The Tenafly Road Se.

By Adrienne Morris

MW01154177

---

THE ONE MY HEART LOVES

**First edition. October 2, 2018.**

Written by Adrienne Morris.

*"Place me like a seal over your heart, like a seal on your arm; for love is as strong as death, its jealousy unyielding as the grave. It burns like blazing fire, like a mighty flame. Many waters cannot quench love; rivers cannot sweep it away. If one were to give all the wealth of one's house for love, it would be utterly scorned." Song of Solomon 8:6*

# Chapter One

Lucy McCullough paced the floor of the dreary room she shared at The New London School for the Blind, fretting over the tardy livery driver. The hallway clock rang the hour. Out the window and across the busy New London street a choral group sang Christmas carols in the lashing rain as Lucy's stomach fluttered. Taking a seat at her desk decorated with paper flowers and angels for the holiday, she strained to read a letter from Buck in the dimming light of late afternoon before folding the worn piece of plain but expensive stationery. She tucked it in her pocket with a sigh. Never mind, Lucy knew the words by heart. How many times had she run her slim fingers over the ink, hoping to absorb just a little more from the stilted words Buck used?

> *Dear Lucy,*
>
> *I think of you often and hope you are getting on satisfactorily in your school work. The bank keeps me busy. Please send word as soon as you arrive in town.*
>
> *Sincerely,*
>
> *Buck Crenshaw*

Though Buck had written with great regularity in the past three months and Lucy could find no real fault in his missives—some were long and tedious lists of current events and some were short notes about the weather—she ached for something more intimate. Her friend and roommate, the homely Miss Clementine, joked that Buck often wrote like a distant cousin forced at gunpoint to ask after her. Lucy did not find this amusing. Still a young lady, she longed for the flowers and passionate declarations Clem received from her beau—a sailor from New London—who had one night stood beneath their window shouting up his feelings for all the world to hear. The sailor was drunk, but that wasn't the point.

Poor Clem with her fat nose and thick legs was completely sightless so spared the true knowledge of her appearance. Her beloved, neither handsome nor ugly, saw Clem's heart and loved her for that alone, which to Lucy seemed almost too romantic. Once Lucy complained (a little) that Buck was incapable of writing a good letter. Clem scolded her.

"Sometimes we must give what we want in return. Maybe the poor boy is unused to romance," she said. Ten years Lucy's senior, Clem had assumed Buck to be just as young as Lucy and judged him as if he were a boy in his teens instead of his early twenties. Lucy did not correct her for fear of embarrassment over the true age difference.

Lucy's letters to Buck were long and ponderous tomes, trying in their length and breadth to impress upon Buck that she was becoming supremely educated. She bragged about her grades in History and Geometry, only hinting once that her private study of ancient languages (with the help of a well-worn text Buck had recommended) had revealed them to be beyond her. She assured him that the financial pages of the papers were fast becoming her favorite reading—though her visual impairment made for slow going over the tiny fonts on newsprint.

Lucy kept Clem's advice in mind as she spilled small bits of cheap perfume on the fine stationery Thankful had given her as a going-away gift, and pressed fall blooms—which hadn't aged well—between the pages of her letters (as if her flowery words were not enough).

None of it seemed real. Not even the deaths of her aunt and uncle. She pulled her crepe armband around her black mourning dress and adjusted her hat when the school matron knocked at her door to tell her the carriage to the train had finally arrived. Lucy gathered up her small suitcase and the bag of fragile, tiny gifts she'd made and smiled one last time in the mirror. In a short while, she would be back in her own cozy room listening to William whistling somewhere in the house, and she would see Buck.

She hoped to spend time with her grandmother too. How odd to imagine Sarah living in the old folks home near the railroad tracks and William in charge at Tenafly Road! The telegram sent in October announcing that William and Thankful had married the previous Saturday at the Englewood Hotel with only the smallest reception had shocked and hurt Lucy, who had always dreamed of being in her cousin's wedding. She imagined William with only Mr. Adriance at his side and imagined the Crenshaw brood doing their best not to show their great disappointment in Thankful's marriage to a vegetable farmer. Who married on a Saturday—the unluckiest day of the week?

Why must William choose a girl with so few accomplishments and such high opinions of herself? He acted far too grateful for Thankful giving him the time of day, but it had always been that way, and Lucy had no power to control it. She hated admitting that Thankful intimidated her. Buck's family was far too stylish and, though Lucy counted herself a McCullough and claimed her family's past glories as her own, she resented the placement of the only respectable McCullough into the care of a shoddy home for the aged.

Lucy committed herself yet again, as she climbed aboard the train, to strive for a more Christ-like disregard for earthly station and status. Thankful might have the prettiest dresses, but Lucy would have the prettiest soul.

And what did Buck think of Thankful's quick wedding? He never once alluded to it in his letters, but then Buck alluded to nothing of any real merit. Lucy unbuttoned her luxurious beaver fur cape (a cast off garment sent by Mrs. Crenshaw) at a window seat on the train across from an admiring young man. She did not consider herself beautiful but regarded her pleasant features as gifts bestowed to her by her dead parents. No matter how nervous or confused or alone she was, she possessed an innate sense that the world was basically good and that beneath people's problems lay much nobility. Her father had been an optimist as well.

She didn't fear the darkness of death, only the fading of light to her eyes and what that might mean for her impending marriage. The idea of burdening Buck worried her. The Weldon family always swayed like a door slightly unhinged. Lucy had avoided the anger and sadness in the house because she made certain to be of no trouble. She'd always made her breakfast, plaited her hair, and whispered her morning prayers long before anyone else even blinked a bleary eye open.

Aunt Kate never needed to remind her of chores because Lucy always sensed every last need of her surrogate parents. When she found herself troubled by the endless upkeep of the big house, she'd remember to offer it all up to God and soon derive heroic pleasure in doing the dishes.

At school in New London, Lucy became the most admired and depended upon girl, and she liked it. But there was a difference. While each student suffered under varying degrees of handicap, they held no claim on her. They liked, even loved, her enthusiasm for music and ideas and clubs and jokes, but at bedtime they fell asleep dreaming of family at home.

Lucy had enjoyed this first semester at school where she did not have to worry every time a door slammed or a person stumbled on the steps, for those things were unheard of here. She had time to linger on her own thoughts until she fell asleep. Here for the first time she experienced the life of a child. In the yard surrounded by a low fence she sometimes caught the glances of boys her own age as they leapt from one boyish game to another, and she wistfully admired them. Buck was better, she reminded herself, and childhood was fleeting for all.

She played in her mind how her first meeting with Buck might go. In these daytime dreams, she was exceedingly dignified and mature. Buck, unable to wait, would run to embrace her before her feet landed on the platform. They would stroll arm in arm and tell each other their most confidential secrets.

When the train rolled up beside the station with its steeple roof and warm gas-lit windows, even the evening rain could not take away from the love Lucy held for dear little Englewood. William stood beneath a large black umbrella as the icy rain poured from the bleak evening sky. A small rush of melancholia stole over her for a second at the memory of her aunt and uncle, but she forced it away when she saw her cousin's smile. Black suited William.

"Lucy's back!" he said as he helped her on the steps and into his arms.

She squeezed him even as she glanced out of the corner of her eye for Buck.

"I'm so happy to see you, Lulu," William said, taking up her suitcase.

"For a fortnight only, I'm afraid," she said. "I've found employment in a house on the water."

"But it's certainly cold against the water this time of year," he said. "What could anyone want with you in January? I'm disappointed now."

"A good family wants me to mind their children most evenings as they're on every board in New London, and I'd like to pay some of my way."

"Why didn't you tell me? I'd have found a way if you needed anything."

She smiled at the idea of the two of them against the world until he said, "Yes, Thankful and I would do our best."

She buttoned her cape against the wind. "Well, I've already promised myself."

He shrugged.

"I'm so thrilled to see *you*, Willy," Lucy began, "but I was expecting ..."

"Yes, *I know*. Buck," he said. "I was told to tell you that he's ill."

Lucy paled.

William handed her his umbrella impatiently. "Nothing serious, but the Crenshaws decided that he shouldn't be out in the weather if he's to be of any use over the holidays."

"He should have sent me word," Lucy complained but checked herself. "Well, I hope he's better soon. Have you seen him at all?"

William shifted her baggage in his arms, nudging her toward home. "No, he's swamped, I hear, changing the world one bank account at a time."

She ignored his sarcasm. "And where is Thankful?"

"At home. She promised to make things nice and cozy for your arrival. I was at the farm until just now with Mr. Adriance—I ran all the way here to make it in time."

"So, you nearly forgot me!"

"No, no, of course not." He tilted his head to check her mood under the dripping umbrella. "I haven't gone and hurt your feelings, have I? Oh, do cheer up. It's Christmas."

Lucy forced a laugh. "Yes, you're right. I was just teasing you." It was a great relief to see him so cheerful. She sighed. "You look very well, Willy."

"I'm well—and dirty."

The rain flew at their faces all the way up Demarest past Saint Cecilia's Church, where the Angelus chimed as they passed.

"Isn't that lovely?" Her voice trailed in the wind.

"Yes, but it's Catholic. I like our church better," William said, though he and Thankful had avoided services on Sundays despite how it embarrassed Margaret that her family's pew remained so empty.

# Chapter Two

Lucy shivered, tired, cold and expectant as they turned the corner onto Tenafly Road where the once-white house came into view. "Oh, no! What's happened to it?" she cried.

"Oh. You mean the house?"

"Yes! I mean the house! It's dark! Is it purple?" Lucy squinted her eyes.

William stopped. "No. Of course it's not purple! That I wouldn't allow, but Thankful convinced me—and I agree—that navy blue is a solid color for a house. You can't tell from here, but the doors are a cheering red. You'll love it in the daylight."

"But it's always been white with green shutters."

"Yes, but times have changed," he said, somewhat hurt and apprehensive now. "It's like starting fresh."

"I don't want to start fresh. What's wrong with tradition and stability?"

"Thankful thinks new is good and I agree," William said firmly. "I thought you'd be happy I've made progress. I paid for the painters and everything out of my earnings."

"Uncle John said painters cost a fortune. And everything now is about progress. I hate it!"

"Well, Papa is gone now."

They stood in the rain a long while until a carriage on the drive interrupted their thoughts. Thankful jumped out in dismay. "Dreadful rain! And you're both here so early!" She ran toward the house, leaving the horse's reins in William's hand. "Come Lulu—let's get out from the weather!"

Lucy stood a moment waiting for William, but he shooed her in as the rain poured off his sodden hat. He laughed as if used to being the barn boy to his wife. Finally, Lucy ran for cover into the house. The front hall was almost as cold and dank as outside.

"Lucy! Oh, dear, we should have gone around the side! There's new rugs right there, and you're soaked through!"

Lucy stepped back out, but Thankful grabbed her before turning on a gaslight in the hallway. "Oh, I remember that cape. It was once so fashionable, but here—give it to me and I'll hang it in the mudroom. Josephine has the night off, and my shop was just overrun with last minute shoppers buying cards and such."

Lucy glanced around noting the old whatnot in the corner and the sturdy coatrack, always so covered in clothes, were gone. The wallpaper had changed and the family portraits no longer lined the staircase wall. A magnificent mirror had taken their place and in it under the dim light stood a drowned girl.

Thankful pulled her again. "Where is that William? He gets insulted if I tend the fire, but it's freezing in here. I hope you're not too hungry, dear. Josephine was given the night off quite unexpectedly by your cousin, and while there's food for our feast tomorrow, there's not much prepared for tonight, I'm afraid." Thankful pulled Lucy into the organized kitchen and looked around as if she'd never spent a day in it. "I'm sure there must be cheese and crackers at least. Now, if only I knew where ..."

Lucy opened the breadbox. It was bare.

"Oh, don't act so disappointed," Thankful scolded but with a tinge of guilt in her tone. "It's difficult managing a career and a home, but then you'll never need to worry about that."

"What do you mean?"

"Never mind."

"And who is Josephine?"

"Oh, a colored girl from the fourth ward. She's so sweet. You'll like her tremendously." Thankful rested her hands on her hips. "This house has always needed a girl, but your aunt and grandmother were so queer about it. I adore this house, but it suffered under great neglect. The men took days scraping away the soot on the woodwork. I can't wait to show you how beautifully it's all coming along—especially the parlor and library. Mama insisted on the newest paper for the walls and ceilings—gold stars like the clearest night sky! You'll *love* it! But right now we need to bring you up to the guest room so you can change your things."

"But Willy's got my bag ..." Lucy said in a small voice.

"Oh, never mind that! I've got tons of things and it's only three months mourning an aunt or uncle. Black doesn't suit you anyway." Thankful embraced her, delicately avoiding her wet clothes. She took Lucy's hand and led her up the darkened staircase to the room that had once belonged to her aunt and uncle.

Lucy stopped in confusion. "What about my old room?"

"Lulu, it was so tiny—the size of a wardrobe, really. We thought this room would be a nicer one for you to stay in on your visit."

"But ... I couldn't, I ..."

Thankful lit a delicate hurricane lamp and then another as she dragged Lucy in, exposing a room bearing little resemblance to the one so comforting to Lucy in childhood.

"Don't you love what we've done?" Thankful asked with bright, hopeful eyes.

"But ... it's so different."

"Yes, it is." Thankful spoke now in a clipped tone of high annoyance. "That's the point. William suffered such sadness every time he passed this room. I couldn't bear it. Every piece of furniture went to a good home—I can assure you. They were so old-fashioned, and we wanted a different mood for visitors. William loves it now."

"Does he?" Lucy was dumbstruck. "If you wouldn't mind, I'd rather my little room—if it's no trouble. I'd be afraid to put something out of order here."

"Don't be silly. You must make yourself quite at home here."

"Good. Because this is, in fact, my home still," Lucy said, moving toward the door.

Thankful pulled her close as if she were still a child. "Lucy, don't be a baby. This room is thoroughly adult, and you'll come to like it in time as William has."

"I wish I had been consulted about my aunt and uncle's things. I have nothing to remember them by now and certain things were promised to me."

"Oh, yes, I made sure to put aside a few bits of jewelry for you—the rest was of little value—and William saved you some pictures in a box somewhere."

"I will thank him for that," Lucy said. "I want to go to my room now."

Thankful pouted with an anxious flutter of her lashes. "Lulu, this is all quite awkward. I understand you're upset with the changes, but think of poor William. This house meant different things to you than him. He is better for not having to be constantly reminded of the past. I'm afraid your room was packed up and sent to my parent's house when I moved in. I plan to share so many of my nice things with you on this visit. We used your room as a wardrobe, but please take a look at the gorgeous gowns I picked for you to wear to the parties this week. We've set it up for you to enjoy a merry time even if Buck is ill."

William raced up the stairs now and entered with a proud smile until he saw Lucy crying. "What's happened? Oh, I knew she wouldn't like the room," he said to Thankful.

"I do like it," Lucy said, sniffling. "And you have every right to change everything—it's yours after all—but I didn't realize how much I'd looked forward to seeing the old things."

William came round and held her. "I stowed every little thing in the attic for you to go through—down to the tiniest hairpin. Do you imagine I've got no feelings at all?"

Lucy wiped her eyes. "I shouldn't behave this way, but it's as though my home has been robbed from me. It didn't occur to me that I'd be a guest here from now on. I loved my room and my bed."

"We have nice new beds now," William said.

"But wasn't it all expensive?"

Thankful sighed. "I appreciate that you and William shared everything in the past, but we are grown-ups now. Our finances are private, dear, and soon—even though you're very young, you'll be expected to behave with maturity as a married woman in important banking circles. Never ask about other people's money. It makes you appear ill-bred, and Buck will be disappointed."

William stared at Thankful for a moment. "Now don't be so hard on Lucy. I should have warned her."

"Warned her? I thought she'd be happy that the place finally looks respectable!" Thankful sobbed.

William took Thankful's face in his muscular hands. He had changed so much in the last three months. This intimidated Lucy. "Thankful, you've made a beautiful home for me, and now I want a peaceful time with you and Lucy." He kissed Thankful's forehead and she smiled. Then William turned to Lucy. "I'll bring you up to the attic as soon as I start a good fire."

Lucy rushed to William and hugged him. "I've missed you so much! I've missed everyone so much!"

Thankful turned away from the two, puffing the pillows on the bed. The affection between them troubled her, and she scolded herself. Hadn't she gotten everything she wanted? William. And there he stood, gently caring for his cousin. Lucy was no threat, but Thankful hated the history they had between them and hated the idea that Lucy, through Buck, would travel in the circles Thankful now missed.

William in his tattered and wet black suit embarrassed her. Thankful imagined the warmth and elegance of even her parents' home at Christmas, which was not nearly as sumptuous as the homes on the top of the Palisades. The marble mantelpiece draped in garland with silver candelabras lit with red candles. The stacks of gold-papered gifts beneath the understated tree decorated with fragile, white angels and lambs came to mind as she considered the misshapen tree in their parlor with its faded paper ornaments and German painted balls that sheltered only a scant few boxes wrapped in newsprint, for William insisted on his family "traditions."

Thankful then reminded herself how upsetting it must be for her husband this first Christmas without his parents. She almost cried at this but decided she needed to be less sentimental for everyone's sake. Someone must remain strong with the Crenshaw family coming for Christmas Day.

She gave William a compassionate smile and made her way to the frigid kitchen, trying not to be annoyed with William for giving Josephine the night off. She waited for inspiration until he trotted down the stairs to make the fires. A can of sardines, a bowl of olives, and a few mealy apples was all Thankful could muster.

William flung open the door with a grin. "Isn't Lucy the picture of health? I'm so happy she's home, aren't you?" He kissed Thankful quickly before exiting to the mud-room for kindling.

Thankful searched for the holiday platter William had mentioned they used in the past for celebrations, admiring for a moment how orderly things were since Josephine had taken over the kitchen. She congratulated herself for demanding a helper. In the parlor she found the unusual cheeses Mr. Adriance had given them as a gift. She unwrapped one resentfully. William told her days ago of his plans for expanding a herd of goat and sheep for dairying. She had not been impressed.

"Don't goats stink?" she'd asked. And this was where the shoe pinched. William. Farming. Shepherding. What about William the artist? All the debt they took on to improve the house on Tenafly Road did not make up for the facts that they did not live in the first ward and that William was a farmer! The bohemian lifestyle of an artist made allowances for romantic impoverishment, but a farmer's poverty bespoke a lack of intelligence and dignity Thankful detested.

There was more to William than muddy boots, but Thankful could not convince him or anyone in Englewood of it. She imagined the false concern of the ladies up the hill at how far she'd fallen. Her only relief from these thoughts came when occasionally William dressed for church and caught the admiration of the girls and women. He was by far the most attractive man in town. Girls fawned over him no matter where he was, and in those moments when William seemed so bashful and handsome Thankful remembered her luck.

She did not feel lucky now though. Only two days before, William had agreed to a spontaneous and rare day of fun—riding out on their horses. The weather had been warm and dry for December as they cantered over the acreage that made William a land-rich man. It had been ages since she had worn her blue riding habit, and in the frolic of their reckless style of riding even William's floppy hat from the West did not bother her. But after a few hours he had seemed restless. Thankful pretended not to notice.

"Thankful ..." William ventured, with something on his mind.

"Oh, William, let's ride into town and take tea at the new little shop ..."

William had scratched his sweaty neck. "That sounds fine, but will you come with me to check on the barn for just a few moments? I'd love for you to take an interest in the animals."

Her stomach dropped at the idea that, even for one day, he could not put her first. She had forced a polite smile.

William's face lit up, and she scolded herself for being so mean deep down, but when he dismounted near the dirty barnyard she hesitated.

"Oh, dear, my nice boots ..."

He helped her down to his side. She waited with her arms folded as he ran off to get hay for the sheep and cracked corn for the chickens fluttering up and over the fence. She suppressed a laugh at the cheerful little birds waddling out to them as William scattered corn.

"Here, Thankful, feed them a bit."

"No, never in these gloves!" she said, unable to stop being peevish.

He shrugged off his disappointment and was soon caught up in the joy of seeing his little flock of sheep looking so healthy as he whistled to them while shaking hay into a rack. Thankful stepped over a cow pie and stood before the gate he'd shut behind him. She sighed at his calm, kind face and the funny way he talked to the animals.

"Did you happen to notice the paints I put on your desk? Mr. Demarest gave them to me for a song," Thankful said.

He nodded but turned to a goat nibbling his sleeve.

She continued. "Now that's a pretty scene right there." She pointed to a stand of trees up by themselves on a rise of pasture. "You could paint it on your noon break." She waited a while for him to respond. "William, why aren't you listening?"

He shot her an impatient glance.

"Willy," Thankful said, her voice raising slightly. "Don't be angry with me. I suppose I still find it so hard to understand why you'd throw away so much talent on this."

"I *know*!" he shouted. "Haven't you let me hear about it enough?"

She had ruined the day. "I promise I won't make another peep."

William glanced again at her, face hardened as he latched the gate. "We'll see."

"William, you know I love you, don't you?" she asked, following him toward a shed.

William moaned. "Yes, I know, but you're annoying me, and I want peace for once."

"Shall I go home by myself?"

"I don't care what you do! Just leave me be!" He waved his arms and cursed under his breath as he grabbed a hay rake.

"Please don't be so angry!" She sobbed. "Won't you forgive this misunderstanding?"

"This isn't a misunderstanding," he said, wiping his brow with his sleeve. "You want me to be someone different."

"How can you say that after all I've done for you?"

He rolled his eyes. "And what have you done but complain?"

She hit his arm. "You take that back! Is it wrong to push your husband toward greatness? Is it my fault that the habits of success were never instilled in you?" She slapped her hands to her mouth. "Oh, Willy, I'm sorry! I didn't mean that. I just get so angry seeing your old lovely drawings and ..."

"Throw them away," William said. "I'll do it myself if they cause such grief."

"No! I love them so much—I want more!"

"Well, you can't have more," William said. "You'll have to settle for enough."

"Crenshaws never settle!"

William looked at his wife's beauty. "Your family thinks you have."

Thankful hesitated a moment. "Yes. But I know better."

William slipped back into mildness. "You don't act like it."

Thankful embraced him. "Please, let's not talk like this any longer."

"Fine," he said, pulling from her gently. He kissed her forehead lightly and called the chickens. "Pick one."

She brightened. "Oh, those ones there are so very pretty."

"They're Dominiques."

"That little plump one." Thankful laughed. "She looks like she's in her Sunday best. I pick her."

William grabbed it and settled it beneath his arm, petting it for a moment. Thankful took a step toward him with her hand outstretched to touch the hen, but before she placed a single finger on the fine black and white feathers William with a quick jerk broke the bird's neck. "Supper," he announced with a vindictive grin.

Thankful cried out and turned to run off, but he grabbed her arm.

"Oh, come now, Thankful ..."

She pulled free of him. "I never thought you'd be so low as to kill such a trusting little thing!"

William looked toward the barn, gathering his patience. "How do you suppose it's done? Now help me take it apart."

"I will not!" she shouted. "You did that out of spite!"

"No, I didn't," he said, cutting the bird open for Thankful to see. He pulled the guts out and threw them to a few waiting kittens. He skinned the bird now.

"You can bring so much beauty into being, but you never want to, do you?"

He glared at her. "Ask yourself the same question." He yanked at the last bit of feather-covered skin and tossed it in her direction. "Feathers for your hat."

*The question*. The question William asked of her had started in the last months as more of a shy hint here and there. These hints Thankful resented and ignored. Hadn't she told William she did not wish to be a mother? And wasn't it enough that she'd whipped William's life into order while managing a moderately successful shop of her own? She enjoyed the quiet nights in the parlor with just William, even though on drafty evenings the sound of the wind caused just the smallest bit of restlessness. When had she ever had one person to herself? When had she ever had the peace that may have allowed her own thoughts to rise to the surface (no matter if now these thoughts led to a certain dissatisfaction)?

It was on one of these blustery nights as William stoked the fire looking particularly handsome that his hinting had solidified into a real and expressed plea. Why, when they finally had each other, did William have to upset the blissful peace with the idea of a child? "Thankful," he said, "you know the telephones coming in around us might make letters obsolete and then what? I love your shop and I wish you could always have it as a hobby ..."

Thankful threw her knitting—a vain attempt at pleasing him by using wool from his flock—into the fire. "And maybe you should have your farming as a hobby. The side yard is completely overgrown."

William laughed, tossing a log in on top of the wool. "You'd enjoy that wouldn't you? Then you'd have me under your thumb every second."

"How cruel you are sometimes." She pouted, sitting back in her chair with folded arms.

"The only real wealth we have is through the Adriance place, however distasteful that is to you. You find Mr. Adriance common, but he's given us a great gift."

Her eyes welled with tears. "Well, it doesn't feel like one. You're always there, and I hardly have any time with you. All you do is talk about it and never listen when I tell you about the goings on at my shop. Now I'm not even enough for you because you want a baby!"

He threw his hands up as if finished with her for good.

She gasped. "Don't be that way!"

He turned away from her, staring at the Christmas tree covered in decorations they'd fought over but letting his eyes rest upon the one they both liked—a simple manger scene carved from ivory and inherited from William's grandparents. Taking a deep breath, he faced her again, confused and frustrated. His words and actions were always the wrong ones. "Thankful, I love you and want you to be pleased with me."

"I am pleased!" she cried. "I need no one else."

"Well," he said, scratching his head as he approached her, "I won't ask you for a while. Maybe you'll change your mind, but ... Thankful, could we at least spend more nights ... together?"

"Oh, Willy, I'd love that too."

"But we hardly ever do. Is there something wrong with ...?"

"Oh, no! Of course not! Not at all." She rushed to him now, wrapping her arms around his middle, looking up into his mellow eyes. "It's just that I'm so afraid of a baby and it all going terribly wrong."

William pulled one of her curls with a look of great seriousness. "I promise I would never abandon you and a baby to the drink."

She stared at him. "I never even imagined that."

Now it was Christmas and it didn't much feel like it though Margaret had sent her a few of her very favorite Currier and Ives Christmas china pieces. Up at the Crenshaw house, Thankful knew her mother would sit for tea as she directed the stable boys hanging yards and yards of fragrant garlands sent up by the florist next to Thankful's shop. Special Christmas jars would come from another year in hiding to be filled with the most delectable cookies one could imagine—and the candies!

William had brought home spice drops and orange slices from Demarest's store, but they were ordinary candies not worthy of the chipped piece of fine crystal he dumped them into—a simple Weldon tradition. When he suggested that she'd had far too many pies made for their budget and the number of guests they would be entertaining, she gave him a superior stare and wondered aloud if he'd had much experience being a housewife, to which he sighed and resumed his whittling by the fire.

And that was another thing ... he never read the papers. Thankful had acquired a taste for news and politics at her grandmother's and considered an uninformed man to be lacking in an important way. When she mentioned women's suffrage William smiled, benevolently offering to use his vote for whomever Thankful liked. He considered one politician as bad as the next, which Thankful *knew* to be *not* so.

Some politicians supported unions—Thankful did not. This was a free country and anyone of merit should rise to the top and keep what they earned. Hadn't her very own grandmother done just that? Even in her seventies Martha continued to try new things and to work hard for every bit of finery she owned. Thankful wasn't sure what William thought, though she detected a small bit of disappointment in her when she insisted that no one should be forced to give over their fortunes to people who didn't want to work as hard.

"Is a banker more important than a farmer?" he asked pointedly.

"Let the market decide!"

William laughed.

What from a distance had seemed so quaint about his upbringing now, when attached to her reputation, felt like an embarrassment. On all the past Christmas visits to the house on Tenafly Road, she'd never noticed the chipped china, the chairs with uneven legs, or the way the window panes had been sloppily painted in the corners. Even the way William reminisced about his "Papa" seemed homespun. "Father" sounded far superior, and although Thankful had always considered John Weldon a dear old man he was no Doctor Graham Crenshaw.

These things Thankful pondered as she cut slices from the summer sausage and threw them, along with Mr. Adriance's cheeses, onto one of the old platters she'd found on a high shelf. She wasn't hungry anyway, and William never should have given Josephine the night off. Didn't they pay her well enough? A woman with five children should take the extra work. Thankful vowed again to herself that the child she'd gotten rid of would be the only one. It was selfish and nearly immoral to bring so many starvelings into the world and expect others who had more control to pay for them.

Thankful's reserve of charitable thoughts stood at an all-time low this evening as she remembered the money she owed Mr. Demarest for the gift she'd gotten William and the money William had secretly spent on his cousin. Lucy had never asked for it, but he confessed to sending her money the last few months for books and such. It annoyed her that he had kept it from her, but then she probably would have talked him out of it.

What did Lucy really need schooling for? Wouldn't it have been nice to continue school herself? Thankful had always been at the top of her class. But then she remembered Buck and his reputation and considered that this schooling gave Lucy an extra year to grow into a woman. Thankful nicked her finger with the knife and mumbled something quite beneath her as William pushed into the kitchen humming a Christmas tune.

She turned to him with a sigh as he sat a box upon the table. "Willy, we'll catch our deaths if you don't build a fire soon."

He frowned good-naturedly and pulled her away from her work. "Come now, Thankful. It's Christmas, and I can't bear two girls acting sorry for themselves."

"And why should Lucy be sad?"

"She's gained the world," he said, "but lost all that matters to her. She has me, but it's different now—she says."

Thankful wiped her sticky hands on the fine apron William had given her. "Well, it's a shame that money is being wasted on her if it's not making her happy."

He stood with his arms crossed.

"Oh, that came out wrong, Willy. I just mean she will have to grow up fast. Marriage is a serious thing. She'll realize soon enough that everyone can't keep doting on her. You're mine now, and she'll have Buck one day."

"I don't like being owned," he replied sharply. Catching sight of the sloppily laid-out platter, he pushed past Thankful and arranged the food in the way his mother would have done.

Thankful came up beside him. "That's not a fair thing to say."

He leaned against the counter. "We've been so caught up in our happiness we didn't consider Lucy's feelings about all of our changes. We should have invited her back for the wedding."

"That's ridiculous," she said. "And nobody asked me if it was all right to store Lucy's things in my room up the hill."

He cried out in exasperation. "You offered your room!"

She played with a loose curl. "I suppose I did, but I assumed she'd be grateful! Mama sent her truckloads of my things without even asking! No one even comes to visit!"

"Is that what this is about?" he asked. "You've got your whole family coming here tomorrow, and up until now you wouldn't think of having anyone until the walls were just so."

"But always in the past the Crenshaws are together for *every* day of the holidays!" she sobbed.

"Fred has every right to invite your family west. I told you you could go if you wanted."

"But I don't want to go without you."

"Well, I'm a farmer now. With responsibilities."

"That come at a cost!" She picked up the platter, but on second thought slammed it back on the counter and threw herself into the old armchair, crying.

"Yes, there is a cost, and you knew of it when we married," William said. "A short while ago you were happy anyone would marry you."

She pounded her fist against the chair arm. "Take that back!"

William looked at the ceiling. "All right. I will. That was cruel, but ..."

"But nothing!" she cried. "I don't even want a trip west. It's not that. But we're so responsible now that it's no fun."

He laughed. "Wasn't it fun to paint and hang paper and change everything? Because if it wasn't then it's a costly mistake we'll be paying for."

"I didn't know I'd have to choose between decent living conditions and a little company now and again."

He rolled his eyes. "And tonight we have company, and we treat her to this little pile of scraps and a cold house!" He stormed out of the kitchen for the parlor.

Feeling sunk and miserable, Thankful listened to him throwing wood into the fireplace. The box on the table caught her attention now. Thankful ran her hand over the plain paper wrapping.

William came back in search of more kindling on the porch. "That's for you—go on and open it," he said gruffly as he passed her.

She considered not opening it, but her curiosity got the better of her. She untied the ribbon and pulled the top off to find a pile of old sketchbooks. She flipped open the top one and found drawings of friends from long ago school days and then ones of her. For every page of friends there were two of Thankful—young and merry—her dark curls unruly even when pulled back with ribbons and bows. Here was a picture of her sharing sweets with a friend. Here was one of her lingering beneath the old maple out in front of the post office before it had been struck by lightning. "I must have been only eleven or twelve," she said to herself, though William had re-entered the room.

"Go on, there's more," he said, pleased to have surprised her.

The sketchbooks as William's talent matured told more about Thankful than she wanted to know. "Willy, you make me so beautiful. They're all quite untrue."

"It's how I see you."

She cried now. "No, William. I'm not a nice girl, am I?"

"Maybe not," he said. "But you could be. You once were."

"Won't you ever draw me again?" she pleaded. "I'm so disappointed that the artist in you is gone."

He picked up a stray piece of kindling that had fallen. "When I look at those sketches or any drawings of mine, I can remember exactly how I felt at the time—I don't want any of it back."

"Not even me?"

He pondered. "That Thankful was a dream. I don't need to draw what I already have in front of me."

"Is it because I'm so ugly now?"

He smiled, shaking his head. "One day, you'll live up to your name, and I mean to help you on that score."

She huffed. "It's not nice to lecture me that way. I wish I'd been named something less descriptive."

William sat now, piling the little pieces of wood on the clean table. "You spend all of your time wishing, don't you. Are you never satisfied?" His voice was soft but impatient.

"Oh, William, it's true! Why can't I be happy?"

"You can if you choose to," he said, tapping a piece of wood.

"It's not that easy, you know," she explained, sitting opposite him. "I try to be bright and cheerful and do fake it terribly well all day at the shop, but ... I feel so restless—like something's missing."

William shifted a minute and glanced at the mantel clock. He stood and gathered the wood again. "Maybe a baby is what you miss."

She jumped out of her seat. "Must you? I try to tell you something and you bring that up to spoil everything. I told you I never wanted children!"

"But I didn't think you meant it!" he said. "I can't help being disappointed. I've tried to stop thinking about it, but I feel that if we don't have any children what's the point?"

She gasped. "You only wanted me to be a vessel for your child?"

"What?" He hardly understood her words. "No! That's not it! It just seems like, well, that we're failures in some way. I don't know ..."

"Are we really failures by saving a child from this miserable world?"

William took a moment to regard Thankful in hurt exasperation. "I didn't think all that we had was so miserable and I wanted a child because it's natural to want to create something from love—and see what we'd look like in a little one—something just ours and no one else's. I thought it would be lovely."

"What if we sold everything and ran off to ... France!" she offered. "Just us!"

He said nothing for a long while. "I don't speak French."

"Well, I do," she said haughtily. "And we could see fine art and eat at the cafes ..."

William pushed the swing door to the hallway. "I haven't any patience for this talk anymore. I let you have complete say in this house and let you work in town and ..."

She stomped her feet and followed. "You *let* me? My pay brings in money."

"Not much," he mumbled as he threw the kindling into the hearth in the parlor and set about building the fire.

"You were given land and a house for free! Don't act superior!"

He stood very close. "I insist on you behaving while Lucy is here! And I *like* farming!"

"That's because you're a coward!"

"You're a horrible wife and ungrateful," William whispered.

Thankful burst into fresh tears. "Yes! I am! Just divorce me! I know you want to."

He shook her. "What is wrong with you? It's impossible to make you happy! What I really want is a drink and you're the one driving me to it!"

"Oh!" she moaned. "Don't say that!"

"I'll say what's true. You make life miserable. I walk on eggshells. I check your moods and still I can't do anything right!" William stormed away from her. "I'm going out!"

"Not to the Liberty Pole, I hope!" she said, coming to his side.

"I'll go where I like!"

Just then Lucy arrived in the doorway wearing one of Thankful's castoff wrappers, looking innocent and beautiful. Her eyes welled with tears at the sound of their arguing. "Why do you both act so mean?"

"You'll understand someday," William said, glancing at his wife.

"I don't want to understand," Lucy said. "If you leave this house tonight and get drunk, I'll go back to school on the first train. Don't test me because I *will* do it."

"Are you threatening me?" William asked in surprise.

"It's no threat," she said, her eyes set firmly on her cousin, "but I will not stay to witness you destroying yourself."

The crackling fire finally began to give heat. The three stood silently until William went to the flames and adjusted the logs. "Well, I wasn't *really* going to leave. I was angry." He turned to them. "I'm sorry. To you both."

Thankful stared at Lucy in wonder as if Lucy had wrestled a lion. "I'm sorry too, Lucy. I should have planned tonight better." She sighed. "Forgive me, William."

William smiled in resignation. "You're lucky you're beautiful," he said, taking up Thankful's soft hand to kiss.

Lucy laughed and suggested popcorn. They lit candles on the piano Margaret and Graham had bought, and Thankful plunked out carols for them to sing. Not another harsh word was spoken. Lucy, after a long day of travel, finally gave in to her exhaustion and said goodnight before making her way up to her aunt's bedroom, but she couldn't sleep. She pulled on another set of stockings in the frigid room and laid an extra blanket on the bed before sitting at the fine desk pushed against the window. Pulling a Christmas postcard from the pile of expensive stationery, she dipped her pen and wrote:

*Dearest Buck,*

*How funny it is to be just down the hill from you yet unable to see you after all this time apart. I do hope you are feeling better. I appreciate you not wanting to spread illness, but I would love to meet you anyway. This house is so very empty with only William and Thankful. It makes me think I would not mind having all of those children you wanted.*

*I must confess that our secret engagement seems nothing more than a dream to me. My bedroom here has been changed into a closet full of Thankful's lovely clothes. She's organized dresses for me to borrow for every day of visiting this holiday. I will admit that even though Thankful assures me my dance cards will be full, I would trade it all for one dance with you.*

*Sincerely,*

*Lucy*

# Chapter Three

Lucy lay in bed shivering and listening to the sound of the rain-turned-to-sloppy snow as it fell from the roof onto the sodden ground. The bedding she hid beneath was soft and luxurious, but not very warm. During the night she'd searched in vain for the well-worn quilts and woolen blankets of her youth but figured they had been hidden or thrown away to the rag men. Her stomach growled.

A few moments before she'd heard movement in the kitchen below, and now the aroma of coffee brewing slid beneath the door of her room. She threw the blankets off and searched for the morning robe Thankful had mentioned she should wear. The slippers at her feet had embroidered squirrels and chickadees upon them, and Lucy stood admiring them with a smile. Thankful *did* have good taste.

On tiptoe she passed the bedroom on the first floor that had once belonged to her grandparents, and where William and Thankful now slept, and pushed the swing door into the kitchen.

A diminutive black woman in her late twenties started at the creak of the door. "Oh, I wasn't expecting anyone up this early, miss."

Lucy rushed to the hearth, rubbing her hands together before the fire. "I can't tell you how grateful I am for this fire! You must be Josephine. I'm Lucy."

"Lucy." The woman studied her. "I'm happy to meet you, Miss McCullough. The coffee is nearly done."

Lucy with a sigh flopped into and curled up on her grandfather's chair, the only piece of furniture still left from the old days—three months ago.

"Oh, miss, you shouldn't sit there when I can bring out coffee to you in the dining room," Josephine said uneasily.

"But it's so cozy in here—if you don't mind," Lucy said, staring happily into the fire. "My grandmother and aunt spent all of their days in here and it makes me feel close to them."

"But the dining room is best," Josephine said, with more force. "Mrs. Weldon wouldn't approve."

Lucy stood. "Well, I don't care." She skipped to the stove, resolving to remain cheerful, and poured herself coffee as Josephine hovered. Lucy spilled a small bit of sugar on the counter, and Josephine wiped it up with her rag. "How is it, Josephine, that you're stuck here on Christmas morning?"

"What do you mean?"

"It's unchristian to make you work Christmas morning," Lucy said, taking her seat again.

"I get paid twice for it so I don't mind." Josephine tightened the bow of her apron and went back to kneading the yeasty dinner rolls. A bird sat dressed for roasting near the stove.

"I'd like to make a pie if I may."

Josephine stopped again, this time not as obligingly. "Miss, we've plenty of pies and fixings made already. I've worked to the bone all week making things just the way Mrs. Weldon likes them and keeping this place spotless. We have *enough* pies."

Lucy sipped her coffee. "I'm perfectly willing to take the blame for making a pie. This is my home until I'm married, and I'll help you in any way I want."

"But, Miss McCullough, you'd help *best* if you'd go to the dining room."

Lucy turned to Josephine and noted the distress in her dark eyes. Impulsively she took Josephine by the hands with a look of sudden shame. "I understand, and I'm sorry. I was being a spoiled child. I know it must be difficult to work for Thankful."

And there stood Thankful with a sickly-sweet smile at the door.

"Merry Christmas, Josephine. I do hope you'll like your gift. It's there on the pantry shelf."

"Oh, ma'am, I'm sure I'll love it."

"And Josephine ... we'll be taking breakfast in the *dining room* as usual," Thankful said. "But do be a dear, and open your gift first. I'm terribly excited to see if you like it."

Josephine complied with an enthusiastic grin. She ran to the pantry and brought the ribbon-bedecked box to the pristine counter, pulling the top off with a gasp. "Mrs. Weldon! This is just the thing to wear with the dress you gave me. They'll all be jealous at Sunday services." She placed the enormous orange hat on her head, primping in the window's reflection.

"You look stunning," Lucy said. She hated orange, but upon Josephine's head it looked the height of sophisticated elegance.

Josephine smiled at Lucy and turned to her employer. "Mrs. Weldon takes such good care of me," she said, wiping her eyes.

Thankful beamed triumphantly, taking Lucy by the elbow. "Let's leave Jo alone now—in *her* kitchen."

William, in a plaid robe Thankful insisted he wear, sat sleepily in his chair although he'd already been to the Adriance farm and back. "Merry Christmas, Lucy," he said, looking awkward at the head of the table.

Thankful guided Lucy to a chair at the center before taking her own seat at the other end of the long table. Josephine carried coffee on a tray and served it out before leaving again. William pushed the coffee aside and poured himself a large glass of milk, filling it almost to the top.

Thankful glared at William as he emptied the glass without taking a breath. She huffed before sipping her coffee.

"Just this once," Lucy asked William, "can we sit closer?"

William looked to Thankful, who held her ground briefly. She was torn between wanting things done in a certain way and feeling foolish for making them strangers at table. "I suppose it is silly being so formal, just us three who've known each other for years."

William jumped up with a grin to help Thankful and Lucy with their chairs. They laughed a little before going back to sipping their coffee in uncomfortable silence.

"The hat you gave Josephine was pretty," Lucy offered.

Thankful nodded. "Yes, well, despite what you may take me for, I can be as generous as you, dear, little Lulu."

Lucy, noting the condescension, considered how noble it would be to ignore the comment but couldn't. "Yes, it's a splendid hat, probably an old one from your collection. Wouldn't it have been better to buy her something useful? For a poor lady with family, there must have been something more fitting."

Thankful laughed, giving William a grown-up and annoying look. "Oh, Lulu, how funny that you've suffered under trying financial circumstances your whole life, but as soon as you imagine you've moved up in the world you tell others how to spend money. Would it have been better if I'd given Jo a lump of coal for heat or an apron? Or is it only you who should get my hand-me-downs?"

"I've never asked you for a thing. We were never poor, and it's extremely rude to insult my upbringing and William's parents. I won't have it in our house!"

"Lucy, don't make a spectacle of yourself," William muttered.

"How can you let her be so mean?"

"Let's have a nice day," he said, stirring his coffee.

Thankful leaned in closer to Lucy and grasped her hand. "William's right. It's Christmas. One day, Lulu, you'll understand the ways of the world."

"I understand right now!"

William pushed his chair back from the table. "Lucy, I'm afraid you *don't* understand. This is Thankful's home now, and she went to a lot of trouble making it nice for me—and you—and all you do is find fault."

"Willy, does a servant really need a special hat?" Lucy asked. "How can you afford it?"

Josephine stood at the door with poached eggs and toast—nothing like the usual McCullough Christmas morning feast. Lucy kept her eyes down in humiliation at having been heard out of context and noted that Josephine placed her plate upon the table less than gently.

William cleared his throat and lay a cloth over his lap. "Mr. Adriance tells me to wish you both a merry Christmas."

Thankful spoke through clenched teeth. "That's nice of him."

William took a few bites of his breakfast.

Lucy surveyed him. "I thought you didn't like poached eggs."

William sighed in exasperation. "No, I like them just fine now that Josephine makes them." He shoved more in his mouth while staring out the window.

Lucy moved the food around on her plate with reddened cheeks.

"Don't you like them?" Thankful asked. "You should. They come from William's hens."

Lucy livened. "Oh, really? How fun!"

Thankful smiled, but her eyes gave away something different. "It's cute how you admire every little thing William does."

Lucy straightened in her seat. "Of course I admire him. Don't you?"

William stood now. "It's time we opened gifts."

Thankful poured another cup of coffee. "Josephine has scones."

"The scones can wait," William said sternly.

They moved to the warm parlor and seated themselves in silence. Lucy squinted her eyes at the new wallpaper and smiled at the tree. "Oh, how I love the old ornaments!"

"We're lucky to have any of them after the time you crushed them in your crib," William said, laughing.

"But you brought them to me and blame me even now when I was only a baby!" Lucy grinned. "Remember when Aunt Kate made those cookies, and you imagined one looked like a little face and felt sorry for it so you kept it in your sock drawer for months?"

"That cookie had a sad look." William laughed. "That was the only year everyone was truly well after coming back east, and we sang carols in the kitchen—even Grandmother."

"Your father wrote those little stories about us that year too. I wish I would have saved mine," Lucy mused. "Only he could have made me so brave and good."

William warmed to the subject. "The thing I liked about his stories was that he never made anyone too brave or too good. Thankful suggested I re-read his books these last months, and they're far better than I remembered."

Lucy nodded in approval at Thankful's suggestion.

William got up to throw a log on the fire. "Maybe I just miss him now and the stories bring him back."

Thankful retrieved two small packages from beneath the tree. "I found these in your father's study while packing it up," she said with genuine excitement. She handed the gifts to Lucy and William.

Lucy opened hers first. It was her aunt's blue earbobs. She unfolded the note and read it aloud:

*Dear Lucy,*

*Please remember the beautiful woman who always loved you so much when you wear these. I should be proud to know that my mother's one luxury enhanced the beauty of both my most favorite girls. Remember me too.*

*Yours with great affection,*

*Uncle John*

"Oh, I've always loved these earbobs! How could I ever forget you, dear Uncle?" Lucy said, sniffling as she put the earrings on.

"They suit you," Thankful said. "They must be a hundred years old."

"Yes! Isn't that delicious?" Lucy gushed, running to the mirror and admiring them up close.

William hesitated when the attention of the girls landed upon him. What if the gift was stupid? What if it was maudlin? What if it hurt too much?

"Go on, William," Thankful prodded. "It's taken every ounce of my strength to keep them secret this long."

William grinned at his pretty wife and carefully opened the paper. A little pile of medals sat all tangled together. William read his note in silence.

"Oh, that's not fair!" Lucy said. "Let us hear from Uncle John."

William coughed. He hated reading anything aloud. He smiled and began:

*Dear William,*

*When you were a child I almost couldn't stand to look at you. Your beauty hurt me. You were an undeserved gift, but you also looked like an untarnished repli-ca of me. A father can never tell his son how deeply blessed he feels to have a boy. One day you will understand, but for now I can say that these medals never held a flame to the satisfaction you have given me. You were always a gentle soul—never vicious, never cruel. You have finally become the man I always hoped you would be and the man I always wanted to be. I may have gotten the medals you felt you needed to be a real man and here they are now, but I can rest in peace now knowing that you fought against a far greater foe than Southerners or Apaches. You fought the Weldon curse and won. May God bless you the rest of your days, and I will be waiting for you.*

*With great love,*

*Papa*

William closed the paper around his gift and folded the note putting them both on the table he sat beside. "The fool." He laughed, uncomfortably, while wiping his nose, "I *do* miss him."

Thankful kissed William's cheek and knelt beside him. "Dear, sweet Willy, forgive me for sometimes forgetting what your father saw in you!"

"Don't be silly, Thankful," he said with a shy grin. "We'd better open the rest of these things before the Crenshaw clan descends upon us." He pulled a tiny box from under the tree and handed it to Thankful

"But you already gave me the sketchbooks!" Thankful said as she unwrapped the box. Inside was a gold locket. She glanced at William.

"Go on. Open it," he said.

Thankful opened the square locket which resembled a miniature book that enclosed ten gem tintypes—one of each member of the Crenshaw family including Thankful.

"I know how you sometimes wish you were still up there on the hill with them all," he said. "I appreciate you coming down here for me."

Thankful kissed the locket and embraced her husband. "I've always wanted to be here! But you understand me terribly well. I *love* it! I will always wear it."

Lucy handed out her sloppily embroidered hankies and pressed flowers framed in dark wood. Thankful handed Lucy her gift. A pair of new earrings from a fashionable shop in town met with a polite thank you. She opened an envelope and pulled out a piece of newsprint in embarrassment.

"It's a bicycle!" Thankful explained. "I couldn't bring it inside or you'd guess immediately what it was."

"Oh, how ... interesting," Lucy said, staring at the picture.

"Don't you like bicycles?"

Lucy looked to William for help, but none was forthcoming. Lucy was the farthest thing from a suffragette and spoke strongly against bloomers of any sort, but there was something more obvious. "Thankful, cycling must be so fun, but I'm afraid you don't quite perceive how awfully bad my eyes have gotten."

Thankful covered her face in shame for a moment. "Oh, Lucy, I'm mortified! It's true, I didn't think! I enjoy it so much and imagined us as friends riding out sometime! It was so unthinking and foolish and expensive! I'm ashamed. Please forgive me."

"There's nothing to forgive," Lucy said. "I appreciate the sentiment and the earrings are lovely."

William squirmed in his chair, slightly annoyed at Thankful for buying Lucy a separate gift without conferring with him. "Thankful, don't fret. Now where's your gift for me?" he asked with a happy grin.

Thankful shrank back into her chair. "Oh ... you won't like it, and I wish I had had more time to exchange it. I sincerely do. Perhaps you'll let me take it back and give you something in a few days."

"Don't be such a baby. Let me see it."

"Willy, I ..."

William retrieved the box from under the tree and shook it with a laugh. "Nothing fragile, I hope."

She shook her head in dread.

William opened the box, and his smile disappeared. Pulling out tube after tube of expensive oils and squirrel hair brushes, he remained calm and quiet until the last one lay upon the table. William stood and left the room then. Lucy looked on in confusion as Thankful threw the paints back in the box, her hands shaking.

"The paints are quite nice," Lucy said.

Thankful whimpered and ran to the porch where William stood smoking a cigarette. "I bought them a while back, dear! I didn't have time to return them. Forgive me!"

William turned to her. "It takes everything in me to stay sober."

"And I'm so grateful!"

"No, you don't understand!" William said. "I'm not doing it for you. I'm doing it for me. Only I can take care of myself. I've loved you forever, Thankful, but maybe we're not any good for each other. I can't spend my whole life not being enough for you."

"You *are* good enough!"

"I hoped I might be, but I'm not," he said in his soft-spoken way. "There was a time I'd have settled for just you, but I want more for myself. I want a wife who loves me no matter what. I don't want our marriage to turn into what your parents have. I don't want to be belittled by you and despise you for your pettiness."

"And your parents were better?" Thankful cried.

"Mother and Papa weren't the perfect people I wanted them to be, but they never spoke an unkind word about each other."

"Your parents were fakes!" Thankful replied, with a stomp of her slipper.

"They were quiet people who took their medicine without complaint." William blushed at his unfortunate choice of words.

Thankful kept herself from using the clear pathway to a grave insult. She held her tongue for a moment. "William, please don't leave me. I couldn't bear it. The constant nagging you about art will stop. I promise."

"You always promise."

"I mean it this time," she said shakily.

William flicked his cigarette into the slush off the porch. "I don't want to ruin Christmas for Lucy so I'll come back inside, but you have to do something for me."

"Anything."

"I don't want you to return those paints. Use them."

Thankful laughed in annoyed disbelief. "What for?"

"For you. I don't care what you paint, but I want you to paint something, and we'll hang it in the house."

"I'd be humiliated!"

He raised his brows with a grin. "Then you'll know how I feel."

"But your work is *good*."

"Well, maybe yours will be better than you think," he said, wrapping his strong arms around her. "When you finish your painting, then I'll think about painting mine."

Thankful rubbed her face against William's chest playfully. "Oh, William Weldon, you *will* be sorry! Miss Hayes back at school said I had the worst sense of color and design she'd ever seen, and I'll make sure I hang the monstrosity over our bed."

"Hey! You promised we'd get a mirror," he whispered.

Thankful slapped him, laughing. "I never said any such thing!"

Lucy peeped her head out from behind the door. "Will we be off to church soon?"

William shook his head. "Sorry, Lucy, but we're staying home to prepare for the supper guests. You don't mind, do you?"

Lucy glared at Thankful, who didn't notice. "I hope *you* don't mind if I keep the tradition," Lucy replied, closing the door again and running up to the guest room. An ornate, red dress hung on the door of an armoire, but Lucy refused it. Her mourning outfit, still damp, would have to do. She pulled her braided hair up over her head like a Scandinavian princess. Her own hat was too sodden, so against her feelings she propped one of Thankful's atop her head and raced down the stairs, took a cloak, slipped into boots and grabbed an umbrella before William and Thankful could notice her gone.

The ground glistened white and gray in the bright sun, annoying her eyes. The small veil she pulled over her eyes was of little help, but never mind, it felt good to be out in the neighborhood she loved so well—even if her boots kept little of the cold and wet from her feet. By chance, Mr. Adriance and his horse—an offspring of her aunt's Handsome—trotted up as Lucy negotiated the icy patches and avoided puddles on the road. "Young lady, today's not the day for walking to church. Would you take a ride from an old friend?"

She laughed, nodding enthusiastically. The old man jumped down to help her aboard, smiling the whole time. Adriance tucked a blanket around her wet skirt, and off the two went.

"And where is William this morning? Back to bed?" Adriance asked.

"Oh, Mr. Adriance, I do hate to speak ill of anyone on Christmas, but William would never miss church when his parents were alive. Thankful seems positively opposed to any traditions we have, and I don't know how I'll keep my temper today!"

Adriance chuckled. "Marriage to a pretty girl changes things, but you'll see. One day you'll marry a boy who will want a few things done his way, and you'll compromise."

"Never," she said. "Well, not about the important things like God and church and Christmas. My husband would never ask it of me."

Adriance chuckled again and glanced at her sideways before tipping his hat to a man on the street. "Dreams differ from reality, Lucy."

"You may be right, sir, but I don't have to like it."

"Nope. I suppose you don't, but I hope you won't be too hard on your cousin. William only wants to please his girl, and don't you want him to be happy?"

"Yes," Lucy said with a sigh.

"You say your prayers for them both, and they'll come back to God."

She nodded politely but said no more, resolving to pray for William only.

The bells of her beloved First Presbyterian Church cheered her as the enormous building on the hill came into view. Lucy wondered what denomination her mother had been and if her family sat this very moment in an Illinois church wondering about a far-away granddaughter. Mr. Adriance spotted the old men he usually sat with as they entered the church but then hesitated a moment.

Lucy thanked him and assured him that she could find her way to the Weldon pew, but when she reached it she was surprised to find it filled with strangers. Before she could decide what to do, a loud and familiar greeting arose from the Crenshaw pew. There Margaret stood twisted toward Lucy while waving a delicate hankie. Lucy giggled as Margaret pushed past her children and ran down the aisle to greet her with a warm bear hug.

"Oh, my little flower, come sit with us. This is your place now," Margaret ordered, pushing Lucy up the aisle.

Lucy happily assented, for the first time feeling truly welcomed back. Graham sat on the other side of his three youngest children, who were not so young anymore. He waved affectionately as did the children. Lucy scanned the fuzzy crowd before taking her seat.

Margaret sat at the aisle and whispered, "Oh, dear, don't cry. Buck isn't here. He's awful sick—keeping nothing down. A feeble constitution like his father. It'll be your job to keep him fit one day." Margaret squeezed her shoulders. "It's so good to see you."

"And you," Lucy replied.

Margaret took her by the chin. "You are a handsome one. Now, where are Thankful and William? It shouldn't take this long to hitch their carriage."

Lucy shook her head as the chorus began to sing:


*Christians, awake, salute the happy morn*
*    Whereon the Savior of the world was born*
*    Rise to adore the mystery of love*
*    Which hosts of angels chanted from above*
*    With them the joyful tidings first begun*
*    Of God incarnate and the Virgin's Son*

Throughout the service Margaret talked—much to the annoyance of the nearby congregants. "Lucy, is it true that Thankful has duck prepared for supper?"

"I believe so, Mrs. Crenshaw," she said, still hungry after the light breakfast.

"Well, I'm glad I had our girl bake a nice honeyed ham to bring down. I do so hate duck," Margaret confided.

Lucy cringed. "Did you ask Thankful if she'd mind?"

"Whatever for? It's a surprise, and I'm sure no one minds extra food after the holidays. It saves the pocketbook."

Lucy inched away from Margaret. It was becoming quite close. "She has planned it just so."

"I'm glad to hear it," Margaret said. "I wondered if she would ever embrace her womanhood. I look forward to this evening. You must love the way Thankful has completely erased the morbid Weldon décor from the McCullough house."

Lucy pretended not to hear.

Margaret sighed. "But, no matter. Before long you'll have a place of your own, and we'll decorate it, you and I, and I venture a guess that we'll have substantial funds to play with. Buck is making a *real good* showing at the bank. They don't care a fig about his looks in their backroom. Bankers have bigger things to mind, of course, and Buck is a hard worker. I've never seen the likes of it, even with his father."

"Maybe he's worked himself sick," Lucy whispered.

Margaret shook her head and looked down at Lucy with a pitying bit of condescension. "Oh, no, dear. This isn't a silly novel. It's been ever so mild this fall and the waters have never frozen yet. One of Buck's new friends has a yacht, and they had it out these last Saturdays. Buck's come in all hours of the night. It's what brought on the catarrh and stomach complaints. Brandy can do that to a man if he's not careful."

"Late nights?" Lucy's blood went cold.

"Be a big girl now. All men have them," Margaret said, waving her fan now.

Lucy felt spiteful. "I suppose even Doctor Crenshaw?"

Margaret laughed. "Oh, not him! The doctor only stays up late with sick customers. He's a homebody, and honestly I'm happy about it."

"Of course," Lucy said, shivering in her wet clothes. The music seemed overly joyful, and she just wanted to go home. The idea of debauchery on the high seas disconcerted her greatly.

Margaret looked over Lucy. "Dear, it's almost been three months—your mourning attire is a bit extreme for an aunt and uncle. Bright dresses will make you so much more attractive."

"Uncle John and Aunt Kate were like parents to me."

"I'm your Mama now. You'll be family soon enough." Margaret squeezed her again. "How is Josephine doing for Thankful?"

"Quite well, I believe."

"Good. I arranged it, you know. I believe very strongly that the Negro women should be given the means to empower themselves. The men—well—I don't know any, but I do hold it against that Milford Streeter for starting Buck's unhingedness. But don't worry, Lucy. He's nearly his old self now—thank heavens. And no matter what happens, remember that we'll always see that you're rewarded for your efforts with him."

"I need no reward, Mrs. Crenshaw," Lucy said, taken aback.

Margaret laughed. "All women need reward for staying with their Crenshaw men. You'll understand by and by."

# Chapter Four

Mr. Adriance drove Lucy home after church, but the happy feeling of their earlier ride had disappeared in the icy rain. The old farmer's horse limped up the hill. Lucy tried to make Adriance drop her off so he could take the poor animal directly home, but he would hear none of it. As they pulled up the drive at Tenafly Road, the horse stumbled and collapsed in the snow. Lucy and Adriance jumped from the carriage. The limp had been warning of a greater problem. The horse died.

Lucy cried and pet the horse's head, kissing it and praying for its safe passage to heaven. Adriance pulled her to her feet. "There, there, Lucy. You're right. He's in a better place now." He glanced up to the house. "Now do me a favor and go get Willy."

She ran up under the front porch and pulled at the locked door. Thankful came to the long window and motioned for her to go around to the kitchen. Once inside and breathless, Lucy called for William from the mudroom with mud and ice dripping from her skirt.

Thankful came to her instead with hands on hips. "And what on earth is the commotion? William's napping. He works hard enough, you know."

"But it's Mr. Adriance ..."

"What about him?" Thankful asked impatiently.

"He's in the drive with a dead horse."

Thankful pushed past Lucy and leaned out the door. "My Lord, why did he bring it here?"

"He drove me home—he insisted."

Thankful glared at her. "Why is everything so difficult? Today is my family's day and now how will they come up the drive in less than an hour with a dead horse blocking the way?" But then she laughed fatalistically. "Land sakes, what a mess! Mama will never let me hear the end of it."

"But your mother would understand that you have no say if a horse dies on your property."

Thankful sighed. "Oh, you don't understand my mother. I'm a bundle of nerves."

"Shall we get Willy? He'll know what to do," Lucy suggested.

"Get dressed in something warm, and I'll get your cousin," she replied, her temper now under control. "I'm sorry that I've been so irritable."

Lucy smiled. She admired Thankful's sophistication and wanted to like her. "I'll wear your earrings today."

Thankful kissed her forehead in a matronly way, which at once annoyed and comforted Lucy.

There was a knock at the door then, and Adriance stood looking haggard and sad in the cold. Thankful let him into the mudroom but no further. "Oh, Mr. Adriance, poor man, I'll fetch William now."

Lucy stood near the kitchen hearth until Thankful left the room, then ran to Mr. Adriance, dragging him in by the fire.

"The floor, miss!" Josephine hissed.

"Never mind it, Jo," Lucy scolded. "Do you want this man to die his death because of a clean floor? Mr. Adriance needs a drink of something fortifying."

Josephine's humanity awoke. She poured tea and set a scone on one of the nice plates, pointing Mr. Adriance toward the table.

Lucy demanded he take his coat off, and Mr. Adriance was in no hurry to disobey. He bit into the scone, his face lighting up. "A bit of heaven, this is!" He licked the creamy butter from his fingertips.

Josephine, puffed up now by his kind words, passed him another before William came in. "Mr. Adriance, what a morning for death," he said sympathetically. "Take your time. I'll run out and get our team ready to drag the old boy around back till tomorrow. Not to worry."

Thankful came in now, looking at the clock and fretting.

"Thankful, why don't you dress for company? Jo has everything under control here, and Lucy can go up and help you," William suggested. "I hadn't even thought how it might be for you at Christmas, Mr. Adriance, with no family. Forgive me for not inviting you sooner, but I hope you'll stay for supper. We have plenty of food."

Thankful looked pained at the thought.

"No, no, son. I've already added enough excitement to your holiday," Adriance said, though his fingers rested on his scone.

William looked softly in Thankful's direction. She sighed. "Mr. Adriance, it will offend Josephine if you don't stay, but I warn you that my family is coming."

Adriance laughed. "Well, then I accept, but of course I'll go home and change out of these things."

"Just sit here till I take care of old Jim on the driveway, and I'll take you back to clean up."

"But William," Thankful whispered, "My parents are due any minute now."

"Thankful, please stop worrying and go get ready," he said, nudging her out of the room.

Lucy followed.

As they reached the top step before the wardrobe that was once Lucy's room, there came a knock at the door. The Crenshaws had arrived. Lucy ran down to let them in as

Thankful slipped into her new gown, nervous tears in her eyes as she listened to her family pile into the front hallway.

"Land sakes, Lucy, is that what you're wearing for our Lord's birthday?" Margaret asked. "Now, Abby, don't cry over the dead horse and spoil everything. We all must die sometime—hopefully not in such an inconvenient way."

"William will get the horse."

"Yes, yes, I know, dear. We met him on the way in. Graham is helping him now in his Sunday finest. That's what we get for throwing out our traditional Christmas at my house. We've always come down here the day *after* Christmas, but the doctor says we must learn to be more open-minded. And where's Thankful whom I haven't seen at all this holiday?"

"She's dressing."

"Now? I've never seen the likes of her laziness. Mark my word it will bring this house to ruin if she doesn't shape up. Thank goodness none of her friends ever come this far down the hill for visits! A dead horse in the drive on Christmas!" Margaret shoved the children into the parlor and waited to be seated.

"Please, Mrs. Crenshaw," Lucy said, "make yourself at home."

"If I wanted to do that, I would have stayed up at my house as I always have." She glanced around at the sparse Christmas decor while pulling her fingers from her gloves.

Josephine came in now with hot strong cider and offered Margaret a cup she took gratefully, before sitting herself on the powder blue couch she'd helped Thankful pick out. Nathan, the quietest of the Crenshaw boys, stood behind his mother looking most uncomfortable while the two youngest girls sat by the tree, pulling at the homemade keepsakes on the branches.

Lucy went to them. "Girls, maybe you'd like to help Miss Josephine in the kitchen."

The girls turned in unison to their mother, who shook her head. "I'm sure Miss Josephine is not paid to babysit, Lucy."

"Then I'd prefer the girls not touch the tree," Lucy said.

"Well," Margaret huffed, "I've never seen this side of you before. Rudeness toward guests is quite unbecoming. I wonder what Buck might say about it."

"I suppose you may wonder as long as you like since Buck didn't see fit to join us for Christmas," Lucy said, her cheeks rising in color.

"The poor boy is ill—working himself to the bone to make a life for the two of you," Margaret replied, astonished at this turn of events, looking to her offspring for support. "I always saw you as a compassionate girl, but now ..."

"Forgive me, Mrs. Crenshaw, but I had been looking forward to seeing Buck all this autumn," Lucy explained with a slight quiver in her voice, "and those ornaments are special since Willy and I made them with dear Uncle John many years ago."

Margaret's indignant demeanor melted. She spread her arms wide calling Lucy to her breast. "My poor darling, come sit at once. In this we share a great sorrow. I too am having trouble being here—without Katie, my dearest friend—and whilst I love the new way it's all done here—I miss Katie's homey, foolish little touches. Wasn't she the worst baker after all?" She laughed and cried.

Lucy nodded and laughed too, allowing herself to be smothered in this sturdy woman's arms for a long while. "I miss them so much, and Buck too."

Margaret squeezed her. "There, there. Don't miss my son. You'll have a lifetime with him," she said with the smile of someone many years into a less than perfect marriage. "But let's do our best to be strong for William and Thankful. My daughter was worried that you'd not like all she's done, and she so wants to have a good girlfriend." She whispered now, "Has she given you the bicycle, yet?"

"Yes, I'm afraid she has, and I wasn't as excited as she hoped," Lucy said feeling gloomy.

"Oh, well, never mind," Margaret said, brightening. "You have a month to make things up."

"No, only a fortnight."

"One week?" Margaret frowned. "That won't do. We'd planned a trip out to see Fred in St. Louis, and Thankful is very disappointed not to be coming along. I'd hoped you'd keep her company."

"I'm very sorry, ma'am," Lucy replied simply.

They listened to the men in the yard. Nathan excused himself to join his father outside, and the younger girls slipped into the kitchen seeking Josephine and sweets. Thankful entered the parlor now, flush with nervous excitement. "Mama, merry Christmas!" She bent and kissed her mother.

Margaret appraised Thankful. "The dress suits you," she said as if it pained her.

The cranberry-red velvet reception gown with its embroidered white flowers falling over the shoulders and neckline and the perfect amount of pure white lace at the neck brought beautiful color to Thankful's already splendid face. Her black curls were held in check beneath a white silk scarf acting as a turban of sorts but tremendously becoming on her. The simple bustle accentuated everything admirable about her shape. Lucy touched the lavish fabric between her fingers in awe.

Thankful hardly noticed Lucy as she stood before her mother expectantly. Margaret said nothing more. William strolled in now with Graham and Mr. Adriance in tow. He smiled at his well-dressed wife, but saw the upset in Thankful's eyes. "Happy holidays, Mrs. Crenshaw," William said.

"It's our Lord's special day," Margaret scolded, "not any old holiday."

"Yes, ma'am," William said. "Mr. Adriance will be joining us for supper."

Josephine stopped mid-pour of the drink she'd been trained to mix for Graham and turned with dismay toward Thankful who nodded back at her in resignation.

"Mr. Adriance," Margaret said with her nose in the air as the man came over to greet her.

"It's mighty kind of the two young ones to invite me to share this day with your family," Adriance said merrily. He enjoyed ruffling the feathers of the big bugs up the hill.

Margaret smiled back. "Indeed."

Thankful took charge. "William has cigars in the library," she said, urging the men to leave at once, though she pulled her father aside and kissed him before he exited. Thankful turned back to her mother and sisters with a sigh, not realizing until now how Katherine and Sarah had served as the quiet warmth of Christmas past. A day of mindless though judgmental chatter lay stretched out ahead of her. Lucy stood by awkwardly and still in her shabby clothes. Thankful worried it reflected poorly on her. "Lulu, please dress, for heaven's sake."

Lucy complied but suffered the intense embarrassment of being ordered by her equal. Once in the hall, Lucy slid the pocket doors shut and stood regaining control of her temper. She couldn't help but overhear the men in conversation.

"Yes, my son Fred says everyone will give in to standard time in a year or two, but I find that hard to fathom," Graham mused. "I don't like the railroads having that much to say in our lives, but Fred says I'm old-fashioned."

"Young people are all for this progress, but I say you'll have more cases of upset in your practice, doctor, with people coming and going all the time like machines held to such a strict schedule," Adriance added.

"I've seen it in my very own family," Graham replied. "All sorts of seductions enter the minds of the young when they can jump on a train and travel over hill and yon. We doctors have a name for it—neurasthenia."

Lucy could hear William clear his throat before Graham continued. "Speaking of medicine, Willy, what ever happened to your grandfather's medical books and journals?"

A long pause hung in the room as the occupants scanned the empty shelves.

"Oh, well, Thankful and I ... well, they were worth a fair lot, sir, and neither of us have any medical interests so we sold them to the traveling shoemaker, Mr. Giles." William cleared his throat again.

Lucy shook at the revelation from outside the door.

Graham spoke Lucy's thoughts. "You must be joking! Whatever Giles gave you for them, I would have doubled or tripled."

William spoke defensively. "We received a pretty penny, sir. Enough to buy your daughter that fine Christmas dress."

"A dress? Hasn't she plenty of those?" Graham asked. "William, those books—some of them were hundreds of years old!"

"Thankful said they looked shabby, sir."

"Shabby?" Graham cried. "More like priceless! You've made a grave error. There are men in Manhattan who have known about your grandfather's collections and would have paid you enough to live a comfortable life for many years."

"How was I to know it?" William asked.

Adriance spoke now. "Well, never mind. The boy's done good work on my farm, and he'll still have that land as a comfortable thing to fall back upon. I'd have done the same thing I bet. I've no use for book learning."

"Well, then you're a bigger fool than I took you for, Adriance," Graham said hotly, but checked himself. "Forgive me. It's just such a terrible blunder the two of them have made and in my mind doesn't bode well for them."

Adriance chuckled. "Oh, come now. You blow it out of proportion. Giles has a big family and could use the extra income when he resells them."

"He'll probably use the *shabby* books for fire starting," Graham grumbled.

"Doctor Crenshaw, I'm terribly sorry I didn't offer them to you," William said, "but it seemed in bad taste to do business amongst family, and we felt the money was more useful to us."

"Dresses are useful?" Graham asked.

"My parents lived as miserable paupers, sir. I won't have Thankful live that way," William said firmly.

"Well, son, then I will take whatever steps necessary to leave the two of you to your own poor judgment."

"Sir, please, don't ruin Thankful's day. She's planned this for weeks. Now I understand your anger, and I promise you I will be more careful with our money from now on. I just hated seeing those old reminders every day. I don't want to be shackled to the past, and I don't care that much about money."

Graham softened slightly. "You will care one day, William."

Lucy hurried up the stairs and into the guest room. She stared out the window through tear-clouded eyes. How could she ever bring herself to enter the study again? This was no longer her home.

Lucy heard wheels outside of her window as a rented carriage came up the drive. For a moment when she pulled away the curtains, Lucy thought Buck had arrived. But no.

Fred in uniform, looking the dashing rogue as usual, jumped from the carriage as it pulled to a stop with India and little Sam in tow. Meg and her husband Royal followed. Lucy waited until the carriage pulled away before quickly dressing into the gown Thankful had laid out for her—a simple frock that clasped up the front with a slight, demure bustle at the back. Screams of delight carried up from below as she adjusted her hair and put on her aunt's earbobs. With one last check in the ornate full-length mirror and a quick pinch of her cheeks, she descended the stairs to meet the crowd.

Margaret clutched Fred in her arms, crying hysterically.

"Oh, Mama," Fred complained, "please calm yourself."

"But darling, you've shocked me to the core with this splendid surprise. I had resigned myself to a quiet and gloomy Christmas, but you've rescued it as you always do!" Margaret sobbed, wiping a tear before composing herself to take a good look at everyone while holding onto Fred as if she might collapse. "Meg, come to Mama at once! You write every day, and you kept this trip a secret! For shame! For shame!" she said as she took her daughter into her arms.

Meg, who had always been the plainest of the children, looked even plainer now with obvious weight gain showing in her best homesteading dress and with her curls pulled into a tight bun at the neck, but her eyes glistened with a happy confidence.

"Mama, it was so very hard not to tell, but Fred and I knew you hated the West and that you'd rather Christmas in Englewood any day," Meg explained. "Mama, soon you'll be a grandmother—again, I mean!"

Margaret squealed and shook her head in wonder. "Merciful heavens! I'd never have guessed that Meg would find happiness on a bleak piece of western real estate with an ex-soldier—didn't we always see her as a spinster, Graham? But here it is! Royal, I've never seen Meg so fat and happy. Though Thankful is the one who never ages, Meg has the finest complexion and it's all your doing, and a grandbaby to boot!"

"Thank you, ma'am," Royal replied, his round, sturdy face ablaze with the attention.

Meg beamed at him. "You should see the house he's made for us out of mud and covered in grass!" She laughed. "It's as cozy as can be, and the barn he's built is like a castle gleaming on the prairie!"

Margaret frowned. "I should think a proper house would come first. Haven't I seen pictures of grimy children with gaunt expressions in those sod houses in the magazines? I'm not sure I approve."

Meg kissed her mother. "Well, you must." She laughed again. "It's temporary, but I love it! The Irish linen tablecloth you gave us dresses the place up so much—it's so romantic."

Margaret smiled at her daughter's excitement and turned to Graham, who stood near the door. "Is this really our Meg?"

Graham shook Royal's hand before embracing his daughter. "I couldn't be happier for you both."

India, with Sam hanging on her arm, stood beside Fred, her eyes fixed on him as if he were her lifeline. Margaret turned her attention to them now with a sneer. "India, I hope you are well this holiday season."

"Quite," India replied with equal hostility.

"Sammy, don't you remember me from only a short while ago? I'm your grandmother," Margaret said as she split the sea of people and picked the toddler up in her arms. "Let's go find Aunt Thankful and some cookies for you."

India stepped in front of her. "Oh, we don't allow him any sugars."

Margaret looked as though the end times had arrived. "No cookies at Christmas is a sacrilege!"

"Fred has been having trouble keeping his weight down of late, and we don't want to burden Sam with something that runs in the family, so ..."

Margaret spoke past India to her son. "What is this girl on about? This boy looks malnourished in my mind. Our family has always been the picture of good health. Mind me, deprive this child of sweets and you will produce a sour adult—look, he's already lost that roly-poly happy face he once had."

Fred took Sam from his mother and placed him on the floor. The boy ran to his young aunt Abigail.

"Mama, we're in the modern age," Fred said. "India has read the latest on health and such. The boy is fine."

Margaret rested one hand on hip and the other she pointed at Sam while addressing her daughter. "Look, Meg, and see for yourself that I am right and promise you will not starve your baby of everything delightful in this world."

"Mama, stop it," Fred demanded. "And where's the banker?"

Graham spoke now. "Buck is on the mend."

"When is he not?" Fred complained. "What's he done now?"

"Overwork is all," Graham replied. "And you've worked yourself up to a captain already."

"Father, I know that tone. I don't care if I've earned it through politics. The Indian wars are nearly over so I have to make my way somehow and St. Joseph politics—while not as exciting as Manhattan's—suit me fine for the time being. India has found her place in the suffrage movement as well."

"And temperance, Fred," India added with pride.

"No worries here, my dear," Fred replied, lighting a cigar. "This is a dry house."

William said, "Oh, no, please enjoy the cider and punch."

"I would have thought it a temptation," Fred replied, puffing away.

"No. It's not," William said flatly, wondering where Thankful was. Backing out of the crowded room he nearly knocked into her.

"Willy! What are we to do with so many guests? I *knew* you shouldn't have invited Mr. Adriance," Thankful whispered.

"Thankful, we'll make do. Tell Jo to make more potatoes because the goose may be too small."

"Mama sent down a feast to outdo ours!" Thankful cried.

William dragged her into the library. "Now, Thankful, don't cry."

"But, it's all ruined. The table is too small, and Mama is beastly to have brought ham—it's everyone's favorite!"

"But if you knew that, why did we cook goose?"

"Because! We *always* eat ham at Christmas," Thankful cried. "I wanted this to be different and *ours* —and now there's Fred and India!"

"And Meg and Royal."

Thankful sighed. "Yes, them too, and I am happy to see my sister."

William wiped Thankful's eyes and looked into them in his soft, Cheshire-cat way. "Then why don't you just enjoy her. Let the rats fight it out as always."

Thankful sniffled but smiled at him. "You're right. What does it matter when we have each other?" She made for the door but William pulled her back.

"I don't care what anyone says. You look like something out of a dream today with your hair that way, and the dress takes my breath."

She giggled at him. "I love it when you seem so young and innocent."

"That I'm not." He winced.

They made their way back into the hallway as Lucy descended the stairs. She refused to look at them until Thankful spoke. "Lucy, will you do us a favor and help Jo in the kitchen? We've been overrun with guests."

Lucy glared at Thankful. "It's Josephine's kitchen, I'm afraid," she said before slipping into the crowded parlor.

"Here is my little waif back from the big city and doesn't she look darling!" Margaret said, waving Lucy over to her.

Lucy walked across the room and kissed Margaret.

Fred passed India a drink, eyeing Lucy. "You're all grown up, Lulu. How's school?"

Lucy smiled shyly. "I'm enjoying it."

"What do they teach you?"

"Well, The New York Point System for reading and history and ..."

Fred's interest had moved on to other things. "Father, how is Buck really?"

"He's Buck," Graham said simply.

Margaret whispered in Lucy's ear. "Wouldn't it be nice if you helped in the kitchen like the old days? Take Sam and Abby before they break something in here, won't you?"

Lucy stormed to the tree at once and took Sam's hand. She turned from Thankful's self-satisfied gaze as they passed each other in the hallway. Josephine appeared to be quite harried now and when Lucy offered her aid she gratefully accepted it. Abby and Sam sat at the fire eating cookies and giggling over childish things. Lucy forgot her resentment once back in her old favorite place.

"I do appreciate your coming in to help after the way I behaved this morning, miss," Josephine said sheepishly.

"Never mind. Change is always awkward, don't you think?" Lucy mashed potatoes in a floral apron.

"Poor Mrs. Weldon tries so hard to scrub Mr. Weldon's past from this house," Josephine whispered. "She makes herself crazy."

"The Crenshaws are crazy. Wait till supper!"

Josephine smiled, covering the slight gap between her teeth. Her high cheekbones and round eyes kept her face young and attractive.

Thankful rushed in now. "Jo, are we ready? My father's hungry."

"Yes, ma'am. I couldn't have done it without your dear Lucy."

Thankful looked as though she might say something tart but did not. She nodded at them both and left again to usher the family into the crowded dining room. William pulled open a few windows for air and the racket of chairs being pulled and pushed signaled the first supper drinks and raw oysters.

In all the hurry there was no setting left for Lucy, but she hadn't time to notice helping Josephine in the kitchen. Royal and Fred talked about things military—Fred expounding on the state of the higher-ups, Royal agreeing with a pleasant smile. Margaret doted on Sam while chatting with Meg about babies and housekeeping and William sat taking everyone in with heightened nerves and a strong desire to drink it all away. Adriance and Graham talked local politics and joked about the pains of aging. Thankful, clinking her glass, called for a toast when William wouldn't. She waited a moment, hoping one of the men would take the lead. Her father refused to make eye contact, and she knew William would die first, so she began. "Merry Christmas everyone. And here's to those who couldn't join us today—alive and dead."

This seemed a negative note to end upon so she continued. "God has been exceptionally good to us this year and here's to another, just the same." She remembered William's parents too late.

The guests sipped from their glasses.

Fred spoke now, leaning back in his chair. "Well, William, you and my sister have turned this place into a nice little home."

William nodded and smiled carefully.

"So when are you going to give my parents more grandchildren?" Fred asked.

Thankful spoke. "There's more to life than just children. India agrees."

India nodded. "Yes, if one can't afford them or if the parents are unfit in some way, then it's best to leave breeding up to others."

Fred laughed. "The Middlemay mind has not left India completely."

"We *can* afford children," William said.

"Oh, land sakes, Fred mentioned you're quite sensitive about things," India said. "I never meant to insinuate anything about you and Thankful. Forgive me."

William took a drink of water. Thankful signaled for Josephine to pour him more and for everyone else's glasses to be topped off with wine. "India, I understand what you mean. There are so many children suffering under bad parenting—even abandonment—but of course I'm not talking about *you*. At least you *finally* came to love your son."

Graham rolled his eyes and took a long drink and signaled Josephine to fill him another. "Maybe we should talk religion or politics."

Margaret moaned. "Oh, Graham, must we? I'm happy talking about babies. Meg will have twins! It does run deeply in our family. Buck says he'd like a dozen." Margaret glanced around the table. "And wherever is Lucy?"

William jumped from the table to fetch her with reddened face and hard jaw.

"Willy, where are you going?" Thankful said, reaching her arm out to stop him, but missing as he passed into the kitchen. Lucy stood at the stove sifting flour into gravy while whisking it. Her contented smile disappeared at the sight of her incensed cousin.

"Are we paying you to serve?" William asked, his voice just above a whisper.

"Willy, I'm fine in here," Lucy said, grateful to be away from the guests.

"No. I won't have it. We will not give them reason to look down upon us! We're just as good as any of them."

Lucy smiled. "Better."

William shook his head. "This isn't a laughing matter. Will they make you the housemaid up at the big house?"

"Buck wouldn't allow that."

"*You* shouldn't allow it!" William said, helping her pour the thickened gravy into a china server. "You don't know what Buck might do. He's a Crenshaw after all."

"As is Thankful." Lucy laughed. "What have we gotten ourselves into?"

William resisted, but smiled. "Come on then. You'll sit next to me."

William squeezed a small chair from the writing desk next to his own and moved his setting in front of Lucy discreetly (though Thankful took note jealously) and Josephine brought another for William as Fred ranted about immigration.

"We don't need any more uneducated rascals filling up the country with popish ideas. Haven't we enough trouble with what's left of the Indians and the ex-slaves? Mark my word, the Indians will be a drag on society for years to come no matter how we set them up with land, and after all that happened at West Point to Buck, I'm convinced that even the negroes best and brightest have years of moral evolution before they catch up with even the dumbest white—and I worry if they all come north to fight for the manufacturing jobs, what will happen to our great cities. And that Streeter never once seemed grateful for Buck's misguided friendship."

Meg spoke timorously now, knowing Fred's words aggravated her husband. "Well, maybe something is owed to the former slaves for the generations of oppression."

Fred laughed, but was quite serious. "And for how long will we owe them something?"

Meg hesitated, glancing once at her husband who remained quiet. "Well, maybe forever."

Fred leaned forward with sharp movement. "Forever?! How silly we Christians have become! So the blacks are to stay permanently victimized? What about Uncle Lucien and Uncle Nathan? They fought and died for the blacks and what do they get for it?"

"I suppose a pension if they'd lived ..." Meg replied.

"But what about their children? And their children's children?" Fred asked heatedly.

"I don't know," Meg wavered, regretting entering into debate. "Uncle Nathan had no children."

"He never got the chance, did he?" Fred said. "I never owned a slave so I owe nothing."

"But we as a people ..." Royal ventured.

"Why is it all right to make blanket statements about whites but not about darkies? New Jersey was a free state."

Margaret hissed at him. "Fred, enough of this talk!"

Fred ignored her. "I bet there's not a single black who'd be happy to go back to the Dark Continent. Things may not be the best here, but Africa's no picnic. I wouldn't want to sleep with lions all about."

Royal spoke again. "Come now, Fred, you must feel some shame for the way we've treated the Indians."

"Personal shame? No. I've done nothing to them. I was taught as a child to dust myself off when I lost a game and get on with it."

"But pushing them onto little bits of land to live in squalor is hardly a game," Margaret said.

"I believe in charity," Lucy said.

"And good for you," Fred replied. "That's your right, but don't force it upon the rest of us and for God's sake don't let the government get involved."

"I agree with you there," Royal said. "There's far too much waste and corruption, and the Indians are just as bad. I bet most will sell off their allotments if the Dawes Act really plays out. They're just not suited to farming and the big bugs will have their land before you know it. Better to send them to schools to learn a trade and move them to the cities."

William tapped his fingers on the table in frustrated anxiety. "I'm a good farmer."

"Oh, you're not a real farmer and you're hardly Indian," Thankful said, blushing with embarrassment.

William mumbled, "One-fourth Indian."

The clock ticked, and a pan dropped in the kitchen.

"Indians are romantic," Lucy said.

Fred choked on his drink. "They killed your parents!"

"Oh, but they're not all that way," Lucy said. "I must forgive them anyhow, or I'd be eaten with bitterness. I do hope every one of them could turn out as William has."

"You forget his white blood," Fred said dismissively. "You're just like my mother imagining Indians on Cortez's lost horses doing no harm, but have you studied in your history books about the Aztecs? I forgive your youthful ignorance, Lulu, but the Indians are capable of real cruelty and great waste of God-given resources. It's a shame, but the government cannot take the place of God and even God has said the poor shall always be with us. Let your charities help, but government officials are the furthest people from God that I know."

Graham said, "Fred, I'm surprised. If you're against government, why do you play at politics?"

Fred laughed. "It's fun sport." He saw his wife's expression of dismay and patted her hand. "Of course I do work for good also—especially for women's rights. And why not? India is brighter than most men I know."

India held her head up with a satisfied air. "My Fred sometimes comes across too harshly. He's been quite a friend to the Indians out west.

Everyone around the table looked on dubiously.

"The ones who don't stay stuck in the past, mind you," Fred explained. "I never imagined I'd say this, but even with his addiction, Willy's father was more of a man than most. He never drew attention to his Indian blood, and in one generation his son here can sit at the head of a fine table with the likes of us."

William shifted in his seat, but then laughed as they all did at Fred's backhanded compliment. "It's nice to have some things remain the same."

Thankful did not like her brother's remarks about William and stewed over her duck (which was greasy).

Margaret pulled Sam onto her lap after listening to him whine relentlessly for his mother's attention. "Now be a good boy and don't ruin Thankful's meal." She wiped his mouth a little roughly, and the boy continued to complain before tapping his grandmother's spoon against the china. Margaret pulled it from him with an exasperated kiss and handed him over to Meg. "How he settles down with Meggie!" she said. "If he isn't the picture of Buck at that age, though. Don't you agree, Graham?"

The doctor hesitated, taking another sip of his drink. "Yes, it's remarkable."

"It's that same thin, starved look," Margaret continued. "You know, India, that Buck was the skinniest child and such a picky eater."

India snapped her finger at Sam, who slid from Meg and joined his mother. "We feed him the healthiest of diets, Mrs. Crenshaw. I oversee everything. The newest science says children shouldn't be spoilt with rich food."

Margaret clucked her tongue, shaking her head. "I don't abide by every new fad, young lady, and your child looks malnourished and is happy to steal cookies from the kitchen. He wouldn't be such a little thief if his hunger was satisfied."

"Mama, stop talking," Fred warned. "I don't like to threaten but this visit will be a short one if you insist on making India uncomfortable. It's not fair to Thankful, who's gone to a lot of trouble. And as far as Sammy goes, he may resemble Buck an awful lot, but I won't permit him to behave like him. He needs to act like a little man—no whining, no spoiling."

Meg made a sad noise. "Oh, but he's just a little thing yet."

Fred turned on her. "Yes, that's what was always said about Buck, and what is he now—an invalid not even here for Christmas."

"Fred, please don't speak ill of Buck," Lucy said politely, but firmly.

Fred's tone changed at the sound of Lucy's voice and simple plea. "Lucy, you're right. It is Christmas after all. My apologies."

Lucy pushed her seat out in the still coltish young way she had. "No need to apologize. But would you do me an unusual favor and help me collect the dishes for poor Josephine so she can go home early for Christmas?"

Everyone around the table thought it a queer request—and one that humiliated Thankful—but Fred stood with a grin. "Let's all help out—like roughing it—come now everyone, it'll be fun and then Josephine can leave right now."

Josephine stood near the door, aware of Thankful's unhappiness but hoping for an early exit. The family stood at once, taking up their plates and heading for the kitchen with much chatter and laughing. Thankful slumped in her chair with her face in her hands. Josephine laid a timid hand on her shoulder. "Ma'am, I won't go if it upsets you."

"No, Josephine, you must or everyone will say I'm a wicked employer! Please forgive me, Jo," Thankful cried. "I only wanted things to be perfect."

"Never mind, ma'am. Listen to them laugh. It'll be all right."

Thankful peered up at Josephine. "No, you don't understand how they'll punish me with this for years to come. But you go now. Enjoy what's left of the day."

Josephine didn't wait to be told again and slipped out of the house and back toward her own family, happily carrying the large hatbox and leftovers Margaret hastily gave her on the way out.

Thankful stood before the mirror, wiping her eyes and listening to the family she no longer felt a part of. Everyone—including William—sounded happy, but she was full of loneliness and despair. Even a simple dinner party was beyond her. She choked back a sob before entering the kitchen with a false smile. William came to her side, at once perceiving her fragile mood.

"Thankful, I love you," he whispered.

"Why?" she asked, but didn't wait for an answer and busied herself with the others.

By now the world outside was dark, and William set about lighting the parlor with a fire. Lucy lit the candles on the tree as the guests crammed themselves into the small space with relaxed countenances and full bellies. Margaret sat at the piano and played Bach and Handel before switching to carols. Even Sam settled in Meg's lap and fell asleep. The evening passed pleasantly until Margaret's fingers gave out. They applauded her enthusiastically. Graham pulled his wife up from the stool, giving her a warm embrace and kiss.

The Crenshaw children still found it hard to believe their parents were somehow finally happy together. They drank it up, not saying a word for a long while.

Lucy interrupted the reverie with a smile. "Isn't that just the sweetest picture?" she asked, her eyes on Meg and Sam.

"Meg has become an excellent woman," Graham remarked with a mix of love and regret that he'd so undervalued his daughter. "She'll be an excellent mother too."

Royal's face shone with pride. Margaret agreed with her husband. "She's the only one of the twins to do things as they should be done, and we all must admire her for it."

"Don't be so stupid, Mama," Fred said, angrily. "You do realize the baby was conceived in a sod hut, don't you?"

Margaret stared at him. "Yes, even I understand it, Fred, but none of *us* can say we did things in the right order as they did."

Fred spoke fiercely now. "How dare you speak of such inappropriate things in front of a lady!"

"Who's the lady, son?" Graham asked with sudden venom. "Certainly not your wife who'd steal Sam away from Buck the way she did. Meg is the only woman of excellence in our family, and I'm sorry I never told her that!"

Meg begged, "Father, please!"

William, too, "Doctor Crenshaw, let's finish the night off well. Thankful's tried her very best to please you."

"A wife who allows her husband to sell off his fortune for a dress is a foolish wife indeed," Graham said, his natural soft spot for Thankful causing the words to fall heavily upon his daughter. "She'll be the ruin of you, Willy, if you don't take a firm hand."

William stared into the fire, collecting his thoughts and worrying how his words might upset his wife as he was certain from past experience that he was bound to say the wrong thing. "Thankful is a good girl."

"Thankful was a good girl—once." Graham poured a drink. "She will lead you, with her pretty ways, to do things that are not good for either of you. Be strong, Willy, for both your sakes."

"Sir, we've all done things that fall short of the glory of God ..." Lucy said.

"And what bad thing have you done, young lady?" Graham asked, his face florid with heat and drink.

Lucy retreated into the shadows.

Thankful stood alone by the nativity scene William had carved for her. She'd forgotten to place the round baby in the manger. "Father, when will you love me again?"

Graham laughed a sickened bitter laugh. "I've never stopped loving you."

"But you and Mama hate me for what I made you do to the baby," Thankful cried.

Graham suddenly sobered up, her words going too far. "Thankful, not now. Not here."

Fred asked, "What did you do to the baby, Father?"

Margaret broke first in a torrent of emotion. "We thought taking it was for the best! When I touched the pink hands, I begged your father to do something, but the tiny little boy couldn't survive being brought out into the world too young! We—I begged your father to do it and when it was done, it was too late!"

"Margaret! Shut up!" Graham said.

India rushed to Thankful. "You were right to do it. Another unwanted baby in the world to feed. You had to care for yourself. I'd have done the same thing if it hadn't been for Middlemay and Fred!"

Thankful pushed India away. "No! It's evil what I did—what I let my father do! The baby still moved!" she cried.

Fred spoke. "Willy, of course my sister told you ..." In a rare display of sympathy and regret Fred shook his head with a sigh.

"You killed a baby on purpose?" William asked, his eyes wide and his mouth unable to formulate another word.

"Yes!" Thankful cried. "And who would have loved him? Not me! Fahy used me and deserted me, and I never wanted any of it!"

"It was a little boy?" Lucy asked, feeling keenly for the baby.

"Yes, an unlovable little wretch!" Thankful sobbed.

Margaret slapped Thankful's face hard. "No! It was not! The boy was handsome and doomed, and I can never forgive you for what you did to your father and that child!"

"But ..." Thankful said, trembling, "you demanded it."

"Every time I deliver a baby, I envision that little boy," Graham said. "For the longest time when I woke from slumber I was afraid to open my eyes for fear I'd still be in an awful field hospital with my brother during the war, but now it's that perfect and doomed baby who greets me each day. I'm sorry, Thankful, but it's true. I blame us both. I hate ..."

Thankful glanced around the room. In the firelight there was not a single look of friendship. "You hate me, Father?"

Graham turned away from Thankful and went to William by the fire. "William, my daughter has chosen to include and shame all of us with this secret. I'd hoped she'd want to spare you. We can give a quiet divorce if you'd like, but I ask as a father who still must provide, not to expose to anyone the shameful thing I've done. I've built my practice on a high regard for human life."

William stared blankly.

Fred signaled India to gather their things. "It's time we leave."

A log in the fire sparked. Graham, Margaret and the children gathered at the door.

In a hush and hurry the house emptied until only the three—Lucy at the tree, Thankful at the parlor door, and William by the fire—remained.

Thankful met her husband by the hearth. "Willy, let me explain ..."

William stopped her. "You lied to me—and I trusted you. You could have told me a hundred times before we got married. No wonder your parents were so quick to be rid of you—and I play their fool!"

"It's true they wanted me gone, but Father loves you ..."

William waved Thankful off. He made as if he might leave but turned to her. "Where did you put the baby?"

Thankful glanced at Lucy trying to slip out of the scene. "What do you mean?"

"I mean what I just said," William said. "Was the baby given a burial at least?"

"Willy ..."

"Where did you dump him then?" William asked. "You think me killing a chicken for supper is bad ..."

"Oh, Willy! My parents—they took care to ..."

"To hide the evidence? Damn it, Thankful! A baby! And it was nearly due, wasn't it?"

Thankful sobbed. "Why do you care so much? It wasn't even yours!"

"How heartless do you think I am?" William asked. "I hold life dear! I can't stay here with you!" William rushed past Thankful, grabbed his coat and slammed the front door behind him.

Thankful turned to Lucy, her curls falling from the stylish turban she wore. "I truly want to die."

Lucy ran to her, taking her hands. "You don't mean it."

"But I do!" Thankful sobbed. "I've done the unthinkable, and my father doesn't love me."

"God will forgive you ..." Lucy said.

"Not that *father*! I meant my *real* father—Graham Crenshaw, you foolish girl!"

"I know who you meant ... but maybe you need something more than the doctor's forgiveness."

"Lucy, I know you mean well, but you're young and innocent and wouldn't understand."

"I understand that you were scared and hurt and alone," Lucy said. "Even a child can understand how that feels."

Thankful sat on the ornate wooden bench beside the door, and Lucy followed suit. "Lucy, you're very pretty. Do you know that?"

"Thank you."

"But being pretty doesn't do anything for you. I hoped it made me special and invincible. Now I'm a murderer!" Thankful cried again, so violently it scared Lucy, but she stayed close, with her hand firmly on Thankful's back. "Everyone hates me!"

"I don't hate you."

"How could you not when I've been a brute to you? And I don't even understand why."

"You wanted Willy all to yourself," Lucy said with a sad smile, "but so did I."

Thankful laughed a little. "I've resented your goodness, Lulu—that shows how low I've become."

"I resented your beauty," Lucy admitted.

Thankful pulled Lucy's glasses away and looked in her eyes. "Do you think I'm evil?"

Lucy considered a moment. "No. You were wrong and selfish to do what you did, but not evil."

"Do you forgive me?"

"I have nothing to forgive," Lucy said. "We're all called to love one another, and I'm sure I could like you, Thankful, if only you let us become friends."

Thankful sniffled. "Friends?"

"Yes, but you must go to God with what you've done—for forgiveness."

Thankful looked momentarily annoyed, but said, "Yes, I do remember hearing that your mother was very pious."

"I've heard that too and take it as a compliment to be compared to her."

"I never liked that about you, Lucy," Thankful confessed, "but somehow tonight I see you might be the very friend I need."

"I'd like for us to be close," Lucy said, just then hearing movement on the porch. "There's Willy. Should you go see about him?"

Thankful peeked through the curtain timorously. "I'm not brave enough."

Lucy squeezed her hand and left her to her own thoughts. After a few deep breaths Thankful stood and with great dread threw her cape over her shoulders before joining William on the slippery porch. William's gold eyes shone in the moonlight. His long fingers dangled from his frayed coat sleeves. Thankful sat beside him careful not to touch him with her skirt, certain William would cringe from her. Thankful watched the mist of her breath in the cold air but felt nothing of the temperature. William smoked a cigarette—something Thankful always complained about, but now understood this habit as his source of comfort—a comfort she'd never even attempted to give him.

William did not turn to her but asked, "Why did you never tell me?"

She shook her head, unable to be honest with him.

"You let me think that I was the only one saddled with heavy mistakes" he said. "You always acted like I was lucky to move up to you—though I never quite did, did I?" He did not need an answer.

"You're better than me, Willy! I never showed it or acted like I thought it, but ..."

"You're a liar, Thankful. I'm no better than you, but I'm no worse. I loved you as an equal, but you'll never consider me as one. Nothing I do is as refined as you like. But I'd never kill a child. My parents went to their graves with giant holes in their hearts over my sister. Babies are gifts."

"We wouldn't be together if I had kept Fahy's child," Thankful said, certain the remark would settle things.

"Then you don't understand me at all," he said. "Do I care what everyone thinks? When have I ever cared? I only cared what you thought. I would have raised the child as my own if you loved me."

"That's easy to say since it's too late!"

"Do you really love me, Thankful?"

"Of course I do!"

"Then don't ever lie to me again."

"So you won't divorce me?"

"This marriage is for life. When will you believe me?" William asked, sighing as he threw his arm over her shoulder.

She leaned into him, momentarily relieved. "I don't care what the family says about me anymore as long as you don't think any worse of me." Thankful felt his breathing catch on her words and looked to see his expression. "You *do* think worse of me for what I did, don't you?"

"Thankful ... I may have fathered a child with Ginny, remember," he said matter-of-factly, which bothered her.

Would William's child visit someday? Would William, upon seeing the handsome child, fall in love with Ginny and desert *her*? There was a time when Thankful was so very much better than Ginny, at least better looking, but now this ugly, uncultured girl of the West had something William longed for—a child and possibly a respect for his simplistic way of looking at the world. Thankful's mind raced. What did she and William have in common? Nothing came to mind. They were both good-looking. That was all! But she *did* love him.

"Thankful, what are you thinking?"

"I'm petrified of the future. What if I lose you to it?" Thankful said, her voice hollow in the frigid air. "What if you like that child better than me?"

William laughed in a disconcerted and confused way. "I don't know her."

"So you *do* know it's a girl?"

"No. Land sakes, Thankful," William grumbled. "I only imagined it was."

"So you imagine things about Ginny and the baby?"

"Yes. I mean, no. Not exactly," he stammered and lit another cigarette.

"What *do* you mean?" she asked, her temper and hurt bubbling over in a superior tone.

William's eyes darted her way, but he couldn't face her. "Ginny wanted children—so occasionally I just wish …"

Thankful jumped up as if to run from him but couldn't do it. "Go find her then! Go be with that whore, Ginny!"

He yanked her back beside him. "Don't test me, Thankful! Ginny may be a whore, but you're a murderer. I never loved Ginny. I love you, but to my mind there's something queer about a girl who doesn't want children."

"I'm not a murderer!" Thankful sniveled. "At least I didn't imagine I was until it was too late to fix anything! But you don't understand …" She hid her face in William's chest. "You could just desert your mistake—I had to carry mine with me! I had no one to help me, no one to talk to! It never occurred to me that I'd fall in love with the baby! He looked so perfect, but it was too late!"

William relented. "Thankful, I'm sorry."

"Why? For telling me the truth about myself?"

"I always hated people calling my father a morphine eater as if that was all there was to him," William confided. "I shouldn't have used the word murderer."

"But I am one. I will always be one and will never deserve any good thing."

He unwrapped her hair and smoothed her curls. "No one deserves anything."

"Willy, I'm afraid of a baby with you. What if God sees fit to punish my actions through it? What if it comes out all wrong? Maybe, India is right—that some people shouldn't have children."

"India's words are evil," he said. "Lucy may be completely blind someday—we knew it since she was little. India's friends would rather she had never been born. I love that girl." He wiped his eyes. "If it wasn't for Lucy I'd still be drinking, and I wouldn't have you."

"Then I owe Lucy my life."

"Even if our child wasn't perfect, I'd love it the same."

Thankful's eyes filled with tears, knowing he would love a child in a way she had never experienced in her own life. "You make my heart burst! Perhaps a baby is just the thing for us."

"Do you mean it?" he asked, searching her face.

His eyes sparkled, and Thankful wondered how she could ever say no to him.

"Then let's try right now," he said, taking her up in his arms, slipping slightly on the icy porch.

"No, Willy, not tonight," Thankful said. "I'm so tired from the day."

William set her down again, but his eyes betrayed hurt and annoyance.

"Oh, please don't look at me so!" she pleaded. "I want to be right next to you all night and know that when I'm weak, you're strong."

"Well," he said, looking up at the starry sky and then back at her, "I can't be expected to be patient forever."

# Chapter Five

The enormous new grandfather clock that Graham had given his wife for Christmas struck eleven as the Crenshaw family poured into the toasty parlor lit with precious globe gaslights and a welcoming fire kept bright by a hired girl. The spicy scents of clove and citrus mingled with the fragrant pine of the tree. Margaret smiled with satisfaction.

"What a difference from the Weldon home," she said.

The others heartily agreed as they shook off the cold and damp, picking over superior-quality finger food and the best eggnog they'd ever tasted, though none of them were truly hungry or thirsty. Abigail, Maddie, and Sam found cozy spots near the fire and listened with dreamy eyes to adult talk they hardly understood.

"So you see now, Fred," Margaret began as she nestled into her wingback chair, "why your father and I have struggled to forgive Thankful. Of course we're pleased that William had no qualms about marrying her—how could he? We all know who he was out west and will keep quiet about it, but it's best to leave a pleasant distance between us. They have the fourth ward and we have the first. We wouldn't want Maddie and Abby admiring Thankful too much and becoming infected with her rebellion."

Fred stared into the fire with furrowed brows. India's growing enthusiasm for birth control and abortion and her less-than-satisfactory mothering of his son worried him. At this moment, Fred was aware of a keen sense of jealousy toward Royal. This average man of little means would show him up most certainly in the area of reproduction if Fred could not change India's mind.

Though his father had never even hinted at any need for grandchildren, Fred considered it his familial and patriotic duty to procreate as much as possible—just like his parents. He'd always imagined a wife of better intelligence than his mother to keep track of his tribe while he conquered the world, but India showed no desire. He'd read Darwin's ideas and feared India was that type of female in the natural world who was without the essential temperament for reproducing the species. White women who cared more about their waist size than human production would eventually leave the country to the immigrants and the natives.

The idea of failure was too much for him. India smiled his way as he considered these things. How could such a stunning specimen of womanhood make do with only one child? Sam pulled on Fred's jacket sleeve now and it annoyed him. Buck had sissified the boy in that first year, and Fred found he didn't like him much but picked Sam up in his arms with a sigh and announced the night finished. The tired family assented to his judgment, taking up candles to their rooms as was their Christmas tradition.

Buck had not been asleep in his room, but could not, upon seeing that Fred and Meg had made a surprise visit, bring himself to face them. He was recovering from bronchitis and exhaustion, but he'd almost convinced himself to make a showing at the Weldon home until he'd heard Fred's voice in the drive earlier in the day. When a small, thin boy had poked his head out from the livery car and glanced up at the window, Buck's heart throbbed and all of his mistakes and weaknesses came to the fore.

Despite months of Margaret's not-so-subtle expressions of doubt about the engagement, Buck had, with heroic resolve, almost convinced himself that he hadn't made a mistake promising himself to Lucy. Perhaps Lucy wouldn't seem so naive as he imagined her now, and it would not be much of an embarrassment to marry such a young girl—*who was also going blind*. And wouldn't Fred just pour on the agony this Christmas? Buck must face them all in the morning but not yet. He'd never enjoyed Christmas and half considered it an evil pagan holiday, though his theology of late was muddled by his great financial successes and his new coterie of banking acquaintances dragging him out for suppers and sails on Long Island Sound.

Buck's *friends* mostly skirted bad behavior. The Turner & Lamont cousins attended services on Sunday and even spoke of the duty of prosperous men to uplift the uneducated masses teaming from tenements only blocks away from Wall Street. Yet their religion struck Buck as bland. After all he'd been through at Middlemay, Buck was happy to keep God at a benevolent distance. For now he wanted time to get a firm footing in the material world—his flights into the spiritual having led to solid crashes.

When his door opened a sliver, his eyes rolled in dread until he saw the outline of Meg. He jumped from his bed to embrace her with a happy laugh. Meg laughed too, though quietly as she closed the door behind her and whispered, "Oh, Buck, you look well."

Buck lit his light.

"Meg, you've changed!" he said touching her belly. "Mama must be over the moon."

"Mama's proud of me for once."

"I'm so glad you're keeping it!" he gushed.

Meg stepped back in affront. "Of course! Who do you take me for? I'd never sin against God on purpose!"

He pulled her close again and sat her on his bed. "I'm sorry. I was just thinking about India and Sam."

"Oh, Buckie, we've had dreadful news about ... Thankful."

Buck looked up in surprise.

Meg confided in a disapproving whisper. "Yes, tonight was a disaster. We found out how despicable she is."

"Poor Thankful," Buck said. "We shouldn't judge."

"Oh, please," Meg said in annoyance while taking his hand. "Spare me your religiosity."

He covered his religious disappointments with a laugh. "Especially not on Christmas."

She giggled. She had a sweet smile. "Are you really too sick for the holidays?"

"I'm not terribly bad, but I've never liked Christmas. Thankful and Fred always got just what they liked while we got those off-smelling bars of soap."

Meg shook her head with merry eyes. "What does it matter now? We have what we like, and you've plenty of money to buy soap or anything you want."

"Forgive my silly ingratitude," he said, his face in brighter light would have shown embarrassment at his small-mindedness. "Tell me about your sod home. What an adventure for you."

"I hardly notice it being sod any longer," she said. "It's so cozy I almost hate moving into a bigger place. But Royal has already begun our real home and will start on it in earnest this spring. He'd wanted it done for the baby, but things don't always go according to plan, I suppose. He says I'm a respectable homesteader, what with cooking, making candles and soap even! For pin money I've gathered buffalo bones to send east for fertilizer too. It's jolly fun being out of doors and busy. I'd never come back east to be a slave to society again. I do so hope you and Lucy will be as happy as I am."

"It sounds quite a lot to live up to."

Meg surveyed him. "Have you and Lucy had a falling out?"

"No! Not at all ... why? Did she say something to you?" Buck felt his reserve crumbling.

Meg smiled. "No, Lucy was made quite busy. We didn't get to speak at all. Thankful put her to work in the kitchen. Willy seemed peeved at her antics. Lucy dutifully played housemaid. It was rude of Thankful, seeing that Lucy will soon be your wife. Mr. Adriance was there too and will spread the idea of you marrying a servant girl."

Buck's demeanor changed, Meg's words striking a tender spot. "Adriance has no right to judge Lucy."

"He doesn't judge, but he certainly talks at the market like a little old lady, and won't the girls up here relish the idea of our family sinking fast," Meg said. "I couldn't care a fig about any of it but worry for you and Lucy since you mean to stay here in Englewood."

"This is why I must convince Lucy to move to Manhattan, but she's probably set on Englewood."

"Why don't you ask her?" Meg suggested. "Buck ... when was the last time you spoke to Lucy?"

"Well, I've been rather busy at work of late … and … I don't recall." He glanced at a framed silhouette of Lucy that she sent him from New London. "I guess not since she left for school. I considered calling her on the telephone from my office, but the idea of it seemed ridiculous, though I have sent letters—just little notes hardly worthy of her."

Meg slapped his arm with force. Her expression was a mix of sympathy and exasperation. "What's wrong with you? You don't intend to break the girl's heart, do you? She has always seemed too sweet to be true, but she's cute and refined-looking now. With just a small bit of coaching she'd do nicely on your arm. The idea of you single forever is so depressing as you've got the biggest heart of all the Crenshaws and would make the best father too. Don't turn out like poor Uncle Oliver."

"Since when do you have such strong opinions?"

She looked him over knowingly. "What has Mama been saying to you these past months?"

"Nothing."

"Buck, you're lying. She's turned you against Lucy, hasn't she?"

"No, not at all—well not me against her, but the other way around."

Meg rolled her eyes.

"No," he said, "Mama has made observations … Lucy probably considers it her Christian duty to marry me."

Meg laughed, shaking her head.

"Or, well, what if she goes blind and no longer finds me of much interest—after all, I'm on the quiet side, and I don't have much to commend me. Initially she liked me because I was once handsome."

"You paint a shallow picture of Lucy and a pathetic one of yourself," Meg said. "You forget that you are a successful man now—despite Mama undermining you. Most women find that appealing."

"I should hate to find that Lulu likes me for my money only."

"You spend too much time under Mama's advice. Move to Manhattan—better yet—Brooklyn! Now, are you in love with Lucy?"

"Perhaps she is too young …"

"And you're too foolish!" Meg replied. "She won't be young for long and looks quite stylish in Thankful's old things. Soon William's friends will swoop in and steal your girl. Imagine Lucy on a farmer's arm when she really wanted you."

"I suppose I've talked myself out of the whole idea of love, Meg."

"Then I pity you," she said impatiently. "I'm also disappointed." She kissed him and left him to himself.

Buck opened his armoire where a wrapped package was hidden. He ran his fingers over it. Glancing at his empty bed, he had a fleeting desire to see Lucy in it with her long blond locks undone and her ever so pale skin exposed just for him, but quickly he imagined his own wretchedness and closed the armoire. God had been right about intercourse and marriage. Buck had experienced things at Middlemay that he now wished he'd discovered with Lucy. She had forgiven him for his weakness, but it weighed on him—the stupidity of following free love, when he had *never* believed in free love! Why had being Richard's favorite overridden his morals? No amount of money could change that.

# Chapter Six

The beginnings of a new day fell lightly on the ornate frames and unusual figurines that sat upon the dresser in the guest room where Lucy awoke from a fitful sleep. William stumbled around in heavy boots downstairs even before the first seam of orange light appeared in the east. Lucy remembered in the past how she'd wake to him stumbling home and considered how far William had come working with animals on the prettiest farm this side of the Hackensack River. The possibility of meeting Thankful in the hallway kept her in her room until the aroma of coffee and sweet muffins baking overrode her dread. She tiptoed down the stairs, relieved to find Josephine alone in the kitchen.

"There you are! I didn't get to thank you for being such a help yesterday." Josephine clasped Lucy's hands in hers. "Sit right down in your grandfather's chair and let me get you a good cup of coffee."

"But I don't want any trouble for you."

"Oh, don't you worry," Josephine assured her. "I'll take the blame. Mrs. Weldon is wrong not to let you have your memories. She's young and stubborn sometimes, but she has a good heart."

Lucy worried a little, but not enough to leave the comfort of the old chair that still smelled of her grandmother's perfume and her grandfather's cigars. Josephine pulled the tartan throw around Lucy's skinny legs and tucked her in like a child.

"Is Thankful awake?" Lucy asked in a whisper.

"She's not well. Poor thing." Josephine poured herself a cup of coffee and sat on the ottoman at Lucy's feet in a friendly, informal way. "She works herself into a frenzy and then when things don't go just so, especially with that family of hers, she falls ill. If you ask me, Willy should have taken her somewheres west or north or south—any place but in her mother's backyard. But who am I to say?" Josephine sipped her drink and shook her head.

Lucy ran her fingers over the warm cup. "It's very good that you're here for her. You may be able to help her."

"I don't need any help!" Thankful said with swollen eyes.

Josephine jumped up, nearly upsetting Lucy's drink. "Ma'am!"

"Go ahead and sit with dear little Lucy. I'll get my own breakfast!" Thankful cried, banging her cup on the counter and spilling coffee as she poured it.

Lucy ran to clean Thankful's mess.

"Get away from me. You're as blind as a bat. You can't fix my messes!" Thankful yelled, ripping the rag from her hand.

Lucy stepped out of the way, but Josephine hovered over her employer. "Ma'am, please," she purred and after a few seconds, Thankful's demeanor changed. She sobbed like a despondent child in Josephine's arms. "There, there, young lady. Everything is fine."

"No one loves me!" Thankful cried.

"Everyone loves you, silly," Josephine said, taking Thankful's red face in her hands. "We all love you—Lucy and me and ..."

"But I mean the important people!" Thankful simpered.

Lucy could take no more and left for her room, but before she made it up the stairs, a knock came at the door. She peeked through the window beside the door. Margaret waved enthusiastically. Lucy opened the door with a sigh.

"Didn't Thankful warn you I'd be here early today to take you for a dress fitting for the New Year's Ball?" Margaret said in high annoyance, smacking her gloves against her hand like the task master she was. "We have visiting today also, and you're not even dressed!"

"Thankful didn't say a word," Lucy replied, stiff with anger.

"She is unreliable. But never mind, let's go up and get you dressed," Margaret said, nudging her.

"Thankful is upset in the kitchen. Would you like to spend time with her? I can manage dressing for the day."

"The way you dressed yesterday has convinced me that you still need a mother's hand, young lady, and it's quite rude to direct your future mother-in-law to the kitchen."

"But Thankful ..."

"If I didn't take seriously the word of God, I'd never even try forgiving that girl her sins. Leave Thankful be in her misery for today. It will teach her a lesson," Margaret said, still with her hand firmly at the small of Lucy's back.

Lucy hesitated but the excitement over the New Year's Ball and dancing with Buck softened her resolve.

Before long Margaret had her young charge squeezed into an exceptionally tightened corset under one of Thankful's castoff dresses that had only been worn once.

"This suits you far better that it did Thankful. If it weren't for your spectacles, you'd give Thankful a race for the money, but looks aren't everything—Graham and I are no great beauties, but our children are exceedingly handsome—except for Buck, of course, but that's his own doing, I'm afraid."

"I like the way Buck looks very much," Lucy said as they walked out to the waiting surrey.

"Well, you're nearly blind, my sweet," Margaret said with a laugh, but Lucy wasn't amused.

"How is Buck feeling?" Lucy asked. "I wish he wrote me a little more."

Margaret took offense, rolling her eyes. "Crenshaw men aren't sissies. Don't expect much in the way of love letters. I've raised them to be better than that."

"My uncle's letters to my aunt are priceless to me."

"And sadly we all know exactly what sort of man your uncle was," Margaret said. "I don't mean to speak ill of the dead, dear, and I admire your devotion to family—it will serve you well when you become one of us, but you have to give up your childish notions to survive this life."

"I only wonder why Buck should hide himself from me when I've looked forward to seeing him for months."

"Take my word, Lucy. For now, enjoy your freedom. Forgive me when I tell you I advised him to allow you this time to grow into a woman. He worries what people will say about him taking you so young."

"He does?" Lucy asked, stabbed through by the words.

"Just a little," Margaret glanced over, her brows arched. "Don't you think it good of him to care what others think of you?"

"I'm not sure."

"Of course you're not," Margaret said with a sympathetic smile. "I loved your aunt dearly, but you fail to understand how the course of Aunt Kate's life was set by public opinion."

"What do you mean?" Lucy asked, her temper rising.

"There was a scandal early in her life that caused her to be an outcast—but for me. I stood by her, and I will stand by you—that you can trust, but my son is better than your uncle, and he will not stand for any scandals that cause you to suffer embarrassment."

Lucy smiled at Buck's gallantry.

"This is a serious matter, Lucy. Through no fault of your own, you were born with diseased eyes. Everyone knows why in this little town, but there's something about you that people like. Buck, on the other hand, has never been popular so I do understand his very pragmatic reasons for marrying you. And I believe you understand why you are jumping at the idea and I don't judge you for it.

"Someone will need to care for you, and you can't depend upon Willy—who knows how long he'll stay sober? But I've advised Buck to solidify his work relationships this past autumn and allow you to enjoy the only bit of independence you're ever likely to have. Your sight has worsened, though you hide it well, and I'm happy you will be made comfortable throughout your life. I would have made the same decision if I were in your position. It's a *good* decision. And we told Buck that if he ever hurts you by running off on one of his crazy whims, we will take your side in it because my husband and I have a soft spot for you."

Lucy listened to the sound of the horses hooves muted slightly in the slush. "Ma'am, what does pragmatic mean?"

Margaret smiled painfully as if Lucy had only now shown her true lack of education. "Dear, I wouldn't worry about details ..."

"No, the word doesn't sound nice, and I'd like to understand what you mean."

Margaret blushed and hemmed and hawed, snapping the reins on her horse's back just a bit harder. "I only meant to say that Buck is doing the sensible thing for everyone. I did the same with my husband. I'm not sure I ever felt a strong and deep abiding love for the doctor, but more like, well, a sense that this was a good pairing up. Living with my father—it was something I wouldn't wish on anyone. For a long while I resented Graham for his lack of romance until I realized that it was me who had made the simple decision to marry for stability and *that* Graham gives me in spades—and more. I've always had fine things and a fine-looking house and children going to good schools."

"So you don't love Doctor Crenshaw?" Lucy asked, the cold making her voice sound fragile.

Margaret pulled in front of the dressmaker's shop. "No, I do love the old man, I just ... it just took me a while to grasp his true value." She lowered herself to the sidewalk and tied her horse, beckoning for Lucy to join her with an undisturbed grin, oblivious to the effect of her words.

Lucy stayed put until Margaret came to her side. "Lucy?"

"I appreciate the value of Buck already, but if he only sees me as a pragmatism then ..."

Margaret urged Lucy onto the pavement in haste. "Dear girl, don't mind my words. I have the worst habit of saying the wrong thing. Buck has never been pragmatic in his choice of girls so possibly I'm wrong, but he once proposed to Fred's dear Rose (may she rest in peace) on a whim, and then there were all sorts of liaisons with women at that horrible Middlemay establishment—so all I was saying is that finally Buck has settled for a girl who won't get him into any trouble." She patted Lucy's hand. "You'll just be devoted and grateful."

"Grateful?"

Margaret sighed theatrically. "Must I mind every word? This was supposed to be a happy day of shopping like mother and daughter. Will you ruin it with your questions?"

Before Lucy could answer, the door to the dress shop swung open and a trim old matron with a snug vest and silver spectacles waved to them. "I had almost given up on the two of you! Come inside, Margaret, I've set out my very best fabrics for Lucy to look over." She beamed at Lucy. "My word, you've grown into a fine young lady, but why look so glum?"

Lucy mustered a polite, thin smile and allowed herself to be taken in by the women. Mrs. Tabitha Swindel was the finest seamstress in all the county and much in demand. "Five more minutes, Margaret, and I would have had to cancel Lucy's fitting."

"Mrs. Swindel, if you're too busy, I won't trouble you," Lucy said, trying to hold back emotion.

Pushing up her spectacles, Tabitha glanced back and forth at the two. "Margaret Crenshaw, what have you said to this young lady?"

"Tabby, I'm not paying you to mind my business," Margaret said lightly as she ran her hand over a bolt of silk.

Lucy asked, "Mrs. Swindel, are you in love with your husband?"

The seamstress laughed. "Yes, of course. Oh, dear, are you having second thoughts about Buck?"

"You've heard about me and Buck?" Lucy asked in surprise. She turned to Margaret, who was paying more attention to the yards of silk and serge. "It was to be a secret until my birthday."

"Don't blame Mrs. Crenshaw, dear, it was Buck himself who couldn't keep it to himself, but I assure you that I've told no one," Tabitha said.

"He never mentioned he'd spoken to you," Margaret said in a huff.

"I suppose he's old enough to not tell you everything," Tabitha replied. She took Lucy by the elbow to show her the lace she planned to use. "Poor Buck, as bashful as ever, came in one day a few months back. He confided his plans and wondered if I could gather up the best things for a wedding gown."

"Buck only wants to dress me up so I won't look like I come from the wrong side of town," Lucy said.

"Well, then he sure fooled me," Tabitha said. "The boy's face was the color of that red over there."

"Buck's face is always red since his accidents," Margaret said.

Tabitha brushed Margaret's words aside. "Lucy, the young man was all smiles talking about you and his big plans to make you happy."

"Really?" Lucy gushed, desperate for reassurance. "Did he seem pragmatic to you?"

Tabitha gave Lucy an odd look. "He seemed intent on you having a wonderful gown."

"Tabby, please let's stop confusing the girl," Margaret implored. "You said you were busy and so are we. Take Lucy's measurements."

The seamstress popped open her watch. "Yes, let's get to it or this girl won't have her dress for the ball."

After a full day of visiting and enduring introductions to the most important ladies of Englewood who were only mildly interested in Margaret and even less interested in Lucy, Margaret drove back to Tenafly Road. The driveway, crowded with stylish carriages, was lit brightly, as was the house.

"Thankful didn't mention she'd planned a gathering without me," Margaret said.

Lucy remembered suddenly that she was supposed to be home to meet Thankful's friends at a card party this evening. "You can just drop me here. I'll walk the rest of the way," she said to Margaret, eager to be away from her. "Thank you."

Margaret muttered something about her ungrateful daughter and snapped the reins. Since coming back, Thankful had reminded Lucy many times to use the side entrance only. Tonight Lucy let herself in the front door. A few people from town hailed Lucy into the parlor. William, sitting with old friends from his days at the Kursteiner School for Boys, looked up from his cards with a grin, and for a second Lucy's spirits lifted. She started to say something to a young man she recognized from a visit to the doctor's office, but Thankful interrupted her.

"Lucy, haven't I told you to keep your dirty boots off the front carpet?"

"Oh, leave her be," someone said good-naturedly, but it was not enough to stop Lucy's temper from boiling.

"Willy, where are the letters your father sent Aunt Kate?" Lucy asked, trembling.

William glanced around, hating scenes. "I'm not sure right this minute, Lulu."

"Stop calling me a child!" Lucy stomped her foot.

Thankful came to her side and took Lucy by the shoulders as if the two were friends. Lucy shrugged her off. "I want the letters right now. This is still *my* family, and I have a right to them!"

"Lucy," William said, not moving a muscle, his hands still holding the cards he'd been dealt, "I told Thankful to burn them."

"I don't believe it, Willy. I know Thankful made you do it!"

"No, it was me," William replied. "Why must I keep in writing what my father was?"

"What he was?" Lucy stood shaking. "You don't see what he was. He was a loving father and husband and ..."

Thankful whispered, "He was a morphine eater, dear."

"*You* stay out of it!" Lucy shouted again.

The guests moved to get up, but William stopped them. "No! I will not have my little cousin ruin a perfect night. I did what I thought best for the memory of this family. When I have children, I want to shield them from how wretched things were. I don't want those horrible girls up the hill to ever have written proof of where you came from, Lucy. I want you to start fresh with Buck."

"I can't!" Lucy cried, aware that most people in the room would only just now learn about the secret engagement. "Buck doesn't love me!" she announced before running to her room, tracking mud the entire way.

Thankful excused herself from the parlor, sliding the pocket doors together before racing up the stairs and barging into the guest room. "Lucy, you *will* marry Buck!"

Lucy wheeled around with wide eyes. "What?"

Thankful grabbed her, but this time there was no sense of friendship in her grip. "You will not break my brother's heart! I knew you were too childish. How can Buck be so foolish?" Thankful cried.

"Let go of me. I wish you would leave!"

"I wish *you* would!"

"You hate having me here," Lucy said, "but I will never abandon my cousin."

"Don't you understand anything?" Thankful ranted. "Willy needs to be insulated from the past. I watched him out west. You don't understand how terribly undermined he was by his parents, and you are a reminder of them."

Lucy sat on the edge of the bed with her arms wrapped around herself, trembling. "No. Willy and I are close."

Thankful stood over her not saying a word for a long while until Lucy had the courage to meet her eyes.

"Lucy, I don't mean to hurt you, but these past months without you here have been such a healing time for William. I've never seen him so happy, and I want you to be happy, as well."

"No, you want me gone."

"No ..." Thankful paced the floor, anxious to get back to her party and not sure how to end this discussion on a positive note. "Lucy, listen. Buck cares for you deeply, and when you are married, I will invite you to tea, but Crenshaw men hate needy girls so take heed and don't push him with expectations that he should put you first, because you'll be disappointed, and he'll be made a caged animal."

"I haven't even seen Buck. How would I push him?"

"He's avoiding you, that's plain, so you must have done something," Thankful said, her hand to her chin in thought.

"I only sent him weekly letters."

"Oh, no, that won't do. Crenshaw men don't do written correspondence. They're very reserved in that way," Thankful confided. At once she felt guilty and satisfied at the sight of Lucy squirming. She hated herself for it and hated Lucy for making her act so. "Lucy, if you do anything to break Buck's heart I will tear you apart."

Lucy stood up to her now, and though she shook there was a fierceness in her posture that took Thankful aback. "I would never think to hurt Buck. There is something tremendously wrong with you, Thankful, and I will pray that, whatever it is, God will take it from you and give you peace. I have done nothing to merit your abuse and wonder how Buck has ever managed to get out from under the awful cloud of horrible Crenshaw women! If Buck chooses to ignore me, then it's his loss, but for now I will not be forced from my home by you or anyone!"

William stood at the open door with a wary look and a hint of anger in his voice. "Thankful, I tried, but everyone has gone—the two of you shouting made things unbearable."

"Oh, William, I'm sorry!" Thankful cried.

"Stop the tears—it doesn't help anymore," William said but with a look of confused sympathy for her, which annoyed Lucy greatly.

"William, I will not allow Thankful to come between us!"

"Lulu, I never guessed that by marrying Thankful I'd have to take sides … I just want peace."

"Peace at any cost, Willy?" Lucy asked, her stomach tight and her throat in knots knowing by his posture what he would say.

"Yes, at any cost," he said, confirming her fear. "I don't want to lose you, but if you and Thankful can't find it in your hearts to get along what can I do? I've gotten what I've always wanted, and I won't throw it away."

"You don't want *me*?" Lucy sobbed.

William came to Lucy and took her hands in a way that signaled their old embraces were over and a new reserve had taken their place. "Don't take it that way. It's not what I meant. It's only that I need to be the kind of man who comes down strongly for his wife."

Thankful, upon seeing that she'd won, put away her weapons and could allow herself to see the real state of the poor orphan before her. "Lucy, I'm so terribly sorry for you. All these changes that didn't occur to us to ask you about must be hard to take, and I sincerely apologize."

William smiled benevolently at his wife. "Lucy, Thankful is trying."

"Lucy, you do realize that William credits you with sobering him, and you wouldn't want for us to be responsible for sending him back …" Thankful began, but saw William's hurt expression. "I mean, I would never want for our fighting to hurt him—or you. I will admit now and never say another word about it that I have held a grudge against you for bewitching my brother—your age being a rather awkward thing—but who am I to judge? I shouldn't care what others think. I should be more like you Weldons."

"Thankful," William began, "do you mind giving me a moment with Lucy?"

William had forgiven Thankful again, so she easily assented and closed the door behind her.

William waited until he heard Thankful talking with Josephine downstairs before speaking. "Lucy, what Thankful said is true. You saved me from my demons."

"No, God did. I prayed for you every day."

William shifted the conversation uncomfortably away from prayer since his went mostly unanswered, and he wasn't sure he believed anyway. "What's this talk about Buck not loving you?"

"He doesn't want to see me, isn't that obvious?" Lucy said, throwing herself onto her bed.

He sat beside her. "Buck's sick."

"No, there's more to it than that."

He shrugged. "You girls imagine men always have things going on behind the curtain. There's no behind the curtain for men. Buck's been sick—he's sickly. That's all there is to it."

"Just because you're simple doesn't mean everyone is," Lucy said without thinking and blushed.

William didn't take notice. "Don't be too hard on Thankful—for me. She's just jealous."

"Of what?"

"Of you. Thankful sees in you everything she once was."

"Thankful was never me."

"She was innocent and happy once and dreaming that I'd be that way too, but I took us both down and when she sees you she's reminded of it all."

"You can't take the blame for everything," Lucy said. "Why do you love her, anyway? She's caused so much suffering."

"I understand Thankful better than she does, and one day I'll convince her of the truth."

# Chapter Seven

A great storm blew in the next day covering Englewood in a thick blanket of snow. A skating party had been planned by the civic-minded residents of Englewood. William was hired with other young working men to clear the pond. Thankful groused at William for shoveling when her sneering peers would be looking on as they waited to glide over the ice, but William promised to be back to fetch her before the party goers even arrived. Noon came and went. She primped before the hallway mirror, occasionally glancing in irritation at Lucy, who, with not a care in the world, sat knitting a scarf of crimson by the parlor fire while humming incessantly.

"Lucy, whatever are you humming?"

"Was I humming?" Lucy asked as if woken from a dream. "Oh, 'The Holly and the Ivy,' I suppose. Grandmother used to sing it every Christmas morning."

Thankful sat beside her. "Where is William, I wonder? He's been gone for hours, and here we are missing the festivities."

Lucy's needles clicked rhythmically.

"I don't know how women keep track of the stitches." Thankful stood again and paced. She ran to the window at the sound of bells on the road, but alas it was someone else's horses trotting by.

Lucy tucked her handiwork into her knitting bag. "We could always walk into town."

Thankful instinctually resisted the suggestion, but this waiting was too much for her. "Do you think so?"

"It would save Willy the trip back, and I don't mind walking."

"I'd wanted to arrive with William, but ... the day will be nearly over and when will I have the chance this season to show off my fur?"

Lucy sighed at yet another new item of clothing for Thankful but rose from her seat and began dressing for the cold.

"Lucy, don't wear that hat. Here's a nicer one, and take this cape."

Lucy loved Thankful's black watch tartan cape and happily borrowed it. The two warm and rosy girls, braving the snow drifts and laughing as they slipped along, almost forgot how much they didn't care for each other until they came in sight of the crowded pavilion and freshly cleared pond already alive with laughter and mayhem. Lucy found her way to the tables laden with warm refreshments and offered her assistance as she didn't like to skate alone. Thankful, after a few vexing moments, spotted William chatting with his friends as he finished the last of the shoveling. Thankful noticed the ragged scarf he'd wrapped on this morning and wanted to pummel him.

Thankful's thick fox collar puffed and flattened in the wind as she strode up to the group. One of the other men tapped William's shoulder mid-sentence, and his relaxed smile faded as he turned to face her. He pulled his hat low over his eyes, which annoyed her further. The men made way and greeted her quietly. She ignored them and came right up under William's nose. Despite her anger she still noted how handsome he was.

"William, I waited *all morning*."

"You look like an angel," he said as his male friends scattered.

"Stop flattering me," she said. "I wanted to make an impression and now it's ruined."

"Oh, here we go again," he said, rolling his eyes as he turned back to shoveling.

Thankful grabbed his arm but William pulled from her.

"Please, Willy, why won't you try to understand me? I've so looked forward to us impressing everyone today. I want everyone to see how happy we are."

William stopped and stared. "But we're not, are we? I'm not."

"Please don't say that!" she cried. "I so wanted ..."

"You so want *everything*! Want! Want! Want!" William ranted. "Look at everyone. Do you see those smiles? Why don't you ask them how to be happy?" He grabbed her collar. "Do you think I don't know how much this costs me? Do you think I want to be out here freezing my ass off for all of your fancy friends? But I do it for you, and you can't allow me five minutes to talk to my friends! We could be out there skating right now, but you want so much!"

"That's not fair! You insisted on buying me this fur!"

"I hoped you'd be happy!"

She wiped her eyes and looked around at her old acquaintances all paired off. She spotted Meg and Royal now laughing at the edge of the pond and pointing to Nathan being dragged down by a clumsy girl. "William, can we start this day over?"

"I'm afraid not," William replied wearily. "I'm going to get my pay and head home. My head is killing me."

"No, don't leave. I'll come with you."

"Thankful, please stay here. I need time to think."

"About what?" She followed him.

He grabbed her by the arm and whispered, "Stop making a scene. You look beautiful, and you wanted to show yourself off. Go ahead and do it."

He let her go with a little shove. She stood breathlessly watching him storm off. A young man of means clumsily made his way to her in his skates. "Mrs. Weldon!"

Thankful offered a polite smile.

"Mrs. Weldon, I was wondering if you might do me a favor. I get rather timid around pretty girls ..."

She brightened a little.

"I haven't the nerve to do it myself, but would you see if Lucy McCullough might go round once or twice with me?" he asked, the color rising in his face as he adjusted his scarf.

"Lucy's engaged, did you know?" Thankful said. "To a much older man and it's quite scandalous, really."

"No, I didn't know," the boy replied, glancing over at Lucy, who chatted with a whole group of young men and women near the refreshments. "Maybe, I'll just ask her myself."

Thankful fled behind a great spruce and burst into tears. *Why am I so mean?*

Lucy, despite being surrounded by eager young suitors, kept her eyes out for Buck and wondered too where William had gone. She skated over to the edge of the pond where Meg and Royal stood. Meg laughed as she took Lucy's outstretched arm. "I mistook you for Thankful in that cape for a second, but it suits you."

Lucy twirled with a laugh. "Thank you!"

They watched the skaters fly by and listened as the musicians started their festive tunes. "Lucy, how is my sister?" Meg asked.

Lucy shrugged.

"She was so nervous the other evening," Meg said. "I want to forgive her for the horrible thing she's done. I hope you will never tell a soul. My father would be in a lot of trouble."

Lucy turned to Meg in surprise. "I'd never gossip about your father! Thankful is a very unhappy person, and I feel sorry that no one stopped her from doing what she did."

"It's her fault! We were raised better. It serves her right!" Meg said, lowering her voice when a group of ladies looked her way. "My parents spoiled her and now they pay the price."

Lucy looked back to her happy peers and wondered what she was leaving behind in marrying so young. "How is Buck?" she asked, regretting it immediately.

"Oh, Buck's the same as ever, coughing and wheezing. You'll have your hands full nursing him one day," Meg said but caught Lucy's worried expression. "But he's a good boy. We all love him, and you won't be alone."

"You make him sound utterly pathetic," Lucy replied in annoyance.

"Don't be angry," Meg scolded. "I'm allowed my opinion about my own brother."

"You all have always thought less of him than you should."

"Royal, listen to this—Lu imagines she knows something of the world," Meg said. "Dear Lucy, Buck is doing quite well in the city from what I hear, but he's always been a bit queer. Don't take it so hard."

The young man of means had finally gotten up his nerve and came to Lucy's side. "Miss McCullough, would you care for a go around?"

Lucy jumped at the idea. The young man struggled to keep up once they got going. As a child Lucy's uncle had taken her early on Saturdays to have the pond to themselves. Lucy had excelled at skating, and today, as she called and laughed to her friend, other young men took notice and lined up to take turns whirling Lucy around the sparkling ice.

Thankful almost left the scene but saw Royal and then Lucy making Meg sit on a snowy bench. She walked and then ran around the cleared sidewalk.

At the sound of Thankful's voice Lucy turned to her. "Thankful, your sister is suddenly ill! Nathan and his friend went to get her a ride."

Thankful brushed Lucy aside. "Don't worry, Meggie. We'll have you home and comfortable in no time."

Meg stared up at Royal.

The ex-soldier's face so usually puffed up with a content expression was deflated now but he kissed her, trying to hide his concern with a thin smile. "She's not close to due yet," he confided to Lucy.

"Don't worry," Lucy said, feeling Meg's forehead with concern. "Doctor Crenshaw will save the day. I'm sure of it."

Royal nodded but said nothing more, searching beyond them for the promised carriage. Moments later, Nathan arrived with a sled and team borrowed from the baker up the road. Everyone helped Meg in and jumped in themselves before racing up to the Crenshaw house. The stable hands met them at the gate and Lucy jumped out first, taking two steps at a time up to the front door. Margaret called for the party to come round back, where Graham met them at the door, taking Meg into his own care as she looked up at him in frightened awe. Royal demanded to come with his wife, but Meg begged him to give her privacy. "Now the pressure's on for a name, Roy!"

Thankful ran to Graham. "Father, may I help?"

Graham brushed Thankful aside. "Lucy is who I want. She's got more experience working with me. You see that your mother is made calm."

"But, I don't want to ..." Thankful began but remembered what William had said earlier. "Yes, Father." She could hear her mother's agitated voice above in the parlor and with heavy feet went to her at once.

Margaret paced like a tiger in a cage, but Fred and India would not permit her to leave the room. Upon seeing Thankful, Margaret's eyes widened at a new idea. "It's your fault!"

Thankful shrank back at the door.

Fred tried to quiet his mother but she would have none of it. "You have cursed your sister! If the baby dies, it will be as punishment for what you made us do!"

India rushed to Thankful to shield her. "Mother Crenshaw, let's not fall prey to superstition."

"You're right, India," Margaret said, wringing her handkerchief. "God would not allow for any more childbirth mishaps in this family. We've had our share—Fred's beloved Rosie first and then this! Oh, Lord save us and don't allow Thankful's evil deed to inflict pain on our dear Meggie!"

"Mother Crenshaw! I must ask you to stop abusing Thankful, who was only an unfortunate victim herself. If only she'd known how to protect herself better ..."

"Dear India. I do not recall ever telling you to call me *Mother*, so please don't. Thankful knew what *all* women know. The best form of protection is a strong will to do right. Men only get what they want if you let them. Thankful should have known better, and she knows that now. I have no reason to sugarcoat anything. My daughter made sure to remind me on countless occasions the bad mother I was."

Thankful pushed past India and out the front door. Buck, who had been napping, wandered into the parlor now with a thick cough still troubling him. "What's all the commotion?"

"You dumbass," Fred said. "Meg's gone into labor."

"But it's too early," Buck said still groggy from his father's cough syrup.

"Tell me, Buck, will you ever get out of those bedclothes?" Fred asked, impatient with his family.

"India's seen me in worse," Buck replied, wondering if there was coffee to be had. "I should go find out if Meg needs anything. Father may like for me to help."

"He already has help in Lucy," Fred said.

Buck's groggy demeanor changed. "Lucy's here?"

"Yes, so I wouldn't go down there looking as you do. Father won't be impressed."

"Yes, you're right. I should stay out of it," Buck replied, swallowing hard on his cowardice.

Fred looked his brother over. "Why are you avoiding Lucy?"

Buck opened his mouth to speak, stricken by Fred's words. "I'm not avoiding her."

Fred laughed, folding his arms before him and leaning into India confidentially. "Buck's always been afraid of the *ladies*."

India smiled sympathetically as Buck's temper rose. "Buck, Lucy's a fine catch for you. She's a strange mix of old-fashionedness and naiveté that's adorable for you. Now if only someone would rid her of her need to be so very good and self-sacrificing, she might be bearable to the society ladies Fred tells me you've been seeing so much of lately."

Margaret arched her brows in reproach. Buck shot Fred a hateful glance.

"I haven't been spending time with any ladies," Buck said, "except for at the socials I must attend for my career. I never should have said anything to Fred about them."

India laughed. "Good for you, Buck. You always were so insecure about your looks, and now I'm sure you finally understand that women find you quite adorable despite the scars, especially since you're making a name in the right circles. I always knew you'd make something of yourself."

Fred huffed now. "India, is it necessary for you to become Buck's flag waver?"

"Oh, don't be jealous."

"India, how is it you raise the temperature of men so easily?" Margaret wondered.

The party ignored her.

"I'm not jealous of Buck," Fred continued. "Don't be ridiculous, India. Just because he's making money at the moment doesn't mean he won't find a new way of fouling it all up. Even if he doesn't, I'm pretty certain that he's already messing something up with Lucy. I told him how foolish it was to get involved with the Weldon family."

"She's a McCullough," Buck said, but weakly.

Fred laughed. "Okay, whatever you want to say. But Lulu's not one of us from up here, and after spending so much time with the *real* ladies of Manhattan, you worry that Lucy will have nothing in common with them."

"I don't care about that," Buck said.

They all laughed at him.

"I'll protect her from it all."

Margaret came beside Buck and put her arm around him uncomfortably. "Dear, it's been what's worrying me ever since you decided to get the girl's hopes up. You seem to consider her a little child to protect."

He pulled free. "No, you twist everything. I'll speak with her now and put things straight." He left the room to the sounds of his family's derisive laughter. Why had he been avoiding everything? Lucy was too good for the society girls. She wouldn't fit in, and it had been selfish to ask her to marry him on a whim. She was too young. Her letters stroked his fragile confidence, but her devotion did appear childish and too over-the-top good. Things could never work between them. A society girl he didn't really care for would be best.

He liked his job well enough, didn't he? The men he worked with and spent weekends with this past autumn were like the friends he'd had that first successful year at West Point. *That was probably enough*, he thought as he made his way down into the guest room, where Meg had been taken. Buck hesitated at the door and touched his hand to the knob when Lucy suddenly opened it from the other side. She stopped for a second but brushed past him in search of more blankets for Meg, who'd gone quite cold in bed. Buck followed her with his eyes and finally with his feet, trotting after her. "Lucy!"

"Buck, your sister is very sick, I think."

"Is she?" Buck hadn't even thought about Meg, really. "Is there anything I can do for you?"

"*Me?*" Lucy stared at him. "Your father needs help."

"Yes, of course, I didn't think ... it didn't occur to me that Meg ..."

Lucy refused to respond to Buck's blundering talk as she grabbed the blanket from the bed in the next room, where Fred and India had slept the previous night. He tried to take the blanket from her, but she hardly noticed as she raced back to Meg. He followed but stood at the door of the crowded, busy room. Royal stood at his wife's side now, his eyes full of worry, but Meg smiled, holding his hand.

"Buck!" Meg cried out, "You mustn't see me like this! It's embarrassing!" she said, but her attention faded as Buck came beside her.

"Meg, how bully!" he said. "Soon there will be a little one right here for us all to hold!" His thoughts of Lucy and society and banking slipped away. He noted the strained look on his father's face so unlike the confident and calm expression he had witnessed on the many house calls Buck had gone to with the doctor. "Father? She's doing fine, right?"

Royal turned to Graham too, waiting for an answer.

Graham said nothing for a long while. "We'll have to see."

"Father?" Buck asked again.

"Buck, go up and be with Mama."

"But I'd like to stay."

Meg turned to Buck and whispered, "Buckie, please fetch Mama for me."

Graham almost stopped him, but agreed. "Yes, get Mama."

He ran upstairs in a daze. The others understood in his panicked expression that they were needed downstairs and ran past him. He followed at a dumbfounded distance, a distance full of dread. This time upon entering and squeezing into the room, he noted Nathan, Abby, and Maddie peering with big eyes from the bench they'd been ordered to sit upon. Margaret knelt down beside Meg. "Graham, do something! She looks so different!"

"I can't." He remembered Thankful's baby. The doctor couldn't touch this daughter for fear of the same outcome. "Margaret, call for Doctor Banks."

"No! I won't have that old man in here for Meg," Margaret began, but the panic in her husband's eyes frightened her, and she ran to have word sent to the old doctor.

"Father, what's the matter with her?" Fred demanded. "Don't just stand there!"

"It's far too early ... there's nothing I can do."

Royal stood transfixed, saying nothing, just holding Meg's hand in his own. Lucy made her way between everyone almost unnoticed as she spread the blanket over Meg's middle. India whispered something to the younger siblings, and they followed her out into the hallway. Fred paced the tiny room before shaking his father's shoulder. "Get yourself together, Father. Do something! There must be something!"

Buck grabbed hold of Fred and dragged him into the hallway. "Fred, stop it."

Fred cried out. "Poor Meg! She never got a stitch of attention, did she?"

"We need to pray that ..."

"Blast it, Buck! She's going to die." Fred pushed him away. "This is exactly like Rosie. I know what this is. Prayers won't help."

Buck didn't want to hear. He walked back into the room, hoping for a different answer, unnerved by his father's paralysis. "Meg, please be strong. You've only just become happy."

"Buck, tell me you'll look after Royal and the baby."

Buck glanced over at the man he hardly knew and then at his father. He said nothing, gave Meg no assurances.

Lucy stepped up behind Buck and whispered, "There's no harm in telling her what she needs to hear."

He hesitated. If he said anything it might mean he'd given up on her. "Meg, I'll be here to help no matter what."

Meg smiled. "You were always my favorite."

He kissed her hand, thinking that he'd always been so caught up with Fred that he'd hardly noticed Meg at all. "We'll be better friends from now on, won't we?"

"Yes," she replied unconvincingly before turning her gaze upon Royal. "You'll name him Buckminster, Roy. You promised."

Royal nodded with a befuddled glance at Buck.

By the time Doctor Banks arrived, Meg had lost consciousness. The doctor guided Graham to a seat before examining her himself. Everyone had been ushered out into the hallway to keep Margaret from a breakdown in front of Royal. Only Lucy remained in the corner to help the doctors.

"I'm sorry, Crenshaw," the doctor said, patting Graham's shoulder. "You couldn't have done a thing to help, I'm afraid."

Lucy came to the doctor's side. "I don't understand. She was just laughing at the pond."

Dr. Banks sighed. "The baby wasn't where it was supposed to be, I suspect—and there was a rupture then. Sometimes there are no warnings." He patted Lucy's hand and left to give the news to the others before leaving the family with their grief.

The hush broke as Margaret wailed in the hall. Lucy knelt before Graham. "Dear, Doctor Crenshaw, I'm so terribly sorry. Meg was a very nice girl."

He stared at her through his tears. "Oh, Lulu, but my girls are never very nice to you, are they? I'm sorry for that."

She said nothing.

Graham ran his hand over her head. She looked up at him and saw that he hadn't the faintest idea what to do about Royal.

"The Crenshaws will take care of you," Lucy said as she came beside the young husband. "I can't imagine your grief, sir, but I could tell that you made Meg very happy."

"Meg made me ... but now what? Everything's changed and so fast ..."

"There's room tomorrow to think about those things. Today, you must just be here with her."

Both men stared after Lucy as she gathered her things and walked out the door. The rest of the family were struggling to keep Margaret from hurting herself so Lucy was able to sneak out through the summer kitchen and into the blustery evening. Only then did she allow for her own tears. Poor Meg! Poor Royal! He seemed so in love and proud!

Turning toward the stable and the path out to the road, she spotted Thankful sitting on a snowy chair next to the family's private skating pond. Lucy considered slipping by behind the large pines, but Thankful spotted her. She did not move but looked to Lucy with desperate eyes. Lucy went to her.

"Thankful, you'd better go in now."

"How is she?" Thankful asked, knowing the answer.

Lucy stared off toward the Palisades, searching for good words. "Thankful, it was all very peaceful in the end."

"The end?"

"Your sister died and the baby too. I'm terribly sorry."

Thankful burst into bitter tears, hiding her face in her gloved hands. When Lucy tried to get close, Thankful nudged her off.

"Leave me be, Lucy. You will *never* take her place!"

"I had no intention ..." Lucy cried in shock. "Please go be with the others."

"You can't order me!" Thankful said but jumped to her feet and grabbed hold of Lucy. "I'm sorry! Truly I am! But I hate you for being so exceptionally good! I hate it!

And however I try I can't convince myself that you're right for Buck. He's become so respectable these last months and maybe one of us Crenshaws has a chance still of that! I don't mind at all how you came to be blind, but those other girls! Why do you think I did the awful thing I did to my baby? The society girls will eat you alive! And Buck will grow to resent your lack of polish!" Thankful sobbed some more. "You think my words are mean, but I speak from experience. Let my brother have his successes for once. Oh, Meg! Why did she have to go and marry Royal?"

"She loved him," Lucy said, aghast at Thankful's cynicism and meanness.

"Just because people love each other doesn't mean they must produce babies. Why must women always give up everything?"

"I don't know, Thankful."

"You know nothing! You're a babe in the woods! Don't you see all the suffering love causes for women? Meg was a sorry loser in life, and she really believed that would change! I could have told her that nothing changes! We're cursed—Father was always right—he said the Crenshaws were cursed!"

"No, Thankful. Willy loves you."

Thankful turned on her and laughed. "Does he really? All Willy cares about is having a baby! If he truly loved me, he would understand how much I don't want one!"

Lucy stepped back. "I should leave now."

"Yes, you should. This will never be your home. You should know that."

Lucy turned and walked slowly at first, but her heart pounded and her feet moved faster as she turned onto the cobbled road. Her ears rang with the words just spoken to her, and her mind blurred it all into a heavy throbbing lump of confusion. A voice called out, and she turned to see Buck running down the street, still in his sleepwear.

"Lucy! Wait!" His raspy voice was raw with exertion. "I was looking for you and thought maybe I'd ride you home if you just come back."

"No, I'd rather walk."

"Luce, I'm sorry," he began, the wind whipping his light brown hair and the slight fever bringing his face to a rosy, boyish hue which softened her anger. With hunched shoulders he rubbed his arms nervously in the cold. "I mean ...well ... I should have done a better job writing."

"I suppose you were busy."

"Yes ... well, not that busy. I could have ..."

She stared at him. "But you didn't." She sighed. "Buck, go be with your family. Meg certainly means more to you than a silly childish romance."

"Silly?" He stopped still. "Are you ending it, then?"

"You'll be better without me. You don't need to draw me a picture. But I wish you hadn't made such a fool of me these past months. Everyone at school thought it ridiculous how much I talked about being married. They wondered if I had dreamt it all. Now I see they were right."

"No, Lucy, I ..." Buck stammered. "I'd forgotten how pretty you were ..."

"Not pretty enough to compete with Thankful's friends."

"Thankful's friends? She hasn't any. What's that got to do with anything?"

"I don't play cat and mouse, Buck Crenshaw. And what kind of boy talks on the street in his underthings when his sister lies dead?!" A torrent of disappointed emotion overtook her.

"There's nothing I can do for her now, is there?"

"I should think you might at least pretend at being upset!"

"You don't know anything about the way I feel," he said coolly.

"You're right! I suppose I never did!" Lucy cried. "Maybe you are as strange as people say!"

"Maybe you're as immature as people tell me!" he shouted, but it caused a coughing fit.

She threw her hands in the air. "Go inside, you big baby! Whoever let a cough stop him from visiting the girl he promised to marry?" She held back her sobs until she'd run down the hill and around the corner. Buck didn't follow, and she was half glad to be rid of the Crenshaws until she was almost home and bleakly imagining the rest of her days.

Her young heart almost enjoyed the morbidity of her imaginings. She'd stay a totally blind teacher in New London, never to return to Tenafly Road. Let William rot in his own ridiculous marriage to the craven Thankful! Lucy laughed at Thankful's name. Ha! The most spoiled, horrible children were produced by dear Doctor Crenshaw and *...poor Doctor Crenshaw.* Poor Thankful. Wasn't Thankful the blindest girl she'd ever known? And what of Buck? How adorable he looked with his nightshirt blown around his stockinged legs. She smiled, but then remembered the true-sounding words Thankful and Margaret had said over the last few days and she cried.

By the time her old home came into view she'd cried everything out, resolving to leave in the morning. A lonely room at the school seemed better than Englewood. The parlor light blinked at the passing of William's shadow. He met her at the front door.

"Lucy, are you okay? Skating must have ended hours ago."

Lucy ran into his arms. "Everyone's dead! And Buck doesn't care for me any longer!"

# Chapter Eight

If one had been keeping score, Thankful had accomplished a small victory over her mother in the days following Meg's death when Martha Crenshaw decided to stay with her granddaughter on Tenafly Road despite the more comfortably appointed rooms at the Crenshaw house on Chestnut Street. Thankful didn't tell William that Martha had written expressing her desire to stay at *William's house*.

Some wives would have appreciated how William fawned over Martha, but Thankful did not. She watched the reunion from a small distance with her arms folded in hurt and lonely judgment. Look how Martha gushed like a young girl! Wasn't it ludicrous how she smiled so much and laughed too? William was many things, but he wasn't *that* funny. And when had Martha ever hugged her grandchildren with such abandon—hadn't she more self-control?

Right now Thankful hated Willy's big doe eyes as he smiled that irresistible smile. He had even tied a loose knot at his neck to impress the old granny. *When had he ever agreed to dress up for her? Go ahead, Martha, with your scrawny neck and try flirting with him, but he's mine.* These thoughts wrestled with the weak smile Thankful held (to the point of hurting) as her grandmother made her way—with William's help—up the porch steps which remained icy despite Thankful warning William about them. Always he was too busy on other people's property.

"Thankful, how are you holding up?" Martha asked as if she might actually care.

Thankful said nothing while leading her grandmother in and helping her with her cape and hat in the front hall. William ran off to get Martha's bag from the waiting livery driver.

"I hope I'm not too much trouble, girl, but I couldn't bear the idea of your mother and her ostentatious flair for the dramatic," Martha said, but could not hide her tears. "How my son must suffer! I wouldn't have the right words, I'm afraid. I know that you and Meg were close. I hardly knew her, but losing a child is the only truly awful thing in this world that I've not steeled myself against." She dabbed her eyes and walked wearily into the parlor. "This is a lovely room, Thankful."

"I changed everything for William so he wouldn't be reminded of the past all the time."

"That's just as I would have done," Martha said. "But ... my, you have very fine taste."

"William is quite land rich," Thankful said defensively.

"Dear, it's unmannerly to talk about your husband's finances. You needn't explain to me. I trust *William* won't spend foolishly."

"But you don't have that same faith in me."

"It's easier to have faith in strangers," Martha said, taking off her black gloves and sitting before the fire. "Where's the little girl Buck plans to marry?"

Thankful shook her head, shushing her grandmother. "We mustn't talk about it. Buck is such an odd fish, and it seems there won't be an engagement after all."

"But they were already engaged. It's what your father wrote in his last letter ..." Martha whispered leaning close to Thankful, who sat opposite now.

Thankful glanced at the door and then back at Martha. "Seems Buck has gotten cold feet, and I'm glad. Can you imagine if he went off again? I do truly, truly love dear Buck, but if he broke Lulu's heart, how would it be for me living with William, who thinks the world of his little cousin?"

Martha smiled at William's affections. This annoyed Thankful, but she said nothing more because William came in with characteristic shyness. "Ma'am, are you warm enough? How can we make you comfortable after such a long drive?"

Martha beamed up at William. "Sit beside me—Thankful, please make some tea. There now, William. Tell me all about your sheep and the farming you've gotten up to. I'm jealous after your last letter."

Thankful glanced back at the two unlikely friends, unnerved that William never mentioned a correspondence with Martha.

"Oh, well, I remembered you told me you were not one for writing, but I like to imagine you enjoy hearing from your pupils," William said.

"And you are correct, young man. Jane and I love your letters with the little illustrations of the funny mishaps on the Adriance farm," Martha said with an appreciative giggle.

"You draw things for Martha?" Thankful asked.

William looked caught. "They're nothing, I ..."

"Don't be so humble, William! The drawings are magnificent!" Martha said, innocent of the tension William's underused talent created.

"Thankful, I need to go check the animals. I won't be long," William said, making a quick escape.

"Have I blundered into something?" Martha asked in bewilderment.

"I can't believe he's going off to see about animals when Meg has just died, and I need him!" Thankful cried. "Willy cares about everyone but me!"

"Animals need fed no matter who dies, dear." Martha motioned for Thankful to sit. "Dear, don't ruin a good thing by being selfish and needy. It's not attractive."

Lucy slid open the parlor doors now. "Excuse me, I didn't realize ..." She backed away.

Martha stood in all her regal magnificence. "Come to me at once, young lady. You must be Lucy McCullough."

Lucy complied with a warm smile. "Mrs. Crenshaw, I'm so pleased to meet you. I'm sorry for your loss."

"Why, you're rather handsome, aren't you?" Martha said, touching Lucy's unbraided strawberry-blond hair.

Lucy said nothing but squirmed under Thankful's hateful stare.

"William always spoke highly of you," Martha continued. "Seems you saved the lad from a life of drunken debauchery."

Lucy giggled at Martha's directness. "I don't take credit for his change, but we all should save each other once in a while."

Martha gave Lucy an impressed nod.

"Meg will be missed, I'm sure," Lucy said for lack of anything else to say.

"You'll miss her?" Thankful asked, cynically.

"*Thankful*. What an awful way to act," Martha said, though she said this as if Thankful's words were of little interest or value to her. Her attention remained fixed on Lucy "The sad truth is the quiet ones sometimes are neglected. That was Meg, poor thing. I bet she had some good qualities."

"Neither of you has a right to talk about her!" Thankful cried. "She was my twin, and I knew everything about her and, yes, she had many, many qualities that go unappreciated in this world! She wasn't attractive, but ..."

"Calm down!" Martha said in consternation. "I said nothing about Meg's looks and, really Thankful, is that all you ever worry about?"

"No!" Thankful cried. "I'm concerned over a great many things that no one cares about! But I wish everyone would stop acting like they'll miss Meg when they never cared!"

"Land sakes, girl, who are you talking about?" Martha asked.

"All of you! No one sincerely cares!"

"If she isn't the image of her mother." Martha noted this in a dismissive aside to Lucy.

"How dare you!"

"Maybe I should stay at the shoddy hotel," Martha grumbled.

Lucy took Martha by the hand. "No, please don't. Despite the circumstances, Willy's been looking so forward to you being here."

Martha smiled. "Has he now?"

Lucy nodded. "And Thankful ... it would be impossible for either of us to understand the bond she had with Meg."

Thankful rolled her eyes at Lucy who always had the right words. She wiped her eyes, grudgingly admitting to herself that Lucy's words were kind—however they might annoy her.

"This girl is right, Thankful," Martha said. "I can't imagine your feelings of loss, and Margaret was not the mother she should have been with you children ... I should have taken more of an interest in you too."

Thankful sniffled as if she might have regained control, but suddenly threw herself into her surprised grandmother's arms sobbing.

"Now, now, Thankful, oh, there you go. Now let it out," Martha said stiffly, looking to Lucy for rescue.

"Mrs. Crenshaw, I'll get your tea now," Lucy said.

Martha pulled Thankful from her, clasping her granddaughter's hands in her own. "Thankful, shall we help Lucy with the tea?"

"No," Thankful said. "We have a girl who takes care of those things."

"Then I'd like to meet her," Martha said, using any excuse to escape the sobbing and clinging.

"You'd like to meet Josephine?" Thankful asked, fearing her grandmother's appraisal of her house help.

Lucy led them into the warm kitchen filled with the scent of yeast rising.

"How very charming this room is," Martha said with a touch of envy. The kitchen was the opposite of Martha's spartan affair, and her reaction to this room came as a surprise to Thankful.

Thankful blushed with pride. She'd made the place shine with fresh paint and bright curtains at the large window above the sink that framed a view of the garden where Simon McCullough's willow dominated. Josephine almost bowed before the regal old lady, but Martha held out her hand in friendship.

"I see that you keep a clean kitchen. May we impose ourselves upon you today?"

Josephine turned to Thankful, "Shall I bring you tea in the dining room? The fire hasn't been watched in there so I fear the chill ..."

Martha spoke. "Josephine, I find that in times of trouble the kitchen is the most comforting room to be in. If you don't mind, I'll sit here where it's warm after my long drive, and we'll get our own tea, if you'll join us. I'm always interested in how people manage their house."

Josephine stood speechless, wiping her hands on her floured apron.

Thankful went to the cupboard and took out four delicately painted tea cups and set them on the rough and worn table William refused to let Thankful sell. She served the others, even Josephine, tea. They sat in uneasy silence as Thankful brought over cream and sugar, but when she brought out the lovely apple strudel from the pantry, their moods brightened and even Thankful cheered a little as she passed the pastry around on the fine china she rarely used. Martha even took a second slice (an unheard of thing), causing much delight in Josephine who chatted about taking care of *her* William and *her* Thankful.

Thankful wiped a tear at the sentiment.

William stomped his boots in the mudroom and joined them in the kitchen with rosy cheeks and stockinged feet. Josephine doted over him as did Martha, whilst Lucy and Thankful looked on in quiet contemplation. Without the drinking, William was the gentlest soul Lucy had ever known. She eyed her cousin protectively, but relaxed once assured that the other women saw how original and wonderful Willy was.

Thankful sat beside him unsure of his feelings, but just when she felt her panic and uncertainty almost ready to explode in an unseemly burst of new tears, William reached for her hand beneath the table. He held her so tightly in his calloused, warm hand and smiled at her with such compassion she wondered how she ever got angry with him.

# Chapter Nine

Buck stood outside his father's study afraid to knock. The door swung open before he had time to gather his thoughts.

"Son?" Graham said with a mix of annoyance and concern. "Is there something you need?"

"No, Father. I was just worried about you."

"No need," Graham said, walking right past him and down the hall toward the summer kitchen.

Buck followed at a careful distance. "Father, I wanted you to ... know that I don't blame you ... you did everything you could for Meg."

Graham turned on Buck with round, offended eyes and a rush of color on his ears and neck. "Of course you don't blame me. Why would you?"

"I-I don't know," Buck stammered. "Of course, I suppose you're right—but I worried you might blame yourself since—well, that whole thing with Thankful and then this ..." He could feel his words enveloping him in quicksand, but he flailed away. "I mean—we all make mistakes. I mean I forgive you—well only God can forgive you, but I don't hold it against you or anything."

Graham stood, an imposingly stout figure against the slim stature of his son, staring with nostrils flared. "Buck, sometimes I wonder if that poor girl Lucy will ever be able to calm your fragile nerves. You stand here making little sense."

"I wanted to give you a few words of encouragement."

"I'm glad you're prospering in banking because you have no skill at whatever it is you're trying right now," Graham complained too harshly, then sighed at his loss of temper with this odd son of his. "I know you mean well, but I don't want to be consoled. I am responsible for Meg. My actions with Thankful cursed Meg, but I don't want to talk about it." With more warmth he continued, "Your Lucy was a gem the other day with Meg."

Buck coughed. "Father, I don't think—well—I believe Lucy wants no part of me any longer, and really ... it's so soon after Meg to be parading a girl on my arm."

"What do you mean?"

"It's for the best. Everyone says so. Lucy wouldn't fit in." Buck cast his eyes down.

"Fit in?" Graham asked, incredulously. "With whom? Lucy fits in with me just fine."

"Do you think so?" Buck asked, eager for approval. "I thought so too. I thought it might be nice to have someone to take care of and fuss over."

Graham laughed. "Lucy's not a doll, son."

"Of course, Father. Why is it that everyone believes I've no sense about girls?"

Graham smiled but said nothing. The doctor sifted through gone-off oranges left in a bowl by the new housekeeper but grabbed a few Christmas cookies instead and sat at the cook's tall stool.

Buck leaned with elbows on the counter. "Here's what concerns me: What if Lucy doesn't like my friends? I'm a good banker, but there's a social element and ..."

Graham stopped mid-cookie. "Are you saying you want to see other young ladies?"

"My friends have been trying to force a certain girl upon me."

Graham shook his head.

"Father, I haven't done a thing. I would never hurt Lucy that way, but this girl is much sought after and her father has friends in banking and government, and for some reason she has taken to me—though I haven't given her any reason to assume I might care for her in any way other than as a friend."

Graham shook his head with more emphasis now, dropping the cookie to his plate. "No. You're going off on the wrong road—again. It's impossible to have female friends. And I strongly advise you not to marry for banking. Don't sell your soul for appearances."

Buck adjusted his prosthetic as he spoke. "The thing is, I don't really care for this girl in the city."

"I don't understand you, son."

Buck rolled an orange under his hand on the counter. "I wondered if it might be easier."

"For whom?"

"For me, of course," Buck said. "I don't have a good track record—at anything. If things go sour for Lucy and me ... the idea of it seems very hard."

Graham laughed again. "Dear boy, you give me hope yet that one of my sons has a heart. That's exactly the feeling you should have about Lucy. What would be the point if you didn't fear losing her?"

"Father, I didn't write her much. There was nothing interesting to say."

Graham stood to go. "Look at that sad young man mourning for Meg in our parlor. How quickly death can steal our happiness! I'm so grateful that someone took the time with Meg. I never did and now suffer that regret keenly. Lucy's different from our poor Meg. She has a spark about her, and, mark my words, if you don't take her someone else will. There's many young men who'd be pleased just for a dance. I saw the way my young male patients looked at Lulu when she worked at the office."

***

Standing in the blustery cemetery, the Crenshaws, Royal Wilder, William, and Lucy huddled beneath the trees on the handsome family plot Graham had bought when Buck scared them in the West. In fact, the tombstone—Buck's—still stood, much to William's composed amusement. William's parents lay buried over a rise with his uncle and grandparents beneath enormous sculptures and plaques that put the Crenshaw spot to shame. Scott McCullough had been fascinated by death and statuary.

Buck stood aloof, his face wrapped in a thin black scarf ashamed at his cowardly behavior toward Lucy but at a loss as to what to do about it. He gazed at Lucy shivering with hunched shoulders until Martha took the girl beneath her cape maternally. Thankful stood beside William, fully composed and striking in a sumptuous mourning outfit with beaver-trimmed cape, hat, and gloves. Everyone waited for Margaret to explode into anguished wails as she had when they thought Buck had died, but she remained silent between Fred and Graham with a defeated, drooping appearance. Only once she spoke saying, "Will I never have a decent grandchild?"

India stiffened at Margaret's words, holding a simpering Sam in her arms but said nothing.

The mourners lingered until Margaret and Graham backed away. Like horses let out of gates, they raced to their carriages, everyone frozen to the bone. Before Lucy could escape and before Buck might have a chance to speak with her privately, Margaret intruded, calling Lucy to her. "Dear girl, the dress we had made for you is ready for tomorrow night's dance."

"Oh, I couldn't go now."

"I'm afraid my Buck has disappointed you, as I expected. I'd hoped that this time would be different because I truly like you, but my boys are fickle. You needn't miss the dance on account of Meg. She's not really family to you, and we've paid for the dress. It's the least I can do."

Thankful came beside Lucy. "Mama, what are you saying to Lulu?"

"How sorry I am about Buck being a cad."

Thankful led Lucy away from her mother. Lucy climbed into the carriage with a stricken and bewildered gaze. William and Martha stared.

"Lucy, what's wrong?" William asked.

"Mama's rubbed salt in Lucy's wound," Thankful complained, angry at everyone. "Buck doesn't deserve to be happy! Lucy, you're better off!"

"Yes, but I'm terribly disappointed. I can't help it!" Lucy cried.

"What has Buck to say for himself?" Martha asked, looking around, but her grandson was gone.

# Chapter Ten

Lucy had volunteered to stay in William's frosty attic room until Martha left, and she sat empty of hope curled in an Indian blanket. The idea of school in frigid New London, with the sea air blowing damp down every chimney, held no appeal. The friends she'd made there were nice enough, but they lacked something.

No matter how she tried to imagine living in the outside world, she could not find peace. Englewood was her home and would always be even if she must rent an apartment on her own. But what would she do with her life? Would she end up like Grandmother in a home for the decrepit with no one ever visiting? She resolved to go to the old age home tomorrow, ashamed of her own lack of concern for the woman who until recently had been a real force in her life.

Thankful came in without a knock and hung a confection of a dress by a hook on the wall. Lucy said nothing. The peach fabric she'd chosen with Margaret's guidance astonished Lucy now with how well it suited the cut of the gown. The small bit of lace at the lowered neckline gave the dress a grown-up look.

"Do you like it, Lucy?"

She hesitated, waiting for an awful sentiment to escape Thankful's exquisite, dangerous mouth, but the stunning woman in black who often cowed Lucy sat beside her and took in the dress as well. "Mama has always known how to dress us well." Thankful sighed. "I told her you'd go to the dance."

"Why? Is it any of your business?"

"Because you mustn't let a man win. Despite your disappointment this moment, you will one day look back in relief that Buck set you free. You can do anything you like now. And you are still so young. I envy you."

"Why?"

"I wish I'd gone to school or something. I don't enjoy running a shop. It's frivolous work selling little cards and the like. William can pick any career he wants, and no one disapproves. You will be educated to teach the blind. That's a noble thing. Everyone will admire you."

"I don't care about that, Thankful."

"You say that now."

"I will say that always. Don't you love my cousin?"

"Of course! But ... it does seem so unfair sometimes that we're judged by foolish things like housekeeping and babies."

"Those things are important," Lucy said. "I was upset that you changed everything, but I do see that it has been a great comfort to William—and the wallpapers are nice."

"I appreciate your compliment," Thankful said with pride, but it deflated swiftly. "Sometimes life isn't as satisfying as I imagined it might be. It's just, well, William has so many talents, and he can throw them away. What I wouldn't give to paint."

"Well, why don't you, then?" Lucy asked simply.

"Oh, I couldn't."

Lucy walked over to the dress and touched it. "Thankful, Meg left so suddenly. What if you only have a short time? Why not try something new that you're interested in?"

"I couldn't compete with Willy."

Lucy glanced at Thankful. "Why would you compete with him? He loves you and would be happy if you were happy. That's who William is."

"You're right. You are far too good for my brother. He's being a fool. Do me this favor," Thankful said, joining Lucy by the gown and pressing it upon her. "Go to the dance and flirt with boys your own age. I bet you'll have them writing you heartfelt letters all winter, and things will seem ever so much better in spring. I want us to try again to understand each other. I haven't got any close friends. I don't trust girls because my mother has always been such a horribly manipulative woman. I want to believe you are better than that."

Lucy sighed. The dress was the most magnificent creation she'd ever seen. "If I go, will you help me do my hair the way you do yours?"

Thankful smiled at the compliment. "Of course! From now on, I want to live for your successes. Every girl in Englewood will wish they were us! Who needs the Crenshaw family when we have each other?"

"What do you mean?" Lucy asked, unsure of Thankful's motives. "You've just lost your sister so I suppose I understand why you may want company ..."

"No! For heaven's sake, of course not! Meg and I were no longer close. Mama made sure of that and I hated that Meg settled for such a common man." A trace of sorrow appeared fleetingly, just long enough for Lucy to note it before it vanished in a flourish of movement and talk on Thankful's part. "I've been rethinking everything. You're nothing like Meg. We won't allow it. I've nursed a jealousy of your friendship with Willy—yes, I know it's utterly foolish." She ran her fingers over a carved elephant William had made for Lucy years ago that Lucy had brought out of storage. Thankful glanced up to check Lucy's reaction. "But now it's clear that you are the perfect thing for Willy and me. When Grandmother goes back home, I want you to take the guest room back as your own. I'll have Mama send your knickknacks and such now that you're free again, and William and I will take care of you. You'll be welcome here. I promise."

"Thankful ..."

"William has been lonely here without you. It's what's making him so set on having a baby."

"Oh, no ... Thankful, you're making a big mistake! I'll be off to school next week."

"Must you really go back this semester? Couldn't you wait until things are more settled here?"

"Thankful, do you realize that I will need to work?"

"Yes, I understand, but one semester won't hurt anything, will it? Didn't Father vow to take care of you financially if Buck failed you?"

"Thankful, if Willy wants a baby, why not just have one? It would be a blessing."

"What happened to Meg only a few days ago? So vibrant and alive to possibilities for the first time in her pathetic life and now ... and now she's in a cold box," Thankful cried.

"Thankful, I must go to school," Lucy said, determined to escape.

Thankful sighed, plopping herself into William's tattered chair. "Forgive me. I know you're right."

Lucy sat on the floor in front of Thankful trying to regain her equilibrium. "I'm sorry for you, Thankful. You're so mixed up inside, and I do wish to be of help, but I adore babies. I understand how afraid you must be, but what if you don't die in childbirth and a tiny little girl or boy with big gold eyes and your beauty enters the world? Wouldn't you be proud and happy then?"

Thankful let herself imagine the happy scene for a second and smiled but again her feelings were transient. "Mama had us, and we never made her happy. It's too much to push onto a child. I couldn't bear hating it!"

"You wouldn't."

"I hated the lieutenant's baby so much that I let my parents do the unspeakable!"

Lucy got to her feet. She searched her mind for words, but none came.

"You hate me, don't you?" Thankful asked, rising from the chair.

"No."

Thankful straightened herself and stood before the mirror. "I hate myself."

"Thankful ..."

Thankful wiped her eyes with a sigh. "No, Lucy, it's all right. I'll be fine. Let me send you off well. I've had your dance card filled for weeks. Have fun with the boys, and I'll give you a few of my better dresses to bring to school. I'd like to be friends somehow—though I haven't any skill at it."

A vague sense of danger and distress overtook Lucy whenever Thankful confided in her, but it was impossible to avoid her without losing the only family Lucy had in William.

# Chapter Eleven

Snow fell the following morning and throughout the afternoon. Thankful readied Lucy for her dance. William drank tea after shoveling the drive, watching Thankful pull and twist Lucy's straight strawberry hair into intricate braids after an unsuccessful attempt at curls with the hot iron. Lucy grimly endured the rough handling she received with each yank, but William laughed, happy his *wifey* was taking such a keen interest in Lucy.

He didn't say much but hoped the attention Lucy would get at the dance might help her forget Buck's cruelty. William shared her embarrassment as if it were his own and vowed never again to entertain Thankful's family in his house no matter how Thankful might demand it.

One day he and Thankful would have an adorable child and never let the Crenshaws near it. When Lucy yelped yet again, William considered how lucky he was to have Thankful even if she sometimes complained about the money spent on Lucy's schooling. Thankful seemed almost happy just now with pins in her mouth. She glanced his way with a funny smile. It troubled him a little that Thankful did not appear to mourn the death of Meg but told himself that he'd married a strong woman.

He half dreaded Lucy going back to school. The house, even with new wallpaper, was a place of mourning, but Lucy brightened it. Without her as buffer, what would keep his mind off children and loneliness? Yet William also looked forward to having Thankful to himself again and the possibility of a child in the new year. A chill fingered its way beneath the kitchen door, and William roused himself to poke at the fire.

"The weather only gets worse," Lucy said. "Maybe I shouldn't go after all."

William laughed at Thankful's panicked face—perhaps she too wanted a few hours alone with him? "Lucy, Thankful's work would be wasted and the boys would be disappointed."

Lucy smiled despite her dread. Thankful brought her a mirror.

"See that little curl? It's held by that pin so don't play with it."

Lucy fingered the ivory hair comb. "I'm speechless. Thank you so much. You've done wonders."

Thankful shrugged. "You're the one with the hair like flaxen gold."

Lucy blushed William's way.

William smiled. "You're the image of your mother, Lucy." He gave her a quick peck on the cheek. "I'll bring the horse round."

Lucy turned to Thankful. "Will you come for the ride?"

"No, that's all right, Lulu. I have to learn to share Willy. I promised, didn't I?"

The windows, aglow with festive decoration along the way, brought a host of memories for the cousins as they chatted under blankets in the surrey. Lucy leaned against Willy, enjoying his masculine scent. One day she'd find a boy as handsome if she were very, very lucky. "I miss Uncle John and Aunt Kate."

"Me too," William said, tapping the reins. "But we have each other, right?"

Lucy slipped her arm around his. "Yes."

"No matter what, right?"

"Yes," she said with a laugh.

Despite the snow, lanterns flickered from the many sleighs as the wind blew near the entrance of the hotel.

"Willy, won't you come in with me for a few minutes? I'm awfully shy."

He hesitated. "I'm not dressed for it."

"I don't care." She smiled, and it charmed him.

"Well, just for a minute then."

He hitched the horse, and they raced into the warm hotel, laughing.

As always in Englewood, there were new faces but plenty of old ones too. Farmer boys and cultured girls mixed in happy, friendly festivity, and Lucy found her footing quickly. A few girls Lucy sometimes talked to waved her over to them and many a young man's head turned as she breezed by. She teased them and spoke as if she'd known them forever. She was not a coquette, and the boys appreciated that, though William noted tonight they eyed her with an awestruck delight in her appearance.

The first introductory dance was called, and William turned to leave, but Lucy would not have it.

"Oh, please, dance this one with me!" she begged.

William hadn't danced a single dance since the West but couldn't deny Lucy. As they glided around the room, he silently vowed to take Thankful out for some frolic; they'd grown too serious already.

The music stopped, and Lucy embraced him. "You've made this trip worthwhile, Willy. We're very lucky aren't we to have each other?"

"Indeed."

Lucy glanced around and waved at the first boy on her card. The music started again. "I suppose you can go now, dear cousin."

"Yes, I should. But thanks for the dance," he replied. "See you in a few hours. Don't get into any trouble ... are you sure it wouldn't be better for me to stay?"

"This is Englewood, Willy. Everybody knows me." She laughed. Her dance partner waited.

William hesitated. A proper girl came and went with friends and escorts. Lucy was just as good as any of them. William decided he'd stay a little longer. One dance led to another, and he was even asked to dance by a dowdy sister of one of his farmer acquaintances. After a cheerful waltz, he realized how silly it would be to drive all the way home only to come back so soon again. He worried he might suffer for the decision, but it was too late now.

From across the room a man with a black armband came into the light beneath the candelabra and interrupted Lucy's conversation with two boys.

"Lucy," Buck whispered at her neck.

Lucy turned in surprise.

"May I have the next dance?"

Lucy stared at him. "No. My card is full. I'm to dance with Jimmy, here."

"Jimmy will understand," Buck said. The boy came from a poor family on the outskirts of town.

The boy looked to Lucy, acting the greater gentleman by letting her decide.

Lucy slid her arm through Jimmy's. "Mr. Crenshaw, you have no right to act superior to the rest of us and push us around. I will dance with Jimmy and then all the others on my card. If you wanted a dance with me, you should have arranged that with your sister."

"Lucy, please let me talk to you."

"Not now, sir!" Lucy said. She tugged for Jimmy to bring her to the floor and made the boy regret it with her sour face and distracted footwork.

"Are you good friends with Buck Crenshaw? He was quite familiar with you. I think it ungentlemanly," Jimmy said.

"My stupid cousin foolishly married us into that family of snobs!" Lucy grumbled uncharacteristically.

"I'm sorry, miss."

"Oh, Jimmy, forgive my temper," she said. "I just hate how the Crenshaws do and say anything they like and get away with it!"

"It's just the way with the nabobs, I'm afraid. The rich get richer and ..."

"Yes, you're right. Thank you for the dance, but I need to find my cousin at once." Lucy scanned the crowd with Jimmy following her off the floor.

"There he is, Miss McCullough," Jimmy said, pointing to William and a girl in black arguing.

Lucy stopped dead with a moan. "Land sakes, can it get any worse?"

Jimmy still hovered. "Miss, your cousin is preoccupied."

"Another big bug," Lucy said. "Thankful Crenshaw."

"Oh, I see—I've heard stories about her that were less than ..." Jimmy began but stopped at Lucy's horrified look.

"Jimmy Burns, you're no better than they are if you gossip!"

"I meant nothing by it, miss," Jimmy said, realizing his chance with Lucy had slipped away.

She looked past him as Buck strode up again. "I asked Peter Darling if I might take his place on your card," Buck said, his face red with the chase.

She remembered Peter Darling from Sunday school classes as a crass ignoramus. "Well ... I don't appreciate you deciding things for me."

"You prefer my sister picking the dances?"

Lucy rolled her eyes. They fell upon William and Thankful in debate near the door.

Buck looked in the same direction. "So will you dance?"

Lucy held out her hand, trying at indifference, but her eyes, even behind her glasses, gave her away. It didn't help matters that Buck had learned the dances so well at West Point. Closing her eyes, knowing that he'd carry her along, she noted his sure hand at her back and the pleasant scent of his expensive cologne. Lucy would remember this final dance with Buck forever as a fond memory of love lost, she thought morbidly to herself.

"Lucy, I'm glad you picked the peach fabric. You look better than I imagined you would."

Lucy lost a step, but regained it.

"I hadn't any idea what to get you for Christmas," he added, "and Mama and Thankful said you'd need dresses for the holidays. I picked this peach."

"Oh," Lucy said. "But ... you do realize that I only came here as a favor to your sister?"

The music ended, but the two lingered until the next boy came in search of Lucy. Buck waved the young man off. "Give us a moment, O'Brien."

"You shouldn't be so abrupt with people, Buck."

He pulled her to a quiet corner. "I know you've decided to break our engagement, and looking back I see that keeping it secret was a mistake—as if we were ashamed, but ..."

"But Buck, isn't there something wrong with it?" she asked. "Everyone hints at it, and you never wrote. Suddenly you're well enough to come to a dance only two days before I'm to leave again. I see how Thankful is with Willy, and honestly I'm not sure I like how the Crenshaws are. I imagined you were different, but ..."

"I am! I'm totally different from the others! And you're wrong. Father says I'd be making a terrible mistake by letting you go."

"So you *were* planning to cast me off?"

"Yes, in a way. The boys at work—well they run with the same type of girls, and they wanted one for me—but I, well, I was confused."

"*Confused?*"

"Briefly, only briefly. Well, since you left." He loosened his collar.

She tried to storm off, but Buck pulled her back by the ornate bustle and it tore. She whirled around and stared at him holding the fine fabric and embroidered flowers and laughed at the idiotic look on his face.

Buck ushered her out of the light again, protecting her modesty despite the many layers of fabric protecting it already. "I don't know what came over me—I never should have yanked you that way!" he said. "I apologize, and I'll go fetch Willy to take you home."

She smiled in bemused silence as Buck considered what to do with the fabric. Lucy grabbed it from him. Buck in humiliation moved to leave her, but she prevented him.

"Forgive me. I'm just not good at this sort of thing. I'm exceptionally good at banking, it seems."

"That's nice, if it makes you happy."

"It does, I guess," he admitted tentatively as if she might find fault.

"Buck, you should be happy."

"I don't want to disappoint you, Luce. What if the person you care about most feels keen disappointment in you?"

"I'm not your mother or sister. I'm me. A true friend hopes for your success, but still loves you when you fail."

"I should have written better letters."

"Yes."

"I did a few foolish things this fall. I see the way Thankful leads Willy by the nose, and I've been worried lately about the impulsive Crenshaw habit of control. I shouldn't have picked the fabrics for your dress even though Mama insisted. I can't stand living in that house much longer. Will you come for a walk with me?"

"It's cold out and dark."

"I'll guide you, Luce. I want you to see something."

"If you've been drinking this fall or anything ..."

Buck laughed. "What?"

"Your mother said ..."

His eyes clouded with resentment. "I do hope you don't trust my mother."

"I'm not sure who to trust right now."

Buck's hand sweated through his glove as he took Lucy's hand. "I want to confess to you the thing I did that shows that I don't have the faintest idea about girls. Fred has always warned me that I'm too fast about things or at least foolish …"

"Do you have a child somewhere?"

"No. Please just come with me."

Lucy hesitated but Buck's expression intrigued her. Besides, she must get all of this intrigue and childish romance over with before going back to New London. By now William and Thankful had settled their differences and were dancing only two days into mourning Meg. Buck left a note with the young lady managing coats near the door for William before taking Lucy into the frosty air. Walking in the dark always troubled Lucy, who secretly dreaded when all days would be just this way. Tonight she held tightly to Buck's warm arm bracing herself for terrible news. His breathing always sounded so forced in the chill air, but they said nothing for a long while as he led her along Hillside Avenue.

"Lucy. I was given a generous bonus this holiday."

"That's nice, but Buck, my toes are frozen, and I don't like how dark this road is. Couldn't you tell me your secret right here?"

"Just wait a minute, Luce. Here. Follow me close," Buck said, guiding her off the road and up a lane.

They came against a short stone fence with an iron gate that creaked as Buck pushed it open against the snow. He led her beneath arches glistening in the moonlight to the door of a small cottage. Buck fumbled for keys with an expression of seriousness. He opened the door and lit a candle, pulling a wary Lucy within the dark house.

"Remember I told you about this place? My father's old cottage—the one my mother hated and made him give up? It was reckless of me, but I imagined us here—just the two of us. I've been pressuring the old man for months. Finally he relented, but I see by your face you don't like it."

"I don't understand …"

"I know how to buy and sell things. I don't know what makes a girl like you happy."

Lucy stood speechless in the little circle of light made by the candle.

"I told Mr. Fischer that we'd keep the wild roses along the fence because his wife had loved them. I hope you like roses. I also said we'd visit him and your grandmother at the old folks' home on Sundays since he has no family to speak of—if you don't mind. You should see the place in daylight—it's homey, but possibly not as big and new as you might like. We can change it all if you want to."

"Buck, I'm astonished. I hadn't really considered anything past an engagement and walks in town and things like that."

"I *did* do one thing more that might anger you. There was an outing with my mates from the bank, and I drank too much and was sick afterwards. I'm ashamed of myself for that."

"When was that?"

"The third Saturday of October."

Lucy laughed that it stood out so clearly in Buck's memory and was relieved that it had happened only once months ago. "The only disappointment I feel right now is that you imagine me such a harsh critic. I love dear old Englewood so much and this charming house but *you* especially."

His shoulders relaxed and a rare softening in demeanor revealed itself. "I foolishly wondered if a fashionable girl from the city would allow me to avoid becoming too attached ... but I've already become attached to you."

"One thing I would never allow for in a man is a wandering eye."

"My eyes have never wandered. The girl in the city was pushed upon me and quite unattractive if you must know. I mean to be a devoted and faithful husband," Buck said with heroic conviction.

She smiled again. "I love roses, Buck, and I'll love being your wife so much here. I can tell even in this dim light that I won't want to change a thing."

"Luce, I don't want to wait for you to come home. I've been absolutely ridiculous avoiding you this week. I promise never to be so cowardly again."

"Promise me never to allow our families to come between us. I've always dreamed of being with a boy who liked me best above everyone else," Lucy said.

"That will be an easy promise to keep. I can't ask you to give up school for me, but I'll miss you terribly. I think we should plan our wedding."

"Right now?" Lucy asked, her heart skipping a beat.

"No, of course not—it's too cold in here." He took her hand in his and led her back toward town and his sleigh.

The horse shivered in the sleet as Buck tucked Lucy's skirt in and covered her with a heavy wool blanket. He hopped in now, and Lucy imagined how fun marriage might be with him as they rode up Demarest Avenue. After a little quiet, he spoke. "Lucy, thank you for helping my father with Meg."

She again had no words.

"Meg is only gone a few days so it might strike you as unfeeling of me to think of weddings, but it's occurred to me so many times that we have no assurances in life. I couldn't bear the idea of never having you as my wife and friend."

She smiled sadly at him. "Poor Buck, you always imagine the worst."

He dismissed the observation. "I remember that I told you I'd like children, but ... if you're afraid, I'd understand. It's hard going for girls in life."

"If God never allowed for children between us, I could be happy with just you, but wouldn't it be splendid to have little ones running around the cottage?"

He looked warm and happy bundled in his scarf and hat. "I'd love that."

"Meg was the happiest I'd ever seen her this week," Lucy said. "Even if the same thing happened to me, I'd be happy that at least we tried to have children and very truly cared for each other. Royal loved Meg."

"Indeed," Buck replied. "I feel the same about you." He searched for an elevated expression of his feelings. "You make me feel ... there's nothing so very wrong with me."

She laughed. "We shall be the best of friends too."

"I can't tell you how unburdened I am now that I've confessed about the drunkenness and the house. Now we can move forward and be completely honest."

Tenafly Road came into view. Lucy pulled her cloak tighter at the neck. The horse and sleigh stopped at the front steps, and Buck jumped out and around to help her. She took his hand with a giggle, and he laughed when she slipped on the icy porch. They stood awkwardly there before the door, holding each other's hand.

"I hate to say good night for fear of breaking the spell," Buck said with an embarrassed laugh.

"It's no spell. You forget, I've loved you since long before you noticed I existed." She squeezed his hand before letting go.

Buck quickly and imprecisely kissed her face. "I love you, Lucy McCullough," he said before jumping back into his transport. He waved then.

Lucy waved too, no longer cold in the least.

# Chapter Twelve

Lucy heard her name called on the landing the following morning and hurriedly draped herself in her silk wrapper. Shivering, she ran down the stairs to find Martha dressed for travel on the second-floor landing.

"There you are, young lady," Martha said with a benevolent smile. "At your age I was never permitted to sleep in this late."

Lucy laughed. "Mrs. Crenshaw, if you only knew the pleasant dream I was having, you'd understand."

"I like you. You're not in the least bit morose," Martha stated. "I've decided that I'd rather a New Year's supper at home where things are quiet."

"I'm sorry to see you go, ma'am," Lucy replied, only now hearing Thankful crying in the kitchen. "What's happened?"

"Thankful has taken far too much after her mother. I had hopes for her, but I was deceived." Martha turned and walked down the stairs with Lucy. A sleigh waited outside to take the old lady to Peetzburg. "It's good you'll be away tomorrow."

Lucy kissed Martha's cheek.

"I've already said farewell to the happy couple so now it's just you, Lucy. Work hard and stay pure, and all will go well for you," Martha lectured. "Goodbye, dear."

Lucy shut the door behind her and stood in the hallway deciding if she could bring herself to enter the kitchen. She reasoned against it, but before her foot hit the first step Thankful charged out, her face puffed and red from crying. Josephine followed.

"Don't look at me, Lucy!" Thankful sobbed, shoving Lucy out of her way.

Lucy blocked her. "Thankful Crenshaw, I will not be pushed and knocked about by you! Stop this tantrum at once! My uncle and aunt would never allow such behavior in their house, and I won't either!" Lucy said with great firmness. "I appreciate everything you've done for me, but ..."

"You don't appreciate a thing!" Thankful cried. "I let William drive you last night and then you keep him there all night to worry me sick! Meg just died! I shouldn't have had to drive out still in mourning to find my husband!"

"I didn't keep him there!" Lucy said. "Willy stayed because he wanted to!"

"So you're saying he doesn't love me!"

"I'm saying no such thing!" Lucy replied as Josephine looked on in exasperation.

"Mrs. Weldon, pardon me, but you're making things worse for yourself with this fussing. Men don't like that," Josephine counseled.

Thankful sobbed. "I know! I know, but I can't stop myself! Lucy, if you only saw William's face this morning! He won't come back at all now!" She sat upon the stair and Lucy sat beside her.

"Thankful, my cousin adores you, but you're making it hard for him to show it," Lucy said. "You always used to be so happy and lively."

"Oh, I've ruined everything!" Thankful said, crying into her handkerchief. "I've become my mother and worse! At least she never got divorced."

Lucy and Josephine glanced at each other in shock. "You were divorced?" Lucy asked.

"Didn't Willy tell you?" Thankful replied. "Oh, he wouldn't because he'd want to save me from the embarrassment! I don't know how many times I can beg forgiveness."

Josephine lifted Thankful's face at the chin. "Girl, don't beg too much. Every time you beg to a man you lose something in their eyes."

"I've already lost everything."

"But look what you have," Josephine said. "A nice home, a nice man and ..."

"And what?" Thankful demanded. "What have I of my own?"

Lucy was baffled by the question. It seemed an alien concept.

Someone came to the door and knocked. Josephine turned to Thankful for guidance but the door opened and in pushed Buck with a box.

"Good morning!" he said, his smile fading before Thankful's misery. "What's happened?"

"Nothing that you'd care about," Thankful said, rising as she wiped her eyes.

Buck handed Josephine the box. "What has Willy done now?"

"Nothing!" Thankful cried. "Buck, you think me very much like Mama, don't you?"

He looked to the others for help, but they shared his discomfort.

"I came to visit you, sis, and to wish you a happy new year since I didn't get to last night. Here's pastries I took from the house for breakfast."

Thankful motioned Josephine to take the pastries to the kitchen. "I know why you're here. It's not very nice to surprise Lucy in just her wrapper and undone hair."

"Oh, I don't mind that," he said, the color rising in his face as he turned to Lucy, who beamed back at him.

"I guess your fears and foolishness have subsided, and you're ready to play cat and mouse again with poor Lucy."

"No. This time I'm going about things differently. I won't rely on Crenshaw women for advice," Buck said.

Thankful called Josephine back before she had time to enter the kitchen. She took the pastries from Josephine. "We won't be needing these as Josephine is a perfect baker, which you'd know if you ever came to visit me." Thankful paused a moment before handing the box back to Josephine. "Your tribe of children can have these."

"Oh no," Buck said, taking the box back with embarrassment. "You see, while I was ill I read a number of mother's magazines—I was terribly bored. There was a story about an engagement." He opened the box and let Josephine help balance it as he pulled a delicate cake out with a ring of pink stone set in white gold sitting upon it.

The three women gasped. Buck handed it to Lucy. "My father tells me it's a rare ruby from Africa. That's why it's pink."

"It's my favorite color," Lucy whispered, afraid to touch it.

"I talked to my father last night, Luce, and he agreed that I shouldn't wait any longer. I hope you'll take this and marry me." His hand shook as he pulled the ring from the icing and slid it on Lucy's finger.

"It fits perfectly!" she said, awestruck.

Thankful rolled her tear-filled eyes. She'd seen the ring only once before.

"My father's grandmother's ring has been passed down for generations, and he wanted for you to have it," Buck said, his ears burning with excitement and nerves.

"Oh, Buck, I adore it! It's the most beautiful thing I've ever received. When shall we marry?" Lucy looked around, bouncing in her slippers, but saw that her excitement and happiness could only be shared with Buck.

"I want to do it right, so let's plan it properly. I hope Thankful will be a great help to us with her cards and knowledge of fashion."

Thankful stared at him. "How could you do this?"

Buck stared back.

"Meg is only just dead, and you expect me to plan a wedding?" Thankful cried self-righteously.

"Since Lucy has no mother, I hoped you might act as a ..."

"A mother? Are you saying I look old?"

"No!" Buck said. "I hoped you might act as a true friend to me and Lucy and be happy for us!"

"That's impossible! Father promised that ring to me! Why would he be so mean?"

Lucy yanked the glistening jewel from her finger, but Buck prevented her from returning it.

"Thankful, Father said nothing about it," Buck said, wiping frosting on his trousers.

"Of course he didn't!" she cried. "All you've ever cared about is proving how clever you are, or how religious or how sad! Lucy, my brother only cares about himself! Remember that when he runs off to do a ridiculous thing! He was once my best friend yet he knows nothing about me any longer!"

Josephine pulled Thankful aside like a strong-armed mother hugging a raging child. "Sweetie, get a hold of yourself! Don't spoil Lucy's happiness."

"What about *my* happiness?" Thankful sobbed. "I'm left down here in this rotten part of town while Lucy takes my place even with my father! I'm married to a farmer!"

"You're married to William!" Lucy cried. "And you are very lucky to have him! Who else with half a brain would take you?"

Thankful gasped and yanked Lucy's braid.

Buck grabbed Thankful's arm. "Don't you ever touch Lucy again!" He dragged her toward Thankful's bedroom. "You will *not* ruin this! I will not let another Crenshaw take my happiness! Lucy and even William are good people, and I won't have you abuse them. You disgust me! You say I go from this to that, but I keep trying! I don't crumple up in a bitter ball dragging everyone in the mud with me! Is it my fault Father likes Lucy better? Now that you've ruined the sentiment of it, I'll probably just buy another ring—I have the money so you can have it!"

"No, Buck," Thankful said, chastened. "I don't want it. Lucy deserves it, doesn't she?"

Buck cursed and rolled his eyes. He sighed as Thankful's eyes welled with tears yet again. He took his sister in his arms. "Thankful, I never meant to hurt you."

She clung to him, crying still more. "I never knew what you felt like when you were the despised one of the family until now."

He sighed. "Forgive me for not visiting. I should have. I don't judge you for any of your mistakes—you understand that, don't you?"

Thankful looked up into Buck's violet eyes. She saw that he had lied but was grateful for his words. "Please let me help with the wedding plans—ours was so quick—and I promise to behave."

Lucy and Josephine waited at a careful distance. Buck turned to them. "It's up to Lucy."

Thankful untangled herself from Buck and fixed her hair before going to Lucy. She slipped to her knees before the surprised girl and took her hands, wiping her tears on them. "Lulu, please, you must forgive me, please!"

Lucy glanced at the door but saw the way Buck looked at her and relented. She helped Thankful to her feet. "Thankful, I'm no threat. All I've ever wanted was friendship. It's your choice now about that. But I won't tolerate any abuse of my cousin or Buck in my presence."

Thankful resented a scolding from a mere girl but kept her temper for Buck's sake. "You are so very good," she said with the faintest hint of sarcasm. "And I promise to keep my feelings in check from now on."

This wasn't the heartfelt repentance Buck had hoped for, but William barged in from the kitchen, sweating from his work at the farm and surprised by the crowd in the cramped hallway. He looked around trying to get a sense of what he'd stepped into. "I saw Buck's sleigh heading this way and hoped nothing was wrong."

Thankful acted as though nothing happened. She took Lucy by the arm and presented her ring finger to William. "The happiest news, Willy. Buck's gotten up the nerve to really propose to Lulu."

William still sensed something unsettling, but took Lucy's white hand in his own. "Land sakes, that's some gem."

The room bristled with tension. William looked Lucy in the eyes. "Are you pleased?"

"Terribly so."

"Then so am I!" William declared with a grin that warmed even Thankful's heart. He gave Lucy a bear hug and more mildly shook Buck's left hand—William was the one person still alive who consistently remembered his prosthetic. "Buck, you're a lucky man."

Buck nodded, knowing it was true.

"Lucy's lucky too," William added. "I hope you both will be very happy."

Buck stood awkwardly for a second, taken off guard by William's kind words. "Thank you, Willy. It means a lot."

"Buck and Lulu have asked me to plan their wedding," Thankful said.

"To *help* plan the wedding," Buck corrected. The tension returned.

"*Really?*" William asked. He saw that Thankful might begin to resent that they'd had such a quiet and rushed affair. Buck would never settle for that and even he experienced a rush of resentment now—much to his own chagrin. William refocused on his cousin with a smile. "Lucy a bride!" he laughed, confused by his mixed emotions.

"My parents wait to hear your answer, Lucy, so I should rescue them from their nerves," Buck said, clearing his throat. "Father hoped that Lucy would say yes and proposed that if she agreed then you'd all be welcome to come tonight for a small gathering to celebrate before she goes back to school."

"I'd almost forgotten she was a schoolgirl still," Thankful said, but only Josephine acknowledged her quip with a harsh glance. Thankful changed her tone. "Of course we'd be delighted, Buckie."

William smiled Thankful's way, happy to see her excited for Lucy and Buck and seemingly oblivious to Thankful's jealousy. Again they stood quietly.

"Well then, I guess I should get back to my parents," Buck said. He smiled at Lucy and left.

Lucy turned to escape upstairs.

"Lucy?" William followed.

"Let me to my happiness for a few moments, won't you?" Lucy said with a forced smile.

"Oh, of course," he said, befuddled. He turned to Josephine who quickly exited back to the kitchen.

Thankful stood under William's suspicious gaze. He pulled her into the parlor and sat her down on the gold couch. "Tell me all about it."

"About what?" Thankful asked innocently.

"Come now, I haven't got all day. Something is not to your liking, and I can't deal with you moping around."

"You already sound annoyed so I won't say anything."

"Just say it," he urged, his eyes betraying his impatience.

"I shouldn't have followed you to the dance last night ..."

"Yes, we've discussed it enough," he said, making to stand.

Thankful pulled him back. "I can't explain to you this terror I have—a terror of losing you! It's taken over!"

"Your tantrums and jealousy are what cause us such strife. So just stop."

"But what if I can't? Don't you think I try? I used to be strong!"

"It's what I admired about you."

She knew she deserved his anger. "All I have is you, Willy! Father gave Lucy the very ring he promised me many years ago!" she sobbed. "He hates me! I'm trapped in this house, and no one comes to visit because they're ashamed!"

"They're just busy, Thankful," he said, softening at the sight of his wife in such distress. "I'm at a loss with you. I can't live like this. You're never happy, and it hurts me that I can't do anything about it."

"Say you love me."

"That doesn't work anymore."

"Please say it," she begged.

"Stop it, Thankful." William glanced at the door. "My little cousin is upstairs alone when she should be sharing her happiness with us. For one day can we worry about someone else but you?"

"That's terribly unfair. You're *all* I worry about!"

"Then please *stop*!" William shouted, the veins beneath the surface of his forehead blue and strained. He stood and escaped up the stairs.

Thankful listened to the soft sound of him knocking two floors up and being let into Lucy's makeshift room.

# Chapter Thirteen

William did his best to ignore Thankful's sullen presence beside him in their sleigh as they slid up the Crenshaw drive with Lucy fretting in the backseat. The stable hand took the reins from William, and he politely but with much reserve held his hand out for his wife as she climbed down from the carriage. More eagerly William helped his cousin, dressed in a bustled and borrowed suit from Thankful, descend. He didn't like the drab olive color of the jacket and wondered if Thankful had picked the outfit in spite. Lucy's pearl white face shone in the moonlight giving her a ghostly appearance, but when she smiled at him, a fleeting urge to paint again entered his mind.

"Promise to stay nearby, won't you, Willy?" Lucy whispered.

"There's no place I'd rather be," he replied because he meant it, and he sought to hurt Thankful.

The front door opened before they made it halfway up the path, and Margaret hailed them. "Oh, here's my new daughter! Lucy! Hurry inside! Everyone is so happy for something to celebrate!"

Margaret pulled William and Lucy by the hands. Thankful followed.

"Mama, do you have no feelings at all calling her your new daughter after Meg is only gone less than a week?!" Thankful asked holding back tears.

"Dear me, Thankful, you're right! But I wanted to make Lucy welcome! Come inside," Margaret said, only half concerned about Thankful. "It occurred to me today after spending the last two days sobbing and asking, *Why? Why? Why must this happen to me?* I finally realized that Meg would hate for us to stay stuck. She always had a soft spot for Buck—bless her heart—and we should be happy that he'll finally be settled with such a good—and pliable—little girl."

"Mama, we all had a soft spot for Buck but you!" Thankful said.

"Now is not the time to bring up the past! I won't have it," Margaret whispered forcefully before they joined the others in the parlor. "I don't believe in regrets."

"Since when?" Thankful asked.

"If you're going to ruin everyone's night again, then you should go fetch your farmer boy and go home," Margaret said and walked into the full room.

Thankful took a moment to compose herself before entering, then found a place near India and the children—the pariahs.

Graham proposed a toast. "Everyone, gather round." He waited until the family was settled. "I can say with confidence that Buck has picked the very best girl to marry. I couldn't be more pleased—in fact I've *never* been more pleased and excited for a wedding."

The temperature cooled with a few insulted guests.

Graham took the measure of the room and continued. "Never in my life have I met a girl of such refined and noble character as Lucy. If there is some blemish, I'd be hard pressed to find it, and my son of so many dismal failures redeems himself with such a choice. None of us are perfect, but Lucy comes close, and I am tremendously happy to welcome her as a daughter—and relieved that Lucy has agreed to care for my son, whom I care for dearly." Graham glanced around, his unresolved emotions regarding the people surrounding him evident. "Finally, I want to say that despite everything I care for you all. Cheers." The doctor emptied his glass before taking Buck around the shoulders with hearty, though stiff, good cheer.

Lucy stood still, painfully aware of everyone's resentment. William held his glass untouched, and Lucy perceived his temptation.

"Thank goodness you're here," she whispered, delicately taking his drink and placing it on the table. "I wonder if the doctor's words were more to cut his own children than to welcome me."

William bent down a little to say, "A bit of both, Lucy. Welcome to my hell."

Lucy was startled, but William just laughed.

India turned to Thankful who made no attempt at hiding her anger over the speech and whispered, "Thankful, is it true that Lucy's eyes are from the disease of her parents?" India asked this knowing the answer full well.

Thankful almost accepted the invitation to gossip but refrained. "I hope they will be—happy."

"Your parents hardly notice Fred and I are happy."

"Father and Mama see what they want to see, and I'm sorry to say they just see you as a modern, unchaste woman," Thankful said. Her opinion of India remained unfixed and depended solely upon Thankful's mood.

"This one thing we have in common, dear sister," India said, directing Sam toward the other children, who were visibly tired of minding him.

"You and I are *very* different," Thankful said haughtily.

"Yes, I'm not like a caged bird." India took a sip of her drink.

Thankful noted that India might be a tad prettier than she was. "What makes you so free?"

"Fred has admirably progressive views. It's great to be with a man who is my intellectual equal and has the same drive as I do. We are a perfectly matched pair even if your family is blind to it."

"Nobody's perfect …"

India laughed in a dismissive and patronizing way. "It's so sad when a woman deludes herself by imagining that life is as it should be. Do you enjoy being more intelligent than your husband?"

Thankful's heart sank. There was something bitter and true in India's words. "Never speak of William that way again."

"I wasn't speaking of him, sister. Fred has informed on you and has strong opinions about your marrying beneath you. *And* I have a mind of my own. It breaks my heart to see women with potential spending their days fretting over wallpaper swatches and menu planning. I do hope there is something more for you in that little house so far away from the hill."

Thankful glanced at William and Lucy, standing like two lost souls, and cringed. "Willy is an exceptional farmer—and artist."

India waited a moment, choosing her words carefully. "And that's *very* nice." India patted Thankful's hand.

"He should be allowed his happiness, it's only ..." Thankful stopped, feeling somehow that even talking to India was a betrayal.

"And what about your desires?" India asked.

Thankful glanced at her parents. The very word *desire* struck Thankful as scandalous.

"Have you read *The Revolution*?" India asked

"I'm not a revolutionary, I'm just ... lost." Thankful sipped her punch.

"How is it fair that your brother Buck can be so successful with his odd behaviors?"

"Don't speak ill of Buck."

"I don't! But why shouldn't you have the same chance at success?"

"I don't want to be a banker," Thankful said.

"But something! Not just a *wife* or *mother*. I can tell you that the worst thing Fred and I did was keep Sammy. I wish now that we had left him with Buck. Don't act so horrified. I love the boy, but he's such a nuisance, and only mothers are saddled with worry. Fred knows it's unfair, so he's agreed to send Sammy to school as soon as he's old enough. I went away to school and loved it."

"Fred always said he wanted lots of children for the white race," Thankful noted.

India laughed. "Oh, Fred can be utterly disgusting sometimes. He hardly ever means the things he says! I told him that if he wanted a happy wife there would be no more children."

"And he didn't mind?" Thankful asked, eager now for information.

"At first he was surprised, but now he's relieved and, imagine the adventures we'll have with no awkward strings attached. Wouldn't you hate to be your mother with so many children? I mean no insult, but it's rather disgusting to even contemplate such a large family—at least it's quite old-fashioned."

Thankful's tense demeanor relaxed as she leaned in ever so slightly toward India. "I feel ... much the same way about Mama. I'd always wished she'd stopped with the two sets of twins."

India smiled confidentially. "You're so lucky to have a clean slate, and while William is handsome and no one would blame you for falling under the spell of his looks, he certainly will never fill that feeling—you know the one I mean—that feeling that there must be more to life than just watching each other age."

Thankful sipped thoughtfully. "You make things seem utterly hopeless."

"But no, dear sister. You fail to realize there's a new dawn rising. I'm sure that a man like William is fine to wake up to each morning. In that way we are alike. Our men are easy to admire, but does William satisfy you intellectually?"

Thankful laughed, but nervously. She sensed a choice in defining things between herself and William and hesitated, allowing her fears to surface. "I'm not an intellectual, yet ... I'd hoped that William and I might love art together, but now he has no interest in anything I find uplifting or exciting."

India nodded with great sympathy, goading her on.

With great relief, Thankful continued: "I love William and always will, but I am terribly disappointed in him—farming!"

India said disingenuously, "Sister, there's nothing wrong with working the soil ..."

"Well, I would agree if that were Willy's true talent, but he is a brilliant artist. What bothers me most is that he doesn't show the manly bravery to make a go of it," Thankful said. "And I hadn't realized how I'd hate the old house. I imagined it would be charming, and I really did love Lieutenant and Mrs. Weldon, but it's just that without the art William is so—so *ordinary*," Thankful whispered, as Buck came beside her.

"May I speak with you a moment?" he asked.

"Not, now, Buckie," she replied dismissively.

"*Now*, Thankful," he demanded and pulled her into the hallway.

"What's the matter with you?" Thankful wrenched herself free from his strong grip.

"You *know* what," he said. "You're a smart girl, right? Maybe not clever enough to realize that India is not the girl you want to confide in. I never dreamed I'd say it, but I feel sorry for Willy, knowing how little you think of him!"

"Don't act so special, Buck! Only two weeks ago you were seeing Alma Prescott! Mama tells me everything."

"I never let Alma believe there was anything between us," he said. "I've learned the hard way that it's every Crenshaw for himself around here, but I didn't expect you to take Mama's word over mine. I thought you were better than that!"

"Who's the one rushing to marry an infant because you're afraid of accomplished women?" Thankful said.

"You have no right to judge anyone on accomplishments!" Buck's voice cracked in anger. "Willy may be only a farmer to you, but the one thing he does have is a certain, quiet charm with people—even bewitching Grandmother! I look at Mama and then at you and wonder was Mama like you as a young girl? You used to be so kind and different. I pity you, knowing that you've lost the things that made you tolerable."

Thankful trembled. "I wish that you had never spoken those words because you have forever destroyed the only friendship that ever meant anything to me."

"We stopped being friends the moment you saw fit to believe Mama's lies about me. So why don't you take the man you loathe home now and leave me to my happiness?"

William only heard the very last line as he came out of the parlor in search of his wife. "Thankful?" he asked, looking as though he'd been punched.

Thankful rushed upon him. "Buck is wrong! Don't misunderstand!"

"William," Buck began miserably, "I spoke angry words just now, please don't hold them against my sister."

"Buck, don't pretend at caring—I hate that falseness about you. Thankful has told me in so many ways that she's unhappy and so am I, but it's none of your concern," William said. "Please see to it that Thankful finds a way home if she wants to come back. I'm leaving now."

"Oh, Willy, don't!" Thankful said. "I hate them all here! No one understands—you know what they're all like!"

"Yes, I do," William said. He scratched his neck at the collar of the fine shirt Thankful insisted he wear. "I hate even saying it, but Thankful, I think I'd be happier without you."

"But our vows! Good times and bad and sickness and health!" Thankful pleaded.

"You are ill, that's true. I'm trying to be a better man, and I'm just barely hanging on here. You're no help. I can't battle my demons and yours right now. You have Josephine and Lucy and even your mother to listen to all of your complaints and concerns—who do I have? I have to work and listen and put up with everyone's moods and … and … where's my rest? Where are my friends? I'm not allowed to have any! I can't even talk to my cousin without your permission!"

"That's not true! I just need … to be valued *most*."

"I can't do it anymore," he said. "It's too exhausting. I even gave up painting because of you."

"No! You're a liar! I wanted you to be a painter, and you know that!"

"You're so critical and possessive and *crazy*! How could I ever pick up a brush?"

"You twist everything!" Thankful shouted now.

Buck pulled her back. "Calm down, sis."

Graham came into the hall now. "What's going on?"

William stepped forward offering his hand. "Doctor Crenshaw, I'm afraid I have an early morning."

"Certainly, I understand," Graham said, glancing at his daughter.

"Thankful shouldn't miss the festivities on my account, sir."

"Of course," Graham replied edgily. "Buck will bring the girls home in a bit."

William nodded and departed into the dark cold with his coat collar turned up and his tweed cap pulled low. Graham gave Thankful a rueful head shake before re-entering the parlor. Buck made to do the same, but Thankful stopped him in desperation. "I never told Willy to stop painting!"

"Thankful, I'm sorry for you, but I want to get back to Lucy. It's not fair to leave her with the snakes." Buck, with an eagerness Thankful had never seen in him, returned to the parlor.

Thankful sank onto the bench at the door. Chasing William would be of no use. She knew not a single soul in the parlor would care to have their evening ruined with her problems. Thankful wiped her tears in self-pity, disgust and deep loneliness. India sat quietly beside her.

"I'm sorry I got you into trouble," India said.

"No, it's my own trouble," Thankful confessed. "I begin to believe Willy's right, and I'm insane. Do you know that my Uncle Oliver on Mama's side went mad and eventually took his life? So it's in the blood."

"You won't go that far, I hope!" India said with real concern. "Listen to me. Men always belittle what they don't understand. Middlemay was a disaster, but it showed me another way of being for women. No more do I imagine us victims or children. Dear, you may not realize it, but we live at a time where women are finally experiencing growing pains."

Thankful sniveled. "I'm not as childish as I may appear. When I traveled west, I met a girl with new ideas, and she stole my future husband from me. I don't trust modern girls."

"The Crenshaw family has problems trusting *anyone*." India laughed, with uncharacteristic compassion.

"And whom do you trust?" Thankful asked. "Not Fred."

"Thankful, I trust myself, and that is all," India said. "How long will you give away your power to others? I've been in your shoes. I love Fred, but I never fall into the trap of idolizing him. Fred strays, but he always comes back and—here's the secret—I can *do* as I like because he knows I can expose him any *time* I like."

"Isn't it depressing to live that way?"

"Then why am I happily finding success while here you are trapped in this rigid existence crying on your mother's bench? Is it healthy to resent that stupid little girl in the parlor when you have everything you need to be free? Fred tells me William has come into money, and he leaves you to do as you like. Why bother worrying if William is enough for you—become something for yourself." India paused, gazing into Thankful's swollen eyes. "I see that this upsets you—but you must let go of childhood illusions. Romantic love is a trap designed by the Devil to keep women down. Willy wouldn't even notice if you attended a woman's meeting once in a while. Trust yourself above all, dear, and you can have anything you want."

Fred joined them now with some impatience. "Must I run after Sam all by myself? It's not fair to offload him on Nathan and Abby."

"The boy needs discipline, Freddie," India said, kissing him as she passed and dragging Thankful back into the parlor.

Lucy chatted merrily with Nathan, Abby, Maddie, and Sam. They looked at her adoringly as did Graham and Buck. India and Thankful gave each other annoyed glances before Margaret pulled Thankful to her side.

"India is not for you," she whispered.

"*Mama*." Thankful struggled to hide her disdain for Margaret.

"Don't act superior, young lady. I know women."

"Mama, I'm so tired of having such hate for my sex."

"Let's not use that word, dear." Margaret waved Lucy's way, and the girl left her little friends behind to join the older set with a sensitive, innocent smile. "Lucy, dear, Buck tells me you agreed to allow Thankful and me to plan your wedding. I'm so delighted."

Lucy's eyes showed a small panic at the idea. Thankful smiled.

"I helped plan your Aunt Kate's wedding with smashing success. And Buck's colleagues will be judging every little thing."

"A small wedding might be nice—like Thankful's. Willy told me it was the best day of his life," Lucy said.

This wiped Thankful's smile away as she remembered how William had not let her out of his sight all that day, and how he'd done his hair just right. Thankful remembered the gentle way he'd kissed her after the exchange of rings. "Lulu, I'm sorry you missed the wedding. That was a mistake I regret. Your cousin was so handsome. It *was* a perfect day."

Margaret clapped her hands twice, breaking Thankful's reverie. "Well, this is different! This will be the first *big* wedding we get to plan, and I intend to make the most of it—for Buck's sake." Margaret waved at Buck, who eyed the girls dubiously before turning back to listen to Fred rave about mining opportunities in the West.

"I still can't fathom why you left the West behind for *banking*," Fred said. "Even Aristotle said money lending is evil."

Buck laughed. "Since when do you read Aristotle?"

"Oh, I don't," Fred replied, picking lint from his jacket. "I just heard that somewhere, but it fits doesn't it? Christ recommended just giving everything away, didn't he? Not very Christian of you, Buckie." His tone was playful, but he never let Buck stay comfortable for long. Appraising Buck's tailored suit and businesslike haircut, Fred sneered at his brother's success. "You know, Confucius said, 'The gentleman is familiar with what is right, just as the small man is familiar with profit.'" Fred smiled as Buck fumed.

"How pathetic that you'd scour a library for ways to insult me, and I wonder why you do it," Buck said in the whisper that let Fred know he'd struck a chord. "Edmund Burke said, 'The laws of commerce are the laws of nature and therefore the laws of God.'"

Fred shook his head, smiling in his always self-assured way. "So you go to the library too, to rationalize why you entered the profession. *That's* sad. I for one wish you'd stayed with me in the army. There's so many manly pursuits."

"So banking is now a *feminine* profession?"

Fred scratched his chin thoughtfully. "Well, I suppose it's a safe job. Even Father found it tedious *beyond the beyonds*, but if you're secure at the bank, then perhaps it's for the best."

"I see it now," Buck said with feeling. "You're jealous because in these last three months I've made more money than some make in ten years!"

"I don't give a damn about money, little brother. I'm not that low," Fred said in a forced whisper. He didn't want his father involved in their talk.

"You have India's family behind you as you had Rose's, and the allowance you get from Father is fully based on his time in banking," Buck groused.

"Now, Buckie, calm down. Let's enjoy your happy news." Fred grabbed his cup and filled it with punch. "Everyone! A toast to the little couple."

*He calls us little!* Buck said to himself, unable even to enjoy the sight of his future bride as she shyly came up beside him.

"I never imagined that the Weldons and McCulloughs would make such inroads here on Chestnut Street." Fred laughed. "But I'm glad they have. Lulu is a fine young thing as I always predicted she would be. Just the simple soul to steady my little brother here, who's bent on world domination through banking."

Buck spilled his drink a little, shaking in angry mortification. This was the family he was asking Lucy to join? "Damn you, Fred!"

"Now what's this?" Graham asked.

"Buck's being too sensitive, Father. We've just been talking about the banks and the coterie of insiders Buck now associates with. My intention upon entering the political sphere has always been to make sure that the common man—like Willy for instance—isn't trampled on by the big banking interests."

"When did you ever care about people in the fourth ward?" Buck asked.

"You think too small. Not everything begins and ends in Englewood. The Chinks and Irish build the railroads, and the bankers get rich."

"And how do you propose these grand railroad endeavors be funded?" Buck asked. "The amount of money and resources needed boggles the mind."

India spoke now. "Everything should be collected for the common good. The government should protect us from the bankers and the robbers."

Buck laughed dismissively. "Fred, you don't support government takeovers of private property, do you?"

India refused to be ignored. "Private property is theft and unjust."

Fred squirmed at his wife's revolutionary ideas. "Why not have the government regulate things more? I'm for progress and the humane treatment of the underclass."

Graham and Buck laughed now.

"There's no such thing as progress," Buck said.

Lucy took Buck's hand in hers. "I agree with Buck. Even the ancients fell to corruption."

Everyone stared at the new voice.

Fred spoke. "Interesting point, Lulu, but I've embraced the theory of evolution—have you heard of it, sweetie?"

"Yes, I have," Lucy said. "And I wonder if it's unchristian. My eyes will one day cause me to depend more upon others. Some social reformers say that useless people should be done away with. It frightens me."

Even Fred felt a gentleman's embarrassment at having touched on such a personal subject. "I didn't mean to offend you."

"You haven't," she replied. "I admire your optimism and faith in humanity, but I suppose my optimism lies elsewhere."

"Oh, yes," Fred said, misunderstanding, "Buck will see that you're well cared for."

Lucy blushed but said no more.

"Please don't take this the wrong way, dear brother," India purred, "but we are family now, and I wonder how you square money lending with your spirituality?"

Buck hesitated, bracing himself for ridicule. "I haven't figured it out yet, but I hope to be a steward of God's money."

Many eyes rolled.

Fred had a ready comment. "I'm sure God is impressed by music boxes."

"Fred, stop it," Buck said.

"A music box?" Margaret brightened.

"It's excessive perhaps," Buck explained with a sharp glance at Fred, "but I hoped Lucy might like it." Buck paused. "Against my usual caution I was compelled to buy it for her when I came upon it."

Lucy trembled at the idea of foolish extravagance. "Buck?"

"It was meant as a surprise, but I began to second-guess myself, fearing it might not be to your taste. Shall I show it to you?"

The family demanded it be shown. Buck trotted out and came back with the valuable item, carefully placing it down upon the round table in the center of the room. The eagerness of his expression and the sense that Buck was making himself vulnerable to family ridicule heightened Lucy's apprehension even before she had time to appreciate it. She touched the smooth rosewood with matching inlays at the front of the case and lid. Ornate brass handles adorned the case sides and the entire box shone as if just polished.

"It's lovely," Lucy said.

Buck smiled and opened it. With the first clear notes of the fugue from the overture of Mozart's *The Magic Flute*, the family stood captivated by the exceptional quality of the sound and the loveliness of the tune. They listened for a long while before Buck abruptly shut the box as if sharing the beauty brought him a sudden pang.

Graham patted Buck's shoulder in approval.

"Must have cost you a poor man's yearly wages," Fred said, but even India shot him an annoyed look.

"Buck, you remind me so of your father! Useless extravagance! But my heart is bursting at the sound of it, my good boy!" Margaret gushed, giving him a quick hug. "Lucy is a very lucky girl to care so little about looks. She wins a heart of gold."

"And a step up into the finer life," Fred noted quietly to India though just loud enough for Buck to hear.

Buck cleared his throat. "It's time for me to take Lucy and Thankful home now."

Everyone agreed it was late, though Thankful lingered in the hallway, only half-heartedly dressing for the weather. "Maybe I shouldn't go home tonight," she said when Buck hurried her.

"Do you want to give Mama something to talk about? Or Fred?"

Thankful pulled her gloves on and followed him out with Lucy tiptoeing beside them, holding her box with great care. The ride home was cold and quiet and awkward. Lucy wondered if Thankful would give her and Buck a moment before saying goodnight.

When they drove up Tenafly Road, a light shone in the parlor. Thankful moaned in dread. Buck turned to Lucy. "I hope you really do like the gift."

She nodded with a shy smile, waiting for a chance to say something privately to him, but Buck jumped out and helped her down in what seemed a hurry. "Lucy, I need a word with my sister. May I see you tomorrow?"

"Oh, Buck, I'd hoped we'd have a little time tonight ..."

"Yes. Me too."

"I'm leaving on the first train, so I guess this is goodbye for now," Lucy said, as she glanced in annoyance at Thankful, who sat like stone in the sleigh.

"Oh, I'd forgotten! Well, then ..." Buck hesitated. He wanted to kiss her, but William's shadow was at the window, and Thankful was just over his shoulder. He held out his hand and took hers. "Goodbye for now."

Lucy waited a moment, things feeling unfinished, but caught Thankful's impatient stare and ran inside.

Buck looked after her in worry for a moment but climbed back aboard. "Thankful, are you happy for me?"

"Of course," she replied, but her face was tight and she refused to look at him.

"Don't be angry with me," Buck begged.

"Why should I be angry with you? You deserve a good life, I suppose."

"You *suppose*?"

"Well, I don't understand it! It's as if Middlemay never happened and the trouble at the academy and all you get up to! Now you're the star of the family, and it's terribly unfair!"

"What?" Buck laughed, but angrily. "I don't have time for this! Get out and be miserable by yourself."

"So I will!" she cried and jumped out of the carriage, slipping and falling in the snow. Buck refused to help her up, snapping his reins and leaving her there to stew.

Down in the cold snow Thankful sat for a long while, gazing at the stars. William came to the door, but did not meet her in the yard. "Are you coming in soon?" he asked, unable to mask his concern but unwilling to go to her. When she didn't answer, he closed the door but waited in the parlor.

Thankful got up, dragging her sodden skirt in the wet mud by the drive, and slunk up the stairs to the dark kitchen unable to face her husband.

# Chapter Fourteen

As Lucy pinned an amethyst brooch on her high-collared shirt the next morning, Thankful knocked on the bedroom door and let herself in with a cool smile.

"I wanted to make sure that you were ready. Josephine has made you a nice meal to eat on the train."

Lucy smiled back. "Thank you." Eating on the train made her sick. Lucy had hoped that there might be something to eat before she left for the station. "Has William gone off to work?"

"Of course," Thankful said, sitting on the bed. "It's all he cares about."

"That's not true."

"I don't want to talk about it," Thankful said. She leaned over and opened the music box, dragging it frightfully close to the edge of the bed stand.

Lucy came beside it, with a nervous laugh, pushing it back just a little.

"Oh, I wouldn't break it, silly."

"Of course not," Lucy said unable to hide her doubt, "but, I suppose knowing that it's so fine is a bit of a burden."

"Buckie would hate that he's burdened you."

Lucy panicked at the idea of Thankful telling Buck but remembered that she was annoyed at his cool goodbye. She put her jacket on and buttoned it. "I'm ready to go."

"Will you take the music box or should we protect it here?"

"I wouldn't want for it to be broken," Lucy began, "so I suppose I should keep it here."

"I hope you understand that I still plan to save this room for you until you wed my brother—just in case." Thankful felt magnanimous because Lucy was leaving.

"Thank you very much." Lucy took up her bag. "Shall we go?"

Thankful raced the horses past the Adriance farm and into town. Englewood was slushy and damp as the two of them stood waiting for the whistle of the train.

"Tell William I said goodbye, won't you?" Lucy asked glancing up the tracks with a forlorn sigh. She wished she'd gotten up earlier to say it herself, but before she had finished her thought she spotted William's copper hair above the crowd as he made his way along the platform.

"Willy!" Lucy cried and ran to him. "Oh, I knew you wouldn't let me leave without seeing you!"

"Of course not!" he replied with a sad smile. "I expected you to stop by at Adriance's. The old man made donuts and wondered if you'd want a little breakfast."

Lucy took the greasy bag in her hands with a happy laugh. "I shall write Mr. Adriance as soon as I get settled to thank him. He's so adorable for an old person, isn't he?"

William laughed. "Must you go?"

Lucy nodded with a sniffle as the whistle blew far off down the tracks. She tiptoed to kiss William's cheek. He smiled and bent into the tracks to see how far the train was, rubbing his frozen hands together.

The train pulled in noisily, and Lucy climbed aboard with one final wave to her cousin and Thankful, noting how perfectly they suited each other even as they stood apart unhappily. Lucy slid herself in beside a window and opened the donut bag to smell the cinnamon and fried batter. The train jolted forward and someone from the back walked up in a hurry.

"Luce!" Buck whispered with a grin and bright eyes, sitting beside her.

"What are you doing here?"

"I came to see you off but didn't spot you until you'd already gotten aboard. I jumped on."

"But where will you get off and how will you get home?" Lucy giggled.

"Lucy, must you go?"

She took him in with a smile and handed him a donut. "I have to go. I've already started."

"But, do you really love it up in New London?"

"No, but—it's what I set out to do."

"Don't go, Luce."

"Buck ... I'm already on the train and it's moving and here you are upsetting all of my plans."

"Yes. But I don't care. I shouldn't have wasted this week being stupid, and what if we die young like Meg? Then what? Haven't you learned enough about being blind anyhow? If that day ever comes when you have truly lost every bit of sight, couldn't we take care of it then? Why waste time?"

"Schooling isn't a waste. One day you'll not like that I'm uneducated, and I'm enjoying learning for the first time."

"If you stay home I'd find you a local tutor or someone in the city to help you, but you're smart anyhow. I want to set things in order right now."

Lucy hesitated as the conductor walked over to check their tickets and saw that Buck didn't have one.

"Sir, your ticket," the conductor said with a hard look.

"Oh, yes, well, I didn't purchase one, but I got on just now and will be getting off next stop."

"How can I be certain of when you came aboard?"

"Are you serious?" Buck pulled his wallet out. "How much do I owe you?"

"Well, I don't know when you came aboard. I'll have to charge you from Hoboken," he said unsympathetically.

"This is ridiculous, but *fine*—this should cover it," Buck said, giving the man far more than a Hoboken trip cost.

When the conductor tried to make change, Buck waved him off. "We're having an important talk, old man, please leave us be. Just keep the change and buy yourself a new tie or something."

The conductor looked annoyed, but kept the change and exited the car.

"Buck, that was a little rude, don't you think?"

"Yes, I can't believe he made such a fuss," Buck said. "Anyway, Luce, it's for the best if you come back home—for everyone."

"Everyone? What do you mean?"

"I didn't want to have to bring this up, but I overheard my parents talking and it seems William and Thankful may be in some money trouble."

"I'm not sure I like your parents discussing such things!"

"Thankful is their daughter, and of course they're going to be concerned when the two of them sell off family heirlooms. Did you know anything about your grandfather's book collection?"

"Yes, I loved it."

"Isn't it a bit odd that they sold it?"

"It was sad and wrong. And Willy has all of that land now. He insists he can afford my school ..." Lucy said. "Oh, Buck, what if it's true? What must you think of Willy?"

"I think ... that William is in over his head with Thankful," Buck said, taking her hand. "I want to save you the embarrassment of being entangled in their finances."

Lucy turned away from Buck and stared out at the grey countryside.

"Lucy? What's on your mind?"

She turned back to him in such a confidential and trusting way he felt he couldn't possibly love her more. "You have no idea what it's like to be fully dependent on everyone around you!"

He laughed. "Up until quite recently I was seen by my family as the ultimate parasite!"

"But you've gotten a job, and you've become independent. School was my one chance at having something to fall back upon."

He gave her a quick, shy kiss on the cheek. "I'd hoped we'd have each other to fall back upon."

Lucy smiled. "Yes, but, Buck, we come into this so unequal."

"Yes, you are far too good for me. I don't want for money. Companionship. That's what I long for, and I know I will be happy just to have you. If you want school, I can get it for you. I will work to get you anything you want if only you'll promise to care for me deeply."

"Oh, Buck, I do care! I truly do! But how would I explain coming home without humiliating William?"

"We shall say that we wanted to be together and it won't be a lie, will it?"

She giggled. "No, it is the truth! But the semester's been paid for."

"I'll handle that part. Willy will get his money back and not even think another thing about it," Buck said, convincingly. "So will you jump from the train with me at the next stop? Won't it be bully planning our big day?"

She took his face in her gloved hands and kissed him hard.

Buck laughed and jumped from his seat, grabbing her carpet bag and waving for her to follow as the train pulled into the next station.

# Chapter Fifteen

When Buck and Lucy arrived back at the quiet Crenshaw home, it put the couple on edge. The floors creaked under their heels and the sound of a distant tea kettle in the downstairs kitchen seemed lonesome.

"Won't you just wait here in the parlor, Luce?" Buck said, closing the door behind her before climbing the stairs to the family bedrooms. At once he heard some muffled talk and crying in the direction of his parents' room. Buck hesitated outside their door before knocking with his wooden hand, a bit too loudly.

Graham came to the door. His eyes were red but he remained in control of himself. He let Buck in as Margaret lay with her face covered on the chaise lounge. Buck knelt beside her. "Mama, what's the matter?"

Margaret stopped and stared. "How heartless must you imagine me! Of course I still mourn for our little Meggie!"

Buck stood up in embarrassment. "Oh yes, Mama. I'm sorry to have been so insensitive. I beg your forgiveness." He glanced at Graham who looked equally upset now.

"Father, I'll come back later. I just didn't think."

Margaret sniffled. "You never do. That at least we can depend upon in this uncertain life! How is it that Meggie's really dead? How is it, I ask?" She sobbed some more.

Graham rubbed his wife's shoulders as he spoke, "Buck, what is it you need?"

Buck bristled even in the midst of his parents' suffering. Graham always assumed he *needed* something and Buck was suddenly troubled at his own lack of real mourning for his sister. "We can talk later ..."

"No, now's as good a time as any, son," Graham said.

"Well, Father, I've been a little rash, and my timing now seems cruelly insensitive though I imagined I was doing the right thing ..."

"Sakes alive, what have you done now?" Graham asked in exasperation.

Margaret stopped crying and sat up, readying herself, wringing her handkerchief.

"It's Lucy, Father. I've convinced her to withdraw from school for now. I ... I thought it best."

Graham waited for an explanation with interest.

"You see, Father and Mama, I shouldn't like to wait—in case—well, in case the worst happened. I mean, death, really. Seeing how quickly Meg went—and I took to heart your words, Father, and feel Lucy to be very special—my one chance at happiness really."

Margaret and Graham glanced at each other but in no way showed their feelings at his words, so Buck continued. "Also ... I thought it best that Lucy stays out of William's finances."

Margaret looked to the doctor with just the smallest glimmer of excitement in her eyes. Graham's forlorn expression vanished as his mind worked. "That's excellent news, and I fully agree that Lucy needs rescuing from the situation on Tenafly Road. Most definitely."

Margaret stood up and motioned for Graham to fetch her robe. "And where is Lulu now?"

"In the parlor. I didn't know what to do with her."

"Oh, Graham, if this isn't the best thing for us just now! I will pour every ounce of my energy into this wedding!" Margaret cried. She kissed Buck and raced from the room to talk to Lucy.

Buck stood uncomfortably. Graham was always so ill at ease with him. "Well, son, you have made your mother very happy."

"And you, Father?"

"Lucy is a fine girl. I only worry how you'll handle William's feelings."

"We've already decided that I will reimburse him for the school."

"That's a good idea, but will he be happy for Lucy?"

"That's none of my concern. I care only about Lucy and me."

Graham shook his head. "You may be able to pay William off, but you will never be able to separate the cousins. They have a bond that none of my children do. Be careful." Graham led him downstairs and welcomed Lucy back from her short train ride.

Soon after, Buck ordered his sleigh and horse pulled round for the ride up to Tenafly Road. As they passed the Adriance farm, Lucy spotted William shoveling the path to the old man's house. "Willy!"

William dropped the shovel and ran out to the road. "Lucy! What's happened?" He eyed Buck with suspicion.

Lucy jumped down with a laugh. "Willy, I've changed my mind about school. I want to be home with you!"

William shifted in his mucky boots and looked up the hill toward home.

"You *are* happy, aren't you?" Lucy asked, taken aback.

"Of course I'm happy," William said with a mix of sincerity and concern. "But we've paid up already, and Thankful ..." He glanced toward home again as if Thankful could somehow see him through the sycamore trees.

Buck came around, pulling out his full wallet. "Willy, here is the tuition money back."

William shook his head, pushing it away. "I won't take a cent of your money."

Buck and Lucy exchanged a pained look. "But we've put you out. Don't be a fool. Take the money," Buck said.

"No. It was a gift to Lucy from me. You can keep it," William said stubbornly. He scratched his head and adjusted his cap, refusing any eye contact.

"Shall we go tell Thankful our news?" Buck asked.

"Well, I still have a bit of work to do here so ..."

"Willy, would it be all right if I brought my things back home?" Lucy asked, in a tremulous voice.

This pricked William's conscience and brought him to his true self. "Lucy, don't for a second think that I'm unhappy with you. It's only that this seems rash to me, and I so wanted to do something for you."

"Oh, Willy, I'm so sorry to disappoint you, but we feel ... so in love and don't want to wait so long. I want a quick wedding like you had."

"Quick weddings aren't always the best thing."

Buck seized upon the sentiment. "Ours won't be too quick, Luce. We mustn't deprive Mama of her plans, and it will take some time to secure the room in the city for the reception afterwards."

"Oh," Lucy replied with a blink of surprise, "I hadn't thought we'd marry in the city."

"Well, of course we will. We must. My associates will come, and it wouldn't do to have them cross the river when the best places are in the city. Plus, they would want to see the ceremony—or I should say that I would want to show you off in the best possible way. The cousins are Presbyterians so it won't be too different from Englewood, and we have our whole life here."

"I'd hope our Englewood friends would be welcome—not just acquaintances," Lucy said.

"Of course!" Buck replied, realizing he was getting ahead of himself. "But we can discuss things tomorrow. Let's celebrate today."

William stood like a weed amongst fine grass ready to ruin the picture Buck had in his head of the perfect day.

"I'd like to tell my sister the news, if it's all right with you, Willy," Buck said in way that meant he would do it no matter William's reply.

William's fists bulged in his pockets, and he nodded, but said nothing to stop Buck. "Lucy, I'm happy to have you home any time you need us."

"Oh, Willy, I'm so glad," Lucy gushed before climbing back into the sleigh.

Buck nodded a goodbye before jumping up himself and setting the horse in motion once more.

Thankful stood at the side door watching Josephine hang the bed sheets to be aired from the guest room on the frozen line. At the sight of Buck's sleigh, Thankful brightened until she noticed the strawberry-blond girl beside him and her shoulders slumped. By the time Lucy and Buck entered the house Thankful's mouth was set firm.

"Has something happened, Lucy?" she asked in a clipped, curt tone.

Buck answered. "Thankful, I've convinced Lucy to stop school for now so we can plan a wedding for June."

"June?" Thankful asked.

"Yes, it's the best month for weddings, my friends say."

"Your friends?" Thankful laughed.

Buck cleared his throat. "I do hope you'll make Lucy quite welcome ..."

"What do you take me for, Buck? Of course, this is her home for now, but the bedding in the guest room is being washed and poor Josephine was hoping to leave early to nurse her sick child. I suppose it can't be helped. I'll go tell Jo the room must be all done up again."

Buck took Thankful aside. "Dear, sister, Lucy has agreed to give up school *for me*, and I do hope she isn't made to regret it."

Thankful softened at Buck's mild rebuke. "Lucy is welcome, and I'm happy for you, Buck."

"I don't mind making my own bed, Thankful. I used to do it all the time," Lucy said.

"That's what help is for," Buck and Thankful said at the same time and laughed uncomfortably.

"Lucy, I'll bring in your bag and be off," Buck said. "Tomorrow's my first day back to work after the holidays, and I need to be bright-eyed."

Lucy said nothing. Thankful stood quietly too until after Buck came and went with a quick kiss for Lucy before he jumped in his sled and turned the corner.

"Thankful, I'm sorry to put you out. I know you'd prefer it was just you and Willy."

Thankful sighed as they walked through the mudroom. "Yes, well, we didn't get a honeymoon, so our evenings alone are all we have ... but you are family, and we must do what we must."

"I promise to stay out of your way as much as possible," Lucy said, but wished she hadn't.

"Lucy, I'm not a monster! It's offensive to act the way you do. You are so young and haven't the faintest idea about marriage and men, but you'll see that extended family can be a nuisance. And you waste your cousin's money flitting from one idea to the next."

"We offered to pay the tuition back," Lucy said, "but he refused to take it."

"*We offered?*" Thankful laughed. "Well, I will speak to William about that! You don't realize how much that little school of yours cost. What a waste to not finish."

"I wanted to make Buck happy," Lucy cried.

"That's very stupid of you," Thankful said in a more sympathetic tone. "Boys never stay happy with you for long."

William came in now, throwing his muddy boots off at the front door.

"I always tell him to come around to the side!" Thankful grumbled.

William had recovered from the news of Lucy quitting school in his gentle, easy way on the walk home and now greeted the two with a look of hope. "So you've heard, Thankful?"

"Yes and isn't it foolish of Lucy to give up a career for Buck?"

William's equanimity left him. "Do you always find fault?"

"Willy, it's all right," Lucy said.

"No, it's not. I'm tired of every happiness being stripped from the land."

"Must everything be about *the land*?" Thankful cried.

William threw his hands up. "I can't take this any longer."

Thankful sought to explain to Lucy. "He always threatens divorce! It's why I can't relax!"

An expensive new necklace dangled around her slender neck, but Lucy decided for William's sake not to confess her mixed motives for leaving school, yet she resented Thankful's extravagances all the more. She determined never to ask her generous but naive cousin for another penny. "Buck is the boy I've always wanted to marry. I don't really have any interest in teaching. I want to raise his babies and be a good mother and help him when he needs it."

Thankful laughed viciously. "Willy, your cousin is such a child! Lulu speaks like in a fairy tale!"

"She speaks like a good wife!" William said. "Lucy, let me take your things up to your room—and I insist that you call it *your room*!" He grabbed Lucy's bag roughly and stormed up the stairs, throwing it in the room and slamming the door before trudging up to his old attic place.

Thankful glared at Lucy. "You come here to show me up saying that rubbish about babies!"

"What do you mean?" she asked, taking a step toward the staircase.

"Do you realize that Buck considered calling your engagement off? I find it repulsive that he will marry you so young. It's embarrassing—and it's not because it's you. I don't mind you, really ... it's just everything."

"Buck told me about his recent feelings, and I understand him," Lucy said with a confidence Thankful found galling.

"You *understand* him?"

"I've felt the same way. You don't seem to realize—or maybe you do—how he and I both take your family's words to heart. You've sought to undermine us. I don't blame you. I am very young and Buck has done silly things in the past, but there's something you must understand about me. Once I've made up my mind about someone I'm quite confident that I'm right. Buck is good, and I'll be loyal to him forever."

Thankful laughed a little, but uncomfortably, and although her inner cynic fought for control she asked with a real desire to know, "How can you be so sure?"

"I'm a McCullough like my father. My loyalty never falters."

Thankful sat upon the stairs with chin in hand. "How is it that you're so young and know so much?"

"You don't see the beautiful things you have. When I left on the train this morning, I saw the handsomest couple I've ever seen on the platform—you and Willy."

"Do you really think that?"

"Of course. I wish I'd been here for your wedding because I'm sure you were such a stunning bride."

Thankful bit her lip, holding back tears. "No one seemed truly happy for us, Lulu. William looked terribly handsome, and I was so proud of him—but my family—well, you know how they are. Everyone loves you including Willy, and all I do is make his life miserable."

"We're to be sisters," Lucy said with a winning grin. She wiped Thankful's eyes. "Willy will love you if you let him."

"But he won't be what I need him to be," Thankful confided.

"Maybe you're the one who won't be what you need to be."

"I don't want to have babies! I won't love them! I won't!" Thankful sobbed.

Lucy brushed the hair from Thankful's face and let her cry on her shoulder for a moment. "Thankful, I agree with you."

"What?" Thankful replied in surprise, pulling back.

"You have a right to your say."

Thankful stared at Lucy in her ridiculous spectacles. "What do you mean?"

"Willy didn't want to marry his mother. He liked that you spoke up for yourself. Aunt Kate loved my uncle, but she resented him too and it was sad. Willy just doesn't like big emotions."

Thankful laughed despite her misery. "Oh, I've made such a mess of things, I'm afraid I can't save any of it."

The two sat for a long time before Lucy stood. "I should unpack, and if you tell me where the linens are kept, I'll fix up the guest room."

Thankful stood now too. "That's very good of you, Lucy. I'd feel bad making Josephine stay. And Lucy, thank you. The room is yours no matter how awful I've made you feel about it."

"We can both make a home here for the next while if you'll only let us."

"You really are too good for my silly brother," Thankful laughed, a weight lifted.

"Well, you're the perfect thing for Willy. You just don't know it yet," Lucy said and went to her room.

Thankful still considered farming beneath William, and that left a sheen of uneasiness over the pretty picture of love Lucy tried to create. Thankful would let herself fully love William once she convinced him of seeing things her way. For now Thankful must convince him not to be angry with her.

She climbed up the attic stairs and took a deep breath before entering his sanctuary without knocking. He looked mildly surprised since she never came up this far into the house. He sat on his childhood bed with one of his father's books opened on his lap. Thankful joined him close enough that he could smell her faint perfume.

"Can we talk?"

William rolled his eyes. "Must we *always* talk?"

She leaned her head on his shoulder. "You miss your father, don't you?"

William nodded, closing the little book as if unable to share that world with anyone.

"Sometimes I forget all that you've lost, Willy. I'm so sorry for that."

William met her eyes for a second. "I have no one when we fight. And this house that you consider so shabby holds the only parts of my parents I still have, and I'm not ready to leave them."

"I've been selfish. Meg and I were never close. I feel a certain loss, but ..."

"I can't imagine how it is with the Crenshaws."

"Must we always speak as if we're parts of feuding families? William, I want to be a good wife. I want ... for us to try ..."

"You mean, try for a ..."

"Yes, let's try right now," Thankful said, unbuttoning William's shirt at the collar. "I so want you to be happy with me."

"But ..." William began, many thoughts racing through his head, but one desire overriding all else.

# Chapter Sixteen

Thankful luxuriated in the calm breathing of her satisfied husband as they lay cozily in William's childhood bed. She ran her fingers over his chest, and he smiled. An animal scuttled over the roof above them, and then came the sound of Lucy on the stairs. She knocked once—and again.

William wriggled free from the happy entanglement. "Lucy?"

"Oh ... I hate to trouble you," she began in the mousy way that so irked Thankful, "but Fred and India are coming up the drive."

William turned to Thankful in obvious annoyance. She shook her head.

"I had no idea," she whispered.

"Okay, we'll be down in a minute," William grumbled, pulling on his loose trousers. He turned back to Thankful, who was still undressed, and smiled. "You look so pretty just now."

"Do you love me?" she asked.

"I wish you didn't have a brother or two," William replied jokingly as he buttoned his shirt and tucked it in before pulling up his suspenders. A quick glance in the cracked mirror let him pull his slightly too long hair behind his ears. "Are you coming?"

"You go, I'll be down in a few moments," she said, unsettled that William didn't actually say he *loved* her and dreading a visit with Fred, who presently made noise on the porch.

William gave her a kiss but missed her lips. Thankful saw this as a sign, but smiled falsely as he left. With a decided lack of energy she pulled her heavy skirt up over her damp underthings and clasped her bodice shut. She glanced in the mirror too, noting her flushed cheeks and flawless complexion. At least she was still pretty.

It was only Fred and India so she didn't bother much with her hair. She was about to leave the room but caught sight of the open book on the side table and went to it. Thankful had read John Weldon's writings as a young lady and remembered them to be mawkishly sentimental. She smiled to herself as she glanced around the little room so full of artifacts and half-realized dreams.

Flipping through the pages of the little book about a far-off army post, she came upon a romantic page and sat for a second to read it: "*The old soldier of the Great War looked upon his bride of twenty years with the same awe at his luck that he had felt the first time he gazed upon her in her green wool riding habit and it filled him with gratitude that she should have accepted him just as he was.*"

She sighed, closing the book. She missed Lieutenant Weldon and wished that nothing had changed since those years long ago when she would come upon the father and son in town and feel such attraction and curiosity.

She steeled herself for the coming awkwardness of a visit with her brother as she closed the attic door behind her. Fred's voice dominated in the parlor as she stood on the landing before Lucy's room, wondering if the girl should be invited to sit amongst the grown-ups. She needn't have worried. Downstairs already, Lucy was bringing in tea for the guests—using that horrid tea set William had insisted they save from Sarah's days as hostess.

"Thanks ever so much," Thankful said sarcastically when joining her, but she saw the happiness her words brought to the girl. "You are too good, Lu." She slid the parlor doors open for Lucy.

William and Fred stood at the fire, and India sat on the edge of her seat as if the bourgeois surroundings of the parlor might contaminate. She stood only when Thankful entered (not when Lucy had come in before her), and this annoyed Thankful despite her own disdain for Lucy. "Do sit, India. What a surprise to have you so late in the evening when our help has already gone home."

"Lucy is a perfect substitute," India said as a little joke.

Thankful noted that Lucy didn't seem to mind, but William swooped in to help his cousin set the tray on the table with an irritated huff.

Fred tossed a sheep from the nativity scene in his hands as he spoke. "So I was just saying to Willy here, that we now have something in common—dead sisters," Fred said with what looked like a tear in his eye. "I was saying we ought to stay in better touch, sis. Who cares about mistakes and all—we're still blood."

"Which mistakes do you speak of?" Thankful asked.

"Do you like cream, Fred?" Lucy interjected.

"William, don't you have any leftover spirits from Christmas?" Fred asked. "No, Lucy, I won't have any cream, *thanks*."

India gave Fred a vexed look. "Lucy, my husband is always so uncouth. I'll take tea with cream and sugar, dearie."

"India," Thankful said as sweetly as she could manage, "we don't need to act as though Lucy were seven."

"I'm nearly fifteen," Lucy stated quietly.

India ignored Thankful. Lucy handed William his tea as he liked it. Thankful opened an antique cabinet of Scott's and took out a bottle for her brother and a glass. Then Thankful got her own tea.

"Looks like we're the poor relatives to Buck—at least temporarily," Fred said after a sip of brandy. "But it won't last."

"Fred, please ..." India moaned. "Won't you bring Fred into the library for a smoke, William? I can't bear him another minute tonight," she said with a tolerant grin.

William stepped forward ready to do India's bidding.

Fred laughed. "What library? I heard all the books were sold off."

William's face reddened. "None of us here care much for medical journals, Fred."

William escorted Fred into the library and closed the door to the women. India leaned in now. "I insisted that we come to see you before we return to the West, Thankful. And I'm glad little Lucy is here too. I have much to tell you both about the world outside this silly little town."

"I like Englewood," Lucy said in a quiet, set tone.

Thankful and India exchanged glances and giggled.

"She *is* young!" India said, with a sympathetic shake of the head. "But Lucy, you're lucky to have a more experienced friend in Thankful. You'll need her."

"Will I?" Lucy asked in a willful way that surprised the other two.

"Oh, yes," India said, the lids of her eyes drooping as her brows arched in condescension. "I've always said that Buck is a fine catch despite his shortcomings, and, he's even rather handsome despite his scars and hand, but he's a babe in the woods when it comes to real life. I worry that you'll be eaten alive by the city girls whom I know all too well. I perceived right from the start that Thankful was as much of a cynic as I am, and that's lucky for you. A girl in your position needs to be realistic."

"I am," Lucy said.

The other two smiled tolerantly at her.

"Anyway," India said to Thankful, as if bored with Lucy already, "I came to give you the magazines I was telling you about the other night. I was once like you—so trapped and miserable ..."

Thankful's expressive face reddened at India's characterization of her feelings.

India read the situation. "Lucy, this is girl talk. Men won't ever understand no matter how they may adore us. Thankful, you must see that there are more ways to be a woman than just being a wife and mother."

"I don't believe in all of that," Thankful said, but eyed the magazines greedily hoping the writings might offer her escape from her despair and resentment.

India handed one to Thankful, but pulled it quickly from her hand. "Will your husband disapprove?"

Thankful laughed. "Over magazines? Don't be ridiculous."

"May I be frank?" India asked, glancing at Lucy before continuing. "Maybe Lucy is too young for what I have to say."

Lucy stood as if given a great reprieve, but Thankful pulled her back down beside her. "Lucy is old enough to marry Buck and will have the same feminine concerns as the rest of us."

India took a sip of tea and set it in its saucer. "I respect the women of our mothers' generation in a way. Of course without them we wouldn't be here ... but we are living in a new age." India looked deeply into Thankful's needy eyes. "Dear friend, my heart bleeds for you. I see as no one else does the true source of your torment."

"I've made such a mess of things!" Thankful whispered with much feeling.

"But how could it have been any different?" India asked, taking her hand. "I hope you won't take too much offense, but your mother has the mentality of a small child ..."

Lucy shifted uncomfortably. "Thankful, we shouldn't listen ..."

Thankful turned on her, but as gently as she could. "Lulu, you don't know a thing about my mama."

India continued, "Fred's told me all about your parents and mine were no better, but we must forgive them their old-fashioned ways. I believe we are the first fruits of an evolutionary trend. Thankful, you understand that there is more to you than just dresses, I hope."

"Yes."

"It's obvious to anyone with eyes that you're meant for more with your beauty and keen intelligence. Such a vision of noble womanhood should not be trapped in the backwaters of Englewood. I pity you, really."

At this Thankful's pride awoke. "I shouldn't like your sympathy, India."

"And you won't have it for long." Here India whispered, "At Middlemay some women bred and some did not. Think of it! A choice, a freedom! We two are exactly the same, but you are far luckier in one way. If Buck hadn't been such a fool, Sam would be well looked after somewhere in Connecticut, but my thinking hadn't fully evolved, and I let myself be controlled by your brothers. I was fearful. But you need not be! You are in control of your own body."

Lucy shook her head vehemently. Childishly, Thankful thought.

"I don't like your words, ma'am," Lucy said, "and in the Bible it says that a wife is to give herself to her husband, and he's to give himself to her."

India and Thankful were surprised that Lucy spoke so plainly. But India said, "Lucy, dear, you are ignorant and inexperienced. One day you will see that the Bible, though a fine book for morals and such, is only man's attempt to explain things he doesn't understand, and it is a very *patriarchal* work."

"I don't know what that means," Lucy admitted, with so little embarrassment it awed Thankful.

"It means that men rule the world," India said. "But things are changing, and men must make room for us."

Thankful laughed.

India spoke sternly as if their very life depended upon her words. "Thankful, speak plainly. Do you receive any pleasure from your husband?"

"I've loved him since ..."

"No. That's not what I mean."

Thankful glanced at Lucy. "Well, I enjoy being close to him. I think so."

India shook her head with a sympathetic yet patronizing smile. "Thankful, the pleasure I hint at leaves no room for doubt if you've experienced it."

"I love him," Thankful said, but with a desperate question behind it.

"Dear, there is nothing wrong with wanting, expecting more."

Thankful leaned in now. "But I find it difficult to speak to William without hurting his feelings, and I must admit that I'm terrified pleasure might bring a child!"

"Do you really not want a little baby?" Lucy asked, being drawn in by the secrecy of the whisperings that made the proceedings seem adventurous and grown up.

India spoke for Thankful. "Babies are the perfect thing for some women, of course. But pleasure in the bedroom mustn't always bring children. We are so ignorant about our own bodies and yet we're forced to be defined by them! I hardly have time to tell you all that needs to be said, but I will write. Thankful—and Lucy too—there are very easy ways to enhance pleasure. I taught Fred everything—he used to be such a brute!" India laughed.

Thankful laughed too but twisted the napkin in her hands.

India grew serious again. "Before I leave I want you to understand that none of this is your fault. You were led down a garden path with that lieutenant fellow out west because you were raised on silly romance. Please don't look so sad. God uses events to make us stronger. You are good deep down, dear. We were made in the image of God—so says your Bible. That doesn't mean you are just a baby machine. You were meant to create more, to be more, to delight in all the things that men do!

"The Devil has used men to keep us enslaved and the poor men don't even realize how free the modern women can make them. That little seed of dissatisfaction rumbling inside of you is God nudging you toward greatness! There's time enough for children—later if you want to, but I'd feel sorry for you even then. What a waste of talent. The only difference between you and me is that I'm further on the road we're both destined for." India whispered again. "The heights of pleasure I now experience with Fred go hand in hand with the freedom we grant each other and the equality of footing we stand upon. I dare say that I have more political clout in our little town than Fred and does he envy that? No. Fred sees that a happy, intelligent wife is the easiest to care for. Are you easy to care for, Thankful?"

"No," she replied with a blush.

"You will lose William and yourself if you remain boxed up in past regrets. Forgive your mistakes and move on knowing that it was society to blame. You, my dear, can help change society."

"How?"

India tapped her refined chin with her long, perfectly manicured fingers. "How about your little shop? Start a women's group or something."

Thankful laughed. "Now you sound like my mother."

"No, no, no. Not one of those chatty coffee clubs!" India said. "When you've finished reading you'll see what I mean. You can be a truly revolutionary woman!"

"Do you really think so? I'm desperate for a cure for my melancholy ..."

"You are your own master, dear friend."

Just then Fred slid the pocket door open. "India, are you ready? I'm exhausted."

India stood now as if invigorated. "Of course, darling Freddie. It's been a fun visit with my two new sisters."

William followed Fred. "Lucy, it looks like you've seen a ghost."

Lucy jumped from her seat beside Thankful unable to look at her cousin. "No, no, Willy, we had a jolly time. There's nothing the matter. May I go now?"

William looked to Thankful who also had trouble meeting William's suspicious eye. Thankful nodded permission for Lucy to retreat to her room.

India kissed Thankful. "I'll write you. I promise!"

Thankful smiled and escorted her brother and his wife to the door with William quietly following, hands in pockets in the hangdog way he sometimes had.

"See you, sis," Fred said already distracted by the night. India waved one last time as they drove off, and Thankful shut the door, at once feeling relieved and trapped.

Tentatively William stepped into conversation as they went around turning off the gaslights. "So ... you and India had a nice time?"

"It was ... fine."

"Just fine?"

Thankful glanced at him. "Why does it matter?"

"Oh. I don't know. I just thought she'd be a bit too ..." William's caramel eyes always widened when he worried he may have landed in unforeseen trouble.

"A bit too what? Intelligent?"

"What? No!" he said, flustered now. "No, just too worldly and conniving in a way."

Thankful felt stung and discovered, but annoyed too. "No, India's not like that at all, and I do wish you wouldn't always suspect my family of grave faults."

William laughed but the way he tossed his head betrayed his annoyance. "Since when do you consider India real family? Do you forget what she put Buck through?"

"Oh, so now you care about Buck?"

William waved her off. "I'm going to bed. I don't have time for this game."

"So now that *you're* satisfied, off you go to bed," she grumbled.

When William whirled around, she regretted her words.

"What do you mean by that?"

"Nothing. I just shouldn't have to answer to you about my friends."

"Please, have as many friends as you like!" William said. "Maybe then you'll allow me a few!"

Thankful caught herself before begging for forgiveness like she usually did when she saw that she had overplayed her hand. This time she swallowed and remembered India's words. Not everything was her fault! She let William escape into their bedroom. After listening to him fumble out of his boots and sigh deeply as he threw himself into bed (in a way she always found endearing), she climbed the stairs to the sound of Lucy's music box playing and knocked at her door. Lucy let her in, and Thankful noted what sweet features Lucy had without her glasses. Buck and Lucy would have beautiful children. She watched Lucy climb back into bed and restart the box with a demure smile that hinted at self-satisfaction.

"Lucy, do you mind closing the box a moment?"

Lucy listened a minute longer before complying.

Thankful sat on the bed and tucked the girl in with tight precision. "Lulu, did you have fun with us grown-up girls?"

Lucy adjusted the blankets back to her own liking. "Now it's you who talk to me like I'm seven."

"Oh, forgive me. I just worried that things were a little too much for you with India."

"Yes, they were."

Thankful was surprised again by the complete lack of sniveling she expected from a young girl. "Dear, in a few short months you will see that marriage is not as you imagine."

"That may be your trouble but it won't be mine," Lucy replied in a tone Thankful didn't like.

"It's best for you to be told the truth in order to avoid disappointment." Thankful sat beside her.

"I won't be disappointed in Buck—only *your* family is."

"That's unfair and you know it. India is to be your family now, and we girls must come together to help each other."

"Thankful, India is a mean-spirited wretch."

"Young lady, take that back!"

"You are not my mother, and I will not take it back. I like men and boys and you can't make me stop."

Thankful laughed. "You sound ridiculously uncouth!"

"I'd like for you to leave, Thankful," Lucy said simply before opening the music box.

Thankful slammed it shut and put it aside. "How dare you act so superior, you little snippet!"

Lucy's delicate mouth whitened. "I will love you despite your silly name-calling because Willy loves you. Now please leave."

Thankful stood to go but couldn't bring herself to the door. "You won't tell William all that was said?"

Lucy stared at her. "How could I ever bring myself to say anything as mean as ..."

Thankful raced back to the bed. "But, Lulu, if only you could understand the frustration I feel ..."

"Stop! I don't want to hear another bad word about my cousin. He loves you! He trusts and depends upon you and it breaks my heart that you have so little respect for his friendship that you'd insinuate horrible things to that minx India!" Lucy grabbed the music box and opened it defiantly.

Thankful in a fit of rage slammed it shut, nearly catching Lucy's fingers, and pulled it from her with a yank that sent it flying and crashing to the floor. Lucy cried out and ran to the delicate instrument, as did Thankful, but Lucy pushed her aside crying bitter tears.

"I'm sorry!"

"You're spoiled and horrible! Get out of my room!"

Thankful gasped at the sound of William's footfall on the stairs. He entered the room in with wide eyes. "What's happened?"

Lucy picked up pieces of her gift.

"Did I hear fighting?" William asked.

Thankful shook, shocked by her own behavior.

Lucy spoke through tears. "Oh, Willy, won't Buck be terribly angry?"

William bent down and helped Lucy gather the pieces of the box. "What happened?"

Thankful said, "It was my fault. I was trying to talk to her, and she wouldn't stop listening to that infernal box."

"What were you talking about?" William asked.

Lucy glanced at Thankful. "We were talking about boys, and how I don't know a thing about them."

William laughed and touched Lucy's face. "You know enough. Buck will understand that dropping the music box was an accident. It's only money." He turned to Thankful as he stood up, a bit painfully. "Don't go scaring my cousin."

"I was only trying to ..."

Lucy interrupted. "I was being rude with the box."

William yawned. "I need to get up early so ..."

Thankful followed him out but not before embracing Lucy in a stiff hug.

# Chapter Seventeen

Thankful hid in her room the following morning when her mother came and whisked Lucy away to find a nice pattern for her wedding dress in town. She regretted how awful she'd been to Lucy and had a headache brought on by sleeplessness to prove it. Why did Lucy make her so angry and upset? Was it Lucy's unwarranted confidence and optimism?

Lucy McCullough had even won the admiration of Thankful's parents. William was blind to Lucy playing everyone's heartstrings to get what she wanted! Lucy had stolen the engagement ring that by rights should have been Thankful's. Margaret was nowhere to be found when Thankful chose a wedding dress. Thankful ruefully remembered Margaret's bored hostility when she offered her only wedding advice—*dress sensibly. After all, you've been married before.*

And Lucy's damned music box smashed to bits! What would Buck say? Even this brought resentment. Willy would never think on his own to buy Thankful something so fine—and didn't she like music too? Thankful almost cried now, but instead retreated to her room and read from *The Revolution.*

Usually William stopped by at noon for a meal, but today, for the first time, he did not. With each passing hour and then as each painful minute ticked by, Thankful's heart pounded and her head throbbed. Where was he? Was this the end of it all?

The revolutionary thoughts of strange women scared her. She wondered if she were being unfaithful to William for reading the essays on sexual freedom, work, and equality. She paced and spoke peevishly to Josephine and paced some more. She thought a walk might ease her nerves, but then decided against it in the hopes that William might come home after all. When evening came with supper set for three, Thankful and Josephine exchanged worried looks as the steaks were becoming drier on the heat with each passing moment. Thankful sent Josephine home and waited at the dining table stubbornly.

Finally sounds on the drive brought her to the window. Thankful peeped from behind the curtain to see Buck's sleigh. She considered hiding in her room or fleeing to the attic, but Buck came to the front door with Lucy too soon. Thankful waited as the knob turned and Lucy led Buck into the gas-lit hallway. She met them there.

Buck smiled in his painfully worried way. "Mama's come down with a headache, sis, so here I am to drop off Luce."

Lucy thanked him for the ride stiffly before racing to her room. Buck followed her with eyes of concern. He turned to Thankful and whispered, "For the life of me, I have no idea what I've done wrong."

Thankful did truly love her brother, and all of her petty feelings melted at the sight of his distress and confusion. She took him into the parlor. "Did Lucy tell you about the music box?"

Buck shook his head. "I do hope nothing's wrong with it—it cost me in the hundreds ..."

Thankful swallowed hard. "A little box like that?"

"It's one of the first of its kind and made by a European master. I spent months searching for just the right one."

"Oh, dear," Thankful said, trembling.

"What's happened?" Buck asked, his tone less forgiving than Thankful would have hoped.

"Buck, Lucy loved the music box ..."

"*Thankful?*"

"Dear me, Buck. I dread telling you this ..." She knew she shouldn't, but she let the words pass her lips. "Josephine, when cleaning the guest room ... she dropped the box, and it fell to a thousand pieces. For something so expensive it broke quite easily, I'm afraid."

Buck ran his hand through his hair, enraged. "Well, you dismissed Josephine then."

"No, Buck, how could I? It wasn't her fault!" Thankful cried. "Mistakes are made. And ... and Lucy kept it so close to the edge of her table. Such a fine gift shouldn't have been given to a *child*."

Buck sensed something. Bolting up the stairs, he knocked on Lucy's door.

"You mustn't go up there, Buck. It's bad form!"

Lucy with tears streaming down her cheeks came onto the landing still in her day dress.

"Lucy, the music box ..." Buck began.

"Oh, Buck, I should have told you all about it, but I was heartbroken!"

"Thankful says Josephine dropped it. Is that true?" Buck asked with a force and anger that surprised and scared her.

She glanced at Thankful on the stairs. "No. That's a lie. It's my fault it's broke. I was rude to Thankful and then it fell."

Buck looked between the two.

Thankful came up the stairs. "No, Buck, it's my fault. I was so tired of hearing it play that same melody, and I lost my temper and took it from her and it slipped from my hands. Forgive me."

Buck stayed quiet for a few minutes, his violet eyes registering nothing. The girls held their breath. "You both just lied to me." He turned, walked down the steps, and left.

Lucy sobbed, turned back to her room, and slammed the door behind her. Thankful banged hard on the door and finally, losing patience, let herself in. Lucy sat at the window, looking out with her head against the pane. She refused to turn around when Thankful tapped her.

"Please, don't be so sad. We'll fix this. Buck can never stay angry for long. He's soft like that ..."

Lucy turned around now, her eyes shining in anger. "A gentle soul, of all people, shouldn't have his feelings trampled at every turn! How is it you take one of his endearing qualities and use it to belittle him? Buck has always said his friendship with you is very important. I'm shocked at how you speak of him behind his back!"

"Lucy, stop being dramatic! You haven't a clue how siblings behave ..."

"One day I will raise twelve children, and they'll be kind to each other."

Thankful gaped and then laughed. "Twelve? Really now, that's the funniest thing!"

"Why? Buck and I have already decided."

"Buck wants twelve children," Thankful repeated to herself, letting the idea wash over her like vinegar against a paper cut. "My brother is too sentimental about it. Imagine how he'd take you dying in childbirth."

"Why do you always imagine the worst?" Lucy asked, but the color rose in her face. "Thankful forgive my insensitivity."

Thankful stayed quiet unable to retrieve any feelings about her sister. Meg *really* was dead. This week had not been a nightmare but a reality that cut her deeply yet when Thankful gazed out upon the others in her small circle, it was as if they all played pretend even during the funeral.

Thankful and Graham had taken Royal Wilder to the station in a mute state of befuddled grief. It hadn't occurred to anyone that he might want to grieve a little longer in the place Meg called home. The ex-soldier was politely shuttled away with words like, "of course you must want time to yourself," and "time with your own family will do you good," and "you are always welcome, now don't trip on your way stepping up into the train."

Everything shoved under the rug. Everything. And perhaps that was why William had at first allowed Thankful so much freedom in redecorating. He sensed that she would help him to never think about things. The real things. And now they had nothing but falseness between them.

"The worst does happen, you realize, Lucy," Thankful said, feeling a sudden sympathy for the girl who still had faith in the future.

"I've always realized it," Lucy said gravely. "Since Willy first told me that dear Uncle John was not *my* papa. I fear you're right in a way. Maybe I am a little too idealistic. I think my father and mother couldn't possibly have been as good as everyone likes to remember, but it's all I have. *You,* on the other hand, have to sit squarely with your mama day after day ..."

Thankful laughed. "Mama loves you."

"Mrs. Crenshaw loved my aunt too, but I'm nothing like Aunt Kate, and I worry that it won't be long now before your mother sees that I will insist on my way sometimes."

Thankful stared long and hard at the girl who, in her navy and white striped dress and more grown-up hair style, appeared much older than she was. "I don't know what to make of you, Lucy."

"I'm having my own troubles with you, Thankful," Lucy said with a saucy smirk.

"Perhaps you are more modern than I've given you credit for."

Lucy scrunched her nose. "God forbid. I like to think I'm just a girl bred from fine parents."

Thankful marveled at Lucy's ability to turn a tragic upbringing into a strength. "I will make things right with Buck. I promise. You have something that at once repels and draws me in—it must be what Buck sees—except not the repellant part."

"I'm not sure what to say to that."

"We Crenshaws are trained adversaries. I envy what you and Willy have, but I haven't the faintest clue how to get there. Won't you teach me your secret?"

"I'm afraid I don't know what it is, Thankful, but for now we must live together."

"William and I have a bit of money set aside for farm equipment or something—I'll convince William to buy you a better music box."

"No, it wouldn't be the same. You can't buy my forgiveness. Just be kind to William. He's the best boy I know—next to Buck—and he tries very hard."

"Yes, and I can be very brutal. It's a curse—my temper."

"It seems more a habit," Lucy said in childlike simplicity. "Will you unfasten my buttons? I'm tired now."

Thankful undid the back of Lucy's dress and helped her into her nightgown as if Lucy had suddenly become her doll. She tucked her in and Lucy let her—missing Katherine a little just now. "Here, I'll turn off the light and you sleep in tomorrow. Josephine will bring breakfast. Sweet dreams, sister."

# Chapter Eighteen

Lucy couldn't sleep. What if Buck called off the engagement because of the music box? She had heard Buck's words to Thankful "... *in the hundreds* ..." and these words kept her in unrelenting misery. He shouldn't have spent that much—but then she smiled at the thought that he *had* spent that much. She dressed before dawn, tiptoed past William and Thankful's bedroom, and slipped out the side door. She raced through the still sleeping town, determined to talk with Buck before he left for work.

The sound of melting snow dripping off the Crenshaw porch behind the shrubbery made for the only noise before she knocked lightly on the front door of the quiet house. A new maid opened the door with a grim look of annoyance at the hour. "Yes, miss?"

"I'm here for Buck, please," Lucy said, her voice meek with embarrassment.

"Mr. Crenshaw is already off to work, young lady, and everyone else is still trying to sleep."

"Oh, I'm sorry—I'm afraid we've never met," Lucy said, taking the woman's hand. "I'm Lucy McCullough, and I'll be marrying Buck, so we'll be like family then."

The woman nodded with a hint of warmth. "Lucy, yes. They told me about you. Please come in then. I'll see if Mrs. Crenshaw is up yet."

"No! Please don't. I shouldn't have come so early, but I really need to speak to Buck," Lucy said with worry in her voice. "Would you happen to have his address at work?"

"In the city?" the woman asked as if Lucy had asked for directions to the moon.

"Yes. It's *exceptionally* important."

The woman liked intrigue and waved Lucy to follow her in and down to the kitchen where another lady stirred muffin batter. The smell of coffee brought a happy smile to Lucy, and they gave her a cup before taking Buck's card from a board tacked with many other things. His name looked nice on the elegant card, but the address was written in tiny letters and numbers. Briefly the two women and Lucy talked about muffins, coffee, and love before Lucy left for the station with the card she couldn't read.

Once aboard the train, Lucy paid the conductor and asked him if he knew anything about the Wall Street area. Lucy made him understand that she had trouble reading the card, so he sat beside her for a second to get a better look.

"I've made a mess of things with Buck," Lucy explained, pointing to his name, "I'm to marry him, but I got into a quarrel with his sister, you see, and we broke a priceless music box that he had searched all over for—just for me. Isn't that nice? You may know him. He rides the train every day. Buck Crenshaw? Oh, you *must* know him. He's very good and kind. He's got a scar right here and ..."

"Oh, yes, *him*. I do know him." The man laughed. "One day he paid the fare for an entire car."

"That's him!" Lucy laughed. "I'm so lucky, don't you think?"

The conductor stood. "You're perfect for each other," he said with a grin. "A gentleman who rides in the lounge, I'm certain, wouldn't mind escorting you to the address on the card."

"Oh, now that would be bully!" Lucy said, clasping her hands as her spirit rebounded and the light of day cast a sudden rosy hue over things.

The man laughed, shrugging, before walking off with a wink. An old man with a cane met Lucy as she stood upon the platform in Hoboken anxiously scanning the crowd and wondering where she was to go next. The spindly legged man sported a distinguished mustache that not every gentleman could wear well. His eyes were blue and friendly.

"You remind me just of my uncle, though he was much taller and had brown eyes," Lucy said, taking him by the elbow. "Do you really make this trip every day, sir? I'm much younger than you, and I'm already confused."

"My name's Lamont."

"Then you're from Englewood, aren't you? From up the hill?" Lucy brightened.

"Yes, and where are you from, young lady?"

"You may call me Lucy. I'm from Tenafly Road. You probably remember my grandparents Scott and Sarah McCullough. They were big bugs like you, but they built on Tenafly Road which Thankful says was a mistake, but I love it. I like the hill too, but home is home, don't you think?"

"Exactly. Now where are you taking me, Lucy?" Lamont asked.

"Land sakes, Mr. Lamont, don't play. I'd be lost without you!" She laughed. "Now watch there for that puddle, sir. I've always wanted to take a ferry somewhere, but I never had a curiosity about Manhattan. My uncle used to say they were cruel to horses in Manhattan. I hadn't remembered that till just now and hate the thought. If only I could adopt some of them, but I have no land or anything. I like trees too. My uncle said they cut everything down in the city. I suppose my ... my future husband likes trees too, but a man does have to work. My cousin became a farmer. He's a great artist, but ... oh well."

And so it went on the ferry and along the streets of Manhattan which were far noisier than Lucy imagined they would be from across the river. The buildings of brown and yellow stone competed with once proud colonial structures of wood for echoing the busy noise of commerce, the shouting men, the constant footfall of brokers hurrying on the sidewalk, and the tack of horses jangling. The sky hid behind crisscrossed telegraph wire, and Lucy imagined the great and exciting conversations and deals being relayed over them. Could she hear the buzz? Signs swayed from nearly every building. Boys and girls her age called the news and hawked fruit on street corners.

Yelling men rushed horses on as Lucy clung to the old man who pulled her down paths that had first been traversed by deer centuries before the Dutch. Mr. Lamont minded the way as Lucy stared up and around until they came to a quiet brownstone with the shades drawn and not a single signpost to alert anyone to the fact that within worked bankers doing unimaginable mathematical figuring.

"Is this really it?"

Mr. Lamont chuckled. "Shall we go in?"

"Oh, sir, you've been so kind, but I've taken you out of your way, and you don't even know me."

"I've gotten to know you pretty well, Lucy," Mr. Lamont said with a kind smile. "And I work here."

Lucy blushed. "Oh, then, you *do* know him—Buck Crenshaw?"

"Yes. I was wondering when you'd associate my name to that on the card."

"Oh, how foolish of me!" she said, laughing. "But honestly, sir, I paid attention only to Buck's name—it stands out so nicely in print."

Mr. Lamont led Lucy up the granite stairs and into the quiet, dark entranceway. A male receptionist stood at the sight of her and was about to give her a polite piece of his mind as this establishment only rarely allowed females in past the front vestibule, but then he saw Mr. Lamont and his eyes lit with eagerness. "Good morning, Mr. Lamont!"

"Please tell Mr. Crenshaw to come to my office at once," the old man ordered.

The young man nodded, hurrying to carry out his duty. Mr. Lamont took Lucy by the elbow and walked her down a short hallway paneled in ornately carved mahogany. Lucy touched it and smiled at Mr. Lamont.

Leaning in close, she whispered, "Forgive a county mouse her small pleasures! I've never seen such beauty this close up—and the light fixtures must have cost in the hundreds!"

Mr. Lamont laughed and ordered a passerby to bring him coffee for three. Lucy sat at a tea table set by the floor-to-ceiling windows, which cast a grey glow over the otherwise warm room. A single lamp of brass sat upon an enormous and tidy desk, and armchairs big enough to fill an ordinary room sat about at random angles. Mr. Lamont checked a few notes on his desk, furtively smiling at the awestruck girl. The door had been left open, and Buck walked in but stopped at the sight of Lucy.

"Mr. Crenshaw, do come in and join us. This poor girl needed escort this morning, and I had the pleasure."

"Sir, I can't imagine why Miss McCullough would come here ... I won't let it happen again, sir."

"Nonsense! Miss McCullough is welcome any time for a visit. In fact I'd be greatly disappointed if she didn't pop in once in a while." Mr. Lamont beckoned Buck to come to table with them as the coffee was brought in.

Mr. Lamont took the two of them in with a pleasant smile and sat back. "So Lucy tells me you are to be married soon."

Buck took his cup, but put it down again. "Sir, it was meant to stay a private affair at first and then, well now we've changed our plans so ..."

"Well, Buck, my opinion is that when you have good luck, you should celebrate it."

"Sir?" Buck glanced at Lucy who blushed.

"This is a family establishment, remember," Mr. Lamont said.

Buck fingered the scar at his neck.

"Mr. Crenshaw, you've been a great asset to the bank. I will be the first to admit that I told Mr. Turner it was wrong to let in an outsider, but he was dead on about you. The young cousins have taken a shine to you as well—but that you know, going out yachting with them this fall. Lucy is a gem, and I can't wait to introduce her to my wife."

Buck stammered, "Your wife?"

"Myrna is a dear and will love Lucy."

Lucy cleared her throat. "Mr. Lamont, you do forget about the broken music box that cost Buck in the hundreds ..."

Buck cringed, imagining this great man of finance would look askance at such a foolish expenditure. "Sir, I can explain ..."

Mr. Lamont laughed. "My son told me you had an odd fascination with music boxes that I took as a bit queer, but now it makes sense!"

Lucy brightened. "Isn't it just like Buck to buy me something I can truly appreciate even if I lose my sight completely?"

The old man was moved by Lucy's words. "It's the sign of a good man to consider such things, and my wife will find the two of you adorable. Now about the broken box—I should like to be the first to donate a sum for a new one to be had. Of course it won't be as nice as the first, but it shouldn't stand between the two of you when mistakes happen."

"Sir, oh, I couldn't let you ..." Buck said, the scar at his forehead bright red.

"Then let me buy the two of you lunch," Mr. Lamont insisted. "How about Delmonico's?"

Lucy gasped and her face lit with unashamed excitement. Lamont laughed again and Buck smiled.

"Sir, this is all so good of you," Buck said.

Mr. Lamont stood now, as did Buck. "Well, I need to make some money now. Mr. Crenshaw, take the young lady on a walkabout for the morning."

"Sir, I have business to attend to," Buck said, trying to read if Mr. Lamont's enthusiasm for Lucy was genuine.

"Young man, never push away a gift," Mr. Lamont said with authority. Then he turned to Lucy. "See you at church, then?"

"Oh, yes, and thank you ever so much!" Lucy gushed. "Buck must be thrilled to work for such a fine gentleman as yourself!"

The old man sat behind his desk and waved them out with a chuckle.

Once on the street Buck laughed in nervous relief.

"Oh, I hope you're not angry with me, Buck, but I had to see you to apologize about the music box. I never should have kept the news a secret, but I was so mortified about it, and I was angry at your sister," Lucy explained as a man pushing a fruit cart nearly knocked her off her feet. "Manhattan has a distinctive odor."

Buck laughed again and pulled Lucy out of the main pedestrian traffic and beneath the stairs of his office. "I reacted badly last night."

"No, you didn't. Best friends should never lie, and I promise never to do that again," Lucy said with great earnestness.

Buck smiled and kissed her. "Lucy, Mr. Lamont is a very big bug. Did you know that?"

"His office gave me a clue," she said with a smile. "But I would have died of humiliation if I'd known who he was from the start. It turns out he's a fine gent, isn't he?"

"Yes, but *you're* the charmer."

"And do you actually think we'll get to meet his wife? Oh, I don't mind either way. And Delmonico's! Am I dressed well-enough?"

He let his eyes wander over her with a grin. "You look far better in that dress than Thankful ever did."

She grew serious. "Must we wait until summer to get married, Buck?"

"Thankful's making things difficult, isn't she?" he asked knowingly.

She refused to answer, taking his hand instead and swinging his arm a little. "So where will you take me now?"

Buck grabbed Lucy around the waist playfully and laughed. "I should be asking you the same question."

# Chapter Nineteen

The parlor light on Tenafly Road flickered in the snow as Lucy ran up the drive and in through the front door. She quickly unlaced her boots, hung her coat, and started on the stairs, but the parlor doors slid open and William caught her.

"Lucy!" he cried, "Where were you all day?"

Thankful came up behind him looking equally concerned.

"Oh, I didn't think to leave a note I guess," she said.

"I was worried sick," he said. "But you're all right?"

"Willy, I'm better than that!" she cried. "I'm sorry to have worried you both, but I was only going up to see Buck this morning at the house. He'd already gone off to work so I followed him in."

"To the city?" Thankful asked.

"Yes! And it was such a wonderful adventure to remember for the rest of my life!"

William dragged her into the parlor. "Tell us all about it."

Thankful could not hide her surprise and interest and sat close, eager for news.

"We ate at Delmonico's! And everyone was so splendidly kind—nothing like I imagined of New Yorkers!"

William grinned. "It sounds grand. But how did you find Buck's office and all?"

"Well, you'll never guess who helped me—Mr. Lamont—from up the hill—high up the hill! But he was such a nice old man and he works with Buck—by chance! And the office was the grandest thing I've ever seen—except for maybe the museum ..."

"Museum?" Thankful asked, dumbfounded.

"Oh, yes! Buck took me all the way up to Fifth Avenue, and we rode in a stage, with dark blue panels and running gear in red! We bounced like mad over the cobblestone and laughed—you should have seen how Buck laughed!" Lucy all but purred as she spoke. "But Willy, the food! Delmonico's was like a castle with perfect linens and mirrors and carvings and the menu was ... it was too much for my eyes so I had Buck pick me out everything." She paused a moment, reliving the day in her mind. "First I had Bisque of Shrimp, then anchovies on toast, and just a tiny bit of wine. William, you don't mind do you?"

He shook his head, still grinning.

Lucy laughed. "Oh, then there was the loin of lamb with mint sauce—you were right, Willy, that I would like lamb—it was delicious with the fried eggplant and potatoes in a strange but delightful sauce, and for dessert charlotte russe! I couldn't have chosen better myself!"

"What a lot of food for such a small girl," Thankful noted.

William shushed her.

"Mr. Lamont treated us, so maybe I should have eaten less ..." Lucy said with a blush.

"I was teasing," Thankful said.

William rolled his eyes.

"Buck ate so much more than I did and laughed more than I've ever seen him. And to make things even pleasanter, some of his friends sat nearby and joined us for dessert, and if they weren't the nicest bunch of bankers!"

William laughed. Thankful did too, happy that Buck had fallen in with good people for once.

"But Willy, The Metropolitan Museum of Art! Oh, it was magnificent! Buck took me all the way up there before we ate, and I hardly thought of food until the very end. The antiquities and the paintings! It made me pine for the days when you painted!"

Thankful nudged William now, and he softened a little toward her.

"William, do you know of John Kensett? His paintings took my breath and one was of sailing and you know how I love the water!"

"Yes, Lulu, I do. Remember when we built the raft down on the river for your cat?" William asked.

"And you had to swim out to rescue him." Lucy laughed, recalling it.

"We should take a day this summer and go sailing, Willy, with Lucy and Buck," Thankful suggested.

William scratched his neck. "You know there's haying in summer, Thankful—but maybe we can get a canoe and paddle the Hackensack in October?"

Thankful's face clouded, but she sighed and recovered herself, still relieved that William had finally come home after sleeping off their disagreement in Mr. Adriance's barn. Thankful kissed him, and Lucy giggled.

"You are prettier together than any painting," Lucy said.

"Is Buck still sore about the box, Lucy?" Thankful asked.

Lucy shook her head, but nursed a grudge still that Buck should have wasted his time and money. Thankful seemed so nonchalant about it all. It caused Lucy to release the smallest bit of spite. "And guess what else? Mr. Lamont wants to come to our wedding!"

"Really?" Thankful replied in just the right envious tone.

Lucy regretted her words. "I do hope you'll help me plan things so Buck's friends will like it."

"Oh, pooh, the wedding day is for the girl," Thankful said. "Let's not worry about Buck and his chums. The real thing is to impress the women who will pull the strings behind the scenes. Mama blundered through all of that when my father was still at banking and spoiled her chances, so you just listen to me."

"Maybe Lucy would want to do things in her style, which I quite enjoy," William said, a bit sourly.

Thankful stared at him. "Well, I won't run roughshod over her, if that's what you're implying."

"All I mean is that Lucy is a simple girl and that's what makes her special."

Lucy kissed them both. "Don't argue over such trifling things. Today was better than a wedding anyway. I'm happily exhausted so off to bed I go."

William and Thankful watched Lucy leave, both uncomfortable at the idea of an evening together so soon after a fight. William stoked the fire, and Thankful flipped through a magazine but put it down. "I wish you loved me the way you love Lucy," she said.

William poked the fire harder and sparks flew. "Stop it. Can't you let things be?"

"Willy, do you mind if I start a women's group at the shop—one evening a week?" she asked timidly. This annoyed her as she considered that she'd grown afraid of men.

William turned and sat in the chair by the fire looking thin and unhappy. He still had headaches some days, and a sudden sympathy passed over Thankful now.

"What do you want me to say?" William asked peevishly.

"Say what you feel!" she instructed.

"If I say that you should start a group, you will accuse me of not wanting to spend time with you, and if I say you shouldn't, you'll say I'm a brute."

# Chapter Twenty

Saturday dragged its feet in coming, and Lucy had an uneasy sense that spending the time mending her favorite old dresses and going for walks each day annoyed Thankful who was always busy and in a great hurry. Thankful acted hurt by Lucy's lack of enthusiasm for the women's group that Thankful had named "Birds Take Flight on Ladies' Night," but Lucy had not made peace with India's style of talk and wanted no more of it.

Buck had promised to drive Lucy on Saturday to his parents' house for wedding plans. Lucy spent the night in a mix of worry and excitement. Only once did Lucy's mind wander to New London, feeling sorry to have left a family with small children without her help after Christmas.

Buck arrived at half past nine. In the brisk sunshine Buck's luxurious beaver coat shimmered. Lucy teased him as he helped her into his surrey. "You look just like a real capitalist now."

He frowned. "It's only work, Luce. I still mean to be a good person."

She noted that she'd bruised his thin Crenshaw skin. "I never doubted it. The coat suits you, and I'll be warm sitting next to you."

He smiled and tucked a blanket around her. "I want to remind you that this is *your* wedding. Be polite with Mama but don't allow for her to make the plans completely on her own."

"Of course not. But you'll be there, won't you?"

"Yes ... but my voice holds no sway with her. I worry how Mama will take us having the wedding in Manhattan and the reception too. Suddenly there's a long list of friends to invite who must not be left out. This is important for our future, you understand." He said this with serious eyes and a rigidness in his voice as he turned the horses.

"You do understand that weddings are supposed to be fun, don't you?" Lucy cuddled closer.

He sighed and laughed. "If only."

She poked his side through the thick coat. "I will see to it. I have given up school and everything for this and ..."

Buck pulled to a quick stop. "Are you having second thoughts?"

"Oh, no! Not at all!"

"I promise that if it's schooling you want, I'll get it for you, but I hoped we might plan the wedding first. Everyone at work has expectations now. Mr. Lamont has asked me about it twice this week already. I'm under pressure over it."

"Oh dear," Lucy said. "It was silly of me to take the train that day. I would say I regretted it, but I won't lie to you. I'm sorry I've made it hard for you, but it was the best day of my life!"

He grinned. "Really? I'm glad. I worried you didn't like all the noise and bustle."

"Oh, that part—especially the dying horse by the wayside—was awful, but I confess I'd almost forgotten about the poor creature by the time we strolled into the museum. My world opened like the most beautiful flower! And the way you picked the perfect things for lunch!"

He cocked his head with pride. "I've eaten there many times now—and it was just a guess about the lamb."

"Oh, Buck! Imagine all the fun we'll have—the two of us and our twelve children!"

"Lucy, I wanted to talk about that. Meg's death, well, it's made me realize how selfish and unfair that dream of mine may be ... twelve does seem a bit outlandish."

"Oh, Buck, no," Lucy said in disappointment. "I've envied your big family with so many brothers and sisters and have warmed to the idea tremendously. It occurred to me that God is making up for me not having a family of my own by giving me a husband who wants plenty of children."

"Hmm, I'm not sure, but ..." He leaned in confidentially, "I am happy to hear that you're excited at the idea. We should start right away—as soon as we're married."

"Yes! Of course," Lucy said, forgetting all about New London.

Buck gave her a peck, and off they rode merrily reminiscing about art and food and the secret kisses they stole as they wandered Central Park arm in arm.

Margaret, Graham, and an aloof woman with arched, discerning brows sat waiting for them in the library where serious discussion about weddings and receptions awaited. Graham jumped from his seat when Lucy and Buck arrived as if being released from prison. He kissed Lucy's white hand and led her to the best chair—his favorite. Buck went to his mother and kissed her, but she pulled away.

"Dear, sweet, Lucy, this is Madame Rainer," Margaret said with an icy glance Buck's way. "My son thinks we're unable to make proper arrangements for your wedding on our own."

Lucy glanced at Buck, who stared out the window. "Oh," was all she could muster.

Madame Rainer, from her chair beside a small table littered with Graham's natural artifacts and magnifying lenses, adjusted her spectacles. "The best families leave little to chance. Englewood gatherings may be quaint, but things are done differently in Manhattan. Your son was quite right to have hired me. I've helped all of his friends get married, and the write ups in the newspapers are always exceptional."

Margaret moaned. "Who are these friends I keep hearing about?"

"I only accept people I like and your son is a dear," Madame Rainer said, her face still sour.

Lucy rose from her seat and took the woman's hand in her own. "I'm happy for your help, ma'am. I haven't a mother of my own and I like you already. Anyone who likes Buck is a friend of mine."

Graham and Buck exchanged smiles of pride. Margaret sent them a dark look.

Lucy pulled a footstool closer to Madame Rainer and sat upon it. "Please show me how things should be done. I should like for everyone, especially Buck and his family, to be very happy and for the men and women of the city to be delighted also. I realize this is a monumental task, so I propose we decide who needs to be the most happy and work from there."

Madame Rainer flipped open her fancy notebook and licked the tip of her pencil. "Who first?" she asked with a knowing, charmed smile.

"Buck and then Mrs. Crenshaw," Lucy said.

Margaret, even with her arms still crossed in affront, smiled.

"Oh, and my cousin must walk me up the aisle. When you see him, you'll understand why. William is handsome and my very best friend," Lucy said, pausing as Madame Rainer wrote something down. "I love Mr. Lamont, don't you, Madame Rainer?"

The woman confessed, "I've never met him, dear."

"Well, you'll be at the wedding, won't you? And I'll introduce you to him. Of course you've met Doctor Crenshaw, and there's no older men who are better than him, but I'm partial."

"Now, have you picked a gown?" Madame Rainer asked, checking the time.

Buck interrupted, "We have, but I was foolish and rushed in where I shouldn't."

"Can you return it?" Madame Rainer asked.

Margaret sat taller, shaking off the notion. "It's to be designed by a dear friend whom I have great regard for."

Buck cleared his throat. "Everyone wears Worth's dresses now, Mama."

Margaret turned to Buck in shock. Lucy giggled.

Madame Rainer shook her head. "This is no laughing matter. *Worth* is the only way to do things right nowadays. If you are to have the wedding in July then you must be fitted at once."

Margaret burst into tears. "*Nowadays* dear friends who work their fingers to the bone attaching imported lace and things get trampled upon by *Worth's of New York!*"

"Mama, it's a Paris company," Buck muttered.

"Buck! It's rude to correct me!" Margaret cried. "And I don't care about Paris! We're Americans!"

"Mrs. Crenshaw, please don't worry," Lucy said. "Buck's first instincts were correct. I would never even consider returning the blue fabric that you and Buck liked!"

"Blue?!" Madame Rainer gasped.

"Yes, blue," Margaret replied with authority, wiping a tear away. "I believe in the traditional way. Blue means the love is true."

"Yes, yes, I know the old ways, dear Mrs. Crenshaw, but *white is for chosen right,* and everyone now wears white since Victoria ..."

"I like blue *and* I've chosen right—I know that already," Lucy said. "It's decided then. I *will* have my dress made by Mrs. Swindel."

Margaret poured Lucy some tea with extra sugar and handed it to her with a triumphant glance Madame Rainer's way.

"People will talk, but have it your way," Madame said, a twinkle of admiration for Lucy in her expression despite her superior knowledge of weddings.

"Lucy, should we at least consider the Worth styles?" Buck suggested.

"No, Buck. I won't hurt your mother, and I love the blue. You'll see," Lucy said.

Buck, unnerved by Lucy's rebuff, retreated to a corner of the room and flipped open a medical manual.

Margaret enjoyed most everything else. Madame Rainer suggested the most spectacular ideas to make best use of Buck's money. Graham looked on with disapproval.

The doctor whispered to his son. "You had better take the reins or you won't have money left for a shoe shine."

"If they know best, leave them to it," Buck grumbled. "I only want things done *right.*"

Graham leaned over the table between them. "Lucy will look grand whatever the color, and she liked your choice. Now be happy with a sensible girl."

"I don't want her laughed at," Buck whispered, but there had been a pause in the women's talk and all turned to him.

Madame Rainer scolded Buck. "Now, dear boy, I'm impressed by Lucy's strong mind, and *that* will overcome any ridiculous judgments about dress color."

Buck sighed.

"Now about cakes ..." Margaret interjected.

Lucy gave Buck a cautious look and said, "I should like to have strawberry shortcake made with my grandmother's preserves recipe."

"Oh, no, that won't do," Margaret said as if the most horribly distasteful thing had been uttered. "Buck is unable to eat strawberries—he breaks out in rash and his nose drips and oh, it's ghastly."

Lucy glanced at Buck and Graham both shifting uncomfortably in their seats.

"All right, then ..." Lucy continued.

Buck coughed, excusing himself. Margaret waited until the door was shut and spoke in a secretive way. "Lucy, he's not *really* sensitive to strawberries."

"What do you mean?" Lucy asked.

Graham came closer. "The boy was afraid of strawberries as a child and just so awkward about everything, you see. Buck suggested that he was quite unable to eat them and would itch all over. We decided it was best to go along with it—until this day."

"But it's a silly lie," Lucy said.

"Well, of course, but it's never been addressed," Graham explained. "Is it that important to you about the preserves?" he asked in a pained way. "Some things are better left unresolved."

"Really? I don't understand why," Lucy said, the color rising in her cheeks. "Is he sensitive to *many* things?"

"This bothers you?" Graham asked as if examining her for defects. "He does have a true reaction to peanuts, obviously."

"Sir, I didn't mean to anger you ..." Lucy began.

Margaret spoke up, "You don't anger us, Lucy, but you must remember that you've chosen to marry an odd fish—but one who is able to furnish you with the best of everything—including care for when your eyes go very bad. We heard that you irresponsibly ran off into the city and got lost."

"I was never lost," Lucy said. "I was helped by ..."

"Mr. Lamont. We know that and it turned out lucky, but it could have gone quite differently if a different sort of man carried you off."

"It was a simple adventure!"

"We don't think adventurers fit our family, dear," Margaret said.

Graham said, "We just mean to protect you from the uglier sides of the world."

"I've done that for myself all of my fourteen years."

Madame Rainer sat back. "How old are you, child?"

"Almost fifteen ..." Lucy stood now.

Margaret made her sit. "Yes, it is true that Lucy is a bit young—but you know Buck," Margaret whispered as if her son were a sad little monster, "and this is his best hope, we feel. Lucy is not after his money like the Manhattan girls."

"*I* am a Manhattan woman," Madame Rainer said, greatly insulted. "We have money of our own and more charms than ..."

Lucy stomped her foot. "Stop it!"

The women listened.

Buck wandered back into the room with hands in his pockets.

Lucy went to him at once. "Buck and I are going to be the happiest couple in New York and New Jersey and that's all that matters."

Buck smiled.

"I think I'm done for the day," Lucy said and led Buck out into the hallway.

"You're very feisty," he said, a little afraid of her.

"Buck, what other lies do you tell?"

"What do you mean?"

"Strawberries?"

"I've always been ..." he mumbled. "Well, I guess I've always ... I don't have anything to say."

"The truth for starters," Lucy scolded. "What other sensitivities do you have?"

He gave her a sideways look, and she giggled at him. "Well, I don't really like liver or veal ..."

"Then I promise not to cook any of it for you." Lucy laughed.

"Oh, you won't cook anyhow. We'll have help."

"Is there room enough at the cottage for that?"

He frowned. "Do you think perhaps the house too small and rundown for us? Because I was reconsidering and a townhouse in the city would be better. You seemed to love the museum."

"I loved *you* at the museum, silly. Don't dare take away our cozy cottage for a place in the city!"

"Okay, but will you even consider Worth's for the dress?"

"Will you consider eating strawberries?" Lucy replied with a nudge to his middle which he pretended to take badly.

"So I guess it's a blue dress and chocolate cake," Buck said.

She shook his hand roughly, jokingly.

"Now what shall we do for the rest of the day?" he asked.

"Sledding! Let's go sledding."

Buck shook his head, but his eyes looked for convincing. "I haven't been sledding on the hill in years."

"Then that's the perfect thing to do—before all the good snow melts."

"Hmm." Buck considered his age and the small bit of social standing he had and laughed. "It's a bully idea! I'll fetch our coats!"

Lucy smiled at his excitement. "Why don't you invite Nate and the girls, and we'll make a party of it?"

"That's a fine idea," he said, giving her a kiss and lingering a little before taking two stairs at a time to find his young siblings.

Lucy was soon discovered alone by Buck's parents and Madame Rainer on her way out.

"There you are, dear," Madame said. "Next week I'll arrange a tasting at the bakery in the city. Shall we go to tea as well?"

"Buck wants chocolate cake," Lucy said. "I'd love tea, but ..."

"I'll send my helper to escort you to my home in Murray Hill."

Lucy looked to Graham, who gave his approval. "I should like it very much, then, Madame. You've already been quite a lot of help to me."

Madame Rainer nodded at the Crenshaws and let herself out.

"Where's my son?" Margaret asked impatiently.

"Mrs. Crenshaw, please don't be angry at him. You must understand that he wants to protect you from any mean-spirited city folk."

"I refuse to be nice to any of them!" Margaret huffed. "Englewood is a respectable town! We hardly ever have dead horses lying about and not a single dirty orphan like you read about in all the New York papers. We are far too civilized for that, and I mean to make them know it!"

"Margaret ..." Graham began.

Lucy came in close to Margaret. "Let's do what's best for Buck. He tries very hard."

Margaret pulled back loftily. "I don't much like being lectured to by a young snippet."

"Margaret, Lucy is right," Graham said with force. "We both know Buck, and if things were left up to him he'd make a fine muddle of it."

Margaret nodded in agreement and softened.

"If Madame Ranger does something wrong, then the blame falls on her," Graham explained. "If things go well it will be assumed that you knew best."

Margaret smiled. "The doctor makes the occasional good point," she said to Lucy and gave her husband a squeeze. "But ... it's *Madame Rainer*, dear."

The young siblings came rumbling down the stairs now with Buck following.

"And what's all this?" Graham asked.

"We're going sledding, Father, with Buck and Lucy," Abby answered with a shy, happy smile.

Margaret laughed, but with meaning. "Surely the two of you will act maturely?"

Buck looked to Lucy who said, "You needn't worry, Mrs. Crenshaw. I will take good care of your brood."

"Graham, give them money for hot chocolate at the shop," Margaret ordered.

Once out in the chill air, they all spoke at once and laughed and threw snowballs and Buck hardly noticed but his cough was gone. A great many of his friends from childhood were there, and Buck asked himself why it had taken him so long to appreciate sledding. Of course it was far better with a girl, her arms wrapped around his waist and laughing in the musical voice Lucy had as they slid down the well-packed snow bank and tumbled off with no regard for dignity whatsoever.

For a moment Buck's mind wandered to paperwork left undone at the office (before Lucy's arrival home from New London he worked all day Saturdays and on a great many Sundays, though his parents frowned upon such activities on the Lord's Day).

Lucy pulled him back to the present with a tug, and he chased her up the hill with a snowball in hand, his little sister Maddie hanging off his back. At the top of the hill Lucy stood chatting with Abby, who looked up at her adoringly, and Buck forgot the snowball. Abby looked so much like Meg. Why had he never had time for the little ones in the family? Nate was off behind a tree with a few young lads, a cigar being passed around stealthily. Buck would tease his brother about it later. For now he'd wait like a puppy for his turn with the very popular young lady he was to marry.

He didn't have to wait long. Lucy strolled up and whispered to him. "You're so handsome out in the weather."

He stood taller, brushing snow from his shoulders with a grin. A few chums from Kursteiner's School for Boys spotted him and bounded up. "Buckie, good to see you out and about."

He laughed.

The men seemed taken aback by it. They all stood gawking.

"I don't think I know you boys," Lucy said.

Buck coughed. "Oh, I'm rude. This is Miss McCullough."

The men smiled.

"I've seen you at church, Miss McCullough. My little brother has a mad crush on you, I think," one man said good-humoredly.

Lucy blushed. "Do I know him?"

"No, I doubt it. He's got a private tutor—very sickly I'm afraid."

"Isn't that tragic then to only be let out for church!" Lucy said.

The men smiled as one, admiring the girl.

"Buck are you babysitting?" another asked.

"That's insulting!" Buck said.

The man, with pained expression, pointed to Buck's younger siblings frolicking a few yards away.

"Oh, yes. I suppose I am."

"Same old Buckie," the man laughed. "You should visit the field club sometime. It's jolly fun and most of the boys from our class come once in a while."

"I'm afraid work keeps me quite busy these days," Buck said, distancing himself as if a light had suddenly dimmed.

"All right, then," one of them said, feeling the chill. "I guess we'll be off. Nice to meet you, Miss McCullough."

Lucy smiled, following them with her eyes as they sauntered back to the sledding. "Buck, don't you like them?"

He scratched his chin. "They were Fred's friends. I want nothing to do with them."

"They seemed to like you ..."

"Are you surprised?"

"No." She stared at him. "Why would you think that?"

Buck's eyes were troubled and serious. "I should take you home now. I'm finished with sledding."

She didn't question why. The weather had changed, and she wasn't really dressed for sledding. Buck told the young ones to go home and walked Lucy up Demarest Avenue in silent contemplation.

"Buck, what's wrong?" Lucy finally asked before turning onto Tenafly Road.

"Oh, no. Everything is fine."

"My grandmother used to say that *fine* meant bad."

Buck laughed despite himself. He looked at Lucy and spoke cautiously. "I want to trust you with everything. No secrets."

Lucy smiled.

"I was a very cruel child," Buck confessed with extreme gravity.

Lucy burst out laughing. "Is this your news?"

"Well, I wasn't like you—so good and pure and all."

"I'm not so perfect—you'll see," Lucy said. "But won't it be fun to mess things up together?"

He looked at her as if she were a new species. "I hadn't hoped for messes, really."

She squeezed his arm and leaned her head on his fuzzy coat as they walked again. "Oh, Buck, we won't hope for mistakes, but we'll forgive them when they happen, won't we?"

Buck stiffened. "I, for one, never want to give in to mistakes—anymore."

"Then what will we laugh about?" Lucy asked. "You'll see, our messes won't be so painful as long as we have each other."

"I can't even imagine what you mean. I want things done *right,* and I'd hoped you'd want the same so we can finally get somewhere in this life."

"You're too serious—but I'm already exactly where I want to be." She hopped up to kiss him.

He glanced around and kissed her back. There on the porch stood Thankful wrapped in a shawl. The tears on her cheeks shined in the last of the day's sunlight.

"Oh, damn," Buck muttered now. "I knew I should have let her come this morning."

"Thankful wanted to come?" Lucy asked, her face paling.

"Yes, but I told her it was unnecessary. There would be enough women bickering already."

"Oh, that was a terrible blunder," Lucy moaned as they got close to the porch. She saw the resentment in Thankful's eyes at once. Lucy raced up and kissed her. "I would have welcomed you this morning. Buck was foolish not to tell me you hoped to come. I'm so sorry and need your help in the worst way!"

Thankful gave Buck a triumphant, angry look while embracing Lucy. "Come inside now, darling. It's cold out."

Lucy pulled away and went back to Buck. "When shall I see you again?"

"I don't know," he said, insulted. "I suppose I'll see you at church with all the other boys."

She frowned. "I don't like babies, Buck. Thank you for the sledding, and I hope you are in better spirits whenever I meet you next."

He stood transfixed by her as she looked back once with a scolding expression before going inside with Thankful. What had just happened? Hadn't he tried his best to avoid controversy and upset? *Women are impossible*, he grumbled to himself, just now running the wedding numbers in his head. The dress and meal and flowers—not to mention the new idea he had about selling the little cottage for the grand Blauvelt mansion a few towns away confirmed the necessity of greater disposable income. *Well*, he thought, *I suppose I can run home and still get in a few hours of work.*

# Chapter Twenty-One

William sat glum and uncomfortable in the stiff-backed chair by the fire in the parlor doing battle against a tattered book on beekeeping. He had never fully recovered from the head injury in his youth and always struggled to stay focused when reading scientific material. Lucy pushed the ottoman out of its assigned location a little rebelliously and sat at her cousin's knees.

"Is it a good book, Willy?"

He put the book aside. "It's too dull for my taste. How was your day?" He glanced up at Thankful who stood with arms folded in the doorway.

"Parts of it were pleasant enough," Lucy began but turned to Thankful. "Won't you sit with us so I can have your opinions too?"

Thankful sighed as if put upon but went over and sat next to William.

"Buck brought in a lady from the city who knows all and sundry about weddings," Lucy informed them, checking for reaction.

"He *did*?" Thankful seemed jealous or insulted or both.

"Buck said it would put your mother at ease."

Thankful smiled a tiny smile. "That was probably wise, though I should have been there—to help you."

"Of course!" Lucy said. "William, I hope you don't mind that I insisted you walk with me up the aisle."

William's face lit in quiet satisfaction. "I don't mind."

"Good. Because I don't care a fig about much else. I want Buck and you both to have a splendid time and that's all. Your mother stood her ground over my dress, and I'm happy about it. I love the blue and the lace. What color was your dress, Thankful?"

Thankful blushed and looked toward the fire a moment. "Well, we did everything in such a hurry—I wish—well, it was a lovely dress."

"It suited her perfectly," William said.

"Yes," Thankful added, "but it was yellow and my mother, being the beast she is, pointed out an old saying ..."

"A *foolish* old saying," William interrupted gruffly, poking the fire now. "Yellow ashamed of her fellow."

Thankful blushed again. "Stupid, really. Mama gives me a headache."

William laughed, but it had a dangerous edge Lucy hadn't heard since when he still drank. "Yes, and because of the farm and such we had the wedding on a *Saturday*."

"No luck at all, Mama says, if you marry on a Saturday," Thankful said.

Lucy tried to make light. "Oh, that's silly. Who believes such things?"

They all laughed uncomfortably.

Thankful stood. "Well, it was only that my mother shouldn't have said it all on my wedding day, don't you agree? If Mama had mentioned the yellow when I first showed her the dress I might have reconsidered, but she said nothing about it until it was too late, and now the idea is always there."

"Is it?" William asked, his soft eyes lit by the fire and his set jaw working a little.

"Well, in a way," Thankful said, but only glanced at him before turning to Lucy again. "I mean she placed that small doubt, and I think it unkind."

"Of course it's unkind, but you think about it *often*?" William interrogated now.

"Stop it. It's just that mean words stay with a person long after they're said."

He scratched his head. His hair needed washing and a decent cut in town, but he refused to have it done by a professional and insisted Thankful trim it as his mother had done. He picked up the bee book as if he were going to read it, then tossed it onto the table.

"Are your eyes tired, Willy? I'll read it for you a little," Lucy offered, sensing a mood she'd seen in William so many times before.

"No, Lucy, save your sight for seeing things clearly," he said, bitterly. His fingers, with still some dirt beneath the nails, clutched the armrests. "Watch out for the mistakes."

Thankful huffed. "Willy, I hate how you get peevish."

"I hate how you spoil even the best memories," William said. He pushed aside the ottoman Lucy sat upon a little roughly and walked out of the house, taking a light jacket from the new coatrack in the hall.

Lucy stared at the door long after it slammed, afraid to meet Thankful's eyes—afraid she'd be made to feel the blame.

But Thankful sat again. "Don't worry. He'll be back. He always comes back."

"Maybe he won't sometime."

Thankful's eyes reflected a hint of worry. She patted Lucy's head maternally. "We do love each other. You'll understand how things are with my brother soon enough. Men do whatever they like. I'm beginning to hate it."

Lucy said nothing. Hadn't Buck behaved very queerly this evening? "Probably there was no good reason to let Willy know your feelings about the yellow dress."

"Couples should be honest about everything, Lulu."

"Perhaps little things should just go unsaid so as not to hurt feelings."

"I would have expected more honesty from you. Buck hates a liar—though he's not above deception himself. Never forget that he's Fred's twin. I love him dearly, but I wouldn't trust Buck completely. Even if he tries very hard, he can't escape being male and a patriarch."

"A what?"

Thankful pulled out a magazine from under a pile of novels. "Read this tonight."

"I don't like reading articles," Lucy replied, sensing something not quite right about the exchange. "I'd rather sort things out with Buck on my own."

"Are you and my brother having problems so soon?" Thankful asked eagerly.

"No." Lucy stood, eyeing the door. "Thankful, I'm afraid of your bitterness. I'm sorry, but I don't want it to poison my opinion of Buck."

Thankful shoved the magazine under the books again and a few of them tumbled to the floor. "Very well. I was hoping I could count you as a real friend who might take the time to understand all the feelings bubbling up inside of me. I have no one to talk to, you understand. Everyone stands in judgment!"

Lucy went to her at once. "Forgive me. I *will* be your friend. But we mustn't speak badly about Buck. I won't allow it."

Thankful simpered and sat again. "But I'm jealous of the two of you. Buck will do everything right, and we did everything wrong. Now all Willy and I do is fight!"

"I'd prefer a small wedding, Thankful, really I would! Think how silly I'll feel at the Christ Church."

Thankful's perfect mouth opened just a little. "The Christ's Church? However did Buck manage it?"

"I suppose he just asked someone."

"You silly girl! Only the very best people of New York marry there!"

Lucy took a moment to think about it. "Then how much *more* foolish I'll feel!"

"Christ Church ... I just can't make myself believe ... and will you wear your spectacles even there?" Thankful asked, wringing her hands. "Oh, and you must insist that William buy himself a properly tailored frock! He won't listen to me, but it would be mortifying for all of us if William went as he always goes like a western ruffian returned from a bank robbery."

Lucy sat prim and stiff. "William will outshine all the wealthy bankers. I can assure you of that!" She hadn't considered William's style, but now made up her mind to have him dressed even better than Buck if necessary. William had made a big mistake marrying his sweetheart. Thankful had lost every ounce of the plucky, happy girl she had once been. She was beautiful still, but in a defiant, haughty way that chilled Lucy to any idea of real friendship.

If only the wedding were tomorrow! Lucy would never come back to Tenafly Road. And there was the worst of it! Thankful had managed to spoil Lucy's home place. Less than a year had passed since her aunt and uncle died and every last memory had been sold off or redone in such a striving, elaborate way that Lucy was repulsed by it now.

Would Buck turn sour upon marriage? Would she meet Willy secretly behind the peach trees on the Adriance farm to exchange horror stories about the Crenshaws?

A knock came at the door. Lucy ran to it wanting to escape Thankful's envious complaining. Buck peeked in the window beside the door sheepishly and with some trepidation Lucy turned the knob with a sigh.

"Luce, won't you come on the porch a moment?"

She hesitated but still preferred Buck's company to Thankful's. Pulling a wrap around her shoulders, she joined him under the gaslight in slippered feet.

"Luce," Buck began, "I acted like a baby and ungentlemanly too. I didn't like that I'd made a mistake in your eyes. And it annoyed me that you took Thankful's side."

"Buck, I'm not sure we should marry at Christ Church."

"What? Of course we should. It's a big thing!"

"I don't want our wedding to be a show for people I don't care about."

"But Lucy—you don't understand. It's a big thing for *me*. For once I have something so special." Buck touched her face with his characteristic reserve.

"Do you mean me?" she asked, warming to his clumsy tenderness.

"Of course!" He kissed her.

"And what about William?"

Buck cocked his head. "What about him?"

"He'll look dashing when he gives me away."

He still looked confused. "Okay."

"Does William look very much like a bank robber from the West?" Lucy asked.

"I don't know what you're talking about."

Lucy hugged him and laughed. "So you don't mind what suit he wears to our wedding?"

"I hadn't thought about it."

"You hadn't?" Lucy laughed. "That's bully, then. I'm sure we'll find him something that suits the ceremony."

Buck glanced into the house and whispered, "If it's about the money we can arrange something—though it will have to be done on the sly to prevent William's pride from being hurt."

She wished he hadn't said sly, but she understood and kissed him. "Promise you won't turn jealous."

"Who would I be jealous of?" Buck asked, beginning to suspect a Crenshaw woman behind these questions. "Please hang on a bit longer. Soon we'll be in our own home on the hill or somewhere else and we won't have to trouble ourselves with family."

"What do you mean by *somewhere else*?"

"There's a large house—big enough for buckets of children in River Edge near Grandmother Martha's house."

"Buck," Lucy said, her chin set. "We decided upon the cottage, and that's where I want to live."

"But this mansion ..."

"A mansion?" Lucy cried. "What's so cozy about a mansion? I don't want to live so far away from Englewood, and you promised we'd start visiting Grandma at the old folks' home, and Willy—I can't leave him here all by himself."

"He's got Thankful ..." Buck noted Lucy's doubt as she turned her eyes away for a moment, wrapping her shawl tighter.

"You must promise me that in no way are you embarrassed of me or my kin," Lucy said. "You must be certain that there will never be a time that my eyes or Willy or anything makes you wish you'd never married me."

"Lucy, I have perfect vision, if nothing else, and who was it that stood for me all of those many years ago at Christmas? And who is the only one I feel needs to know every bit of truth? I'd be blind not to see how even the very best of men admire you. I will do whatever you say. If you still want the cottage then ..."

"You do remember that it was you who picked it out without any guidance from me."

"Do you resent it? I would understand," he said, seizing upon her words. Maybe she'd still be turned to the mansion.

"No, but I only question why you bought it in the first place if you think it something so easy to cast off."

He stood back and admired her, thinking over what she'd said. "I'm never impetuous, Luce. I would never cast you off. And the cottage ... it has meaning for me. My father owned it and never wanted to sell, but my mother hated it and insisted they buy the house on Chestnut."

"I see."

"Yes, so ... it seems silly now, I guess, but I wonder if my father—and mother—would have been happier there."

Lucy smiled and took his hands, the fake one smooth and cold. "Dear Buck, we will be almost painfully happy there. I just know it."

"Then I won't mention the Blauvelt mansion again—though it does have a pretty flower garden, and we could plant the smelly flowers you like."

Lucy laughed. "The cottage, Buck."

He kissed her and, in the half-light his face looked just as it always had before the rough times of early adulthood, and he was quite handsome. His violet eyes reflected the light and the usual intensity of his manner softened fleetingly when she kissed him again.

Underneath it all the Crenshaws are silly romantics, Lucy thought in happy satisfaction. Realists are terribly dull.

# Chapter Twenty-Two

Spring came on early in Englewood, and the tulips and narcissus poked through the warming earth at the Adriance farm. Mr. Adriance sat in the sunshine hoping to cure the chill he'd gotten back in February. As William weeded his wife's old garden with care, Adriance sighed.

William got to his feet. "Mr. Adriance, would you like me to make you tea or something?" he asked, patting the dirt from his hands on his trousers.

"Sit with me a minute," Adriance said.

William complied. The odor of sweat and dirt brought Adriance to memories of his own youthful vitality.

"Sir?" William waited for words.

"Willy, you're a good man."

William pulled his cap lower over his eyes. "Thank you, sir."

"Are you happy here?"

William looked hurt. "Of course."

"I've never once regretted giving this all over to you. You've done a fine job. Your parents would be proud."

"Mr. Adriance, that means a lot," William said but sensed something awkward working its way out of the old man.

"Willy, some folks consider working with their hands dirty, but we know better, don't we?"

"Sir, if you're huffed about the new gloves I'm wearing ... Thankful got them for me ... so ..."

Adriance chuckled, hiding his annoyance. "Why would I care about gloves? What I care about is that I'm not long for this world, and I worry that you may be tempted to give this all up to make peace with your wife."

"You have no right to say anything about Thankful ..." William began. He scratched his head and wiped his nose on his sleeve before continuing. "Sir, I'm sorry, I ..."

"You can speak plain to me—we're equals." Adriance said but noted William's surprise at the appraisal. "Son, I fear your lack of confidence will land you in trouble."

"Sir, I haven't got anything to say."

Adriance shook his head. "Of course, not. You're your father's son." He looked out upon the carefully tended beds with a wistful smile. "William, some women are never satisfied, but you can't let them spoil things."

"Sir, one day Thankful will appreciate ..." William's words trailed off as he tried to imagine Thankful appreciating anything.

"I hope Thankful realizes she has a lot on Tenafly Road with you," Adriance said, "but I'm already proud of you."

William looked toward the road with a smile. "Sir, I won't ever give your property over."

"Remember what we talked about last week," Adriance urged. "Money management, Willy."

"Yes, I intend to put my foot down, sir."

"Yes, of course you do," Adriance replied, running his bony fingers over his bald skull.

William thought about the expensive suit Thankful had just convinced him to buy for Lucy's wedding. He already owned a suit, but when he had said that to Thankful she had burst into tears of shame. He hoped the new suit might distract his wife from the constant prattling on about the Christ Church.

"How's your little cousin finding the Crenshaws these days?" Adriance asked.

"Bully, I guess. Buck got Lucy a tutor so I never have any time with her. The tutor could come just as easily to Tenafly Road as Chestnut. In fact Lucy tells me the lady lives on Knickerbocker Road, so ..." William stopped what he considered rambling talk, but Adriance looked eager for more so he continued. "And Lucy's even learning the piano with Mrs. Crenshaw—I hope all of it doesn't change her."

"You miss her?"

"A little. Yes," William confessed as if this were a deep revelation. "Thankful does her hair so old—I wonder does she do it on purpose to make Lucy look foolish, but no one seems to notice so maybe I'm just being ..."

"A good brother." Adriance laughed. "I hear they'll be taking up residence at the old gingerbread-and-stone cottage."

"Really?" William was stung that he'd been kept ignorant of important news.

"I only know because Mr. Neigh is a friend," Adriance said, "and I was surprised that Buck convinced him into the old folks' home."

"Oh, I bet Buck strong-armed him some way—the rat!" William let slip.

"More like buried my friend in more cash than he could swim out from under. And he was lonely after his wife passed on, I hear," Adriance said. "How's your grandmother doing?"

William stood to go back to work. "I'm afraid I've been too busy to visit her."

Adriance shook his head. "Come now, Willy. Sundays are free and it would take but an hour to check in on her."

"I hate lecturing, sir," William replied with more anger than intended. Once after a visit to the old folks' home William had ventured to suggest that he and Thankful were set enough to bring Sarah back to her home, but Thankful raged at the idea of the fancy bedroom on the first floor being dismantled and given back to its original owner.

"Haven't we sunk a small fortune into that sleigh bed, Willy?" she'd cried. "And Sarah is so far gone! Imagine her wandering off half-dressed and raving mad like the banshees one sees in awful theater productions! Why, just this week the town inspector asked if we might consider moving that small bit of vegetable gardening out of street view and plant a nice lawn. Can you imagine Sarah planting willy-nilly in the front?"

William couldn't put to words all that swirled in his head at the time, and Thankful's argument had seemed insurmountable. "But Grandmother was the one person who really took time for me as a child ... when I was beaten by the boys at Kursteiner's that first year, she gave me my uncle's coat."

"Young boys shouldn't be coddled by their grandmothers. If we ever were to have a son I ..." but Thankful had stopped herself, obviously not wanting another run-in about babies. "Sarah is safer at the home though I do admit the place isn't the least bit cozy and has a very odd odor."

William's head hurt as he reflected upon her words, which all sounded very sensible. "I guess I've never had peace about tricking Grandmother into going."

"Convincing, William," Thankful had said. "She's there for her safety and it's a bit selfish of you to expect her to come and go now that she's settled."

"But love and safety seem two very different things to me ..."

"William, I love you for being so sentimental," Thankful said, giving him a rare embrace.

When he made art Thankful seemed to admire his sensitivity, but now he sensed that she found him thick and slow. And there was that opposite thing that reared its head too—an unquenchable need in Thankful to be first in his life no matter the hurt it might bring to others.

"You should go through those cobwebbed paintings in the attic before we get rid of them. Make Sarah's room at the home more inviting."

"Would you come with me Sunday to hang them?" he'd asked edgily.

Thankful crossed her arms in hurt. "But Sundays are for us! You promised! I allow for you to feed the blessed chickens and sheep on Sunday already!"

This conversation had been months ago and lately things had changed in a way William felt more uneasy about. Just then Thankful hailed the two farmers from the street as she passed in the old McCullough buggy. William waved half-heartedly and strode up, noting that if he hadn't she'd have continued on down the road. Thankful waited for him to help her down as if this proved some affection between them. William pretended not to notice and lit a cigarette instead.

"Aren't you late for the shop?" he asked curtly.

Thankful seemed surprised at his cool demeanor but she shouldn't be, he thought.

"Well, I was reading and planning for my meeting tonight—you hadn't forgotten, had you?" Thankful asked as she hopped down.

"How could I? It's all I hear about," he grumbled, dusting pollen off a quaint birdhouse handmade by Adriance's wife.

"I didn't imagine you ever listened," Thankful quipped—almost happily.

William glanced her way, a little surprised. "Well, I guess you can be on your way then."

"What will you do tonight, Willy?" she asked, coming up close enough for him to smell her fragrance. Out of doors there were no worries about affection's consequences.

"I'll work here with the chickens and go for a meal in town for a change."

"You never take *me* for a meal," Thankful noted with emotion. "Josephine has already planned a steak."

"Well, I don't want a steak."

"Mr. Adriance, William is wasting his hard earned money by refusing a steak already set out. What do you think of that?"

"I think William can fight his own battles," Adriance replied before going indoors.

"You are being very spiteful about tonight!" Thankful shouted. "I knew you were against suffrage!"

"I couldn't give a damn about voting. I don't vote."

"You are excruciatingly uninformed about politics. It's a scandal!" Thankful shouted.

"You are uninformed about men!" William replied, turning away and brushing Thankful off when she tried to hold him there.

"William you are a patriarch of the worst sort! You have no respect for new ideas and women."

William laughed. "What?"

"Have you ever heard of Victoria Woodhull?"

"Who?"

"See, you know nothing about women! Or the news even! It's infuriating."

"When would I have time to read the papers with you over my shoulder every blasted minute?"

"William, do you really mean that? Do you want me to leave you alone?" Thankful cried. "Then fine, you have tonight all to yourself!"

He glanced back toward the house to see if Adriance was watching.

"Go on, William, get back to your important work!" Thankful huffed as she climbed back into the carriage.

# Chapter Twenty-Three

Lucy let herself in through the kitchen, hoping to go undetected past the parlor where she expected to find Thankful fussing about some small thing William or Josephine hadn't done quite right, but she found the parlor empty and fireless. Had something momentous happened while she took lessons up the hill?

Homecomings lately held about as much charm as getting teeth pulled. A simple glass of milk in the kitchen at bedtime became a trial. Had Lucy placed the glass on the wrong spot at the counter? William, when home, may as well not have been. Thankful stood guard at his cage. Lucy trudged up to her room, content to slip beneath the covers of her bed with no incident, but found William sitting in one of his father's old armchairs placed before her window where it had been for years until banished to the attic.

"Well, Lucy, I don't care what Thankful says. This is a good chair, and it should stay here in this room like always," he said before glancing out the window for Thankful.

Lucy said nothing as she sat on the bed.

"I hope you're not angry at me for being in here ..." William said, leaning forward.

Lucy shook her head. "It's your house, Willy."

"Are you still huffed about that?"

"No. Not every girl gets angry over ridiculous things," she snapped.

William ran his suntanned hands over the ragged edge of the chair's arm. "Lucy, what am I doing wrong with Thankful?" He glanced up hopelessly then back toward the window.

"You're just too good for her."

He stretched out in the comfortable chair. "Lying doesn't suit you. You had better quit it. I keep remembering our wedding. I see everything I did wrong now, but at the time ..."

Lucy lay upon her pillow, staring at the ceiling and impatient for sleep. "Willy, must you always play the fool?" She turned on her side. Her words surprised and hurt her cousin, but she could not refrain from speaking them. "She's bitter and mean."

"And I've made her that way."

"How's that?"

"She loved me a long time ago before I drank. If I hadn't, nothing bad would have happened to her."

"Thankful ran out west on her own. You promised her nothing. I used to feel a little sorry for her, but now I'm sure that her suitor out in Arizona got the best deal."

"Lucy, you take that back! Have you been infected by the Crenshaws with all this study on the hill?"

"You mustn't take all the blame for everything always!"

"I take what's due me, Lucy. You're too young to understand."

"No I'm not!"

"You weren't there for the wedding ..." William said and held up his hand to stop Lucy from responding. "And yes, that was my first mistake. I imagined I could navigate a small wedding on my own at least. I was the one who bought her the Worth dress—have you heard of them?"

Lucy gasped.

"Her mother spoilt it."

"But Willy, those dresses are far too expensive."

"Yes, it came at a dear price, but it was well worth it to get Thankful out from under Margaret's constant interference."

She cringed. "All mothers want to help their daughters pick a gown."

"But Thankful complained so much about her mother's meddling ..."

"But she didn't really mean it."

He seemed shocked and confused at her reaction. "Then why say it?"

Lucy sighed.

"And Thankful said she couldn't bear a reception at Doctor Crenshaw's club," William continued, "though I would have liked to see what all the fuss is over it. I could have made more business for the farm mingling with the nabobs."

Lucy imagined poor William standing like a hair out of place in the club she'd been taken to for lunch with the doctor only last week. Some club members even frowned upon Doctor Crenshaw for bringing in a girl.

"So I arranged an arbor covered with roses—or what was left of them at that time of year to take pictures beneath, and it was pretty until the weather gave out, and we had to skedaddle under the roof of Adriance's barn. Thankful laughed as if it were all a lark, and I imagined we had fun—but she sees it so differently now. I'm flummoxed."

"If only your parents were still alive," Lucy said, wiping a tear at the idea of Willy managing the Crenshaws on his own. "But the ceremony must have been lovely. Weddings always are."

William picked at a hang nail. "Well, that's the thing that bothers me most. We were too late for setting up a time at the big church, and I hoped it would make me feel that Mother and Papa were with me if we had the ceremony at their chapel. It's a charming building—I used to paint it often—and Thankful always admired those paintings."

"But now the chapel's been moved to the cemetery," she said.

"Yes, but on a fine fall day the trees are bright with red leaves, and it's so quiet there. It's an almost sublime location."

Lucy burst into laughter. "Oh, Willy, marrying at a cemetery! Oh, but I love you for it. You told Thankful why you wanted it there, I assume."

"It seemed an obvious thing." He thought a moment and laughed too. "But I guess it wasn't." His eyes became grave. "Lucy, I worry that I'll never be able to conform to the world here in Englewood. I so desperately crave a drink ..."

"No, Willy. You don't. It won't help and you know it. I'd rather you run away and escape us all than have you as you were."

"I wouldn't have any place to go, anyway," William said. "And I do really like the chickens and all. They're comforting to me."

Lucy wouldn't mind a few chicks scratching about in the garden, but Buck wouldn't approve (if he was anything like his sister).

In a few months Lucy would be married to Buck whom she had known forever, but not really at all. She had always followed news of Buck's exploits as closely as she could, but the Crenshaws spoke their own language. It had always been clear that the family had favorites and that even now when it should be obvious that Buck was the only moral member of the family—no one seemed all that impressed. Even Nathan smoked and drank behind the scenes, and, while Abby and Maddie were adorable, they showed all the signs of snobbishness and conniving as Margaret and Thankful.

Comparisons had been a steady diet at the house on Tenafly Road—the people on the hill with their perfect marriages and families seemed to be further away than their physical distance. But having so much freedom of movement as a child allowed Lucy an escape from the fiction of perfection. Many marriage difficulties played out as she hid beneath parlor windows in town at dusk when she and her mates played manhunt.

The women at the shops by day who had seemed so nice often had bitter tongues on an evening with the windows open in early spring. And how many times when sneaking off to the river did Lucy witness a well-dressed man skirting the whitewashed buildings in Undercliff, where the low women were rumored to live? These things she kept to herself, imagining herself noble for not turning into a sinful gossip.

"Where is Thankful?" Lucy asked William.

"A meeting—she's formed a group of women to tear us men down," he said with an air of disdain. He saw a concerned look cross his cousin's face before she turned to a button on her dress that needed replacing. "You don't approve?"

She met his eyes reluctantly. "I'm not sure."

"But you see Thankful's not happy with me, don't you?"

"I don't understand her. She's made a lot of mistakes, and you still keep her. She hardly seems grateful."

He laughed. "I don't want her gratitude. I've made a few terrible blunders myself."

"Yes, but you were drunk."

He scratched his head. "Thankful is nothing like my mother—that's why I like her." Lucy stared.

"Mother did her best, but Thankful—she's strong. I admire her for that."

Just then the door slammed in the kitchen, and they listened to Thankful make her way up the stairs wondering how they would find her spirits. Thankful beamed at them when she threw open the door and jumped upon the bed beside Lucy.

"The meeting was a smashing success!" she gushed, holding her hands to her chest in delight. "The Lamont girls came and the Fosters and the Van Briskies even! The air was filled with high-minded talk, and I felt as if I'd been rescued from a parched desert! And they even liked a poem I'd written ..."

William cocked his head a little. "You write poetry?"

Thankful blushed guiltily. "Well, I keep a journal—I used to write in it before we were married. It was at the shop and we were discussing the great women authors and poets ..."

"Are there any?" William asked, cuttingly.

Thankful would not have her mood spoiled and Lucy, at least, was grateful, because if William and Thankful fought here she would have no place to sleep.

"William, I wouldn't expect you to have read any novels, being so busy with *other* things. But anyway, I am a success for this moment, and you should be happy for me."

"Should I be? How will it affect me?" he asked warily.

Thankful raised her chin with pride. "You've gotten what you've wanted in farming, and now finally I have a chance at success."

"At doing a women's meeting?"

"Yes! And more, though as a man you don't understand. I knew more about the women's suffrage movement than all the other girls, and I could tell that they were a little in awe of me. I'm glad I wore this smart new suit jacket. It was much admired—and you said it was too modern."

William laughed before rising from his chair theatrically to highlight the awkwardness of it being in the room.

Thankful didn't even notice. "One day you'll find that women are equal to men."

"I'd always thought them superior until very recently," he said, adjusting the chair a tad.

Lucy groaned.

Thankful stood now and put hands on hips. "William, it's utterly ridiculous for you to sneak in that old chair when we could have discussed it like two adults."

"Really?" William replied in triumph—he'd gotten her to notice the chair.

Lucy lay back, rolling her eyes at their dramatics.

William spoke again. "Well, I want the chair right here."

"Fine then. If Lucy doesn't mind the musty cigar smell. Do as you like. I intend to do the same," Thankful said.

"What does that mean?" William asked a bit timidly, tucking his hair behind his ear.

"I will not become your mother waiting around in this dark house for you to come home. I won't dote on you anymore."

"You dote on me?" William laughed looking to Lucy for support.

Lucy rolled over toward the wall.

"Yes, and you don't even notice my efforts! From now on you may tell Josephine if you want a steak or not."

"Is this about the steaks?" William asked, his voice rising. "I came home and ate those blasted steaks!"

"Well," Thankful took a breath. "That's fine, but I intend to write and paint and organize for women from now on, so don't depend upon me being here when you get home from your sheep and chicken work."

"I don't understand ... are you leaving me?"

"What?" she asked, guilty for the occasional thoughts of doing just that and seeing how she would hurt him if she ever did leave. For a moment she imagined herself heroic and generous for staying with him. "Of course I wouldn't leave you," she said with little enthusiasm.

William's anger swelled to bursting. "I rescued you from your immoral behavior, and this is what I get!"

"How dare you! You're nothing more than a washed-up painter and drunkard!"

Lucy sat bolt upright. "Thankful, take that back!"

William said in a small voice, "She can't."

Thankful's eyes got big and unleashed a torrent of emotion. She made to kneel at William's feet, but he dragged her to standing.

"Stop it," he said, softly now. "I'm sorry I brought up your past. I had no right."

"Willy, I'm so terribly unhappy. I'm sorry," Thankful cried. "And I don't want to lie to you anymore because I do love you—but I don't want any children—ever. If you make me, I will resent you forever, just like you resented me when I insisted you paint!"

William's disappointment hung in the air as she sobbed with her shoulders hung in misery.

"Thankful, let's not talk about that so soon after Meg's death. I pressured you."

She shook her head adamantly and took him by the shoulders. "No, Willy, never. I won't have children." She drew herself up, her chin shaking and her eyes still streaming.

"You may sleep in the attic tonight! I couldn't bear to have you near me! I thought I married my best friend and a man, but all you want to do is irresponsibly make babies and play with foolish farm animals!"

"Those farm animals pay for your luxuries!"

"You call this life luxurious?"

"*Yes*! We are in debt to all and sundry over this bed and that dress and every stupid little thing!"

Thankful counted in her head all the expensive hair combs and petticoats and grimly realized that even at the Crenshaw home money was not squandered in the way she had demanded of William here, but her unhappiness led her to say, "So, you see, that we cannot afford a child."

"A child costs nothing!" William said.

"Nothing to you if I die in childbirth! Father certainly wouldn't charge you for his services!" Thankful cried. She turned to Lucy on the bed. "And you fill my brother with ideas about twelve children! Ha! What would you know about caring for little ones being the young and spoiled little sister to everyone! You'll see when everyone is crying and wet or when one dies—tell her, Willy, how you still sometimes talk about your little sister in your sleep! There's already too many people in this world and what you and Buck talk about doing is disgusting to me when there's starving children in Manhattan!"

"You care about children in Manhattan?" Lucy asked. Her rare anger aroused now for William's sake. "How dare you send William to his room!"

William spoke for himself. "Lucy shouldn't be the victim of your bitterness, Thankful. And neither should I. You moved here willingly. You knew I was farming."

"You knew I wanted nothing to do with children," Thankful shot back.

"Yes, I guess we are both disappointed then."

"Are you asking *me* to leave?" Thankful asked.

"No. I wouldn't want for people to talk—for your sake," he said in a tone so cold and dead that it frightened Lucy.

Lucy slipped from the bed. "Thankful, leave my room."

Thankful, outnumbered, pushed past William and ran down the stairs to their bedroom, slamming the door behind her. The muffled cries could still be heard through the floorboards.

"Willy, what will you do now?"

"The same as always."

"You won't drink, will you?"

"No," he said. "Marriage isn't all that important after all. I mean, maybe it's okay to just share a house and go about your business. I don't have the patience any longer for the fighting. Let her have her clubs and interests, and I'll get mine back."

"Leave Thankful and adopt a poor orphan. I'd help you care for it."

He smiled an awful, false smile of supreme sadness. "No. It's not the same, is it? You'll see when you have your own, I bet."

"Buck and I won't have so many. It's ... irresponsible, I suppose ..."

"Lucy, I'm counting on being an uncle now so do as you like."

# Chapter Twenty-Four

At the banking establishment of Turner & Lamont, Buck at first kept to himself behind his desk at the back of the cavernous brownstone office. The cousins, a boisterous lot of young men with growing client lists of fledgling mineral magnates, grew curious about this figuring and re-figuring outsider with the unusual eyes who worked well past lamp lighting after the cousins had long since left for the many attractions of Manhattan night life.

Buck noted the initial sneers of disapproval from the cousins. While Mr. Lamont and Mr. Turner held equal stature at the bank, it was whispered (mainly by the women in the family) that Mr. Turner had been surprisingly reckless letting in an outsider. Even Mr. Lamont had quietly looked askance at the new hire when there were so many other young men from the city with better resumes and close relations.

Buck's first few endeavors brought in small though impressive entrepreneurs from good families with high moral character whose businesses were modestly rising just beneath the sight lines. These businesses would afford the bank quiet and respectable profits in just a few short months, but Mr. Lamont had, as a matter of principle, not come into Buck's small, dark area to congratulate him. Buck occasionally caught Lamont glimpsing over at him when ending a droll joke with a silly pun to the cousins, who were not doing nearly as well as Buck.

Buck didn't mind. Even his appearance was different from the cousins and uncles with their thick, blond hair and heavy, healthy, athletic frames. Buck remained weedy and, except for one other fellow, he was the only man amongst them who had darkish hair. No one had violet eyes or visible scars.

The hum of conversation and occasional laughter served only as a backdrop to Buck's figuring and planning, his note writing, and assessing the value of merchants who wanted this house to be their banking home. Unlike the cousins, he had no pedigree, no former knowledge, and no relationships with the men of commerce who visited the quiet brownstone. While this wasn't the richest banking house in lower Manhattan, it was one of the most respected and better for being so impeccably discreet.

He hardly ever considered how odd it was that he had gotten this opportunity because Fred had married the girl Buck had loved at West Point. He hardly thought about the odd times at Middlemay or the silliness of his conversion out west. He considered himself a more mature Christian now. The wide-eyed new convert had adjusted to the realities of life here in the city, where new worlds opened to him—restaurants bustling with exceptional people, museums with art so unlike the gaudy still-life paintings at home, and a sense that slowing down for even a moment was the greatest sin.

The cousins attended their churches on Sundays and met for chess club on Thursday evenings with cigars from Cuba and rugs gotten from dealers who specialized in luxurious oriental furnishings.

With each passing success, the cousins grew more interested in this odd fish, Buck Crenshaw, who wore a perfectly tailored uniform of genteel respectability. There were rumors about his scars and a story about his rescuing two beautiful ladies from Indians. No one liked to ask about his exploits, but each wrestled with feelings of admiration (for his quiet heroism) and a masculine pride that caused them to judge this new outsider with a mix of superiority and contempt.

The cousins hardly identified with Rose Turner's side of the family because there had been a great falling out at a wedding years ago over a spill of brandy and a ruined harpsichord. Rose's mother had been a spiteful woman who did all she could to keep her daughter from the Turner and Lamont boys.

The *cousins* considered it ill-form not to invite Buck along on their great adventures in autumn. It was the year of the yacht and everyone's family had one—though nothing on the scale of J. P. Morgan's *Corsair*! So Buck went yachting—often recalling the apostles on stormy water. None of the cousins knew that Buck dreaded the sea. Life was rudderless enough, but money needed to be made so he sailed with the moneymakers while keeping a wary eye on the changeable clouds.

Buck's salary, by the cousins' standards, was quite low—though again he hardly thought about such things. But this was a moral bank run by a moral family, and Mr. Turner and Mr. Lamont one day decided to reward him, after he landed a client of the highest caliber, with a generous (yet discreet) bonus. The cousins must not be told in order to avoid hard feelings.

Mr. Turner was a lonely old man now with his wife and daughter gone. Only once had Rose mentioned that Buck had first asked for her hand in a silly way years ago, but Mr. Turner romanticized the event and half imagined that Buck was his true—at least better— son-in-law, though he kept a distance from Buck for Buck's sake. Things would not go well for Buck if the others thought he received a certain sympathy from the old man.

And so most of the cousins found it not that horrible a thing to take the ugly pup sailing. Buck's quiet reticence won their respect as well. How awful it was to be around the striving social climbers of the day! Fairly quickly they'd forgotten that Buck had come from New Jersey to join their clan.

Lucy's visit had made a profound impression on the uncles. Mr. Lamont's ferry ride over the Hudson with the young girl had turned the man's heart completely. At church the next week, Lucy had run to Mr. Lamont as if a dear friend and, with no shyness whatever, introduced herself to his frail wife. Lucy gushed about her upcoming wedding and the rose-littered cottage on Hillside Avenue that even Mr. Lamont considered a charming old place. Mrs. Lamont invited Lucy to tea right after services, but Lucy declined—to go visit her ailing grandmother.

Buck heard nothing of that Sunday incident. He had stayed home to work on an account he had not gotten to after coming home too late from chess playing during the week. In truth, chess bored him, but he did have a strong curiosity about the homes of his fellow bankers. The chess matches were held at someone else's place each week (but not at his home on the other side of the river). Not that anyone had said they wouldn't come to Englewood. It was as if Englewood just didn't exist. Buck got off the train in Englewood for peace and the chance to see Lucy occasionally during the week—though not too often. That would change upon marrying, of course. His mother couldn't keep Lucy busy forever.

Not a week went by now that Mr. Lamont didn't stroll over to Buck's desk to chat or to deliver a fine box of Earl Grey tea from Mrs. Lamont for Lucy. And so with Mr. Lamont's approval Buck became one of the crowd and much sought after on business matters—sometimes a lazier cousin might ask him to clean up his own troubles and smooth a few ruffled clients' feathers. He was eager to do it. Success came with the desire to keep it at all reasonable cost. He would protect his morals and decency, but if it took an outsider twice as long to find success he'd work twice as hard to keep it. And wouldn't Lucy be proud?

Buck still pondered the mansion near his grandmother and also a dignified, brownstone in a somewhat declining neighborhood of the city, neither of which he could afford just yet. Money struck Buck now like the waves he'd been knocked over by at Long Branch beach as a child, but now he remained standing at just the right angle—feet firmly in the shifting sands—it was intuitive. He hadn't the slightest intellectual ideas about banking and, even with his late waves of success, his understanding of finance was like sunshine penetrating not too deeply into an ocean of speculation, more conservative transactions and the peculiarities of old Knickerbocker families.

A few of the low-lying cousins grumbled that, with his hard work and devotion, Buck was usurping the less clever of the family. There were sixteen male cousins in all. The banking house had the feel of a club with a nook and cranny given to each of the young men—including Buck—though his spot at the back was smaller and darker with not a window's light nearby. Portraits of the Lamont and Turner men looked down with mild, paternalistic glances from within their gilt frames as the grousing cousins, prevented by their conservative uncles from heedless speculating in railroad schemes and mining expeditions, wondered if Buck wasn't somehow making his success in the quietly cunning way of a Jay Gould, but none could find any fishy smell of impropriety in his work.

A gregarious lot, the cousins talked and talked and it was a matter of family pride that they all must know each other's business and have an opinion. Some bristled like racehorses before a derby under the conservative leadership of the uncles, but the better sort stayed steady all week, slowly and quietly making their fortunes in the dynamic capitalistic economy.

And what was wrong with making one's fortune? Buck deliberated about this at his desk after a shocking incident at Delmonico's with Lewis Lamont and Preston Turner III. The rich sauce on the slimy asparagus he'd eaten sat heavily on his stomach, and his mind wandered to home and the help Mama would find for Lucy's kitchen after the wedding. On Saturdays, after a few hours with Lucy, as real spring came on, he was sure he was doing the right thing by marrying her if for no other reason than to rescue her from Thankful, who lately had become ugly in her bitterness—talking on and on about women's rights. Buck noted that (at least on the exterior) Lucy held no such interests and seemed to take Thankful's militancy with a mix of sympathy and amusement. Buck liked Lucy's young and amused face best. It was as if she floated above the game in some way. It lacked any condescension, and he admired that too, for if Lucy had ever hinted at a real dislike for Thankful, Buck's natural loyalties would have been tested.

There had been one girl whom Preston had set upon Buck in the fall at a card party, who had torn him to pieces when he admitted that he could not imagine a girl in banking—or at least not a refined lady. He had proudly mentioned Victoria Woodhull as maybe an exception, but it had not been enough to prevent the lady's annoyance.

Lately, though, he worried that being married might keep him from his work. On Saturdays with Lucy's little blond head leaned against his shoulder, he enjoyed the day off from banking, but on Sundays and especially on Wednesdays, when work piled up and when lunches lingered on far too long, he considered asking her to wait—a little bit longer—for marriage.

At his desk, Buck fretted over what had just happened at Delmonico's ...

Lewis pushed away his plate and wiped his mouth before asking, "So when do we get to meet your girl?"

Preston, the top thoroughbred cousin, moaned while lighting a cigarette and signaling the waiter for another drink all around. "Buckie, my boy, enjoy your freedom while it lasts."

Buck had laughed in a phony way.

Lewis smacked his lips as he finished his brandy. "Preston, wasn't it you who so badly wanted Buck entrapped by your friend Felicity, last autumn?"

"Yes," Preston replied, "but that was different. Felicity is a friend of mine and my wife's so I knew what Buck would be getting into. We could suffer through marriage together." He chuckled, flicking his ashes. Preston's movements, his voice, and even his hair expressed an easy confidence and optimism Buck admired and resented (a little). "This Lucy is an unknown property."

"Not to me," he'd replied.

"Oh, really now?" Preston said suggestively.

"Buck has known the girl for his entire life," Lewis said, not suffering from the same low sense of humor as Preston. "Uncle says she's rather pretty."

"I would have preferred—I hope you don't mind my opinion—we Turners are strong in our opinions ..." Preston began. "But I would have liked a city girl from our circle much better—for your career. It's nothing personal against your girl, but Felicity had poise and an aptitude for polite conversation and with a wry humor perfect for entertaining our sort—too bad she left for Europe. I find that so many people new to ... money ... make others ill at ease."

"Buck's doing well enough showing us up," Lewis said, nibbling at dessert. "Girl or no girl."

Preston never ate sweets, being a lean man of energy. "Tell me about Miss McCullough. I'm curious."

He'd picked up his fork—sometimes it still bothered him to eat with his left hand in public. "We seem to get on well."

Lewis asked, "How old is she?"

"She's younger than I am."

"What sort of schooling has she got?" Preston asked. "You seem deep—the type who likes novels or poetry or something."

"No, there isn't any time for novels and such."

"That's right. You were a West Point man. Funny, I can't imagine you a soldier."

He'd looked up from his dessert. "I suppose no one could."

"So, what sort of schooling—for the girl?"

"Oh, well, Lucy attended school in Englewood—briefly—and then recently in New London."

Preston sipped his brandy, not truly enjoying it. "What's in New London but whales and the navy?"

He liked Preston and Lewis and felt compelled to be honest. "There's a school for the blind."

The words hung heavily for a second, then Preston said, "Oh, so she wants to help the blind. A philanthropic girl with serious pretensions." He nodded in approval. "I can see that for you, and it's best to keep your wife busy while you work—you won't see her much, I'd say."

"I'll definitely make time for Lucy and the children." Buck would show his father how parenting was done.

"You'll see," Preston warned. "Women want more and more of you until you're ready to scream. How many romantic suppers are we men supposed to endure?" Preston looked to Lewis who shrugged.

Lewis had not been blessed with the Turner looks or a noticeable personality and had given the idea of marriage a pass.

"Lucy isn't like that," Buck said. "She's been known to spend entire afternoons by herself on the river."

Preston gave that bit of information an odd look but continued to pry. "Tell me all about her idiosyncrasies."

"She's not odd like weird or peculiar ... I don't know ..."

"Well, that's a fine kettle then—not really knowing ..." Preston said. "Well, tell us about her family."

Buck rolled his eyes.

"It's that bad?" Preston asked with newfound cheer.

"Technically, she has no real family," he'd replied, pushing the strawberries around his plate (he'd ordered them with cream for dessert but was having trouble bringing himself to eat them). "Lucy's parents were killed by Indians in the Far West."

Both cousins leaned on their elbows. "Well, that beats the Dutch. Do tell."

"There's nothing to say, but that both parents were murdered when she was just a baby. I suppose her father was a good soldier once—in the war."

"How horrible!" Lewis said, leaning in even closer, in case he might miss something. "So who raised her?"

"The Weldons." The tiniest piece of strawberry with all of its mealy seeds stuck on his tongue. He wished he'd ordered the chocolate cake as he always had. "Her uncle had problems after the war. I consider Lucy the only sane one of the lot—to be honest."

Preston smiled in satisfaction. "Clouds on the horizon, I tell you—but then she doesn't have to see them much once you move into the city."

"Her aunt and uncle only recently died."

"How morbid," Preston said. "It seems wherever this Lucy goes, people die."

Buck dismissed Preston's ridiculous comment with a half-hearted wave of his prosthetic hand.

"Did the Weldons die by Indians? Speaking of which, what about the Indians who took your hand?"

He'd hesitated. A newspaper article floated out there somewhere detailing the broken, pathetic wretch he was after returning east so he said something else. "Lucy's uncle was a morphine eater."

The cousins looked deliciously shocked.

"What must that have been like for our dear Lucy?" Preston asked.

"I have no idea," he'd answered immediately regretting his unkind words about the dead lieutenant. "You won't mention I told you that at the wedding ..."

"I'm offended, Buck. What do you take me for?" Preston asked.

"Lieutenant Weldon was a war hero and his wife, Mrs. Weldon—I was quite fond of her, actually. Anyway, Lucy is nothing like them, and I believe she has a very admirable sense of faith."

"In what?" Lewis asked, eyeing his cousin as if to signal the discovery of some small imperfection in their new friend.

"Is Lucy very pious indeed?" Preston asked, peeved almost.

He'd laughed uncomfortably. "No, not terribly so. No, not at all." But he had no idea. Up until this very moment he'd assumed Lucy liked religion as much as he did although he knew he'd been flailing about since Middlemay in search of God—well, more like avoiding Him, being too busy right now—but he imagined Lucy teaching their children about Noah's Ark and such. He tried to recall if Lucy appeared too pious at church, but he'd been so bad about attending since returning from Middlemay.

As if reading his mind, Preston, taking the napkin from his lap and tossing it upon the table asked, "Will you become members of Christ Church, then? It's religious but not morbidly so and everyone's going there now."

"Well, I haven't actually mentioned to Lucy the idea of a place in the city."

"Well, you must," Preston urged. "It's fine for the uncles to stay in the country, but all the younger set stays together in Murray Hill all winter and summers are at Long Branch. You'd be surprised the important people you meet on a beach these days."

"Maybe so, but Lucy has such fair skin—I'd imagine the seashore to be too much with its dreadful sun." He was thinking of Lucy's eyes but also about getting sun poisoning as a child on a family trip to the shore to visit relatives. The burn had been bad enough to fear for his young life, but it had also ruined Margaret's plans, and he recalled how she refused to speak to him for the rest of the summer and the beatings he'd gotten for the smallest infractions for weeks after. "I'd like to see the Adirondacks," he said.

"Saratoga, then?"

"No, more like a nice walk up a mountain."

"No, our friends don't do that."

"Are you sure?" he asked, as an alien sense of class consciousness bubbled to the surface of his calm veneer. "I hadn't heard that the mountains were a poor man's escape." Lately he nursed a resentment toward his father, who'd thrown away social standing when he left banking years earlier.

The young bankers stood and walked toward the exit when a man in shoddy attire stepped before them. "Capitalist ratbag!" the man shouted before throwing an egg at his face.

The host and a waiter jumped upon the intruder, but he wrestled free, fleeing into the busy street outside. Preston and Lewis stood in silent shock as he'd wiped his face with a finely pressed eggshell blue handkerchief.

"Buck, are you all right?" Lewis asked breathlessly.

"I'm fine. It's only egg, but ..."

"Some of these foreigners hate success," Preston said.

"Why?" he asked, truly astonished.

No one had had a good answer, and all afternoon (what was left of it) Buck sat at his desk pondering the odd event, unable to put it behind him, especially since the story made its way around the office.

When the cousins began filtering out for a trip up to Preston's for euchre that evening, Mr. Lamont appeared at Buck's desk.

"Sir!" Buck straightened like a soldier at drill.

Mr. Lamont shook his head with a smile. "Burning the candle at both ends—don't you go in for games?"

He wanted to answer correctly, but he was tired and a little vexed. "Not very much, I'm afraid, sir. I go most weeks, but ..."

"I'm not one for games either—that's a Turner trait. I hear you were assaulted today at Delmonico's."

Buck laughed, picking up his pen as if to get back to work but stayed standing. "Oh, it wasn't as much as that. Trifling, really."

Mr. Lamont soft eyes looked for something in Buck. "But it bothered you, didn't it?"

Again he hesitated, not sure what words were needed to satisfy the older man.

Mr. Lamont sat down and waited for him to do the same before continuing. "You wouldn't be human if it didn't bother you."

"I don't want to sound, well, dramatic, sir, but I've been through much worse so ..."

"Ah, yes. Preston mentioned that you rescued two girls as a soldier. Silly girls going on western adventures get what they deserve, I think—but lucky for them you were there."

Buck cleared his throat. "Happenstance, sir."

Lamont smiled and lit a cigar, crossing his thin legs.

Buck sat primly.

"You're making a fine career for yourself here, Buck, but you mustn't worry about the opinions of men."

Buck loosened his collar, fidgeting for time, unsure about confiding in this man with kindly, pale eyes who even in old age possessed a youthful vigor and optimism. He kept waiting for a false note, but not a one came.

"Sir ... I do sometimes wonder if making so much money is very Christian." He waited for the world-weary look of derision he'd grown to expect from the cousins when mentioning godly things, but Mr. Lamont sat back, leisurely smoking and listening.

"Christ mentions the difficulty a rich man will have getting into heaven," Buck continued with his face down, looking over his work as if before a headmaster with ruler in hand.

"Buck, I like you."

"Thank you, sir."

"My father once told me that it wasn't the riches, but *the man* who allowed himself to be controlled, possessed by the wealth. Money is not evil—it's the *love* of money that ruins a man. I do worry about the general falling away from religion amongst your generation. But it's to be expected, what with science pushing one to ask questions. Americans are becoming too fascinated by wealth and the characters we see flaunting their money every day in the newspapers."

Buck nodded dutifully. He never read anything but the hard news and financial sections of the papers. "Sir, I do hope that the money I make is made as cleanly as possible. I worry that in such a speculative market as we now have in oil and whatnot that some men will be ruined on my account."

Lamont smiled again. "My brother-in-law was right to hire you. You speak truth. I worry, too, that the cousins—every last one so young and together all the time—may become drunk with opportunities."

"I hope, sir, that capitalism is not evil," Buck said haltingly. "I believe in meritocracy without exception and that capitalism is the only right way."

"Here you are until all hours of the night, doing the work of three cousins. You're right to expect reward for it."

Buck's ears rose in color. "Sir, I'm just grateful for the opportunity you and Mr. Turner have given me."

"Yes, but we feel a pay raise is due."

"Sir? The recent bonus was more than generous."

Mr. Lamont laughed and rose from his seat, putting out his cigar. "You had better decide what to do with your money."

Buck scurried to his feet. He had kept himself so busy he hardly knew his own bank account, but felt proud of this new windfall.

Lamont noticed the slightly upturned corners of the young man's mouth and laughed. "It's only money—no need to take it so seriously—but keep this between us. Some of the boys will be annoyed that you'll make double their salaries. What will you buy first?"

"Sir, I was considering—well, I feel I've been given so much—that I should give a bit to the church." Buck said this for effect and because he meant it. "What would be an acceptable gift to Christ Church?"

At this the old man frowned and gave a disappointed once over. "I assumed we'd be keeping you at First Presbyterian in Englewood. My wife's grown quite fond of Lucy and their little teas."

Buck recognized his misstep, but how was he to get out of it? "Oh, yes, that's what I meant," he chuckled falsely. "It's only the cousins talking about the city at lunch to-day—I misspoke. But sometimes I wonder if it wouldn't be easier to live over here."

"As your elder and friend I'll be frank. You couldn't afford it. Not yet anyway. The younger set is dangerously caught up in the wrong things. Safety and rectitude may seem dull at your age, but trust me when I say some of my own kin have come very close to falling away from all that is good." Lamont projected an imposing authority. "I'm happy that you have feelings for your *home* church—not just going where the crowd goes to be seen. It shows a maturity that will one day lead you to high places in this firm. Mark my words."

Buck cringed at his ridiculous and ostentatious imaginings and for having pushed the wedding to be at Christ Church. "Lucy was disappointed when I told her the wedding wouldn't be in Englewood, but I decided it best to keep it simple for the guests—most of whom live in the city."

"That was thoughtful, Buck, but an admirable trait can be taken too far," Lamont advised. "It's *best* to please those closest first."

"I suppose you're right, sir, but in my mind I was *protecting* Lucy from those closest to me."

The old man laughed. "Fair enough. Anything for Lucy—though I can't imagine an awful family producing such a fine young man."

Buck, with raised brows, held back what came to mind first. "Well, sir, you may be overestimating my parents and you know my brother."

"As you age, young Crenshaw, you may come to admire your parents' finer qualities."

Buck scoffed, for a moment forgetting his reserve, but instantly saw that he'd shown too much. "Sir, I'm certain of your wisdom."

Mr. Lamont sighed at Buck's youthful resentment. "Your father is the doctor …"

"Yes, obstetrics, mostly now," Buck said sourly, thinking of Thankful.

"You don't approve of babies?"

A wave of unexpected and sad bitterness led him to reply, "I just think my father doesn't appreciate the responsibility of bringing life into the world." Buck's words came out like poison.

Mr. Lamont eyed Buck with the same non-judgmental aplomb he'd had the whole time. "But Lucy tells me you're one of seven children."

"Even dogs have offspring, sir." He sat again. "I'd rather not talk about them any further, if you don't mind."

"I hadn't expected so much emotion over easy talk, but that's fine. You're a warm-blooded American."

Buck laughed uncomfortably.

Lamont sighed. "I've never met your parents so I'll reserve judgment and for now give them an old person's benefit of the doubt."

Buck's cheeks burned with indignation and unresolved anger that his parents should be given any benefits—but no one knew except his siblings how his parents played each child off the other or the temper Margaret showed in force or that his father might help his sister kill a child. "Sir, I respect your tolerance and hope one day to be able to imitate it."

Mr. Lamont took the compliment in stride. "Most of your generation are sadly devoid of moral aspirations—I'm glad to know you are an exception."

"Your generation ended slavery, and who could have imagined that?" Buck said, not because he really cared, but because it stroked his superior.

Mr. Lamont turned to go. "Slavery never ends, it just moves."

# Chapter Twenty-Five

Thankful fretted at the kitchen window in her purple-trimmed lavender gown. Josephine, discomfited by Thankful's presence in her kitchen, prepared noon dinner for William on this rare occasion when he'd be coming home to eat it. The old ways of large suppers in the middle of the day had given way to the thing called "lunch," and this thing was usually had at Thankful's shop or at the Adriance farm. Josephine enjoyed the freedom she had to get things done in her own way at noon, but Thankful, with all of her grumbling and standing in the way and asking after trivial items left somewhere in the house, threw Josephine off track. She burnt the dainty fried cheese crisps that were her specialty and that William loved with the greens he brought home each day from Adriance's garden.

"Isn't it so like Willy to keep us waiting? I would have imagined that for this day he might do things right at least for Lulu," Thankful said, waiting then for Josephine to agree, but Josephine said nothing. "If I'd have known that I could have kept the shop open today, I would have. By the time Willy comes home we'll be lucky to make the ceremony. You do have a bath ready for him, don't you? We can't have him smelling of swine."

"Mr. Adriance doesn't keep pigs, ma'am," Josephine said, sorting through the remains of her cheese crisps with a deflated shake of the head.

"Oh, Josephine, look at the mess you've made. You may as well throw it out." Thankful popped open her watch though the kitchen clock ticked right above the window. "He's probably doing some unnecessary chores."

"Maybe something's happened, ma'am." Josephine continued to pick out the less-than-scorched crisps with her long callused fingers, unwilling to suffer a complete loss.

"Ha! Well, I won't be the one strolling over to find out after the last time Mr. Adriance spoke to me so boldly. Imagine being asked to leave the premises! Can't a wife visit her husband if he's just walking about doing nothing but watching sheep eat? I assure you that if ever Mr. Adriance needs fine stationery, he'll be sent elsewhere!"

"I suppose, ma'am, that William works mighty hard."

"Even so …" Thankful said, snapping the watch open again with an exasperated sigh. "Oh, and Jo—please remember—it's Mr. Weldon to you."

William's tardiness would have been so much more vexing if Thankful had actually wanted to attend Buck's wedding, but part of her (the larger part) hated that little Lulu would be getting all the attention from Buck's New York crowd. And how did Buck suddenly have a "crowd" anyway? Men got all the opportunities. And wasn't it ridiculous to imagine Lulu fitting in with cultured ladies? Thankful considered all the books she'd read and understood. Her women's group seemed to consider her practically a genius (or did they just love Josephine's refreshments?). Why hadn't Thankful married someone from the city?

Thankful stopped herself—these thoughts led down paths of unhappiness—but on this sunny day (of course!) she dreaded seeing romance on display. She admired herself in the reflection of the window. She had such large eyes and perfect curls! But who cared? As a married woman it no longer mattered. Weddings used to be full of fun and flirtation with dresses, dances, and romantic intrigue. She hardly remembered how little she actually enjoyed them in her younger years. Her mind played out the inelegant dancing of William in the West, and she shuddered. Fahy and Demarest were at least good at a waltz.

"Oh, land sakes! Where is that man?" Thankful huffed with her nose in the air as Josephine cut two slices of day-old bread and spread chicken salad over them.

"Jo, you've done your best this morning, but obviously Mr. Weldon doesn't appreciate your efforts, and there isn't time for a meal any longer—just dump it out for the cats in the yard—and the coffee too. I hate the smell of burnt coffee."

"But, ma'am, it does no harm to leave the plate go a few more minutes ..."

"We don't have a minute any longer. Please do as I say, and then you may leave."

Josephine with her mouth set, keeping back words she might regret, hated wasting the food, but was eager at the chance of an early dismissal. She tossed the coffee grinds onto the chicken and bread and made for the door just as William jogged up and into the kitchen.

"Sakes alive, Thankful, that dress suits you fine!" William said, his cheeks rosy with exertion. He nodded a hello to Josephine. "Am I really late?" He glanced at the clock with a wince. "I'll just have a small bite and get ready."

Josephine stood with the ruined lunch in her hands.

Thankful took it from her and set it on the counter. "Darling, we had no idea when you'd be back," she said, a little sorry now, "but there are those black walnut muffins my mother sent down last week still in their tin."

"I hate black walnuts, and you know it."

"Let's not fight over such trifling things. Give the muffins a try ..." Thankful said while signaling him not to make a scene in front of the help.

He brushed past her. "And no coffee? Damn."

"Well, dear, why were you so late then?" she asked, coming close and rubbing his arm almost affectionately. "We were worried."

"Just a trifling matter—*not that you'd care*," he said with emotion.

"Darling, what's wrong?" she asked with big eyes of concern.

"Can't a man at least depend upon his coffee?" William asked with a wounded expression that at once set Josephine to brewing more.

"No, Josephine. There isn't time," Thankful said, and to William, "I promised her time off early. You wouldn't want a little coffee to keep Jo, would you? We can just stop in town for a coffee at the new café if you'd only hurry."

"Coffee's cheap at home," William grumbled as he left to get ready. His stomach complained of hunger as he washed up in a hurry—to avoid Thankful's "help" getting dressed. The doting had lost its charm once he realized it was more a directing. William slipped out of his coveralls and put on his elegantly tailored suit—his mood brightening at the thought of walking his cousin down the aisle. After a quick check in the mirror, William intended to skedaddle up to his old attic spot, but Thankful met him on the landing.

"And where are you off to now?" she began but saw how well he looked and couldn't help but admire him. "Oh, Willy."

Thankful's old tone pleased him despite the lost coffee. "Why do I have to love you so much?" he asked, taking her in his arms.

His assurance gave her momentary relief from the maddening fear of divorce (even though she longed for escape at times), but then the comment annoyed her. Was he feeling the same confinement as she? And his words made it seem he was forced to love her—that she was a terrible burden. An ounce of honest appraisal brought on self-loathing and anger. Wasn't she the only one who kept the house on Tenafly Road respectable? Wasn't she also the one who screamed and cried over silly things? These thoughts raced by as William embraced her and she replied, "It's terribly difficult to love you too." It came out harshly. She tried to cover by kissing him, but he pulled away—the grin gone.

"Where are you going?" she asked.

"Up to the attic to get something."

"We really haven't got time, Willy. Don't you care about Lulu's big day at all? Coming home so late!" she ranted, unable to stop her mouth, yet knowing her words were wrong and mean.

"Stop your damned lecturing, Thankful! Of course I care about my cousin! Her name is *Lucy*—you do that on purpose, don't you? You think a thick farmer doesn't notice insult?"

"For the life of me, I can't break the habit of seeing her as a little girl."

"You're a liar, now."

She gasped. "Those words are very harsh!"

"You're very harsh! I bet you're picturing how it will look that Lucy is so young, but you miss that everyone loves her and wants her happiness but you!"

"She prattles on about nothing!"

"And that's your reason for making this home into just a house for her these last months? And an unfriendly one at that!" William ranted. "It's why no one comes to visit."

"No one comes to call because I don't want anyone to know how we live with mud and dirt in the mudroom and boots and such everywhere!" Thankful shouted.

"That's what a mudroom is for!" William cried in exasperation.

"Well, it doesn't have to cry out to the world we're farmers!"

"You may not have to worry about that much longer," he said.

"Why?" She softened her tone. "What do you mean?"

"Nothing. You wouldn't understand."

"Willy, tell me ..." she urged, hopeful that he was tiring of the whole farming enterprise.

"I may not be suited to animal husbandry."

Thankful tried not to smile at his elevated work language. "What's happened? Has Adriance found a flaw in you?—because you know I never trusted him."

He shook his head and rolled his eyes, but there was an unsettling amount of emotion in them.

"*Willy?*"

"You remember I purchased that herd of Nubian goats ..."

"Of course—for a pretty penny."

"This morning Pixie had a kid—only one—it seems fine, and Mr. Adriance says he'll bottle feed it for me today while I'm away ..."

"That's good, because you do realize I'd have to draw the line if you even considered missing Buck's wedding over a goat, of all things." She adjusted his collar as she spoke.

"I never said I would *miss* the wedding—but the poor doe will likely die, and I've a soft spot for her—she was always so friendly to me."

"Well ... perhaps it won't die," Thankful said, trying her best to show concern, but with one eye on the clock.

"Adriance doesn't have the patience for sick animals. He sees them as a drain, and I do understand that, but ... Pixie's a good girl." William wiped his eyes. "And she'll be all alone in her suffering. I'm pretty sad about it."

"But this is what you wanted. This *is farming*. In this one thing I agree with Adriance. It's only an animal with no feelings so you should toughen up if you intend to continue." She said this tugging at his collar as if what he was saying was just baby talk.

He stared at her with lonesome eyes. She noted it but was firm in her conviction that if he insisted on being a farmer, he must experience the pain of it—as she did.

At this, he left her on the landing and continued up to his attic. There, wrapped in newsprint painted with delicate forget-me-nots, was his mother's expensive bracelet. His mother had never liked it because his grandfather gave it to humiliate his father, but William wanted Lucy to have something of value. The Crenshaws would dress her well today and not suffer a pinch in doing so, but he suffered no bitterness. She deserved the best. He took his one best thing and planned to give it to his cousin in a private moment before the ceremony.

On his wedding day William had tried to give it to Thankful, but she'd made the face he had lately grown accustomed to—one of disappointed embarrassment—a pained look that in all of his many years of knowing her had never surfaced before. He sat upon his bed remembering the day.

The wind blew, sending shimmering bursts of fall color across the cemetery grounds at Brookside Chapel as Thankful laughingly waved to him when she arrived in her yellow dress—superstitions be damned!

Not a single acquaintance of William's attended (Mr. Adriance had taken ill—or so he said—though he seemed fine the day previous). To be fair, none of Thankful's friends were invited either. Fred and Meg were west, but Grandmother Martha had come, and it had touched William when she'd confessed that it was for him. Martha wanted to talk all about his sheep and the farm.

"Maybe now the two of you will finally settle down," Doctor Crenshaw had said, not quite optimistically.

Thankful and her mother fought after Margaret made mention to the pastor on the very morning of the wedding that Thankful had been previously married to another and divorced, which led to a less-than-warm ceremony with the pastor feeling ambushed, as he was strongly opposed to divorce.

Yet the day was a rose-toned picture for William who remembered his father on a walk in town so long ago, certain that one day Thankful would be a Weldon. After the ceremony he pulled his new wife behind the chapel and kissed her as the others bickered about which surrey to ride in. He wiped her tears away. "It doesn't matter what the pastor thinks—we won't go to that church any longer," he had said.

"Won't we?" Thankful seemed unaware that now they could make their own choices.

Looking back, he understood that it was more a realization on her part that by marrying him, she had given up the high regard of her family and the community at First Presbyterian. William told her that they'd be free of all society, and she seemed happy at first. She asked if one day they might sail on the ocean and see the world, and he laughed and told her they could sail the Hudson every fall after harvest and never get so old as to not swing on swings and dance the dances—but they'd gotten old quickly. William's dances were not good enough so he tired of the effort, and the old swings nestled in the ancient grove on the Adriance farm never got used after the wedding.

The formal luncheon, with all of Margaret's most popular confections on display, went mostly uneaten in the awkward aftermath of a quarrel with the restaurant owner. Margaret nearly made the young new chef cry when she summoned him to the table to imply that he'd virtually ruined the day with his undercooked meat before sending her plate back. Margaret even suggested Graham not pay the bill.

William squirmed at Thankful's side in awe of the neatly dressed wait staff with vast reserves of patience. She seemed to take it all in stride and even joked once about her mother's atrocious behavior, but now William saw that Thankful covered her feelings with false and affectionate good humor. The merry cheerfulness of her youth must have been a facade, and despite his best efforts to discover the source of her unhappiness, he could neither understand nor help Thankful.

On their wedding day, before William discovered the hidden parts of Thankful, they waved goodbye to the family, and having no time for a real honeymoon, they spent their first night together at the house on Tenafly Road in his parents' yellow-papered bedroom still smelling of old-fashioned perfume and cigars. They laughed nervously, undressing in the early evening shadows—each in their own corner filled with memories of physical experiences had elsewhere. The night was less than successful, so Thankful moved their bedroom downstairs because she had inherited some of her mother's superstitions and felt things weren't right because it had been William's parents' bedroom.

Having slept with many a whore, William had gotten used to women pretending enjoyment but didn't want that for Thankful. He needn't have worried. She did not try to hide her lack of pleasure. In his shy embarrassment he had no words to ask her how things might be improved, and before long a resentment settled in for both of them. But on their wedding night it hadn't really been that bad. Ever since that time in the Crenshaw barn when both of their thirsts had been so strong, William had assumed sex would always be that satisfying with her. He thought that the wedding day had just been too grueling for her and that she'd come around with rest.

Even Buck had arrived late to William and Thankful's wedding and left early—preoccupied with work (and a girl in the city). And this actually had been the thing that spoiled Thankful's day—Buck's total disinterest in her destiny. She chose not to tell William about the conversation Buck and she had had while William spoke with Martha.

"Buck, are you happy for me?" she'd asked when Buck sat next to her in William's vacant seat at the restaurant.

He looked at her sideways and tapped his fingers to his lips thoughtfully.

She had asked the question playfully (with just a small touch of needy approval). She assumed she'd get an easy answer, but then Buck never made things easy.

"My only fear is that you're too smart for him. I shouldn't say it on today of all days—and I've been a cad lately, haven't I? But there are so many fine gents in the city now, and I only wish I could have introduced you to them sooner. We'd be together in society, and I wouldn't be so lonely then." He smiled as if what he'd said was somehow complimentary.

But it stung her because she felt she was indeed too intelligent and well-read. Reading well-written novels seemed of great importance to her suddenly. Also Buck had a way of making his loneliness charming and inviting. Wouldn't she like to think of herself as the sophisticated sister of a top-rung financier? And lately Buck was growing into his scars and fine suits. Hadn't they both chosen below their stations in life?

Thankful glanced at her parents resentfully. They'd both come from respectable families, but had failed miserably in guiding their children to the right people. In fact, the unpredictability of their discipline (except Mama's fascination with new ways to cause Buck to suffer) had led to a family of social misfits—herself included. She turned to Buck and laughed, her sour ideas hidden behind a habitual smile, and said, "I suppose you and I will be solely responsible for intelligent conversation when we visit each other after we're *both* married."

Buck smiled expansively. "You know, Lucy writes fine letters and has a different kind of intelligence I admire greatly."

"A different sort? What does that mean?" Thankful laughed with disgust while adjusting a curl fallen from its place atop her head.

"I don't know ... maybe it's a right way of seeing things."

"Lulu's practically blind, so enjoy her sight while you can."

Buck turned on her in surprise. "That was low!"

"Oh, please don't be so thin-skinned, Buck," she said, playing with the button on her glove. "I was being humorous."

"Well, it didn't strike me as funny."

"Then you've become the stuffy banker everyone says you are."

"Who says so?"

"Mama."

He waved her off. "Mama just hates bankers." His hair had turned light from all the recent sailing he'd been doing with Preston and the other cousins. "I'm not stuffy."

Thankful leaned in and whispered, "Mama tells me there's a girl in the city you're keen on. There's still plenty of time for you to escape marriage on Tenafly Road."

"You shouldn't talk like that. Anyway, unlike you, I'll be setting up house on the hill."

"Yes, and I hear you bullied an old man into the old folks' home in order to get your fancy little cottage."

His lips tightened. "He's well-cared for, Thankful—I saw to it."

"And how many times have you visited him?" Thankful asked with a knowing grin.

"That's none of your business."

She laughed. "Oh, Buckie, come in from the cold and join the rest of us Crenshaw cynics."

"No, Lucy won't allow it, and for that I'm grateful."

"Children haven't put away childish ideas yet. Be careful not to put too much confidence in Lucy's adorable romanticism." Thankful glanced around for her husband. William laughed merrily with Nate and Martha about some stupid thing by the dessert table. At once she longed for whatever that stupid happiness was.

Buck sighed and looked earnest. "If only you took the time, you'd see how at ease Lucy puts people. It's very admirable."

"Yes, you already said you admired Lulu, but what about sensible things like age difference? You are exceedingly mature, and she's a baby." Thankful said with a smile as if this were just light banter. "But you never answered my question. Are you happy for *me*?"

Buck paused again, running his fingers over his wooden appendage. "We all hope for things for our siblings, and I had hoped for something different for you, but I guess under the circumstances, you've done well enough."

"I don't know how to take that."

"Take it as a brother wanting the world for you and watching you settle into that shabby house on Tenafly Road. I know you'll make the most of it, but I wish you'd have waited."

Thankful stared, her large eyes tearing up. "That's probably the worst thing you could have said to me on my wedding."

"No. I could say worse, I think." Buck hadn't liked her jab about Lucy's age, and he'd had a few quick drinks. He saw the hurt look on Thankful's face. "I'm only being honest."

"And unchristian," Thankful replied.

"That's bunk after all."

"I liked you better as a Christian, Buck."

"I liked you better as a Crenshaw," he replied before excusing himself. He kissed her forehead and went to shake William's hand before leaving for his bedroom-turned-banker's office.

# Chapter Twenty-Six

Lucy insisted she arrive at the church early. She also insisted that the carriage she arrived in be a simple one despite Margaret's entreaties to the contrary. William had promised to meet Lucy at the church as soon as he could manage it, but Lucy worried he'd be late and felt more worried sitting fully dressed in the hotel room Graham and Margaret had arranged for her. And so Lucy insisted on being at the church.

Despite Margaret's annoyance at being pulled from the festive atmosphere of the hotel where all of her other children were, Margaret admired Lucy as she sat in the vestry and flipped through a silver prayer book set with jewels that had once belonged to her deceased mother, wishing a small essence of her mother lay hidden between the pages. Lucy wore the blue dress with old point de Venice lace at the throat and the same lace in her veil kept in place by orange blossoms and a small tiara. Her strawberry-blond hair, held back in a simple braided bun at her neck, at first struck Margaret as perhaps too simple for a New York wedding, but simplicity had always looked best on McCullough women.

Thankful had not joined the family for supper the previous night as the matron of honor should. Margaret didn't mind watching over Lucy on her wedding day but complained to Graham that Thankful should have taken a more active interest in her duties leading up to this point.

The traditional farewell luncheon given by Thankful had been a stilted affair with only the Crenshaw maids and one of Lucy's childhood friends, though they were no longer close. Maddie and Abigail were still young, silly, and easily bored by the rectitude of the gathering having mistakenly thought the luncheon would be festive. The party, such as it was, sat quietly and uncomfortably beneath the paintings of overripe fruit in the Crenshaw dining room as Nathan was called in to play (awkwardly) on his violin a sweet song before being ushered out. Granted this was Margaret's idea. It had fallen flat because Nathan's red face and hardly concealed admiration for Lucy caused his two younger sisters to titter behind their fleshy hands.

Margaret thought it might have been a better day if they'd gone out to lunch—maybe into the city—but Thankful insisted that if she must be matron of honor, she would have no interference, and, in some ways, Thankful had outdone herself. The floral centerpiece perfectly played upon the shade of the tablecloth and the colors Thankful had chosen for the bridesmaids. Margaret sensed that Lucy wasn't fond of emerald green on the bridesmaids against her powder-blue gown, but the Crenshaw girls looked so fine in jewel-toned colors and it was a very thin fence Margaret walked the top of to keep Thankful in the wedding party at all.

Thankful had come to Margaret one day in late April complaining that Lucy was being obstinate about the cake she wanted for the luncheon and threatened to quit the whole affair. Margaret begged as she'd never begged her daughter before.

"No, you mustn't leave poor Buck in the lurch." What she really meant was that she depended upon Thankful's innate good taste to sway the New York crowd's opinion of *her*. "Let Lucy have her cake, for goodness sake. Save your battles for the wedding day. The luncheon is only family anyhow."

And hadn't Thankful pulled the cake charm predicting she would be the next to have a baby! When Lucy clapped her hands delightedly, Thankful held her tongue, angry at herself for letting such a triviality spoil what she liked doing—planning parties. Yet no matter how she tried to like Lucy, something about the girl ignited such fury in Thankful.

Margaret worried, as she paced on Buck's big day, that Thankful might still do something embarrassing just to upset Lucy. Margaret wished now that she had not pushed Thankful into accepting the compliment of Matron of Honor but had hoped that it would bring Lucy and Thankful closer. It had not.

Margaret peeked out the door, mumbling nervously as the church filled with quiet voices. She dare not step out. Big city society people intimidated her when she thought about Buck being so unfit for making his way with them. The ceremony was drawing near and still there was no sign of Thankful.

*** 

William leaned over the rails of the ferry as Thankful sat within, afraid of wind in her hair as they cruised across the Hudson. Both were lonely for things lost. That William would be the only family present for Lucy today depressed him, and even after months fraught with conflict, it had still been nice to meet his cousin in the kitchen for a snack on a late night when they both couldn't sleep. Now that would never happen again, and although it made sense for Lucy to stay at the hotel in the city the night before the wedding so Margaret could dress her and prepare her for married life with a "talk," it still pricked at his nerves how the Crenshaw clan had captured his cousin.

It pricked Thankful's nerves as well. Margaret had not shown an interest in *her* wedding dress, but Lucy's every move, her every insipidly cheerful tale was repeated by Margaret as if it were a great and precious gem of adorable truth. How Thankful's patience had been worn thin hearing the animal stories Lucy, and now Margaret, seemed to delight in. In actual fact Lucy had only told one story about a little Scottish terrier that saved its human family from a burning building, but Margaret had embellished and repeated it ad nauseam, turning it into a fable about family devotion or something.

Thankful glanced out the window of the ferry, noticing a few sets of female eyes enjoying the handsomeness of her husband, but on this day their admiration held no sway. If only they could see the dirt under his fingernails hidden inside his gloves. As if William could feel her slipping away, he suddenly pulled back from the water and sought her. The ferry was crowded, and he stood with no seat of his own.

William leaned over then and whispered, "Anyway, you do look beautiful."

"And you look the perfect gentleman," she replied with so little feeling that they both retreated to their own thoughts again.

She was anxious to speak with India about rights and such. She wondered how supper in the city had gone last night with Lucy, her parents, siblings, and India (of course Thankful and William had been invited but livestock stood in the way).

William stared bleakly through the crowd and back at the New Jersey shore worrying about his goat—her rough coat and scared eyes haunting him—but Thankful assumed his stare was a blank one, and it annoyed her. What would he possibly come up with to say in conversation today with New York bankers? She hoped he'd remain quiet.

Briefly she wished her sister Meg would have given her the secret to happiness with an earthy homesteader. No Crenshaw had ever looked that content. But then Meg had never expected much, and Thankful could not make peace with low expectations.

\*\*\*

The day settled into a dry and perfect coolness as William hailed one of the better cabs, but as it passed with well-dressed passengers, he suggested the omnibus, now crowded with every description of people. William's rakish smile at the idea of hanging off the side of it charmed Thankful just long enough to climb aboard when once again she wondered how the other guests might arrive at church.

About a block away from the church Thankful said, "Willy, this *has been* a lark, hasn't it? Something we should do more often, but ... it's so pleasant out and, despite all, we're a little early so why don't we walk the rest of the way—it's so exciting in the city!"

William gave her a knowing glance but complied and adjusted happily to walking. Though he wouldn't admit it, he loved the city for its constant refashioning of itself. The buildings erected and torn down on a dime to make way for grander, more ostentatious creations he found amusing (he followed the building of the great museums with secret delight in the papers). If William wasn't always so agitated by Thankful he would have loved planning excursions for the two of them to admire the new mansions. He had no desire to live in one. He liked small things best, but he enjoyed seeing the rich compete in moving rock and pasting mortar. Grand comedy—and beauty too. Uncle Simon's favorite verse came to mind: "What do people gain from all their labors at which they toil under the sun?"

Up ahead stood the church with a great many people on the sidewalk and still more stepping from their expensive carriages. Thankful sighed in relief that they had walked until she spotted Buck and Preston Turner jump from an omnibus laughing in their elegant black suits, white ties, and colorful socks. The idea of Buck being playful without her broke her heart as a flood of childhood memories came to mind. Her stupid pride!

William opened his mouth to speak with a flash in his merry eyes.

"Don't say a word about the omnibus!" Thankful said, but laughed all the same. Perhaps it would be a fine day.

Buck saw Thankful and trotted over, looking a bit under the influence of a big night out with dark-circled eyes and pale cheeks. His rare grin was infectious but pierced her. How much she wanted to embrace him!

"Are you just arriving now?" he asked, nodding a greeting to William who returned it with hands in his pockets. "Lucy must be out of her wits waiting for her cousin."

William took the hint and disappeared into the church, just after a pause to admire the front facade of the building (though, in his mind it was no First Presbyterian of Englewood). Adjusting his eyes a moment, he glanced around at the interior, which had been grandly decorated with flowers and ribbons festooned from top to bottom. A massive sculpture made of white lilies in the shape of a dove hung precariously over where the bride and groom would exchange vows. William cringed at the gaudiness of it and hoped it had not been Lucy's idea. Margaret grabbed him now.

"This late! But what else should I expect from a Weldon! Lucy is desperate for you so come along!"

But when William entered the side room lit with the tinted glass depicting virgins and sinners, Lucy turned to him as if she'd been in a perfect reverie. His painter's eye delighted at the scene. Lucy jumped up to embrace him with a squeal.

"You look so terribly handsome!"

"I'm sorry to be late," he said, suddenly bashful.

"Oh, are you? I hadn't noticed, but Mrs. Crenshaw has been the worrier all morning," Lucy said with a smile.

Margaret smiled too—for Lucy. She shot William a severe look before wringing her hands. "And where is my impossible son?"

"Buck's just arrived, ma'am," William informed her.

Lucy gasped. "It's really happening, isn't it? Up until now I've felt like a dress-up doll, but you'll keep me steady up the aisle, won't you, Willy?"

"Of course. This is the greatest honor I've ever received, and—well—here's something for you so you never forget us Weldons down the hill."

Lucy shook her head, promising with her eyes that the idea of forgetting her family was impossibly silly.

The diamond bracelet shone from its case.

"Dear, you should save the wrapping—it's exquisite," Margaret said with teary eyes. "William, forget-me-nots were your mother's favorite."

"Yes," he replied with simple modesty as he helped Lucy clasp the jewels around her wrist.

Lucy gazed up at her cousin. "Willy, I know this was your mother's—don't you want to pass it to your children some day?"

His face betrayed a disappointment, but he recovered quickly. "Go on, Lucy. I want you to have it and remember how much I care. In case anything happens—you know I'll always be here—I'm not going any place, and you'll always be a sister to me."

"Oh, Willy!" she sobbed and kissed him.

He wiped it away. "Promise you'll visit on occasion."

She laughed. "You can't keep me away! After all, I'll live right up the road—even if Thankful ..." She blushed then. "Nothing will ever stop me from adoring you, William Weldon."

"Good then." He cleared his throat. "Then let's not make a show of ourselves and do this thing right."

Margaret stood back admiring them. "I *will say* that the two of you scrub up nicely. Katherine and Simon would be proud." She sobbed into her handkerchief. "How hard it is to imagine them both moldering in their graves and missing the two of you make your way in the world. God is cruel at times, but let's be happy to spite Him! Off I go to find Buck. Don't touch your hair, Lucy."

***

Buck and Preston took their places as the crowd grew quiet. Buck noticed his father seated in the front aisle but could not look at him, fearing he might find on his father's face an expression of doubt or disappointment in him. The sound of his mother's shoes against the marble tiles and that of Nathan's as he shuffled behind her added to Buck's nervous excitement. They picked up their violins to play.

When Nathan had asked Buck if he could play Pachelbel's *Canon in D* for his brother, Buck hadn't had the heart to deny him though he would have preferred strangers to mess up a wedding march than his own family to embarrass themselves. Buck glanced once at Nathan when the pause before starting seemed decidedly too long. Nathan smiled at Buck, and Buck returned the favor with an encouraging nod.

The music began and at once Buck knew that his brother's playing would win the crowd's admiration, for what he lacked in expression he gained in precision, and what Margaret lacked in precision she gained in emotion. The duet was so exquisitely executed that Buck hardly noticed his two young sisters as they appeared at the back of the church in their striking green gowns. Behind them stood a plain girl Buck hardly knew and then Thankful dressed in a slightly paler version of the green his other sisters and the plain girl wore.

Thankful walked the aisle with chin up and eyelids a touch lowered, displaying with her proud smile a keen sense of being watched and admired. Buck saw her pride and it annoyed him, but like everyone else in the church he saw how well she looked and involuntarily smiled. Despite all, Thankful was his favorite sister and would always be. One day she would understand his marriage and they would all spend holidays together.

A part of Buck wished the ceremony would go no further. Let the world be a happy place full of expectancy. Let Thankful steal the limelight and laugh with him like always. But she arrived too soon at the front of the church, and he saw now that her happiness was a veneer. Was it for his sake or just her own? Buck spotted India in the first row, whispering to another girl behind her. Fred stood with the other ushers, still bristling with hurt and anger at being passed over for best man. In this moment with Preston so serene, so assured, and almost bored, a wistful side of Buck wished he had chosen Fred one last time.

The music changed and two shadows appeared at the back of the church. Preston nudged Buck out of his thoughts and whispered, "Are you certain?"

He refused to answer. His face flushed and a sudden desire for escape rushed over him, but he quieted this with the assurance that if this too failed he could divorce. Taking a deep breath, he fixed his eyes on the future, on the shadows taking more form as they strode forward. He noted for a second that Thankful worried William would bring her shame of some sort, but William, so touched by gold, and so proud of not himself but his cousin, sent a new murmur of admiration along the pews. Buck remembered William in the West and felt a small bit of satisfaction in the part he played bringing William back into the Englewood fold. It was obvious, as William came closer, that he searched for something in Buck just now.

Buck unconsciously imitated his sister's proud pose. Yes, it was a veneer too. William sought Buck's assurance. He sought something in Buck's posture and eyes that Buck could not, *would not* deliver.

This spectacle before a large New York crowd was *what was done*. What was *expected*. Ceremonies hid a host of feelings. Unresolved conflicts hung in the shadows. Buck assumed that, like himself, most people in attendance today depended little on God. Their very lives were at the mercy of the maker of the universe, yet today not a one considered sitting in an ornate building a miracle.

The timid excitement Buck had carried into the church now retreated as he met William's searching face. What sort of show was all of this? What was the purpose? Why love another? Why even take care of oneself? He looked at William and could not understand in him this searching for the welfare of his cousin. Why care? The color left his face for a second. William and then Preston took note. Preston leaned in again placing his hand upon Buck's shoulder.

"Good fellow, it's time," Preston whispered as the heavily veiled form of Buck's future wife waited a few steps from the altar.

Margaret cleared her throat as the music ended. Buck caught her critical expression before slowly taking the three steps to meet Lucy. Each step was as if plunging into a cold spring. He wondered would he trip, would he make it the three steps through this blinding spectacle, would he reach Lucy and feel anything at all?

The veil, so heavy and, in Buck's opinion, ugly, made him think of Catholic processions and weird saints. It was as if a ghost stood before him, and in these fleeting seconds he wondered what more Lucy McCullough kept under wraps. Only seconds had passed. Thankful with sparkling eyes pressed him to take Lucy's outstretched hand (he had not noticed). He did this obediently, unthinkingly. He led the ghost up the three steps. Thankful followed, waited for her cue, and with a solemn and dutiful sweep of her hands she raised the veil and Lucy appeared—herself but different.

Up until this moment he had liked to imagine this girl as a sort of diversion or hobby, something like a good meal or day spent out in fine weather, but not truly a person. No, certainly not a formidable human with desires and a will of her own. He had played this false game in his head and now that game was over. The Middlemay women came to mind. How utterly boring it had all become when their petticoats lay upon the floor beside his little bed.

Surely he and Lucy would not come to that! Lucy did not smile. She seemed a different girl altogether. Her glasses were gone. Could she see the panic on his face? His hand was clammy in his glove. What was Lucy thinking? Now suddenly before the world he really wondered what Lucy thought! How had everything changed so quickly?

"Luce ..." he began for no reason.

The reverend called them to attention. Lucy gazed at the man, but Buck couldn't take his eyes off Lucy.

"Do you take this man ..." the reverend asked.

Lucy solemnly replied.

*Do you really?* Buck thought. *Whatever for?*

"Do you take Lucy McCullough ..."

Lucy turned to Buck with her exposed and clouded eyes. In her expression was an odd mix of tenderness and determination. The determined look on her thin, pink lips ignited something in Buck. She waited still for his words. The reverend, his parents, and the church hung on his silence, on his strange expression ...

"Buck," Lucy said and in that one utterance, in her assured tone with the hint of merriment and good humor that delighted him, he was freed from his dark thoughts and doubts. He did love this girl, this one from Englewood with a ridiculous boat. Maybe one day they would get a houseboat—but no, he wanted more for her than that. A castle with a moat. Yes.

Buck laughed and everyone breathed again, though they thought it strange to see such a serious young man suddenly become someone new. They liked him the better for it. Lucy covered her mouth as she giggled but her eyes told him that she was no child.

"Do you take Lucy ..." the reverend repeated.

Buck interrupted. "Of course. Yes, Of course I do." He said this like a gruff old banker, and Lucy laughed some more.

Buck smiled but allowed for no more laughter. Lucy understood his need for dignity now and bit her lip. Still there was no hint of the child. The lace was ugly but it only made her look more beautiful. Buck kissed the bride in the stiff, forced way everyone expected of him. Lucy understood and her smile as she walked down the aisle on Buck's arm made everyone forget any awkwardness on Buck's part.

# Chapter Twenty-Seven

When the elder Mr. Turner had offered his venerable old home for the wedding reception Buck at first declined in mortification. Mr. Turner must suppose Buck had no money for a nice party some place special. Would Mr. Turner ask for a rental fee?

Mr. Lamont sent Preston to change Buck's mind later the same day over drinks at the Union Club where Buck hoped to be a member one day. It hadn't occurred to Buck that Mr. Turner might take offense to his refusal.

"A reception in Uncle Turner's house would be the first celebration he's had there since Rosie's death. You could bring healing in a way—and wouldn't it read well in the papers heralding your acceptance into our family? Consider your future wife and her chances if not your own. Quite frankly, you're being selfish in your obstinacy."

"Lucy and I have a budget, you see, and ... I'm not comfortable talking about money."

"If my uncle needs something from you, he will ask for it. He knows your salary. Uncle Lamont loves Lucy and they both have more money than they can use. I wouldn't be speaking with you like this if they hadn't sent me to reason with you."

Margaret had at first poorly taken the news of her further lack of control but warmed to the idea that Buck's reception would cleanse the memories of Fred's strained wedding day at the Turner home three years before. Margaret knew, though she would never admit it, that Fred had been a brute to Rosie all along and now her lesser son could mend a fence.

Some families looked askance at dancing receptions but not the Turner clan. Every house in the family was built with dancing in mind. Dining halls could be cozy to the point of confining if it helped accommodate a large parlor. And so it was at Uncle Turner's house. Even the staff dressed with decorative corsages and ribbons for the reception. The buffet table—a Turner tradition—was set in the long and wide hallway. Margaret noted with delight the many delectable items and how they were displayed. Clam broth, oyster bouillon, lobster a la Newburg, chicken croquettes, larded game in aspic, asparagus salad, and more. She gushed over the large chocolate cake standing amongst the more refined desserts and whispered to Graham how anxious she was to try the pistachio charlotte.

After the servants cleared the tables of fine china, Preston led Lucy onto the floor with Buck and Thankful following. No one noticed the cold way in which the four began the dances but the four themselves. Preston did not like that Lucy seemed unimpressed by him. Lucy worried without her spectacles. Buck waited for cutting remarks about Lucy, and Thankful wrestled with her jealousy. All breathed a sigh of relief when the music stopped.

Mr. Turner strode onto the dance floor and signaled for everyone to find their seats at tables squeezed in along the top of the room. "Mrs. Crenshaw, the mother of the groom came to me with a request ..."

The Crenshaw siblings perked at the words, glancing at each other to see if they had been the only one taken by surprise.

"Mrs. Crenshaw is an accomplished musician as we all noted at the church. She asks to play a song for her son and his new wife."

Fred chewed his cigar and tapped his foot nervously, expressing the concern of all the Crenshaw siblings.

Margaret dabbed her eyes as she made her way to the piano in the corner of the room, sat, and smiled a moment at Lucy, not Buck, before setting her fingers upon the keys. "I'm sure you all know this one by Strauss. Forgive me if I bore you, but my new daughter Lucy so loves roses. Lulu dances through life so like an innocent child that this waltz—'Roses from the South'—reminds me of her."

Buck shook his head in annoyance but noted as the first few notes led to the next that Margaret's interpretation of the piece meant for dance was being played with far more sensuality and emotion. This added a new and surprising humiliation, but the guests remained transfixed. When Margaret finished playing, a hush of awe blanketed the reception room. Margaret blushed at the intense sense of intimacy her unleashed talent had upon a crowd of men and women who until moments ago were prepared to dismiss her with a mild, disinterested turn back to their drinks. Margaret spotted Graham wasting not a moment on the opinions of others. She saw through his usual reserve a flash of pride and devotion move across his face. Graham laughed then as if surprised at his luck.

Before anyone had time to recover and register their enthusiasm, Margaret spoke. "Oh, what a triumphant time this is for my son! We never imagined Buck in *banking*. As you all know, my father is a competitor of yours. My husband briefly worked under him but was terribly bored – even while hobnobbing with the best families like the Vanderbilts and Belmonts."

Buck sat in painful stillness even as Lucy clutched his sweaty palm. Fred dropped his head into his hands as Thankful sighed with a mix of sympathy and embarrassment for Buck, peppered with irritation at how Lucy seemed to take it all in stride. Graham's momentary pride in Margaret vanished, and his face projected a lifetime of cruel swings in emotion as his ears turned purple against his starched collar.

"Oh, dear, I should leave the speeches to my husband, but he's so quiet," Margaret continued, almost gasping in excitement and a growing sense she'd done wrong.

Lucy stood at once and the room electrified at the sight of her warm, forgiving smile. "I disagree with only one thing Mrs. Crenshaw says. There couldn't be a better sort of people—however famous or rich—than the Lamonts and the Turners. You've welcomed a poor orphan girl into your lives and recognized the wonderful qualities of my Buck." Lucy turned to Buck, who sat with his mouth slightly ajar, and kissed the scar at his temple before sitting back down beside him with a delicate rose glow on her cheeks.

Mr. Lamont hurried to Margaret's side now. "Dear Mrs. Crenshaw," he began with a booming voice that kept the room quiet. "It's been a pleasure to get to know your son, and I agree that we are not as exciting as Commodore Vanderbilt and his ilk. I will take it as a compliment to our family. I realize now—though I had my reservations about letting an unproven young man into our little bank—that my brother-in-law was right to hire Buck. I promise to take good care of your son," he said, clasping Margaret's hand in his own. "Mrs. Crenshaw you've done a fine job of raising him—and of playing the piano."

The thunder had passed and the rains of praise for Margaret's playing began. Buck could breathe again. Before he had a chance to speak with Lucy, his sisters Abigail and Maddie dragged her away. Mr. Turner came and sat beside him.

"Thank you, Mr. Turner, for everything," Buck said.

"I see this lovely wedding, and wonder where you hid when we were looking to marry off our Rosie." Turner wiped away tears.

Buck had no words.

"Lucy is quite young," Mr. Turner added.

"Sir?"

"I'm happy to hear that you plan on remaining in Englewood. Our family prides itself on tolerance and avoidance of all gossip, but New York is a hard place for young girls. Have you considered sending her off to college or Europe for some polish?"

"Sir," Buck said haltingly, "I convinced her to quit school to marry me. I didn't want to wait."

Turner winced. "I'm surprised. That's rather brash of you." He took a sip of his drink then. "I would have expected the cousins to find you someone less problematic—though Lucy seems a spunky character."

"She hardly needs school when she's already taught me so much about life's little enjoyments, sir." He blushed at his own choice of words.

"I'm sure she has, but for Lucy's sake keep her home—she'll be cruelly treated by the Saratoga crowd. I do wish you'd told me of your plans for your wedding journey. I would have sent you to a quiet place I have in the mountains. But at least Preston will be there keeping a watchful eye over the two of you. Still in all, Saratoga ladies during the summer season have girls like Lucy for lunch, and I'm afraid to say Lucy looks her age and seems oblivious to rebuff."

"It's one of her charms, sir."

The old man laughed the rough laugh of a smoker. "Always remember that the charms of women come at a price—you only have to look at your brother to see that. I opened all of my contacts to him, and still he goes with that notorious Van Westervelt girl."

"Notorious, sir?"

"She's known up Fifth Avenue for her association with abortionists but makes a mockery of poor Rosie by keeping her bastard child and running off to a free love colony."

"Sir, I'm sure she just did what a scared girl would do."

"And how would you know that?" Mr. Turner asked.

Buck muttered, "I imagine she trusted the wrong men."

"The same wrong men as my Rosie. Did you know Fred had at least two other women in the wings?"

"Sir, I believe there was only one, but that's neither here nor there. I hate how Miss Turner suffered under my brother's misbehaving—but I'm not like him. I admired Miss Turner greatly, but then there was trouble for me at West Point, and Rosie saw Fred as the safer one," Buck said, still with some bitterness. "I asked if she'd ever consider me, sir, but she said no."

Lucy slipped up behind them.

"Enough talk for now, son," Turner said. He stood and held the chair for Lucy. "You may have your husband back now, young lady."

She smiled primly and watched after the old man. "You both looked so serious, Buck—is everything all right?"

"Just the past. Nothing really," he replied, but stiffened at her overly solicitous gestures, worrying now that all eyes would judge her immature and brutalize her in their gossipy parlors.

Fred swayed up, already drunk. "This is a damned big party, Buck—it has Mama's paw prints all over it—a bit ostentatious, don't you think? Especially when people go hungry only streets away."

Buck blushed, and Lucy looked across the room.

Fred laughed with glassy eyes. "India is heading a committee for children's welfare."

Lucy spoke when Buck wouldn't. "That's good of her, Fred."

"India's always been keenly aware of suffering."

"That's funny," Buck said, tapping his wooden hand absently against the table top.

Fred's eyes narrowed. "Pardon me?"

Thankful and Margaret made their way over now.

Fred ignored them. "India likes children well enough—like Mama—she always let us do as we liked."

Thankful laughed a little, her guard down after a few champagne toasts.

Margaret glared at her. "And why are you laughing at me?" she asked Thankful.

"Mama, not now," Thankful replied, taking a sip of her drink while admiring one of the cousins from afar.

"No, Thankful, say what you need to say," Margaret demanded.

Thankful didn't need much prodding. "I think Buck would agree that it was feast or famine at home—either Buck was ignored or beaten. The rest of us were mostly ignored, thank God."

A handsome cousin strode up as Margaret spoke. "I may have occasionally lost my temper, but I never denied a child its very existence by aborting—."

"Mama, that's enough," Fred growled. "Are you single-handedly trying to destroy any shred of reputation this family has left? It's why India and I can only stand coming back rarely."

"How dare you!" Margaret cried. "We all know you had to leave on poor Sam's account—with his mother known for all the wrong reasons. Lucy insisted we still invite you and that adventuress India! The true ladies here whisper about your wife in the dark corners this very instant!"

Buck's voice hardly carried over the noise of the full room and the talk. "Mama, please ..."

Fred shoved past Buck as he tried to rise from his seat. "I couldn't care less what these backwards bourgeoisie snobs have to say! I was a fool to have fought Buck for Rosie's hand! A lifetime with her dullard cousins so bent on rules and old-fashioned morality would have killed me! It's all humbug and hypocrisy! As if Mr. Turner didn't entertain women on his frequent trips to Europe! Ha! If Buck had ever had the sense to ask my advice, I would have warned him of the corrupting and soul-deadening forces at work in banking at a small house where you'll always be an outsider! I bet they pay you a pittance compared to the cousins ..."

"That's not so! I've done very well for myself there!" Buck said.

The Turner cousin had heard enough against his clan. His bright eyes were animated with a rare temper, but he spoke with admirable composure. "Fred, you may still hold some bitterness over how the uncles kept you from the firm, but the sordid investment dealings you engaged in (using Rosie's money) with the *fictional* rail line to New Jersey cranberry farmers would have brought our family nothing but embarrassment. But let's stop discussing the past. You have a new life of excitement with the Indians and saloon keepers of the West. This is Buck's day."

"I don't give a damn what day it is—I'll not have someone with the ridiculous name *Herbert* chastise me in front of everyone! How dare you!" Fred said, his chest puffed in indignation.

Buck stood now. "I demand that everyone stop at once! My wife," he liked the sound of it, "doesn't deserve such high emotion. You've all had your chances, and it's time you leave us both alone to our happiness."

Buck took Lucy's hand and led her to the relaxing musicians. "Luce, what would you like to hear? Boys, you wouldn't mind cutting your break a little short for the bride would you?"

Lucy had already charmed them with earlier praise and, now with one smile, they picked up their instruments.

"Thank you so much," Lucy gushed. "Families need a break from quarreling once in a while."

The men laughed and played a sentimental waltz that had been John and Kate's favorite—no one but William and Lucy appreciated its value. As Buck moved Lucy in the waltz, she spotted William with his bittersweet smile admiring the dance.

Herbert Turner, at Buck and Lucy's departure onto the floor, made to escape the Crenshaw clan, but Thankful touched his arm. "Shall we dance? My husband seems to be off somewhere, and I love this music."

Herbert hesitated before chivalrously taking Thankful for the waltz.

She smiled up into his face, but Herbert looked past her.

"Sir, you dance well."

"Mrs. Weldon, I really don't want to offend you, but my skin crawls at your touch. Women should never ask a man to dance. It's unseemly. I promise never to tell a soul what you did with your baby, but I can in no way condone the act or associate with someone who's committed a crime against God." Herbert moved her to the music, but discreetly left Thankful in the shadows at the far corner of the ballroom.

There she stood, shocked at rebuff and on the verge of tears until she spotted William making his way toward her with his friendly smile. William always forgave her, and briefly the love she had kept prisoner in her closed heart sputtered through her veins. A young and sophisticated lady pulled William aside and convinced him to finish the dance with her. William shrugged in an inelegant way, only once glancing at Thankful as if to ask belated permission. She nodded, already annoyed and ashamed remembering his disgraceful dancing in Arizona years ago, but to her surprise he found his footing, and the couple made an artful end to the dance. Before Thankful could get to him, three other flirtatious girls surrounded William, who laughed at their attention.

A new fear gripped Thankful as Preston Turner and his wife, in an elegant mauve satin, garnished in the front with gold and jet fringe, joined the tittering girls. William's lack of polish and verve might go unnoticed by foolish girls, but Thankful understood that Preston and his wife were the center of the social universe at their rung of society and that a conversation with William would bring her precariously close to another humiliation. She nearly tripped over her skirts, moving at a jog, to interfere and save the conversation from being a low comedy of manners but arrived too late. They were already discussing livestock.

"Goats have more personality than cows, but they're not as easy to manage as sheep."

Thankful put her arm through William's. He looked happy.

"Oh, darling, are you boring the Turners with your gentleman's farm tales?" Thankful asked breathlessly. "William has told you all about the real estate boom in Englewood, hasn't he? I keep trying to convince him to sell and move into the city."

William rolled his eyes. Preston smiled contemptuously.

Mrs. Lottie Turner recovered first. "My mother's family kept sheep on their estate up near Rensselaer, and I spent a summer training a goat to cart. Those were the pleasantest days of my childhood. I always considered it such a shame that the boy goats should come to such an awful end, so my grandfather saved one for me as a little pet."

William laughed with a warmth Thankful hadn't heard in months. "Yes, the poor boys are a dilemma, but right now I worry about one doe who's had a rough time of it in childbirth."

"What a sensitive soul. Isn't he, Preston?" Lottie said more than asked.

Preston nodded tolerantly at his wife.

"My uncle is bewitched by Englewood," Preston said. "He's invited us out many times. Do you hunt your land, William?"

"We've got fine mounts if you'd like to come for a sporting day," William said in an easy way that surprised Thankful.

"That sounds bully," Preston replied. "And you could show wifey here the barnyard furries."

William nodded, but before he could reply, Thankful spoke, "And when you tire of the muck and dirt, you can take tea at our humble little home."

Thankful's eagerness did not impress Lottie, who looked askance at the demeaning way she had with William. "I doubt that I should ever tire of being out in the country air. You don't suppose I could have a tall glass of goat's milk on the visit, do you?"

William laughed and turned to his wife. "See, Thankful!"

Thankful wrinkled her nose. "I just couldn't drink from a goat. But I must say, Mrs. Turner, that your dress is so lovely. Did you get it at Stewarts? My mother used to take me there sometimes."

Lottie laughed. "Are you serious? It's gone quite out of fashion to shop there—but I suppose that's unfair—you not being a part of the city crowd." Lottie had not really meant to injure Thankful deeply but saw that she had. "Your dress is pretty too."

William had gotten caught two sentences back. "And that's probably my fault—about the city. I've been resisting visiting."

"Why?" Preston asked.

"My parents passed recently," he explained with a wistful sigh. "The city reminds me of how they tried but obviously failed at civilizing me."

Thankful was certain he spoke *these* words to hurt her.

"Well, you look civilized to me," Lottie said.

William laughed, and Thankful noted Lottie's color rise.

"They used to take me to see art," William said.

Preston grew animated. "What sort?"

"Oh, whatever was being shown, I suppose. My parents were admirers of the Hudson River School, but I've always liked the Europeans best at painting—though Thomas Eakins—I do like him. I don't know how he exposes his subjects' hidden moments with such sensitivity."

"Yes, it's amazing. I've just started a collection. It's small yet. Heade appeals to me as well. Do you know of him?" Preston asked.

William raised his brow in false affront. "Of course. The Luminists. Such moodiness."

Preston's stiff cordiality disappeared. "Thomas Cole's work is grand but bland, I say."

William nodded in agreement. "When I first stood close to a Fitz Hugh painting, I figured there was no reason to paint again."

"You're an artist?" Lottie asked with an excited glance at her husband.

"No, I used to draw and paint a little ..." William said, glancing Thankful's way.

"William has magnificent talent," she said. "We might be convinced to sell an old piece."

"Thankful!" William complained. "I don't paint anymore, and I sell nothing but vegetables."

"William, must you?" Thankful groaned with crossed arms.

Preston looked on in amusement. He had a fondness for artists and fancied himself an egalitarian man. The idyllic life of a farmer appealed him after viewing *The Gleaners* by Corot. "The Metropolitan has been acquiring impressive pieces of late—have you seen them?"

"No," William replied matter-of-factly.

"If you ever do come into the city, call on me, and we'll take a tour. My cousins are so dull about art. I need a new friend for that."

"Thanks for the invitation, and I shall keep it in mind, but this time of year the farm is so busy."

"We'll find a way!" Thankful's words tumbled over William's, and he shot her a look.

An old matron Thankful didn't recognize interrupted now. "We need another couple for the quadrille the bride asked for."

"I didn't imagine Lulu knew what a quadrille was," Thankful said with a giggle, "but we're worn out, aren't we, William?"

"No. I'm not and Lucy mentioned something earlier about this dance so ..."

Lottie took William by the arm. "I'll join you, Mr. Weldon, to make the young girls jealous." She winked at Preston who took it all in stride.

Thankful waited for William to seek her approval, but he did not, so she was left to fume over the turn of events. Preston did not appreciate pretty girls with sour faces and made an excuse to leave her.

"Oh, but tell me how my brother gets on at work," Thankful said at the last moment, graspingly.

Preston warmed to the subject. "Quite well, actually."

"May I ask, how does Buck fit in with—well, with people of such high standing in society?" Thankful asked, knowing she shouldn't but unable to stop herself.

"Hmm," Preston enjoyed being reminded that he was of better stock. "The thing about your brother is ... well, he's of higher-than-average intelligence and works hard, but the thing my uncles and cousins appreciate most is his goodness. I've hardly ever heard him say an unkind word and his integrity, of course, impresses us all."

"I find it impossible to imagine Buck in banking," Thankful said, a resentment rising at the impressive reputation Buck now had. "I should think it rather dull for him—I mean no offense—Buck led a rather wild life until recently. I find it amusing to watch Fred beg help from Buck now on one of his ridiculous railroad schemes or some such thing."

Preston tightened his lips, and his eyes narrowed, glancing at Buck on the dance floor. "Railroads? I wasn't aware of our family taking on railroad clients at this time."

Thankful hesitated a moment but not quite long enough. "Well, Fred is family so I suppose it's different. I'm sure Buck will do no harm, but he's always had trouble keeping Fred's dirty hands out of his things."

Preston's cordial demeanor hardened. "I hope what you say is untrue because the uncles will see Buck booted out."

"Oh, no! I hadn't meant to cause trouble!" Thankful cried as the color drained from her face, and her chest heaved in panic. "I may have gotten it all wrong. I overheard them talking heatedly just yesterday when I went to visit Mama."

"Well, this puts me in a spot then," Preston complained mildly though his eyes and rigid manner betrayed anger.

Thankful gripped Preston's sleeve. "Let's pretend I told you nothing, and you won't get in trouble with your uncles."

"Mrs. Weldon, you fail to understand me. I like Buck and hate to see him go, but my loyalty is with my uncles, of course."

"Then you should understand Buck's loyalty to his family," Thankful said. "And a few thousand would hardly be noticed."

"Then you know nothing of the pride we take in our moral code."

Thankful laughed to hide her fear. "Oh, that's so old fashioned, and I'm sure you've made your mistakes and indiscretions—bankers are famous for that nowadays, aren't they?"

"Not in our bank, Mrs. Weldon. I'm sorry you keep such low opinions."

Thankful held her head haughtily now. "I wonder if your Uncle Turner only hired Buck to avenge his daughter. Fred is no angel, but using Buck, who has such a fragile mind, seems less than morally upright, sir."

"My uncle is the kindest man I know and, if anything, too generous for his own good. We cousins were shocked that he'd invite Buck in after the way Fred broke Rosie's heart—we blame Fred for her death."

"Be serious now!" Thankful exclaimed. "Fred is no murderer."

"Rosie was a sweet, if stupid, girl—and devoted to Fred even after she found out that Fred had had an affair with one of her dearest friends, but when Fred embarrassed her father with rotten speculation, using Uncle's clout, Fred humiliated Rosie beyond repair."

"Oh, how awful—and so like Fred," Thankful admitted.

Preston delicately disengaged Thankful's arm from his own. "I'm afraid it's my duty to see that Buck doesn't get up to any tricks."

"Oh, Buck isn't like that! I only heard Fred harassing Buck for money. Please don't ruin Buck's big day—he can be very fragile."

"What do you mean?"

"Well, he is much better now, but he's been a little—*off*—in the past. I can trust you, can't I? I only tell you this so that you're not too hard on him. I'm sure if Buck's done wrong you can teach him better. After all, he has enough to worry about with a wife on the brink of blindness."

"Lucy is going blind?"

"Mama convinced Lulu to leave her spectacles at home. It's why my husband protects her in the dances—to make sure she doesn't trip and humiliate herself."

"That young girl will have no sight?" Preston asked, wiping his forehead of perspiration.

"Please don't judge Buck harshly for being so softhearted to pity Lulu. But he'd just come back from Middlemay and I suppose felt guilty before God."

"*The free-love community*?" Preston asked.

"You've heard of it?"

"Of course, Miss Van Westervelt. She ..."

"India convinced Buck to take her!"

Preston stared. "You're not serious!"

"For over a year Buck took care of India's child."

"Buck did?"

"Yes. So please be nice to him. He needs a steady income, and he's come so close to being respectable."

"Buck had a child with India?" Preston gasped.

"No! Not at all!" Thankful felt the waters rising. "I shouldn't have told you any of this. You twist everything!"

"I've hardly said a word."

"Now can you see how hard he's had it?" Thankful asked snapping her fan open and shut again. Her breathing quickened.

"I can see that there's a lot more to Buck Crenshaw than he lets on beneath those tailored suits and his feigned shyness," Preston said with an agitated flourish of his hands.

Thankful's eyes raced over the crowd and then back to Preston. "Buck is a quiet and guileless soul. He's just made some foolish decisions at times."

"And how is that supposed to comfort a banker?"

"He is quite serious about banking, more serious than anything else."

Preston laughed sardonically, shaking his head.

"Mr. Turner, I don't like your tone. Buck is trustworthy."

"I'm not so sure any longer, but here's the end of the dance."

Thankful grabbed Preston's wrist and begged, "Please tell no one what I've told you!"

Preston widened his eyes and laughed again.

William and Lottie rushed up in laughter and talk, but their faces fell at the sight of their spouses.

"What's happened?" William asked.

"Dance with me!" Thankful cried and pulled him to the floor.

"This is some honor," William said.

"Stop it, Willy. I've made a grand blunder!"

Lottie Turner quizzed Preston and wore a look of horror now. It had been her practice each season to fall madly in love with the idea of befriending a new girl with little means and much potential. Lucy, with her strawberry hair, unusual eyes, and forthright personality appealed to her. Here was a girl Lottie could help get by, and she had come to like Buck.

"I find it near impossible to imagine Buck Crenshaw could do anything nefarious," Lottie told her husband. "Oh, and you mustn't tell the uncles about any of this—at least until after the season at Saratoga! Poor, poor Lucy!"

Preston put his arm around his wife. "You've had your heart set on adopting the little orphan."

"She's a darling. I want to dress her for smashing success and ... I find her strangely soothing."

"And that may be the very game they're at!" Preston said with emphasis. "Buck seemed the nicest fellow to spend time with."

"Perhaps they *are* nice."

He ran his fingers along Lottie's shoulder, thinking. "If Crenshaw really was a parvenu, would he have suggested climbing a mountain in the Adirondacks over a Saratoga season?"

"He probably didn't know any better," Lottie said. "He seems nothing like his awful brother, frothing at the mouth at our heels everywhere we turned! I'm afraid Buck's mild nature has charmed me too, Preston," she confessed. "What a mess."

"Indeed. Now what shall we do? I knew hiring Buck was a mistake!" Preston fumed.

"Haven't you often lectured me about heeding gossip? And what do we really know about Mrs. *Thankful* Weldon?" Lottie pointed out with a sour look of vexation.

Preston kissed her forehead. "Far too much! Buck's family is a train wreck on all tracks! I truly believe dear Uncle Turner has lost his wits—yet that William Weldon seems a decent fellow. I rather liked the idea of an artist friend."

"And a young country farmer," Lottie said. "He seems genuine and pleasant. I do wonder why he would marry a girl with a name so unsuited to her actual personality. She's dreadful."

"And you don't know the half, darling," Preston said, giving her an affectionate squeeze.

Just then Lucy tapped Lottie's shoulder with her gloved hand. Preston and Lottie turned, faces reddening as their minds raced over what Lucy may have heard.

Lucy shook. "I'm ashamed of you both! I thought you were Buck's friends!"

Lottie shot Preston a pained look and took Lucy's hands in hers, bending a little to meet her eyes. "Sweetheart, dear, things are not as they seem."

"Then how are they, may I ask? Thankful is my sister now, and I won't tolerate gossip from anyone."

The Turners were silent before the young lady with the doe eyes and determined chin. They glanced at each other again, hoping the other would have the right words to say.

Preston sighed. "Young miss, let's not spoil your day."

"No one can spoil it," Lucy said with a defiant toss of her head.

Preston leaned into his wife, relying on her feminine charms.

Lottie touched Lucy's face, a little too familiarly, and Lucy pulled away.

"Oh, Lucy, dear, let's find a quiet place for a chat, shall we? Preston, we must be frank with her."

"But the Saratoga season?" Preston replied in confusion.

"Never mind that, dear," Lottie said in annoyed dismissal of her husband. "Lucy, please come with us."

Lucy's eyes sought Buck, but she followed the two out into the dark, humid city night, tentatively stepping into the shadows until Preston took her by the elbow and led her down the stairs with a sudden surge of compassion for the girl. A bemused Lottie smiled at him. Preston motioned his hand to say he'd explain later. They crossed the street and guided Lucy to a bench beside the park. The street lamps gave everything a blurred glow as Lucy kept her eyes on the mansion across the street, where the small notes of dance music trickled out.

Lucy stood now, shivering in the cool of the night after the warmth of the dancing. "I want to go back inside. Can you please tell me what kind of trouble my cousin is in so I can go find Buck?"

"Your cousin?" Preston asked.

"William," Lucy replied.

"This isn't about him, young lady," Preston said, running his hand through his perfectly trimmed hair.

Lottie pulled Lucy back to sitting. "You see, dear, we like you very much and some things have come to light that cause us pain."

Lucy looked startled. "What things?"

"Is it true that Buck ran off with India Van Westervelt?" Preston asked.

Lucy said nothing.

"You must be frank with us because Thankful has filled my husband's head with the most horrible rumors about *our* Buck," Lottie said.

"Well, I don't believe Buck is *ours* like a puppy dog, and Thankful lies," Lucy said.

Lottie put her arm around Lucy's shoulders. "Lucy, you are so very young, but you must understand that working for our family means being a part of something nobler than just any bank. We value morals, sound judgment, and superior conduct in business *and* our private lives."

Lucy recoiled, as if she'd been given poison. "Buck has fine morals!"

"Dear, we held Buck in high regard until ..." Lottie said, her words like soft butter.

"Until what?" Lucy asked, glancing yet again at the bright lights of the brownstone mansion.

Preston impatiently pushed the pace of the discussion. "Lucy, it pains me to speak so boldly to a girl in your condition ..."

"Please, Mr. Turner, go ahead," she said. "My condition, if you mean my eyes, should be of no concern to you since it is of little concern to me."

Preston cleared his throat, loosening his tie. "Your sister-in-law has given me reason to doubt Buck's trustworthiness. I'd like to resolve this situation as quietly as possible."

"I don't understand," Lucy said firmly. "He's a man of character."

"And how are you so sure?" Preston asked.

"I ... don't know," Lucy searched her mind for a specific example but only the foolish schemes he'd involved himself in with Fred over the years presented themselves. "Buck is ..."

Lottie sighed impatiently at the sight of Margaret across the street craning her neck for a sign of the missing bride hidden behind the long shadows of the socialite couple. Lottie shielded Lucy all the more. "Is Buck in a money deal with Fred?"

Lucy laughed. "They hardly ever speak. Buck would never ..."

"Are you certain?" Preston so wanted to trust her.

Lucy clutched her chest in a heartfelt and immature way. "I trust Buck with my very life!"

Lottie took Lucy's hands in hers maternally. "I fear you've been deceived. Oh, how it breaks my heart! The insight Thankful has given us tonight makes Buck an embarrassing addition to our family—and we so wanted to give the poor man a chance."

Lucy's white face, grew even paler still, but her voice was unwavering. "I'm grateful to you both for giving my husband a chance, but you should both be ashamed of yourselves for trusting the angry words of Buck's bitter sister!"

"Lucy, please ..." Preston begged, taking her by the arm.

"Let go of me at once," Lucy demanded. "I have no interest in impressing you. I only agreed to this city wedding because Buck hoped that you might enjoy yourselves. He looked happier tonight than I've ever seen him because he imagined you might really be his friends."

Preston and Lottie glanced at each other.

"How are we to be certain of him?" Lottie asked.

"I will stand for him with this." Lucy unclasped the bracelet of diamonds.

Preston laughed and looked up into the hazy sky. "Oh, dear," he said, meeting Lucy's eyes once more, "we're not in the business of pawning. Good God."

Lucy held it before them, the jewels echoing the faint glistening of the fireflies in the park. "This is worth quite a lot, and it's very old. I am so certain of Buck's integrity that I will hand over the only family possession I have as a safeguard. If Buck ever discovered you had such a low opinion of him he'd leave the bank straight away. He is just about to make your uncles heaps of money. He'd never take a risk with Fred."

Lottie made to push the bracelet away though she had an eye for antique jewelry. "Please, Lucy, we want to believe you."

"Lucy," Preston began, "it pains me to disappoint you."

Lottie's eyes darted to a figure on the steps across the street talking with a hysterical Margaret and directing her to return to the reception. At once, William spotted the little party just out of lamplight's glow and jogged across, his slight limp more pronounced after a day of work and dance.

"Mr. Weldon!" Lottie gushed breathlessly.

"My wife's made a real hash of things hasn't she?" William said.

No one spoke until after a gold-emblazoned coach pulled away with a guest—a client of Buck's who had done well under his advisement.

William glanced at Lucy. "My wife means well, but talks too much."

"But is she truthful?" Preston asked.

William hesitated, scratching his head with a wince. "I'm not sure."

"Willy! You have no idea what you're saying!" Lucy cried. "You could ruin Buck!"

"Lies ruin things, Lucy," William said. "I hoped Buck had changed for your sake."

"*Changed*?" Lottie demanded explanation.

"Buck has always been led by the scruff. Fred sees to that. He may have started out with good intentions ... it makes no sense for Buck to bite the hand that feeds him, but ... well, I want to protect Lucy in any way I can."

"Mr. Weldon, you may be too late for that. If Buck has allowed Fred even one step in the door, if he's taken on any risky rail securities, however minute, my uncles will see him sacked, and rightly so."

"Of course," William replied as Lucy tugged at his sleeve in consternation.

"Willy, you're very wrong!" she cried.

"Dear girl," Preston said, "maybe this has gotten too big to put off. We must ask Buck all about it."

"No!" Lucy replied. "Please, don't! I beg of you—there must be a way to avoid it. If Buck is innocent—and he is—he would never feel right about the bank again, and you will have brought humiliation to us beyond repair. He has always spoken so highly of you, Mr. Turner, and I think it very unchristian to convict a man without trial!"

"But what am I to do? If he is conspiring with Fred, whom my uncles despise, then what?"

"I will back Buck's reputation with my land," William said suddenly.

They all stared.

"The land I own is extremely valuable. All I ask is that you wait until you know for certain. If Buck is up to anything and you can prove it ... I will sell a portion of my property to your uncles. Mr. Adriance told me that your family has wanted the back meadow for years."

"William! What are you doing?" Lucy whispered.

William spoke to the Turners. "Lucy saved me once. Now I will do the same for her. She believes Buck is innocent. Let the newlyweds have at least tonight." He smiled at Lucy who stood with mouth ajar. "Mr. Turner, if you'd like to come by the farm before your trip to Saratoga, you can see for yourself—the land and such."

"I'm at a loss," Preston said. "This whole thing is so unseemly, but my heart goes out to Lucy who has brought such joy to my aunt and uncle."

"Oh, and Lucy is a joy to me too," Lottie said. "I for one find it very hard to imagine our Buck being bad." She gave Lucy a squeeze.

William looked on dubiously. "Buck will pay in the long run, anyway. I will see to it somehow, but for now I'd rather be left out of any talk you may have with him. He needn't know of our deal unless he's found guilty. And then even this marriage is off to a terrible start. Yet, if he's innocent we'll never speak of it again."

Preston glanced at his wife. "I worry about being dishonest with my uncles."

"No, dear," Lottie noted, "you are temporarily keeping a suspicion to yourself—one that your family will win at no matter the end. And Lucy will have no shame either way."

Lucy chewed the inside of her cheek, remembering only yesterday Buck grumbling about Fred being up to his old tricks ... had he been bullied yet again? "Willy, you can't put your future in danger. You shouldn't."

Preston huffed, "This is why our set doesn't like bringing in people with no history. I've never had to navigate such murky waters."

Lottie took Preston's hand in hers. "Now, we must give Buck and Lucy a chance, Preston, dear, since things are still so uncertain. Imagine a wedding day so spoiled by innuendo! Lucy's heart must be broken and, oh, there's Buck now, looking as guileless as ever."

They all turned as Buck dodged an omnibus before walking up, warily taking in the tense group. "Lucy," he began with a soft smile, "I was worried, but see you are well-cared for. Is something the matter?"

Even William felt a pang of sympathy for Buck.

Lucy glanced at Lottie before speaking. "I just needed air."

"I gladly would have accompanied you," Buck said with a note of suspicion.

"I didn't want to spoil your fun."

Buck found something unsettling in Lucy's demeanor. He turned to Preston. "Has something happened?"

"Something's always happening, Crenshaw, but nothing for you to worry about just now," Preston replied irritably. "Mr. Weldon, would you care to have a smoke with me a moment?"

William nodded, and they walked a little further down the sidewalk.

Buck stood awkwardly among the women, wondering why the men cut him from their company.

Lottie took his arm. "Be a gent, Buckie, and escort us back inside, won't you?"

# Chapter Twenty-Eight

The ferry back to New Jersey, full of late-night workers and theatergoers, was quiet and tense in the deepening fog. Though members of the Crenshaw wedding stood with faces to the shore, there appeared no sign of it. If people spoke, they did so only briefly and solemnly. Bells and horns sounded. Larger vessels suddenly came into view only to vanish again into the dark, dense air.

All merriment must come to an end sometime, Buck said to himself as he watched Lucy speaking with her pensive cousin. Thankful sat too, but at a noticeable distance from her husband. Buck worried for her happiness. He had hoped that once the nervousness of the ceremony had passed he'd be able to relax, but Preston's curt goodbye at the end of the night, and Lucy's clinging to Willy bothered him. Was he just imagining this shift in feelings? Was it just anticlimax after a trying few weeks of entertaining?

He turned back toward the breeze with its faint scent of ocean only a little further downstream. Lucy had spent the better part of the evening with William. Should Buck interrupt them or let them have their final time together? He had no intention of visiting Tenafly Road that often in the future. He was now more determined to have Lucy properly schooled at the best places despite her blindness. He would not have Mr. Turner be right.

Sighing, he regretted agreeing to Saratoga with Preston for a honeymoon. He had no interest in the fast set, and even though his salary could not compete with the Drexels and Trasks—or even the Turners and Lamonts—his sensibilities were more in line with the older, quieter families.

Grandmother Martha confirmed as he sat briefly with her this evening that her side of the family had Dutch blood from the earliest Knickerbocker families and at least one Revolutionary War hero captured and sent to Quebec. Buck almost wished the honeymoon over so he could hire someone to research his genealogy.

"Deep in thought, son?" Graham asked, leaning against the rail next to Buck, his straight hair tousled in the wind. "Lucy was lovely today. You've done well for yourself."

"Thank you," Buck replied stiffly.

"Mr. Lamont has a high opinion of you."

"Does that surprise you?"

Graham turned his head quickly, stung. "Buck ... I always knew without Fred you'd make something of yourself. I didn't expect banking, but ..."

Buck said nothing. His father hypocritically had quit at finance after he'd made his fortune. Buck meant to stay the course and take good care of his clients as well as himself. Graham stared at him still, waiting for him to speak.

"I'll just be glad to get on with things now," Buck said.

Graham laughed. "Enjoy this, son. You have a nice girl. Everybody loves her, and she's chosen *you*."

Buck smiled, glancing back at Lucy now asleep, leaning on William's shoulder. "I'm going to make certain she gets the best of everything."

"Make sure she gets the best of you," Graham warned.

"That's what I meant," Buck replied, stiffening again.

Graham patted Buck's back paternally. "Son, I hope ... I'd really like for us to remain close."

Buck gave his father a hard look. Had they ever been close?

Graham surveyed his son in the brightening lights of the dock. "I never quite know how to read you."

"Well, now's no time for a big talk," Buck replied, "and I'd like to have Lucy in bed at a reasonable hour."

Graham gave him a knowing look.

Buck's face burned. "We have a lot of travel tomorrow. That's what I meant."

"Okay, son." Graham laughed and sought out his bleary-eyed wife who'd been crying over Meg and marriage and grown-up children deserting her and not allowing her to know her grandson who was dreadfully spoiled and needed a grandmother's stern touch.

Thankful looked up with puffed eyes at Buck as he strode over to Lucy. "Oh, Buckie, I'm so sorry for ever being mean to you."

"Thankful, please," Buck replied, "today was a good day, wasn't it?"

She sniffed and wiped her nose. "I hope I didn't ruin it."

"Thankful, the day was so full that frankly, I hardly noticed you. But it's okay. I'd do anything for you," he said softening his tone. He missed Thankful in a way. "You realize that don't you? We're close like Lucy and Willy."

Before she could reply, Buck turned his attention to Lucy, tapping her gloved hand with his own. She woke with a start, as William rubbed his tired eyes.

"Luce, we're almost home. Really home."

For a moment Lucy had forgotten her unanswered questions and rose to embrace her new husband, but Fred strolled up, still tipsy. "I hope you rot in Hell, Buck."

"I'll see you there," Buck replied.

William stood immediately as Fred and India walked off the ferry. "I hope Fred hasn't done anything to spoil your day."

"I should never get involved with him, that's all," Buck said matter-of-factly, though Thankful, Lucy, and William felt the worst confirmed.

"Lucy will be protected," William said with sudden aggression. "I'll see to it."

Buck stepped back, offended. "Of course, Willy. Just as I will see to it that Thankful is protected."

"I've gotten Thankful out of more scrapes than you know," William said, sending daggers through his wife.

"Well, you owe her, anyway," Buck said, "after all you've put her through."

William took Thankful roughly by the arm. "Buck, you owe *me*."

Lucy and Thankful cried for mercy.

Buck continued. "How in the world do I owe you?"

"Please, Willy, let's go home now," Thankful urged, her usual aplomb gone.

Buck stared not sure what to make of his sister. "How in hell do I owe *you*, Willy?"

William's golden eyes softened. "I've ... given over my best friend into your care. That's all. I just hope you understand the value of her."

Thankful and Lucy exchanged relieved glances.

Buck, ready for a fight, took a moment to switch reins.

Thankful tugged at William. "We should go."

Lucy kissed her cousin on the cheek. "I love you, Willy, and I'll miss you terribly this summer."

William said nothing, taking her face in his hands and patting her cheeks playfully before turning toward the gangplank and the waiting livery cab.

As the last of the family drove off, Buck put his arm around her shoulders. Shaking her a little, he nudged her to look up at him. "We'll only be just up the road from them upon our return."

"Yes, but it's not the same, is it? How will Willy and I ever have those funny chats that only happen at odd times when you live with people?"

"Perhaps we'll have our own odd chats over crying babies," Buck said. "Now watch your step, dear heart. I still don't understand why you left our wedding in the dark tonight without me."

"I'm not an invalid, and I may never be," she said, clasping the rail leading to Buck's new Victoria carriage and horse brought by Margaret's stable boy. "It won't do to treat me as if I don't have the intelligence to know right from wrong."

"What do you mean?"

She bit her lip, unable to meet his serious eyes. "Let's go home. I've been so looking forward to finally seeing it."

"Luce, I wanted to spruce it up a bit before we really settled in, and it seemed wrong to have you come by before we were married," Buck said with a nervous laugh. "Isn't it so odd to be really married?"

Lucy giggled at him. "I *do* love you though."

"Do you really?" he asked with a grin of satisfaction. "Because I'm over the moon happy with you."

Off they drove, sitting quietly in the dark all the way until they rounded the familiar corner and were carried up the hill. The old stone wall of their cottage came into view. The lane to the stables glowed with white hydrangeas Buck had planted after consulting with a fashionable garden designer recommended by Mr. Lamont. "How do you like the lane?"

Lucy squinted without her glasses. "It's not how I remembered it."

"No, I had all the old roses dug up. They were terribly overgrown."

"But their delicious smell!" Lucy sighed in disappointment.

"Luce, I'm not a complete imbecile. I hadn't forgotten about your desire for a *smelly* garden, but a lane needs to be orderly for visitors—don't you think?"

"I suppose," she replied glumly. As they turned under the great arbor, she gasped. Even in the dark the scent of heliotrope and roses drifted on the breeze.

"Over there beneath the windows I had Mr. Ormond transplant the roses so you could sniff them first thing in the morning."

Lucy began to cry. "It's so terribly thoughtful—and beautiful, isn't it?"

"Yes. So stop crying," he said a little harshly.

Lucy stopped dutifully, yet taken aback.

He jumped down as a boy came to take the carriage (a boy Lucy knew from the public school). Buck helped Lucy onto the cobbled path and led her to the front door, where a cat with kittens lay unused to company at this hour.

"Darned old cat," Buck complained.

Lucy picked up a kitten, snuggling it to her face. "We'll keep them all!"

He laughed and shrugged, pulling a key from his pocket. He turned the knob and opened the door. "Put down the kitten so we can do this properly," he said.

Lucy kissed it, then stood before Buck gamely. He scooped her up with feigned exertion and once over the threshold he plopped her down on a fancy sofa so he could light the lamps. "I'm having this place fitted with the newest in lighting, Luce—to make it easier on you."

"Buck, I like the lights."

"You know, there's still a nice home in the city a ways off from Fifth Avenue that I think we could just afford ..."

"I like it here," she said. "But, Buck, where are the old rocking chairs by the hearth that I remember? Oh, and I see you've had a wood stove installed in the fireplace."

"You must like it. It's the latest in style and comfort."

"I don't know, I ... and where are the rockers again?"

"Oh, those. Well, I have these cousins who used to invite us upstate, and they'd all sit around in rockers knitting and such—even my uncle. They were odd fish."

"So you got rid of the rockers?" Lucy asked, taking in the many changes to the place she had only seen briefly but had romanticized for the past months.

"No, everything is in the barn. I just wanted our first house to be clean and new. So I take it you don't even like the new sofas." His voice was a little gruff. "You did get your say at the wedding, mostly."

She laughed at him. "You, Buck Crenshaw, are adorable when you pout, and I'm afraid you're right. I should be grateful that you've thought so long and hard about everything, but those old things hold great charm."

"And that's why I didn't throw them away."

"Would you still love me if I brought the rockers back?" Lucy asked with an impish grin.

"Yes, I suppose ..." he said, coming to sit with her at once. "Forgive me for not allowing you any say."

Lucy took his hands—she had a way of not noticing the wooden one. "I hope you will always come to me with your concerns."

"Of course."

"Even if I'm younger than those other girls—the city girls."

"We will make certain that you are able to compete on every level," he said.

"Why should I want to compete?" she asked, withdrawing her hands.

He found the chill unbearable. "Luce, I want ... to make certain that you are not held up for ridicule ..."

"Do you find me ridiculous suddenly?"

He pulled her hand back. "No! Not at all. It's just that Mr. Turner mentioned how good-natured you are and that it wouldn't do with the younger set of women. He said they'd eat you alive, and I can't have that."

"And Mr. Turner is wrong!"

"Wouldn't you enjoy a year in Europe for schooling and culture?"

Lucy folded her arms. "Most certainly not! I'm a happy American. I'm sorry that Mr. Turner's opinions would have you throw me off for a year!"

"No! That's not what I want at all. You do understand that without Mr. Turner's kindness toward me I would not have been able to marry you."

"That, Buck, is another lie you tell yourself! I'd have married you no matter what line of work you took! I'd have had a simple ceremony and lived in one of the camps down by the river."

Buck shook his head. "Well, I never would have done that! You shouldn't aim so low, Luce."

"So I'm low?"

"No! It's just I promised myself that I would show William I could take good care of you."

"And you think Willy's doing a poor job with your sister?"

Buck tossed his head, stood, and went to the wood stove. "I think Willy's a disaster. I'm sorry, but I do. He lets Thankful get away with being a spoiled baby, and he doesn't deserve all that land he's got and ..." He checked himself now. "I suppose he's a fine artist though."

Lucy looked at the wood stove for a long while as Buck brooded, sure that the wedding night was ruined.

Finally, Lucy spoke in a quiet voice. "Buck, you mean well, but William is a better friend to you than you know."

"What?" he asked, looking at the clock. "Can't we talk about all of this another time? I just wondered if you'd like Europe."

"Buck Crenshaw, I want to make very clear the sort of girl I am. I don't want to be educated in how not to be me. If I am ever to go to Europe, it will be with you. If you'd like for me to learn the latest dances or learn another language, I will do that and a great many other things, but the most important thing for me is *you* and that's final."

He mulled over her words, allowing himself to momentarily enjoy them. "My father was right. I am the luckiest man alive. Now let me show you our room."

Buck took Lucy around the waist and led her down a hallway wallpapered in faded rose.

"This is where we'll hang family pictures," Lucy mused.

Buck smiled and opened the door. "It's not grand, but I hoped you'd like the blue ..."

"Toile, how lovely!" she gushed as she entered the bedroom, hands on heart. "Oh, and the furniture is my aunt's!"

"Thankful suggested that you might like something from home," he said, leaning in the doorway.

"Your sister surprises me at every turn," Lucy replied, running her hands over the familiar bedpost. "Buck, do you trust me?"

"I think so."

"Will you trust me with all of your mistakes?"

"You don't like the bed?" he asked in surprise.

"I do. Please, Buck, I thought I shouldn't tell you, but ... how could I give myself to you ..."

"Mama said she explained how it all works."

Lucy smiled. "Yes, she gave me a medical book with *tiny* letters—but I've read novels, you know."

"Well, it's a little different from novels."

"Will it hurt much?" she asked, biting her lip in the way Buck found adorable.

He smiled and ran his hand down her back. "It doesn't hurt for men, Luce, but I'll be gentle, and we have forever to get it right."

"If we are to live together happily, I must tell you something I'm afraid will make things very difficult, but God *did say* the truth sets one free."

"What's this about?"

She took a deep breath and let the words pour out, "Everyone worries that you and Fred are scheming over railroad bonds."

He sat on the bed. "Well ... I'm not, really."

"Are you certain?" she asked, her heart pounding.

"Who told you?"

"Mr. Preston Turner."

"You can't be serious!" he cried, remembering the cool sendoff a few hours ago. "I'm most certainly ruined then."

"Why on earth would you ever trust Fred?"

"I don't! But he was set to make us look like buffoons to the Turners and the Lamonts."

"So?"

"So? How do you think I'm paying for this shabby little house or a trip to Europe or anything?" he ranted.

Lucy sighed. "So ... you said you have no deal with Fred?"

"I will admit that I considered a deal of sorts. I don't want Sam to suffer impoverishment and be looked down upon at Exeter."

"Boarding school? Isn't he a bit young for that?" Lucy laughed.

"Maybe so. But really it was that Fred said he'd tell Mr. Turner of my past problems, and he even said he'd mention your eyes."

"He would blackmail his very own twin?"

"He presented it rather differently, but I understood when he mentioned that he still has friends at the newspaper society pages and with a few assemblymen who'd love to expose any flaw in the Lamonts and Turners. The idea of sullying a fine old family appalled me so I considered quietly helping Fred sell shares to only a few of my clients."

"But then you didn't."

"No, though it was tempting. I don't know how Fred does it, but he's in with some of the bigger fish out west. If Mr. Turner ever found out ... So my intention was to speak with him after Saratoga and let him know what Fred was attempting to do."

"Oh, Buck!"

"But if Preston knows anything, then Fred is more a scoundrel than I thought!" Buck said. "Maybe it's time I expose India's actions at Middlemay!"

"Buck, no," Lucy said. "It wasn't Fred."

"What do you mean?"

"It seems Thankful spoke with Preston."

He looked at her with the eyes of a dumb animal. "Thankful? Why?"

Lucy had no answer.

Buck tore off his tie, tossing it next to him. He stared past Lucy as if she were no longer there.

"Buck, I shouldn't have told you this tonight, I think."

"No, you've every right to know the messy character you've saddled yourself with. So much for a splendid wedding night."

"Things can be mended, can't they?"

"The amount of hatred that exists for my brother was an almost insurmountable barricade to acceptance. Preston and I were becoming friends of sorts. The fact that Thankful, of all people, brought everything to light only makes the story seem more believable. Now it will just look like I've been caught and covered up just in the nick of time."

"Preston and Lottie are willing to wait until things are proven."

"And that's why the clandestine meeting when you should have been enjoying your wedding day," he grumbled.

She rested her head on his slumped shoulder. "Our wedding and my memories of it will not be sullied now that I know you stood for integrity."

"We should cancel Saratoga," Buck said. "I can't bear facing anyone."

"That would be the worst thing. You need to speak with Preston as soon as possible," she urged.

"You really want to go, don't you?" Buck asked. He watched her as she let her hair down and took off her earrings. He had never seen her with loose hair.

"I don't care about Saratoga," she said. "If the Lamonts and Turners want to turn you out on hearsay then I have no time for them, but you can't just give up, can you? Let's decide right now that if all goes wrong, we will pack up our things and move to—say New London. I'll get work and you will too and we'll be blissfully poor in secret. Won't that be an adventure?"

"You love Englewood."

"But Buck, I love you more and the idea of your family always being your worst enemy makes me quite indignant. They've no right anyhow. So no matter what, we two will be friends until the end."

"Even in New London." Buck laughed.

"Even there," Lucy said.

Buck sighed. "I suppose I can live with the utter humiliation and impoverishment. But I can't help wondering where God is in all of this."

"God is right here with us."

He pulled her closer and kissed her, keeping a brave front, but how many times could he bring himself to start over?

She held his face in her hands and kissed him and then again before saying, "You know I will never speak ill of you, ever. I will never desert you."

He laughed off the sentiment uneasily. "So ...would you like to consummate the marriage or should we wait until everything is cleared up?"

She giggled. "You have such a funny way about you. I didn't strain my eyes for nothing reading your mother's manual. When things are at their bleakest, that's when we need to enjoy everything that's wonderful—to even things out."

"Well, I hope it's wonderful for you," Buck said with a smile, running his hand over the hair that had fallen past Lucy's shoulders. "You have a queer way of looking at things, but I like it very much."

She whispered in his ear, "Will we help each other undress?"

Buck dimmed the gaslight, forgetting about the world as she unbuttoned his shirt and ran her soft fingers through his fair hair.

"How long I've dreamed of touching you, Buck."

# THE END

Adrienne Morris is the author of *The Tenafly Road Series*, a family saga following the Weldon and Crenshaw families of Gilded Age Englewood, New Jersey. Her first novel, *The House on Tenafly Road* was selected as an *Editors' Choice Book* and *Notable Book of the Year* by *The Historical Novel Society*.

Authors rely on word-of-mouth! If you enjoyed *The One My Heart Loves* please leave an online review—even a short one! It makes a big difference and is greatly appreciated.

**OWN THE SERIES!**

*THE TENAFLY ROAD SERIES*[1]

*The House on Tenafly Road*[2] *(1)*

*Weary of Running*[3] *(2)*

*The Dew That Goes Early Away*[4] *(3)*

*Forget Me Not*[5] *(4)*

*The One My Heart Loves (5)*

*The Grand Union (6)*

*ADRIENNE'S OFFICIAL NEWSLETTER*[6]

**CONTACT ADRIENNE:**

AdrienneMorris.com[7]

Nothing Gilded, Nothing Gained[8]

INSTAGRAM[9]

BOOK COVER DESIGN by *Samantha Hennessy Design*[10]

1. *https://amzn.to/2LaIjdK*

2. *https://amzn.to/2y7VZUb*

3. *https://amzn.to/2K2gwuJ*

4. *https://amzn.to/2KzvicF*

5. *https://amzn.to/2INoWZZ*

6. *http://eepurl.com/cnCwBP*

7. https://www.adriennemorris.com/

8. https://middlemaybooks.com/

9. https://www.instagram.com/middlemay_farm/

10. *http://www.samanthahennessy.com/*

Made in the USA
Middletown, DE
28 September 2019